POKÉMON JOURNEYS

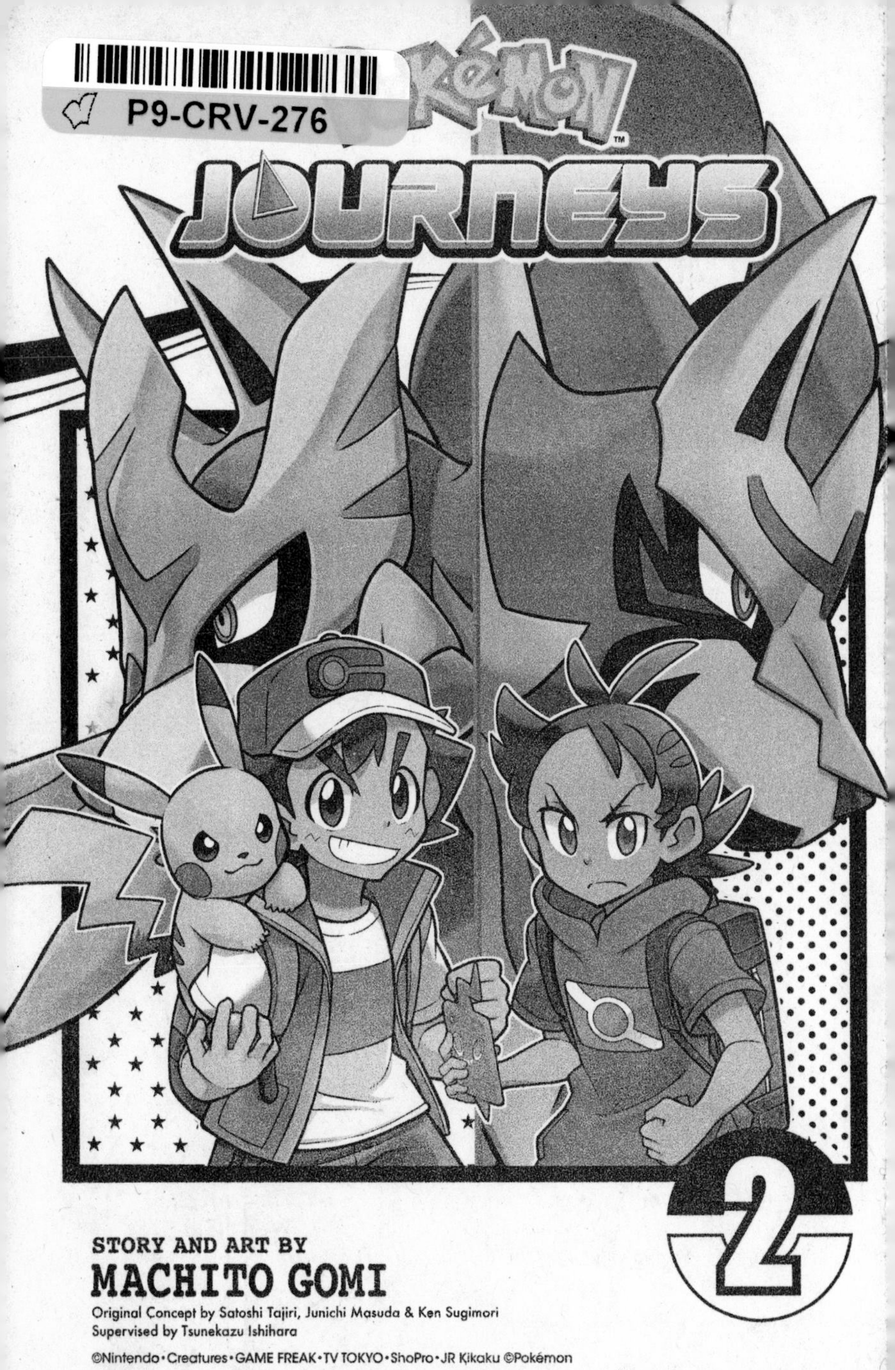

2

STORY AND ART BY

MACHITO GOMI

Original Concept by Satoshi Tajiri, Junichi Masuda & Ken Sugimori
Supervised by Tsunekazu Ishihara

Characters

GOH
ASH'S TRAVELING COMPANION AND AN ASPIRING POKÉMON TRAINER!

ASH
HE WANTS TO BE THE VERY BEST, BETTER THAN ANYONE EVER HAS BEEN!

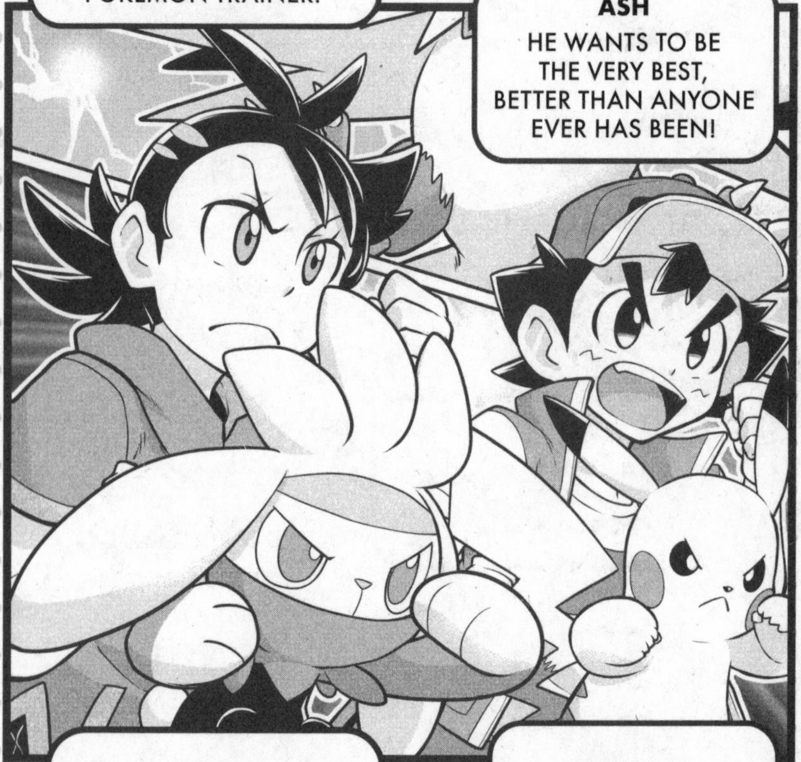

RABOOT
THE FIRST POKÉMON GOH CAUGHT, EVOLVED FROM SCORBUNNY!

PIKACHU
ASH'S AMAZING PARTNER!

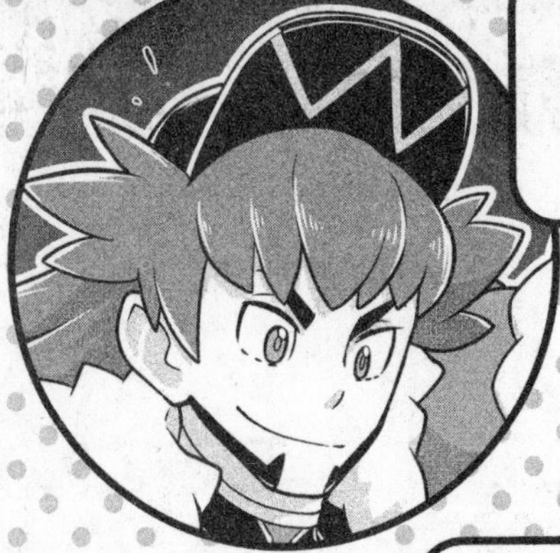

LEON

HE'S THE STRONGEST POKÉMON TRAINER IN THE WORLD AND THE UNDEFEATED CHAMPION!

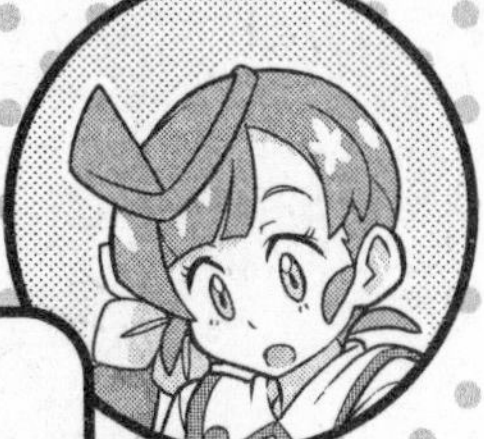

CHLOE

THE DAUGHTER OF PROFESSOR CERISE, AND ALSO GOH'S CHILDHOOD FRIEND.

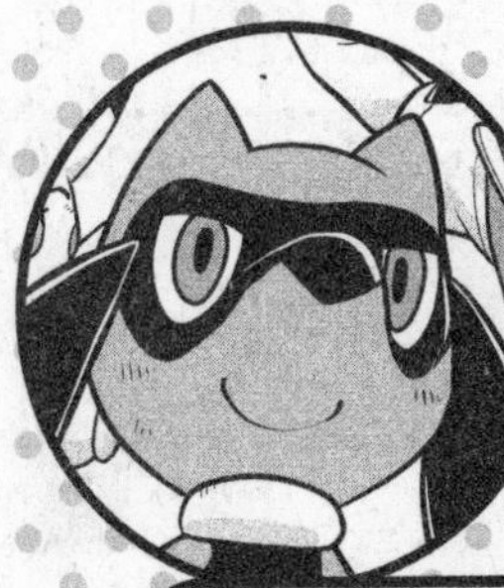

RIOLU

A POKÉMON ASH HATCHED FROM AN EGG.

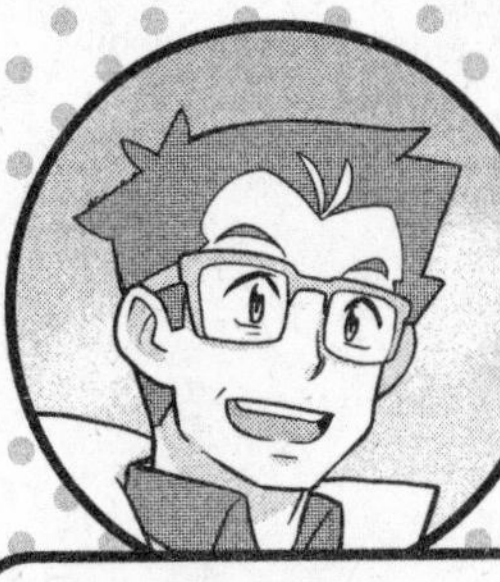

PROFESSOR CERISE

PROFESSOR OAK'S FORMER PUPIL WHO LIVES IN VERMILION CITY.

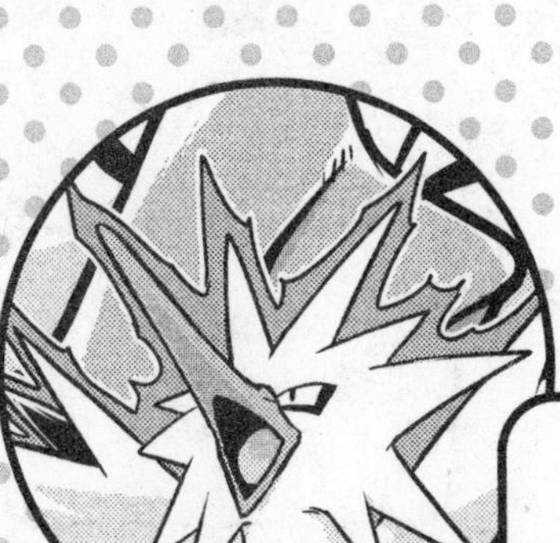

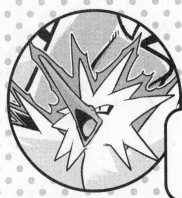

ZAPDOS

A LEGENDARY POKÉMON. IT APPEARS FROM THUNDERCLOUDS.

CONTENTS!

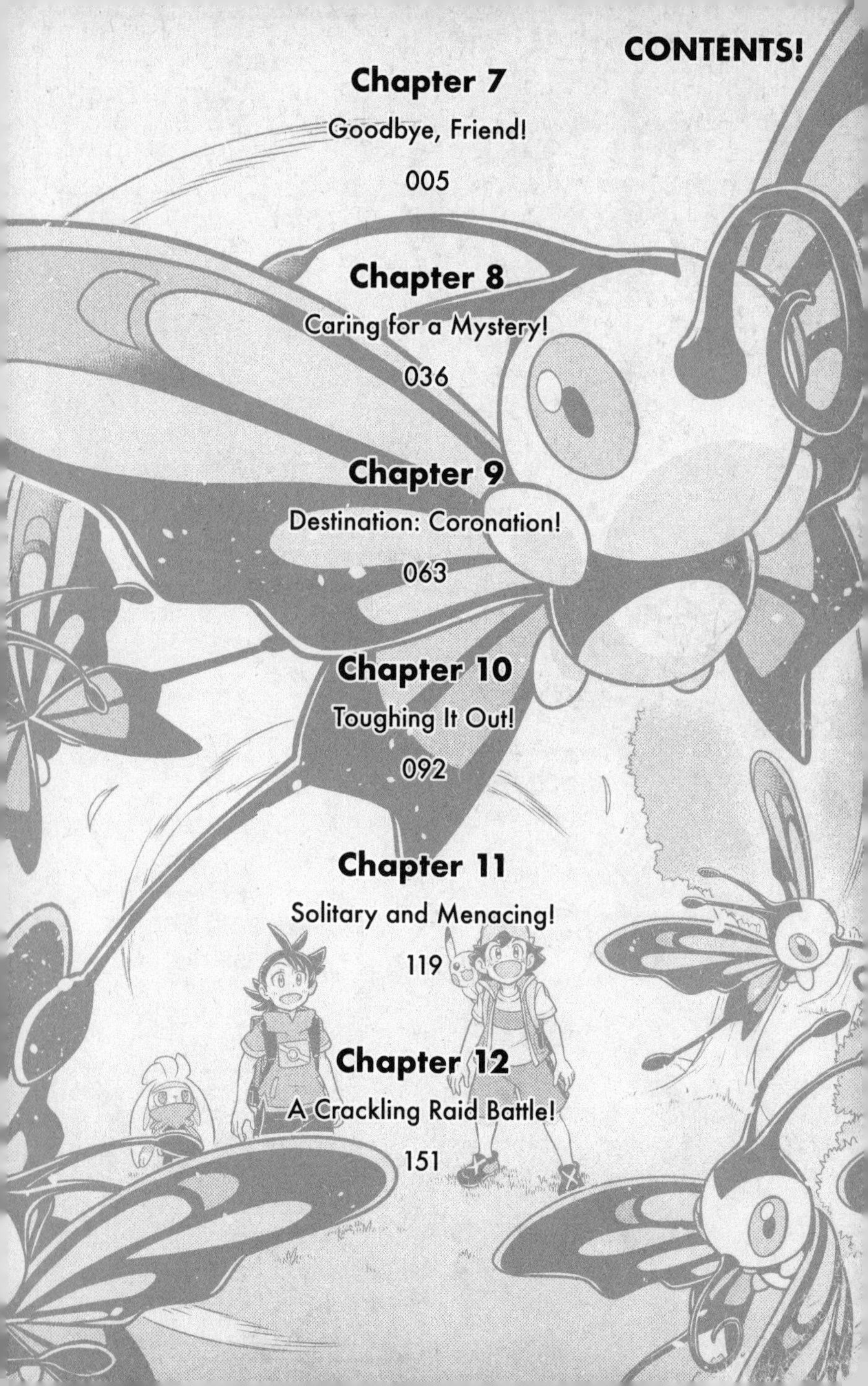

Chapter 7
Goodbye, Friend!

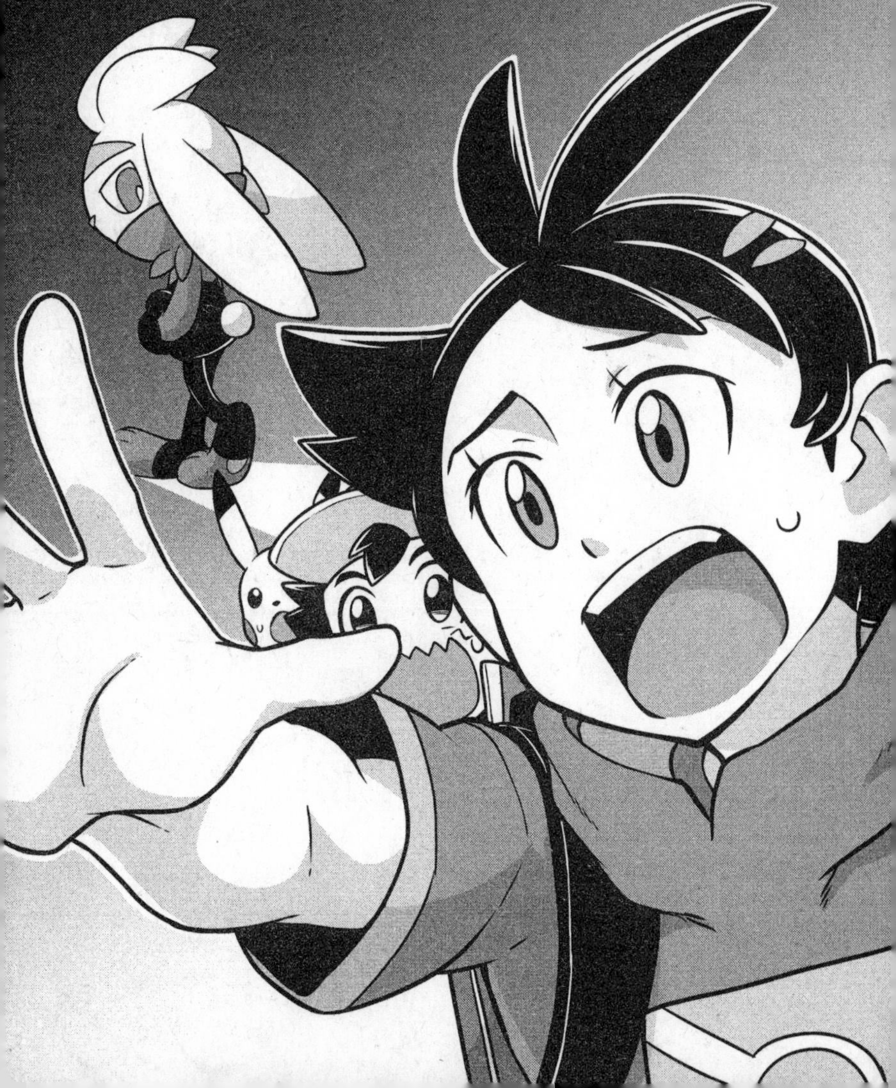

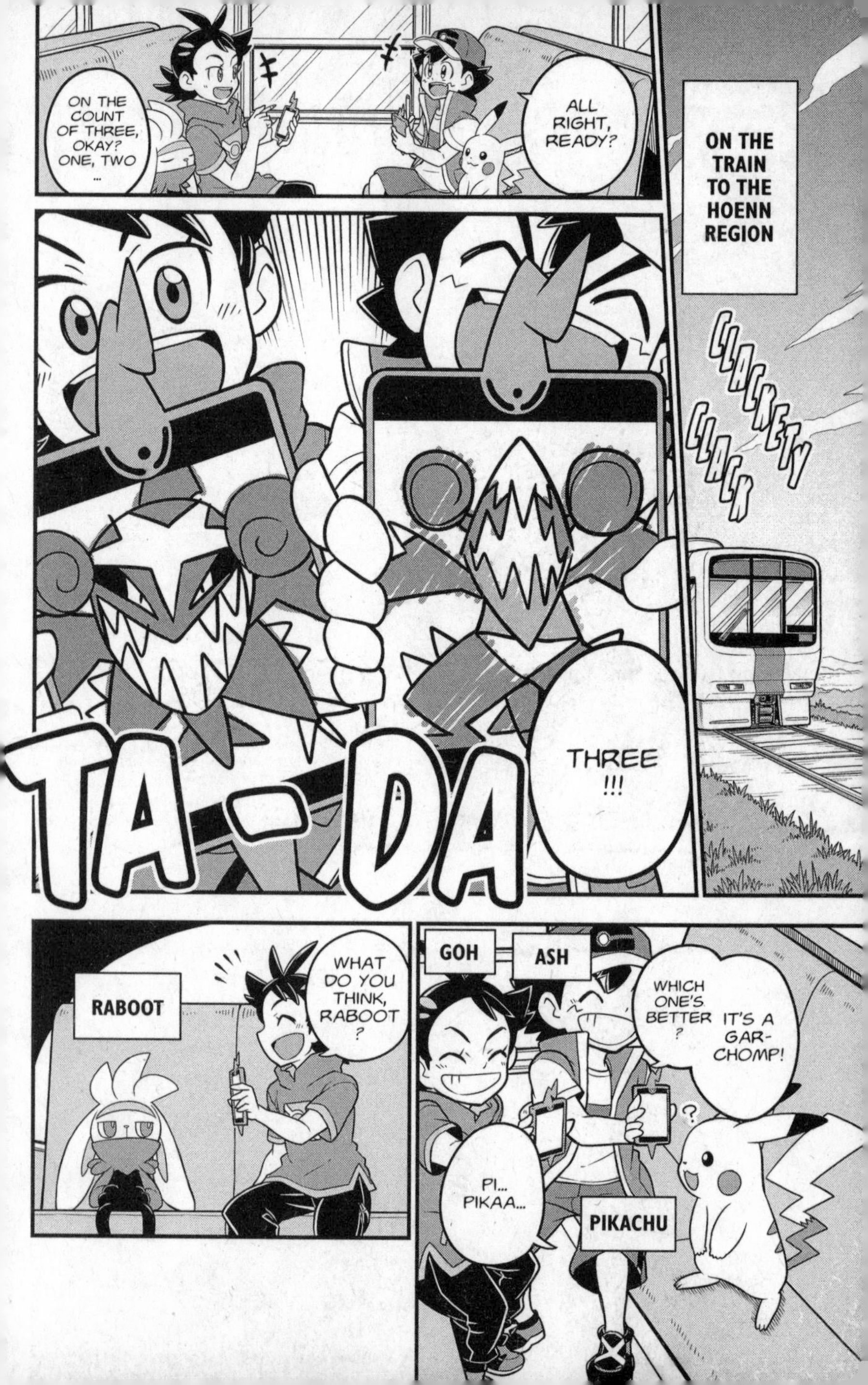
ON THE TRAIN TO THE HOENN REGION
CLACKETY CLACK
ALL RIGHT, READY?
ON THE COUNT OF THREE, OKAY? ONE, TWO ...
THREE !!!
TA-DA
ASH
GOH
IT'S A GAR-CHOMP!
WHICH ONE'S BETTER ?
PIKACHU
PI... PIKAA...
RABOOT
WHAT DO YOU THINK, RABOOT ?

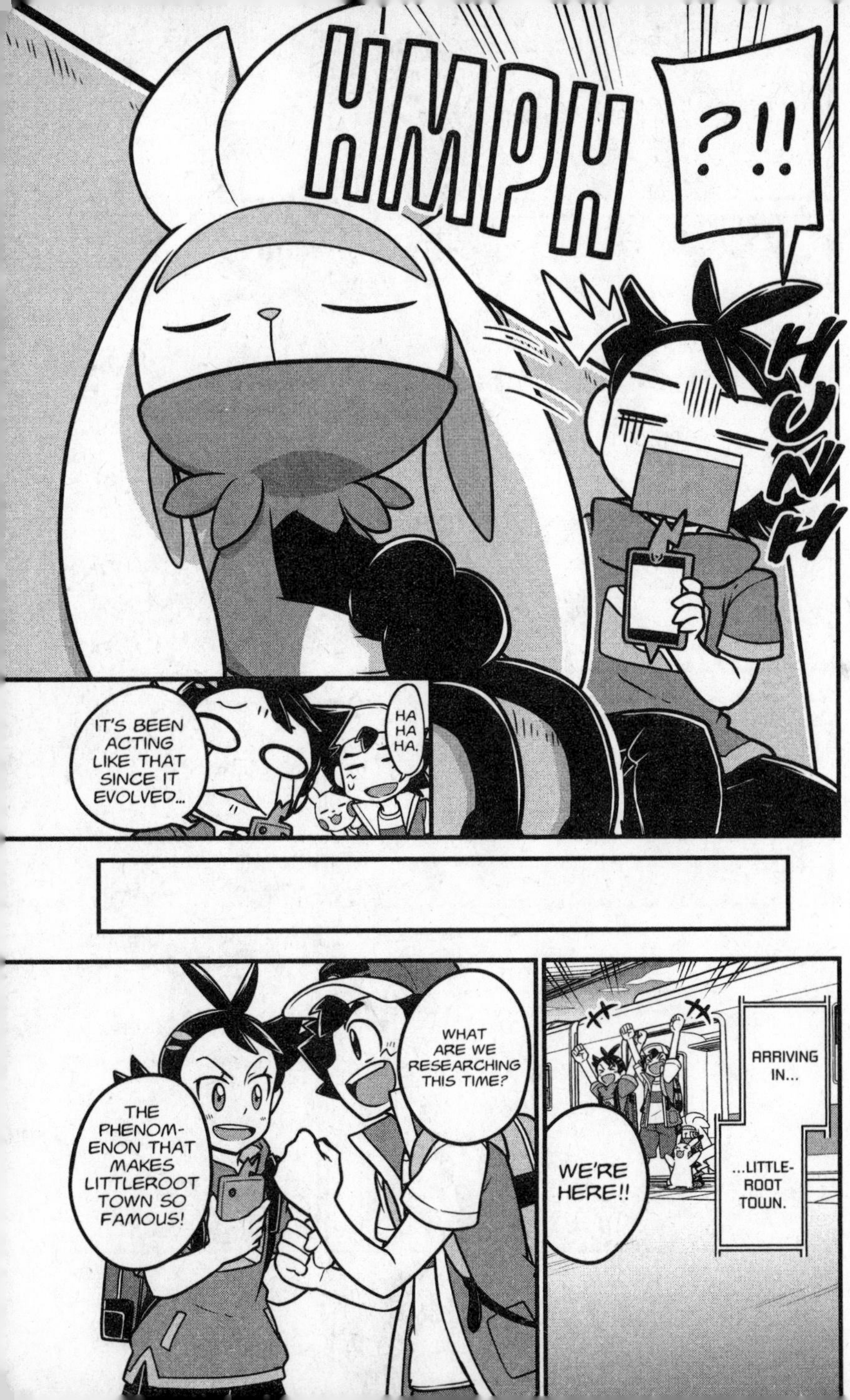
?!!
HMPH
HUNH
HA HA HA.
IT'S BEEN ACTING LIKE THAT SINCE IT EVOLVED...
ARRIVING IN...
...LITTLEROOT TOWN.
WE'RE HERE!!
WHAT ARE WE RESEARCHING THIS TIME?
THE PHENOMENON THAT MAKES LITTLEROOT TOWN SO FAMOUS!

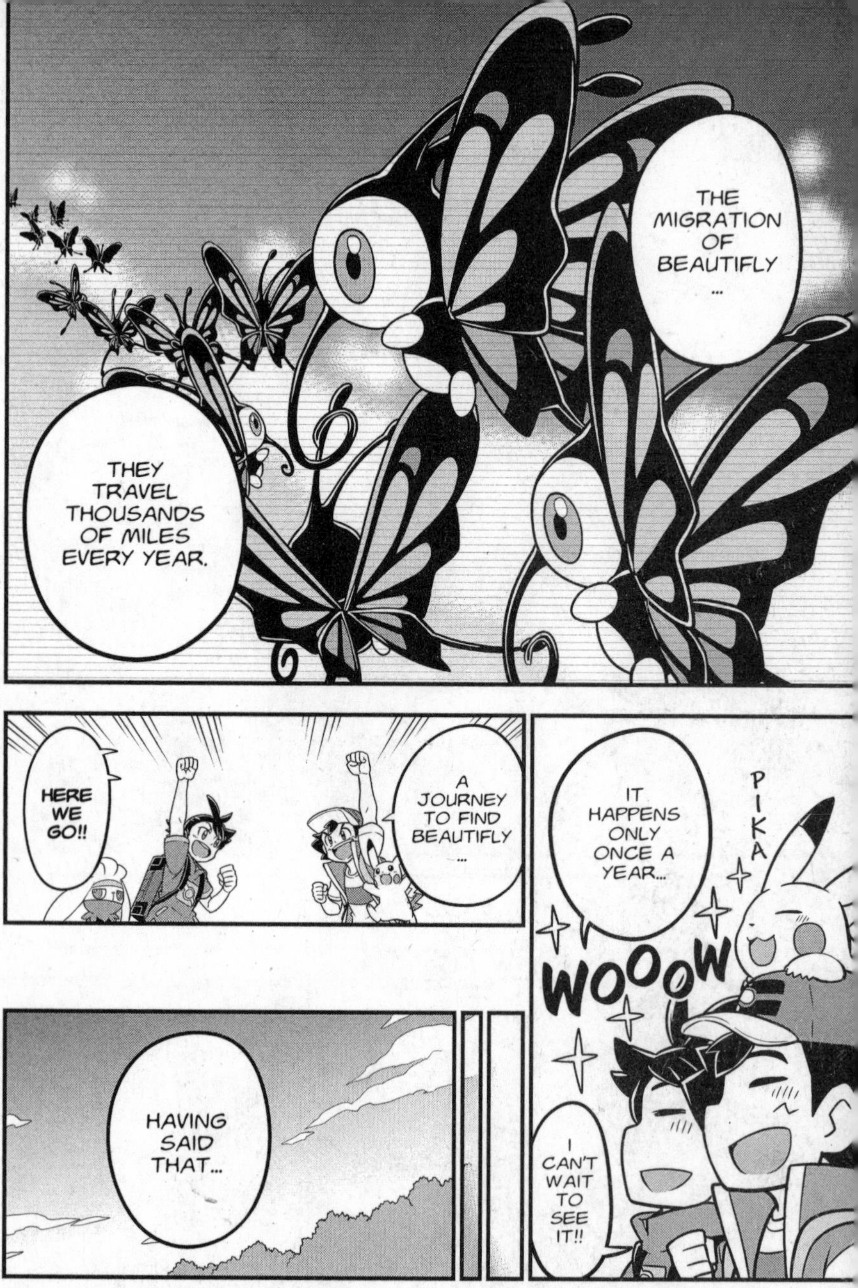
THE MIGRATION OF BEAUTIFLY ...
THEY TRAVEL THOUSANDS OF MILES EVERY YEAR.
IT HAPPENS ONLY ONCE A YEAR...
PIKA
WOOOW
I CAN'T WAIT TO SEE IT!!
A JOURNEY TO FIND BEAUTIFLY ...
HERE WE GO!!
HAVING SAID THAT...

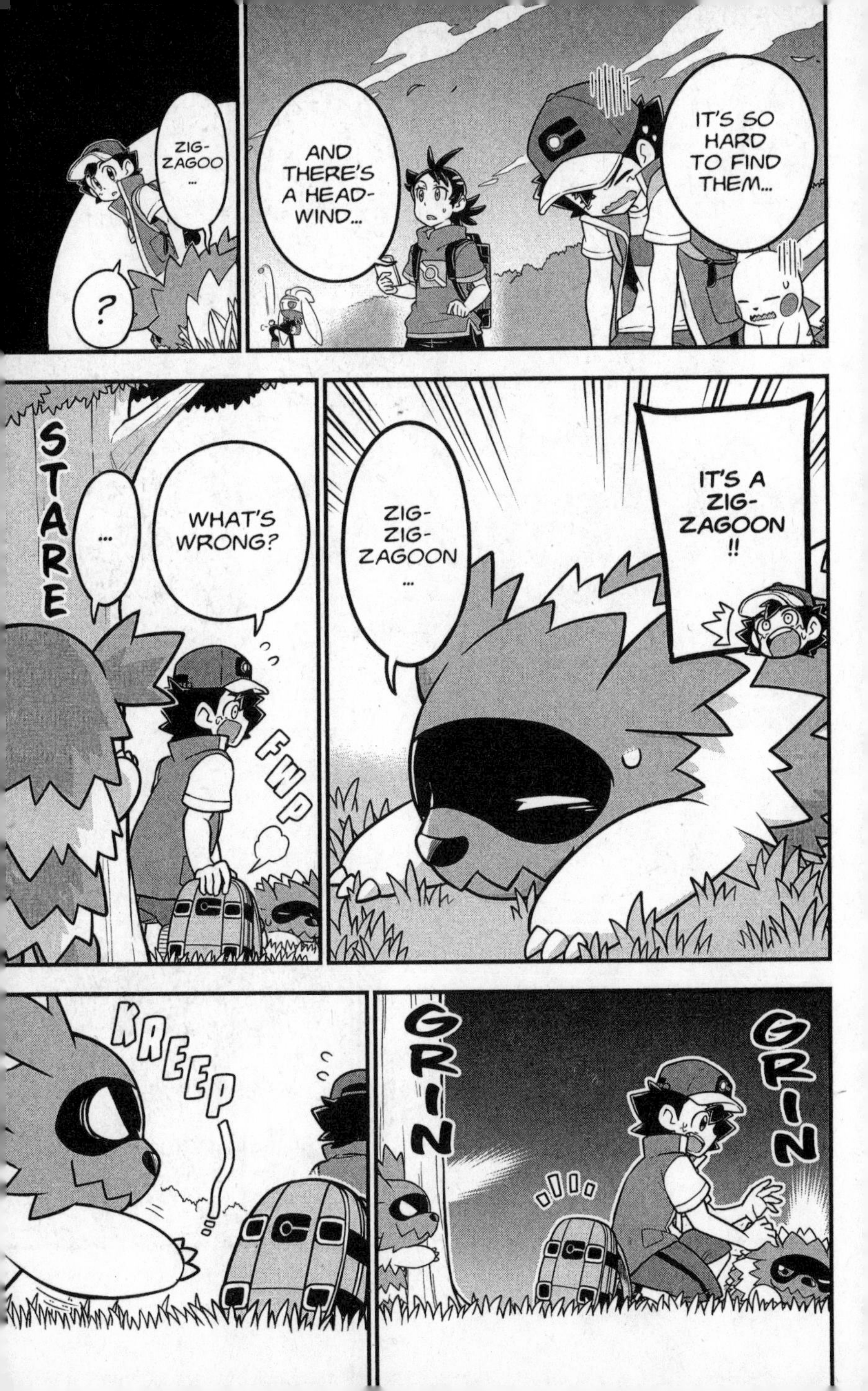

IT'S SO HARD TO FIND THEM...
AND THERE'S A HEAD-WIND...
ZIG-ZAGOO ...
?
IT'S A ZIG-ZAGOON !!
ZIG-ZIG-ZAGOON ...
WHAT'S WRONG?
FWP
...
STARE
GRIN
GRIN
KREEP

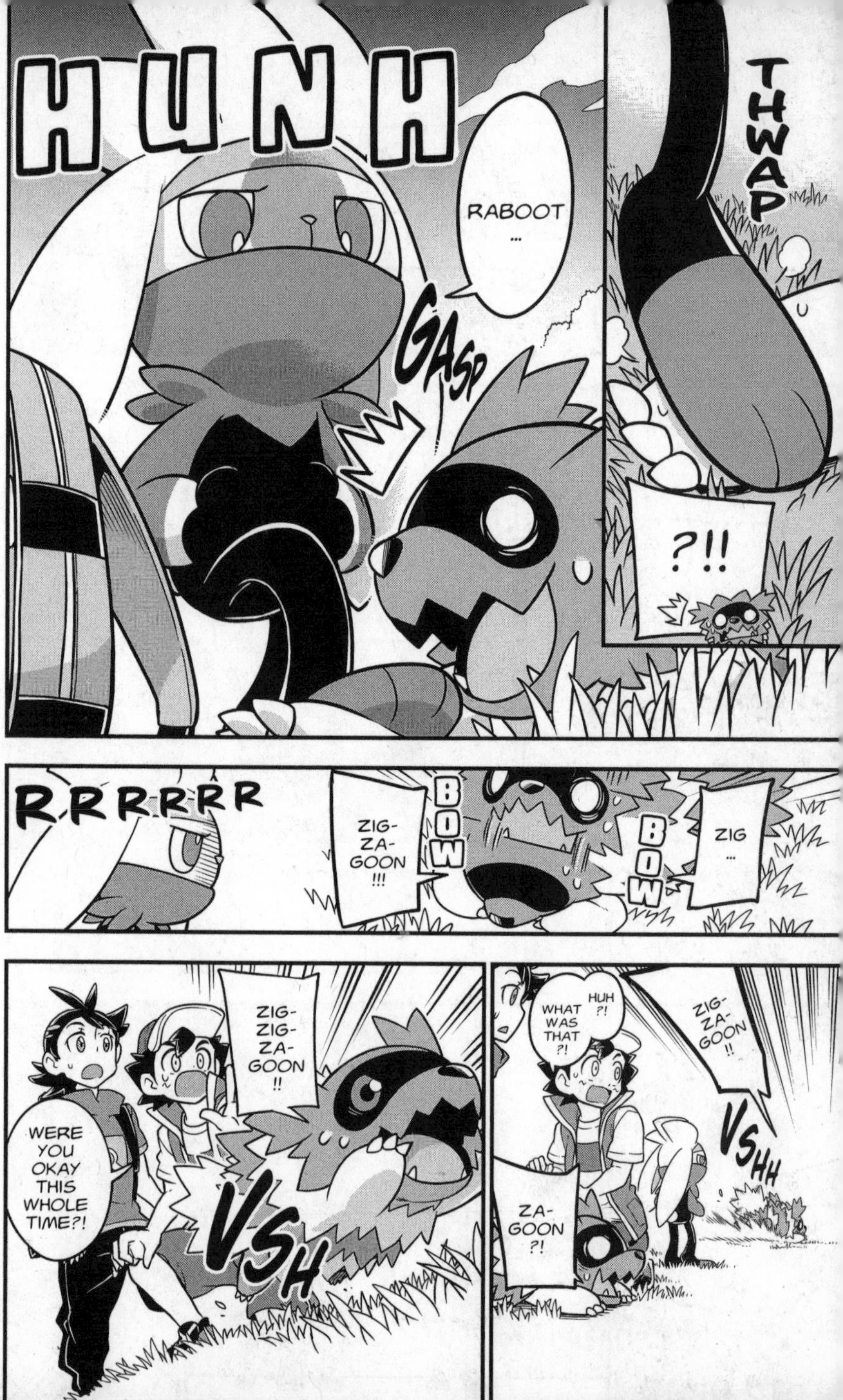
THWAP
?!!
HUNH
RABOOT ...
GASP
ZIG ...
BOW
BOW
ZIG-ZA-GOON !!!
RRRRRR
ZIG-ZA-GOON !!
VSHH
HUH ?!
WHAT WAS THAT ?!
ZA-GOON ?!
ZIG-ZIG-ZA-GOON !!
VSH
WERE YOU OKAY THIS WHOLE TIME?!

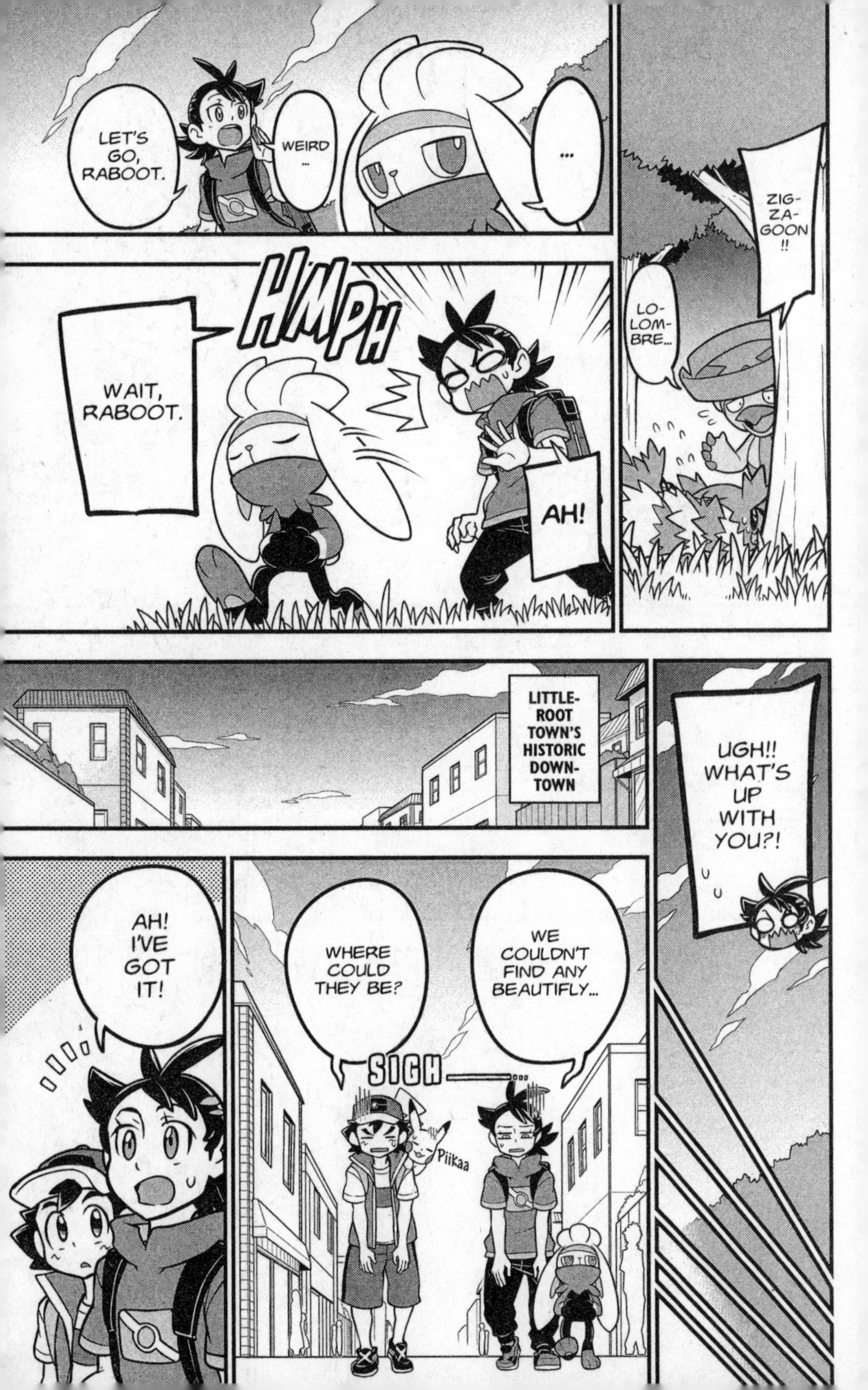
ZIG-ZA-GOON!!
LO-LOMBRE...
...
WEIRD...
LET'S GO, RABOOT.
AH!
HMPH
WAIT, RABOOT.
UGH!! WHAT'S UP WITH YOU?!
LITTLEROOT TOWN'S HISTORIC DOWNTOWN
WE COULDN'T FIND ANY BEAUTIFLY...
WHERE COULD THEY BE?
SIGH—...
Piikaa
AH! I'VE GOT IT!

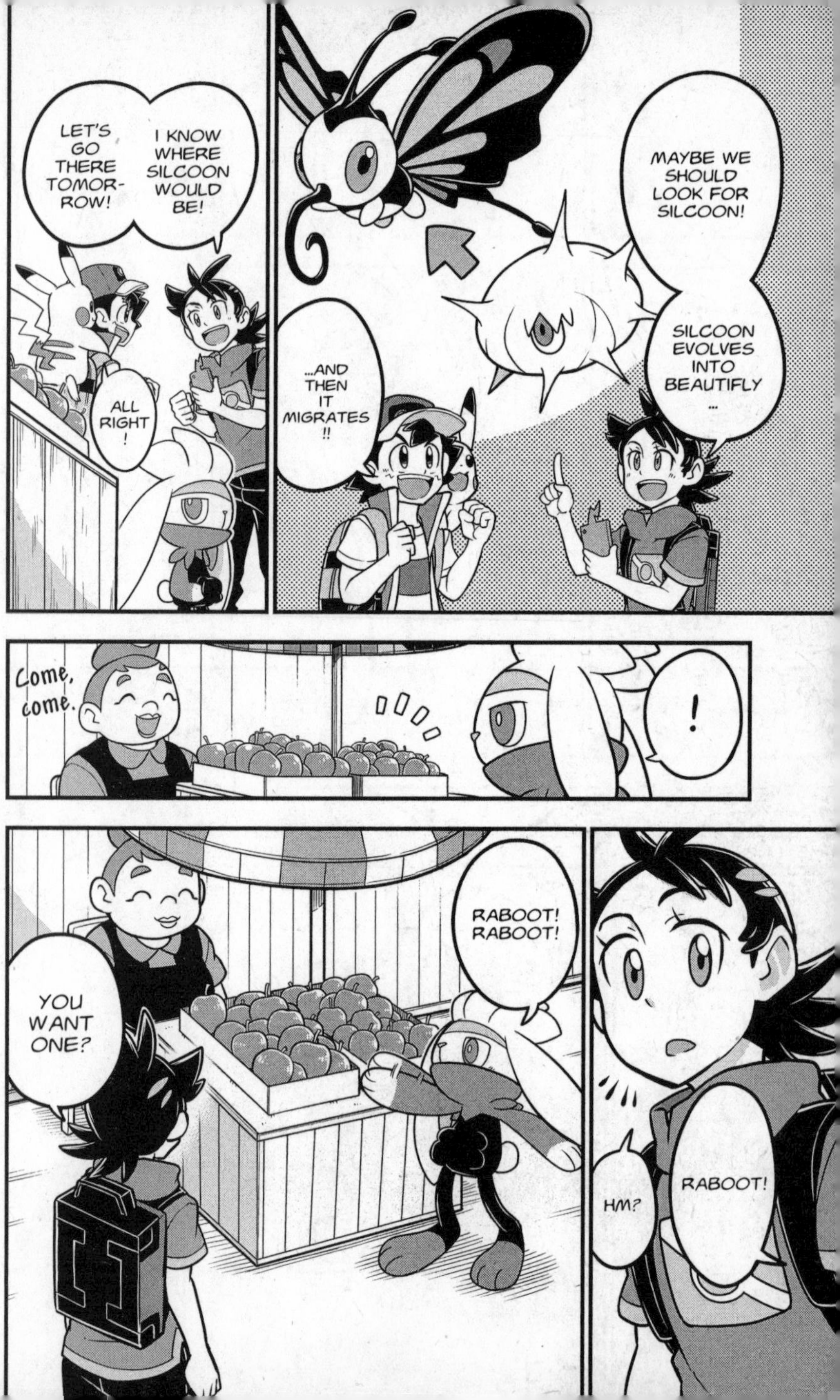
MAYBE WE SHOULD LOOK FOR SILCOON!
SILCOON EVOLVES INTO BEAUTIFLY ...
...AND THEN IT MIGRATES !!
I KNOW WHERE SILCOON WOULD BE!
LET'S GO THERE TOMOR-ROW!
ALL RIGHT !
!
Come, come.
RABOOT!
HM?
RABOOT! RABOOT!
YOU WANT ONE?

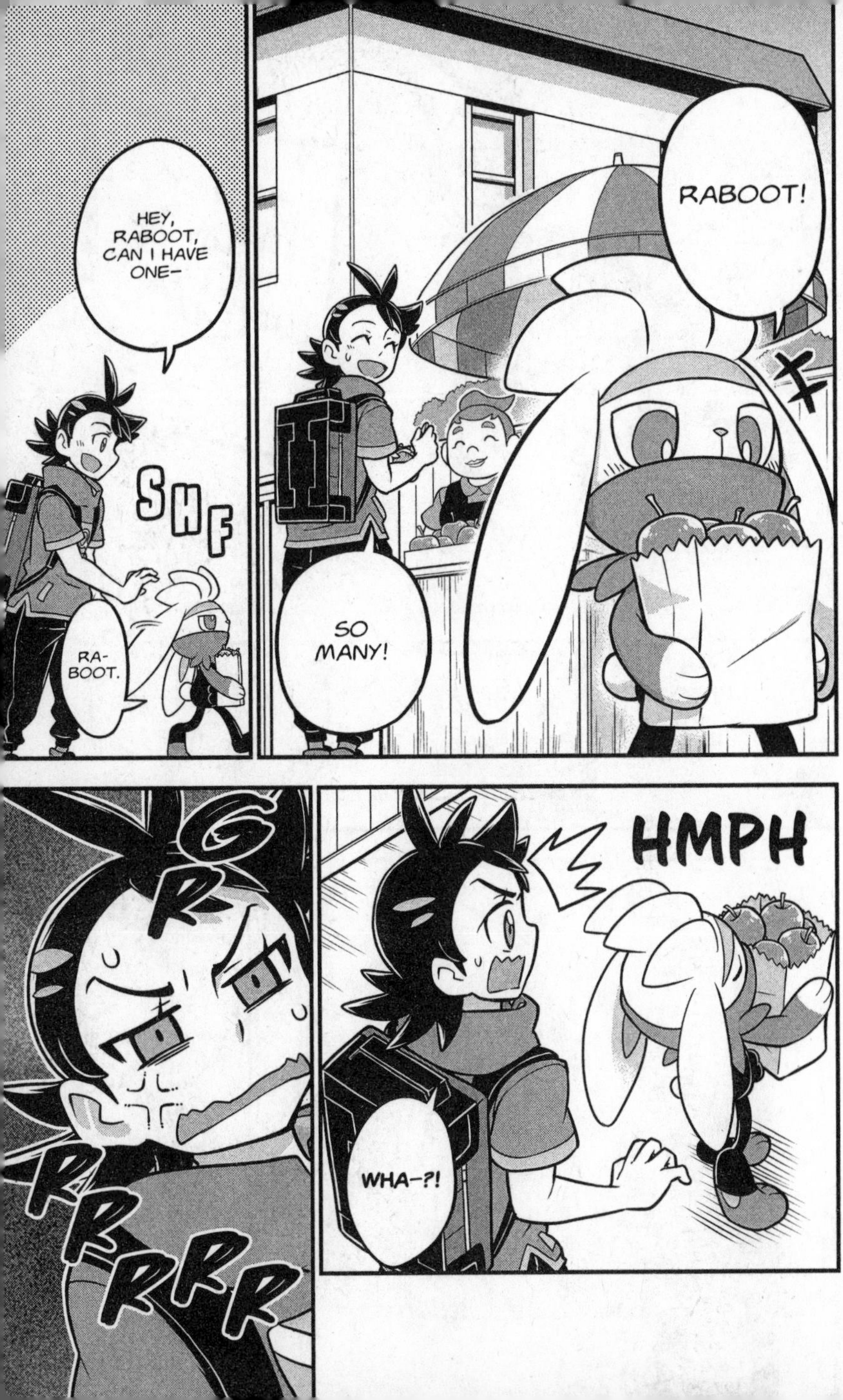
RABOOT!
SO MANY!
HEY, RABOOT, CAN I HAVE ONE–
SHF
RA-BOOT.
HMPH
WHA–?!
GRRRRRRR

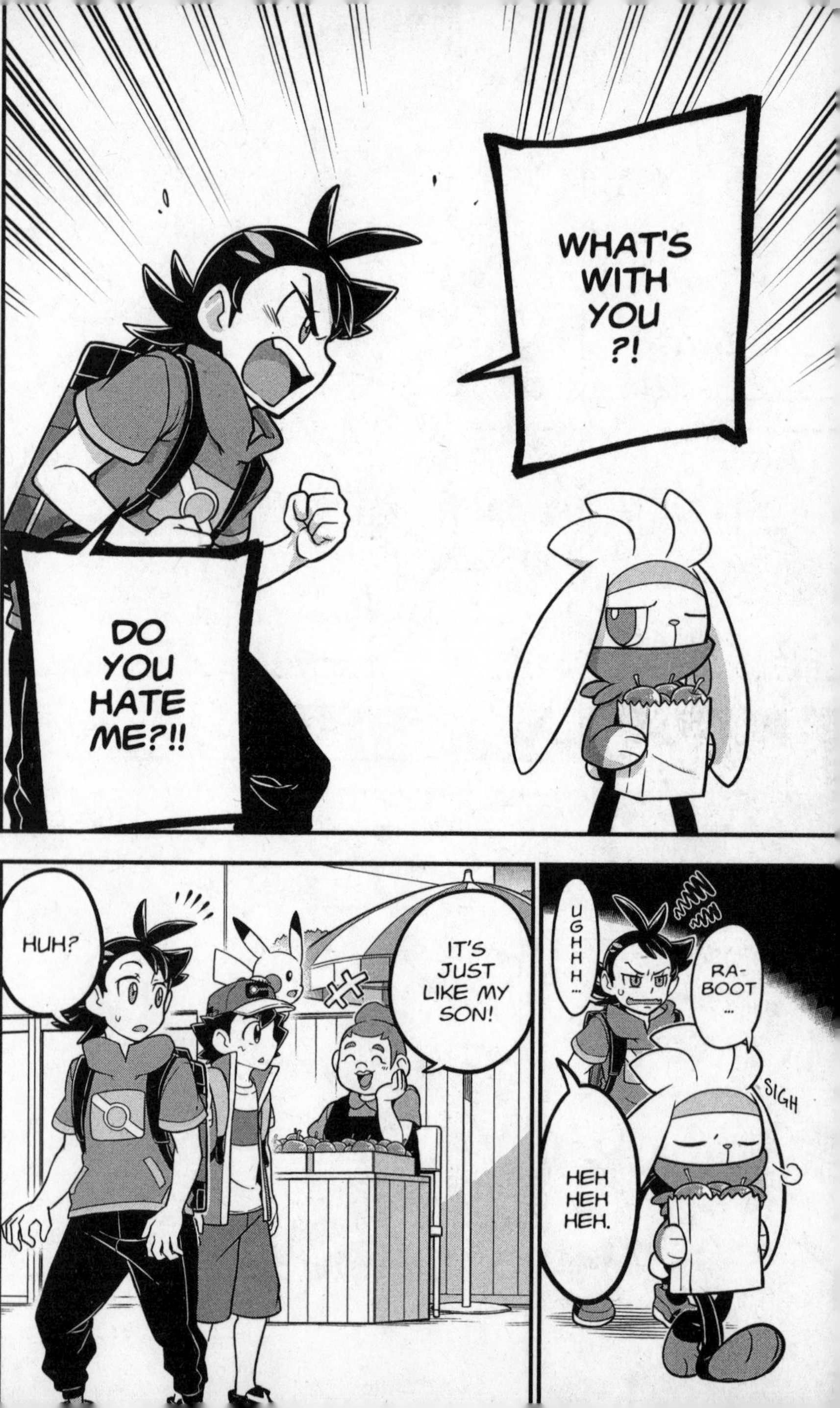
WHAT'S WITH YOU ?!
DO YOU HATE ME?!!
UGHHH...
RA-BOOT...
SIGH
HEH HEH HEH.
IT'S JUST LIKE MY SON!
HUH?

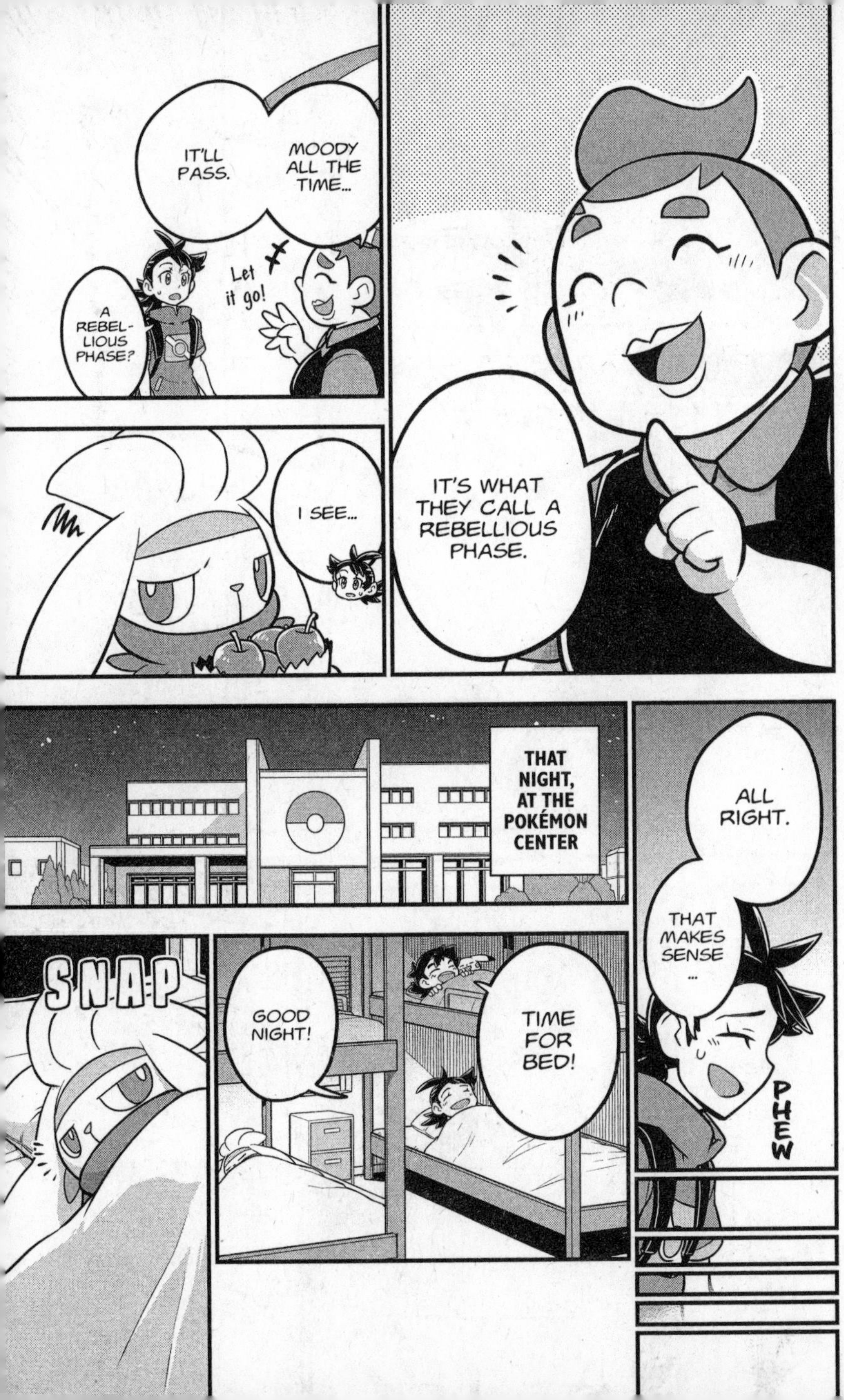
IT'S WHAT THEY CALL A REBELLIOUS PHASE.
MOODY ALL THE TIME...
IT'LL PASS.
Let it go!
A REBEL-LIOUS PHASE?
I SEE...
ALL RIGHT.
THAT MAKES SENSE...
PHEW
THAT NIGHT, AT THE POKÉMON CENTER
TIME FOR BED!
GOOD NIGHT!
SNAP

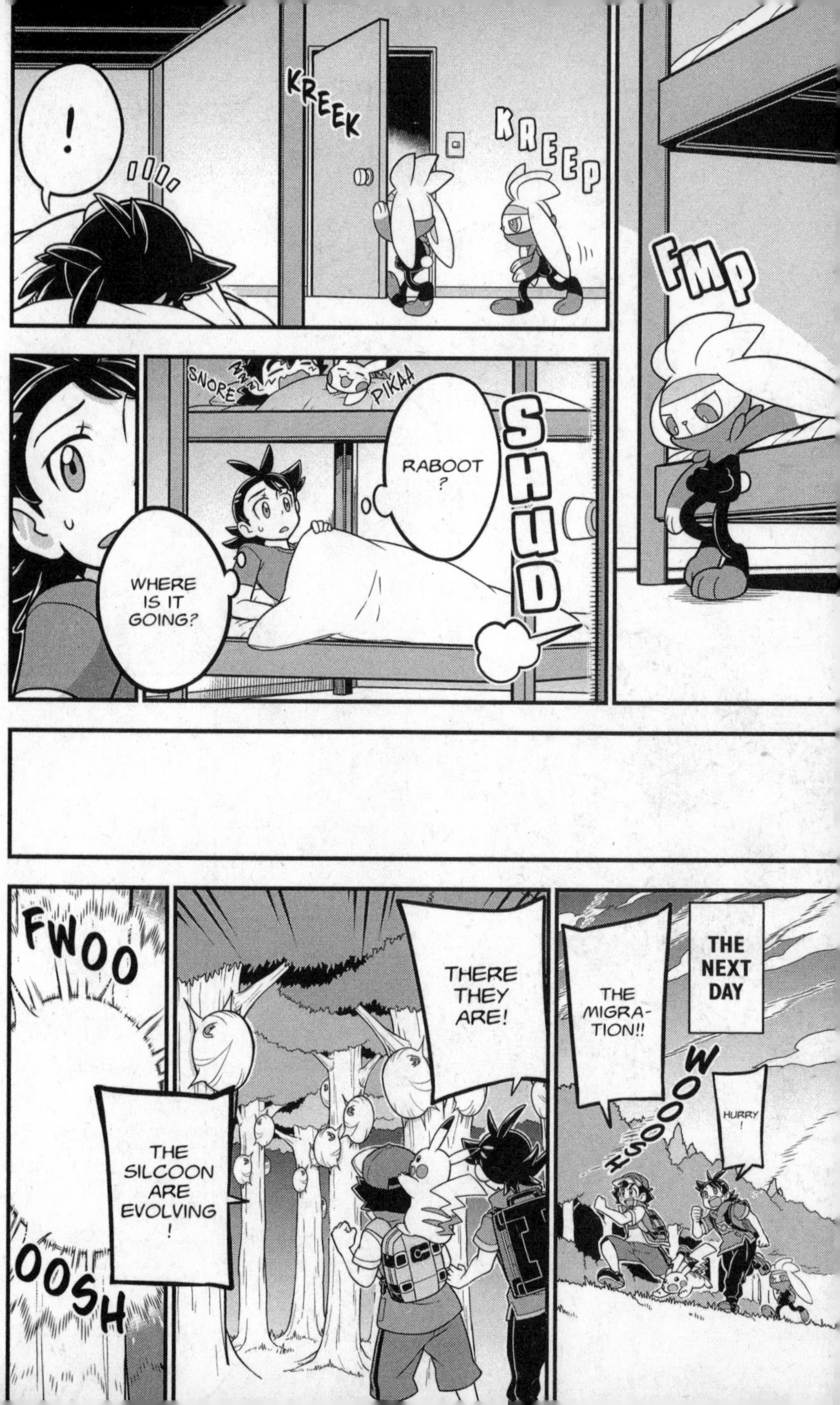
FMP
KREEK
KREEP
!
SNORE
MMZ
PIKAA
RABOOT?
SHUD
WHERE IS IT GOING?
THE NEXT DAY
HURRY!
WOOOOSH
THE MIGRATION!!
THERE THEY ARE!
THE SILCOON ARE EVOLVING!
FWOOOOSH

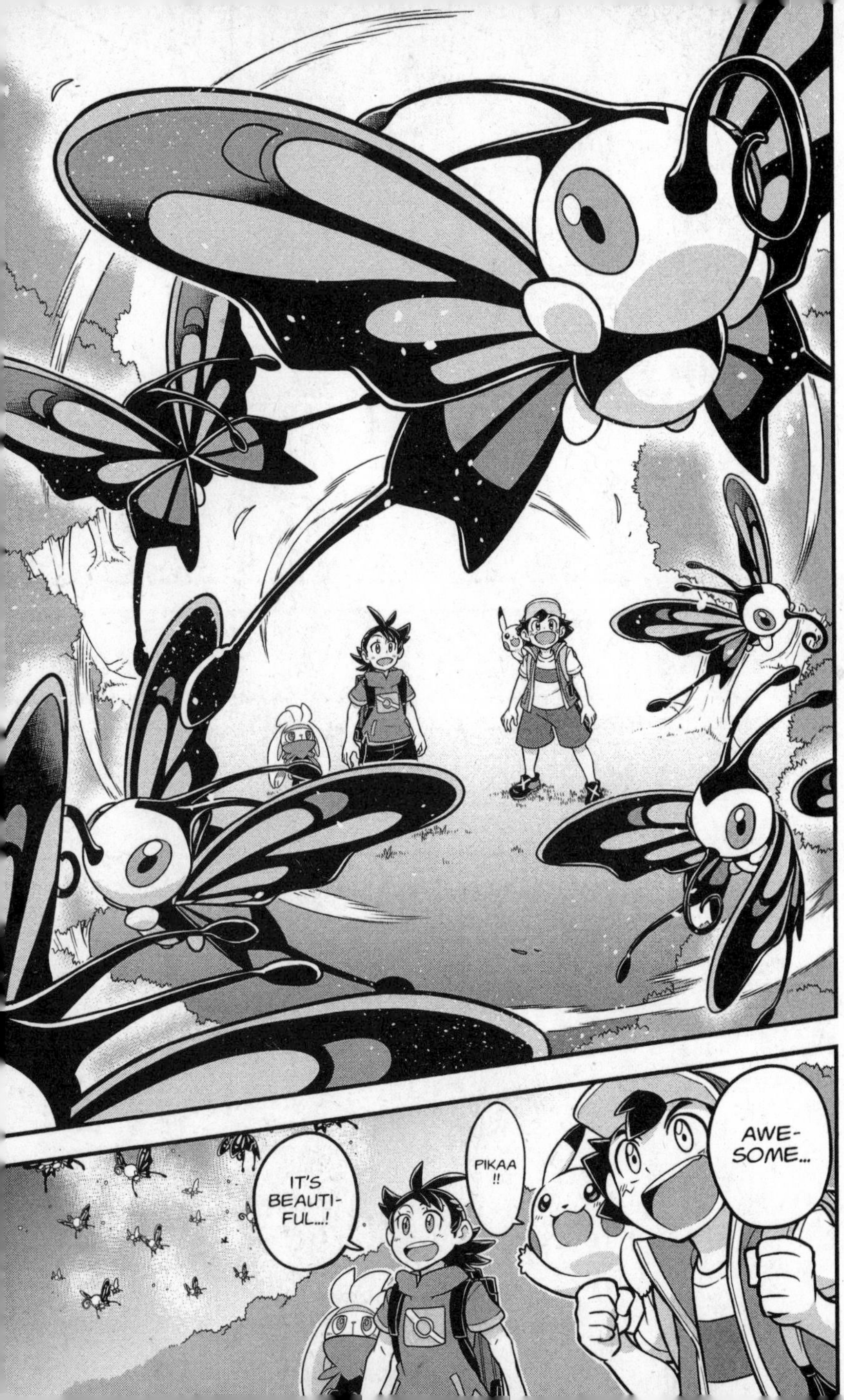
AWE-SOME...
PIKAA !!
IT'S BEAUTI-FUL...!

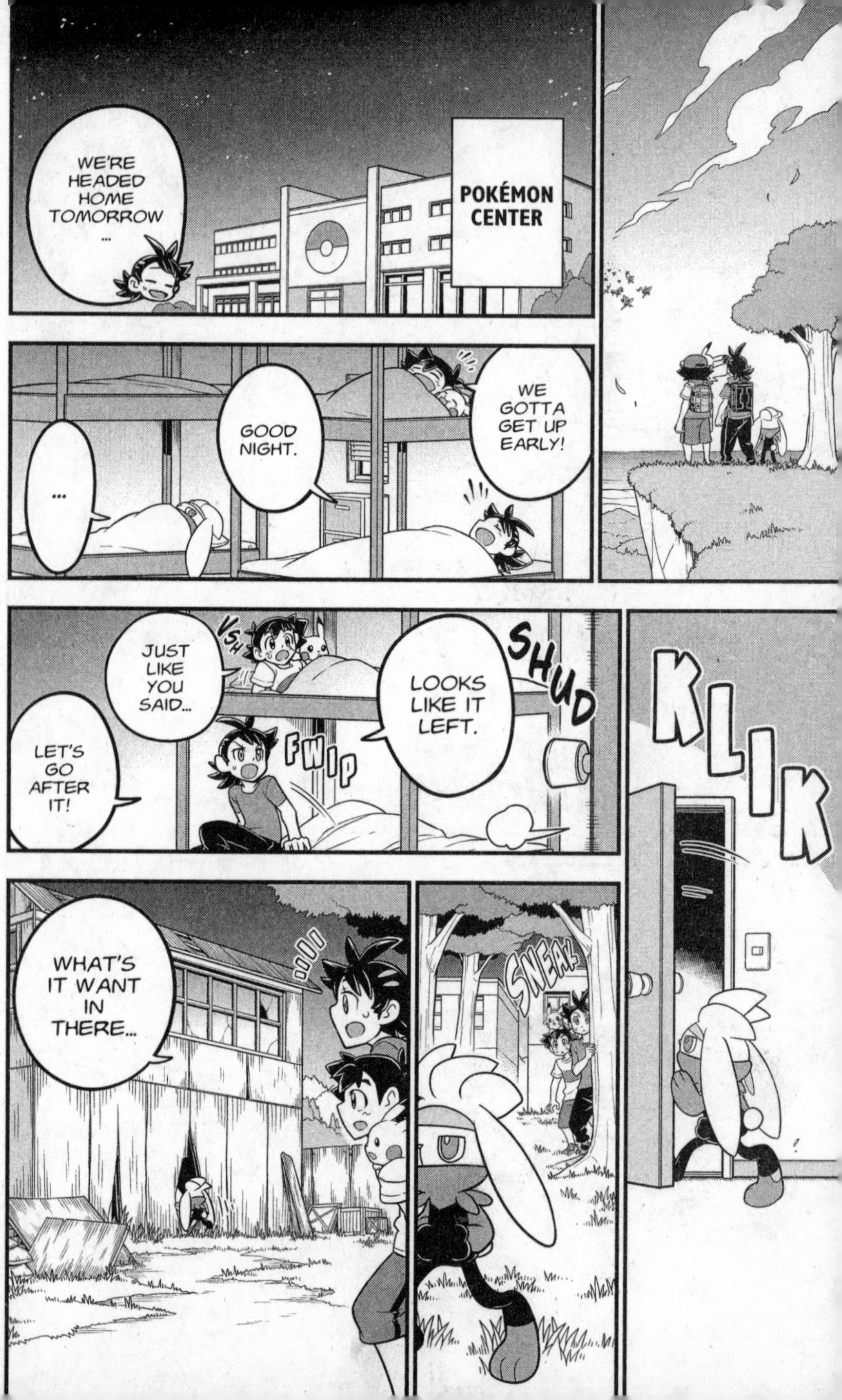
WE'RE HEADED HOME TOMORROW ...
POKÉMON CENTER
WE GOTTA GET UP EARLY!
GOOD NIGHT.
...
KLIK
SHUD
LOOKS LIKE IT LEFT.
VSH
JUST LIKE YOU SAID...
FWIP
LET'S GO AFTER IT!
SNEAK
WHAT'S IT WANT IN THERE...

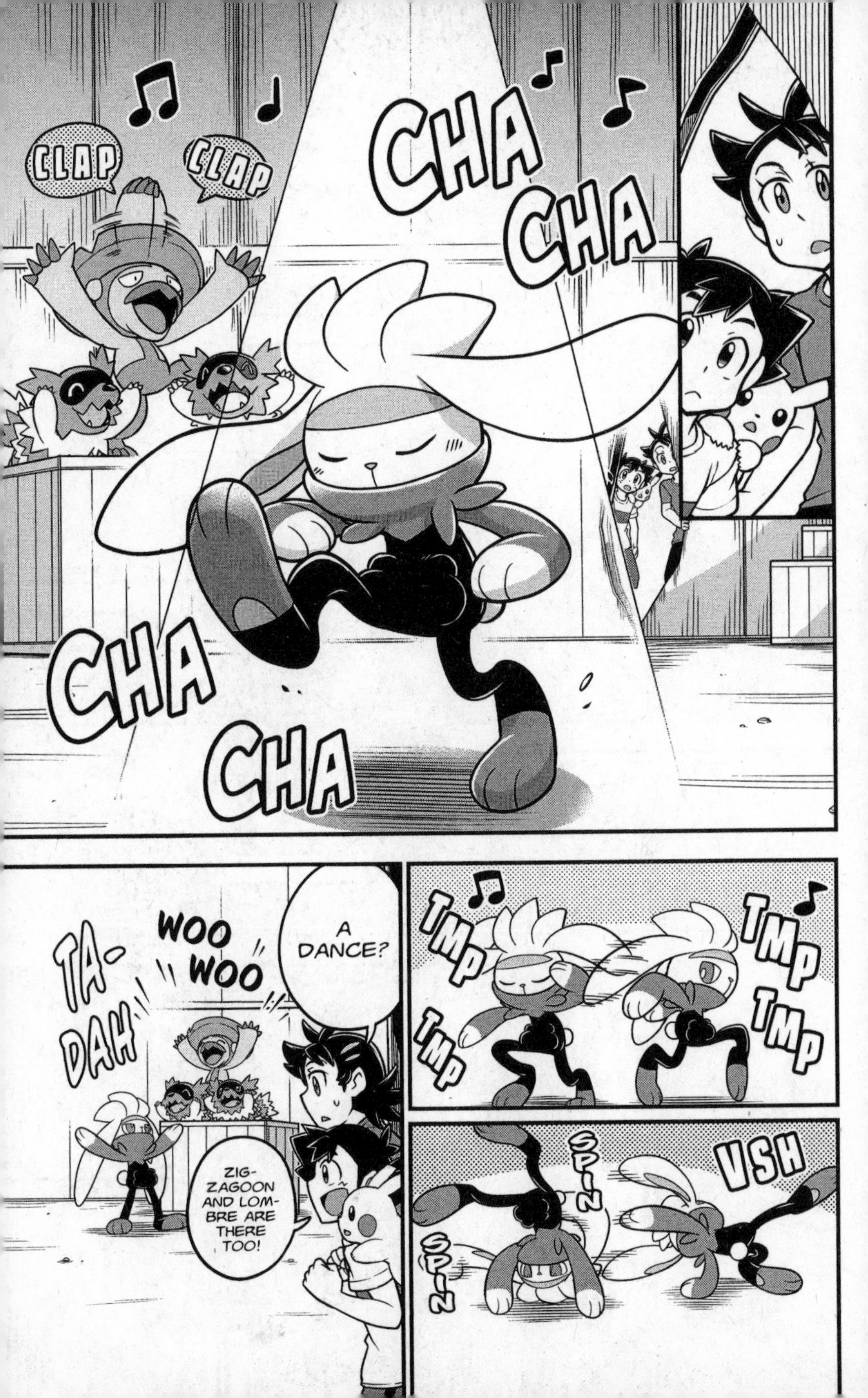
CHA CHA
CLAP
CLAP
CHA CHA
TMP
TMP
TMP
TMP
VSH
SPIN
SPIN
A DANCE?
WOO WOO
TA-DAH
ZIG-ZAGOON AND LOM-BRE ARE THERE TOO!

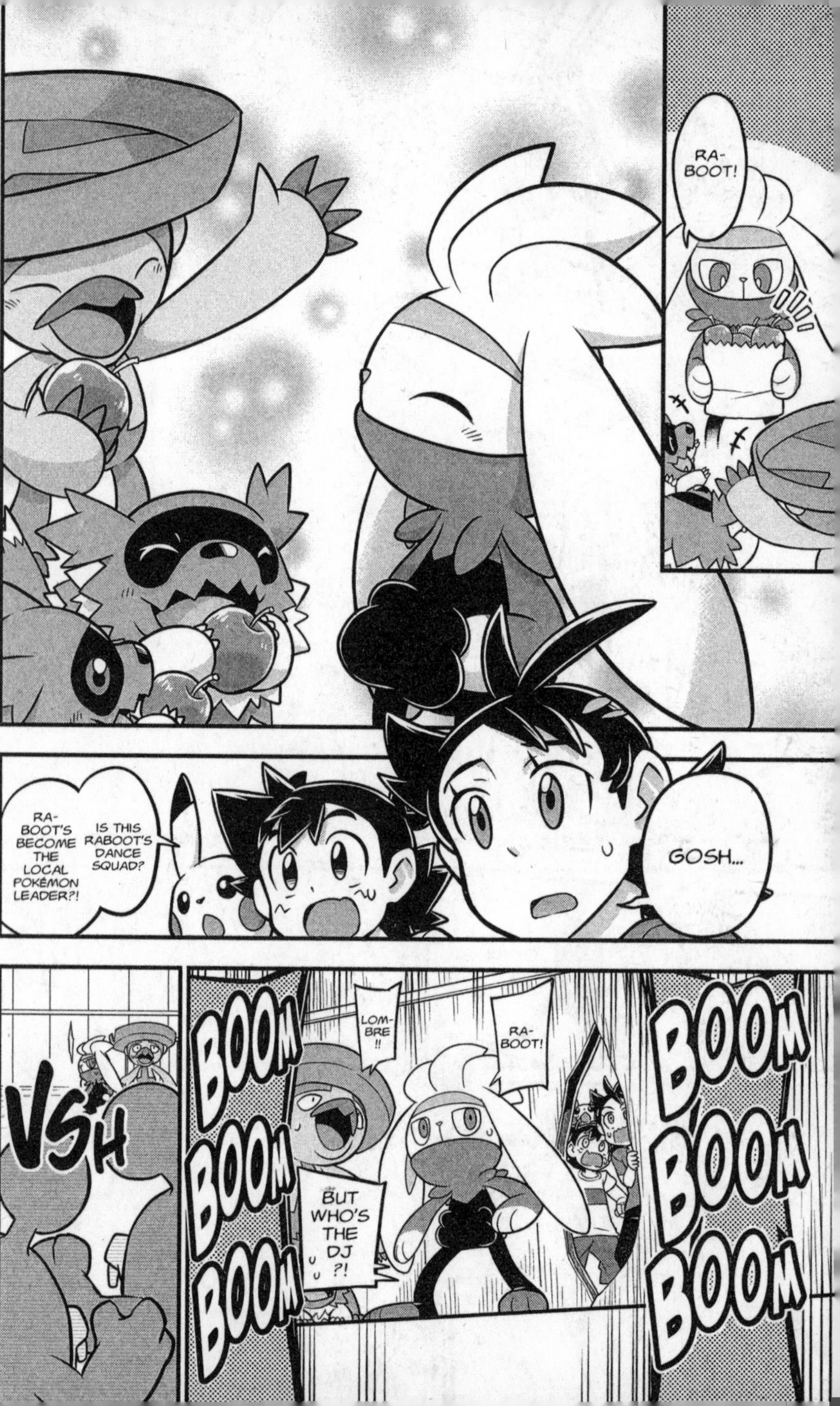
RA-BOOT!
GOSH...
IS THIS RABOOT'S DANCE SQUAD?
RA-BOOT'S BECOME THE LOCAL POKÉMON LEADER?!
BOOM BOOM BOOM
RA-BOOT!
LOMBRE!!
BOOM BOOM BOOM
BUT WHO'S THE DJ?!
VSH

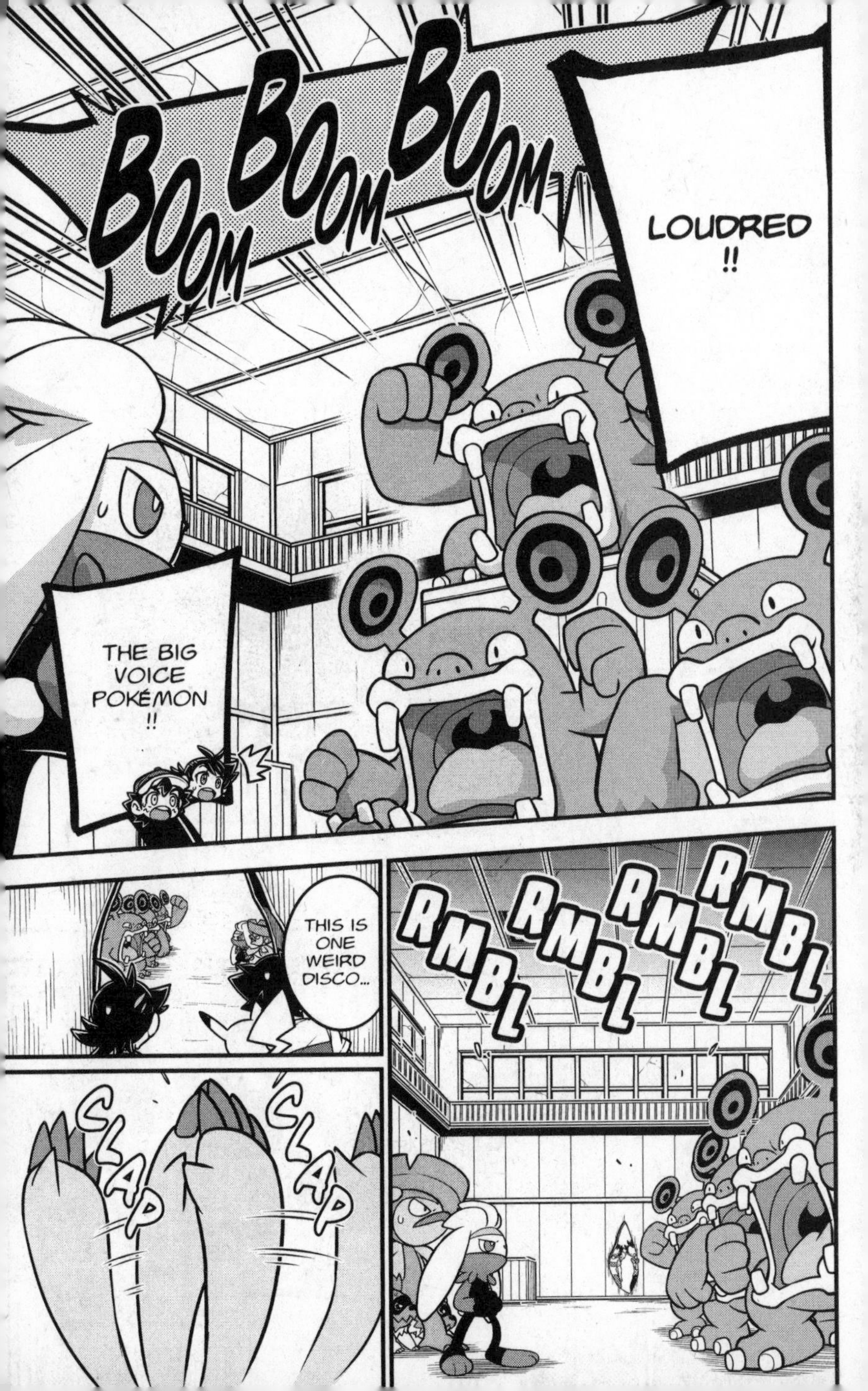
BOOM BOOM BOOM
LOUDRED !!
THE BIG VOICE POKÉMON !!
RMBL RMBL RMBL
THIS IS ONE WEIRD DISCO...
CLAP CLAP

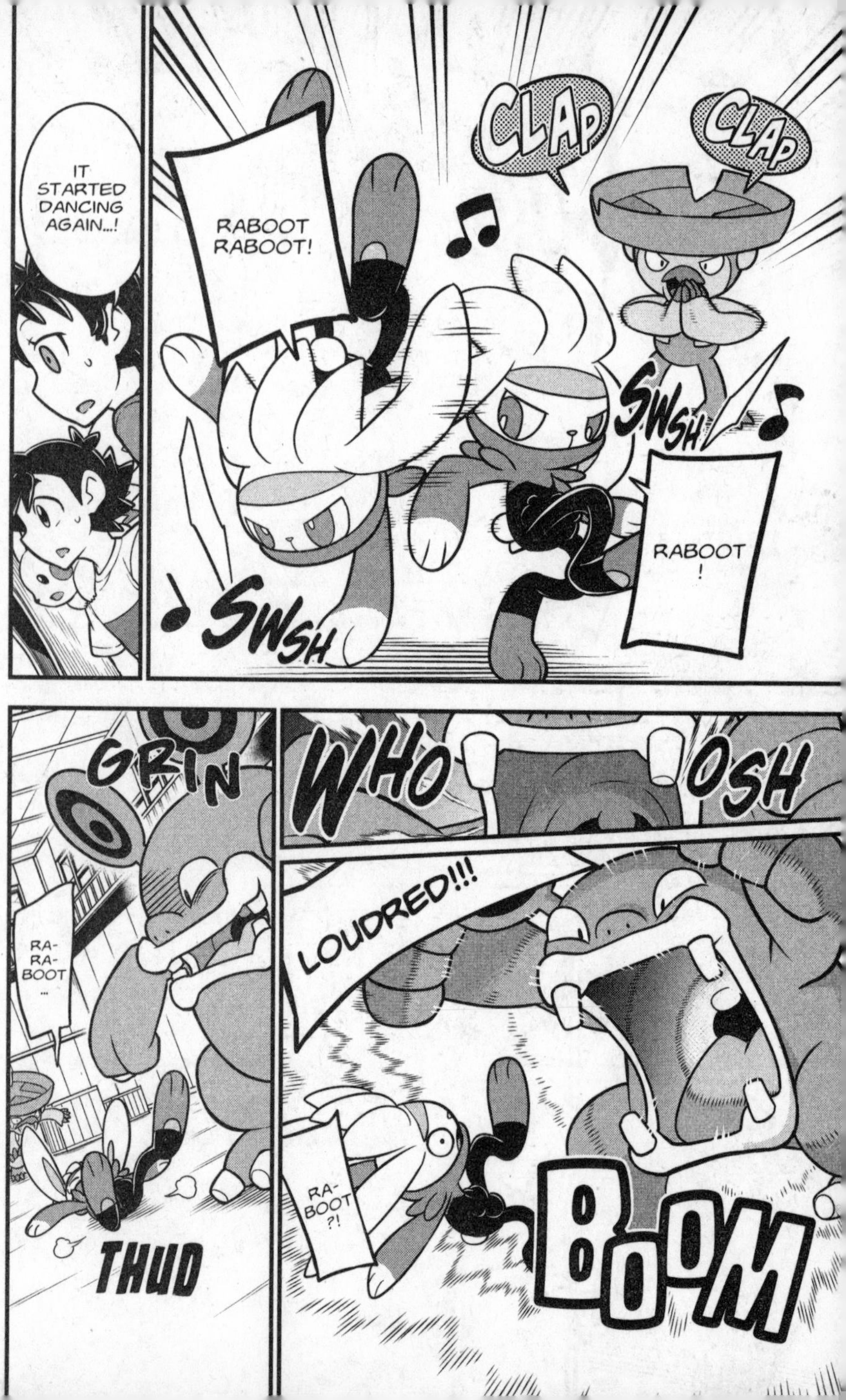
CLAP
CLAP
RABOOT RABOOT!
SWSH
RABOOT!
SWSH
IT STARTED DANCING AGAIN...!
WHOOSH
LOUDRED!!!
RA-BOOT?!
BOOM
GRIN
RA-RA-BOOT...
THUD

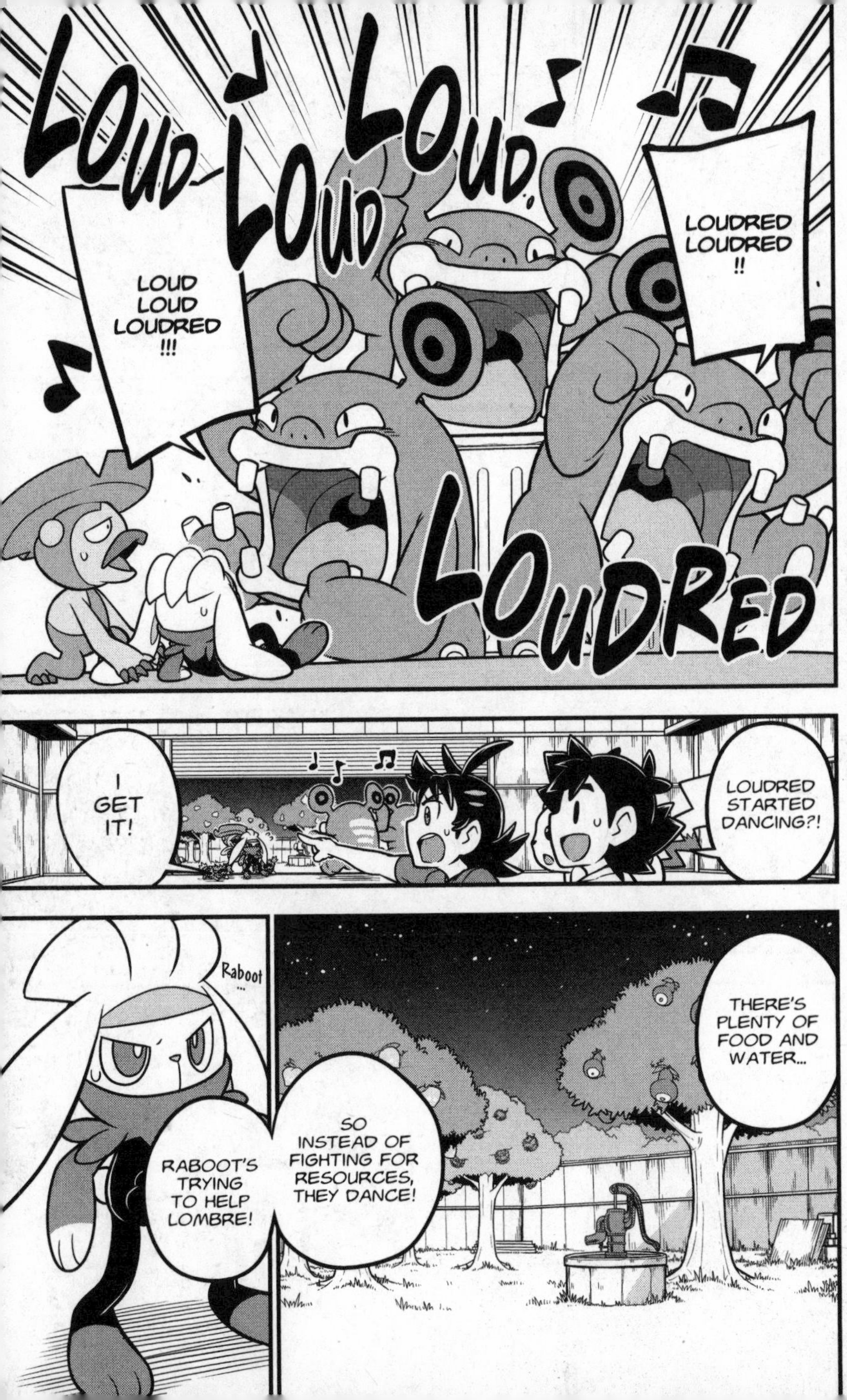
LOUD- LOUD LOUD
LOUDRED LOUDRED !!
LOUD LOUD LOUDRED !!!
LOUDRED
LOUDRED STARTED DANCING?!
I GET IT!
THERE'S PLENTY OF FOOD AND WATER...
SO INSTEAD OF FIGHTING FOR RESOURCES, THEY DANCE!
Raboot ...
RABOOT'S TRYING TO HELP LOMBRE!

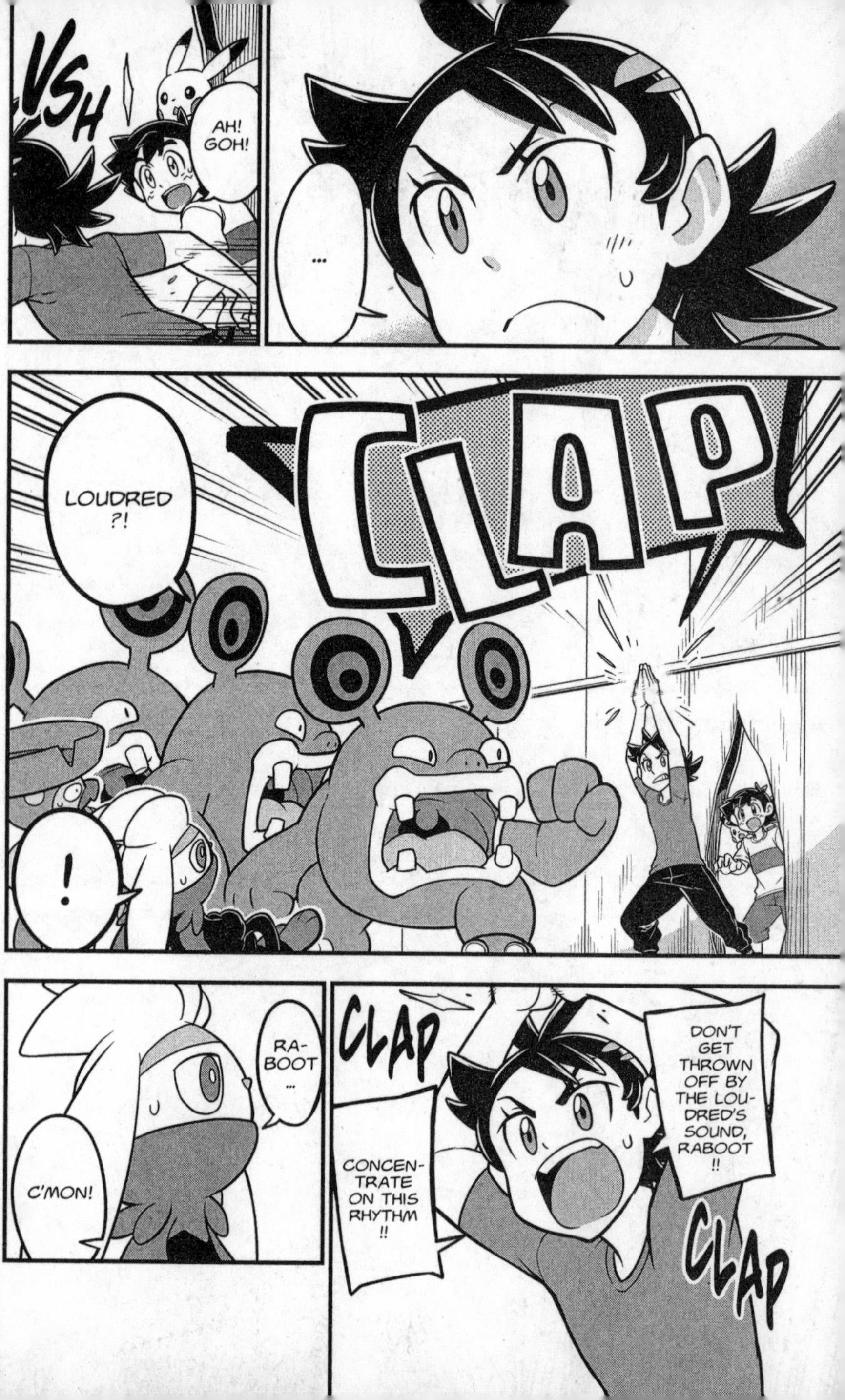
...
AH! GOH!
CLAP
LOUDRED ?!
!
CLAP
DON'T GET THROWN OFF BY THE LOU-DRED'S SOUND, RABOOT !!
CONCEN-TRATE ON THIS RHYTHM !!
CLAP
RA-BOOT ...
C'MON!

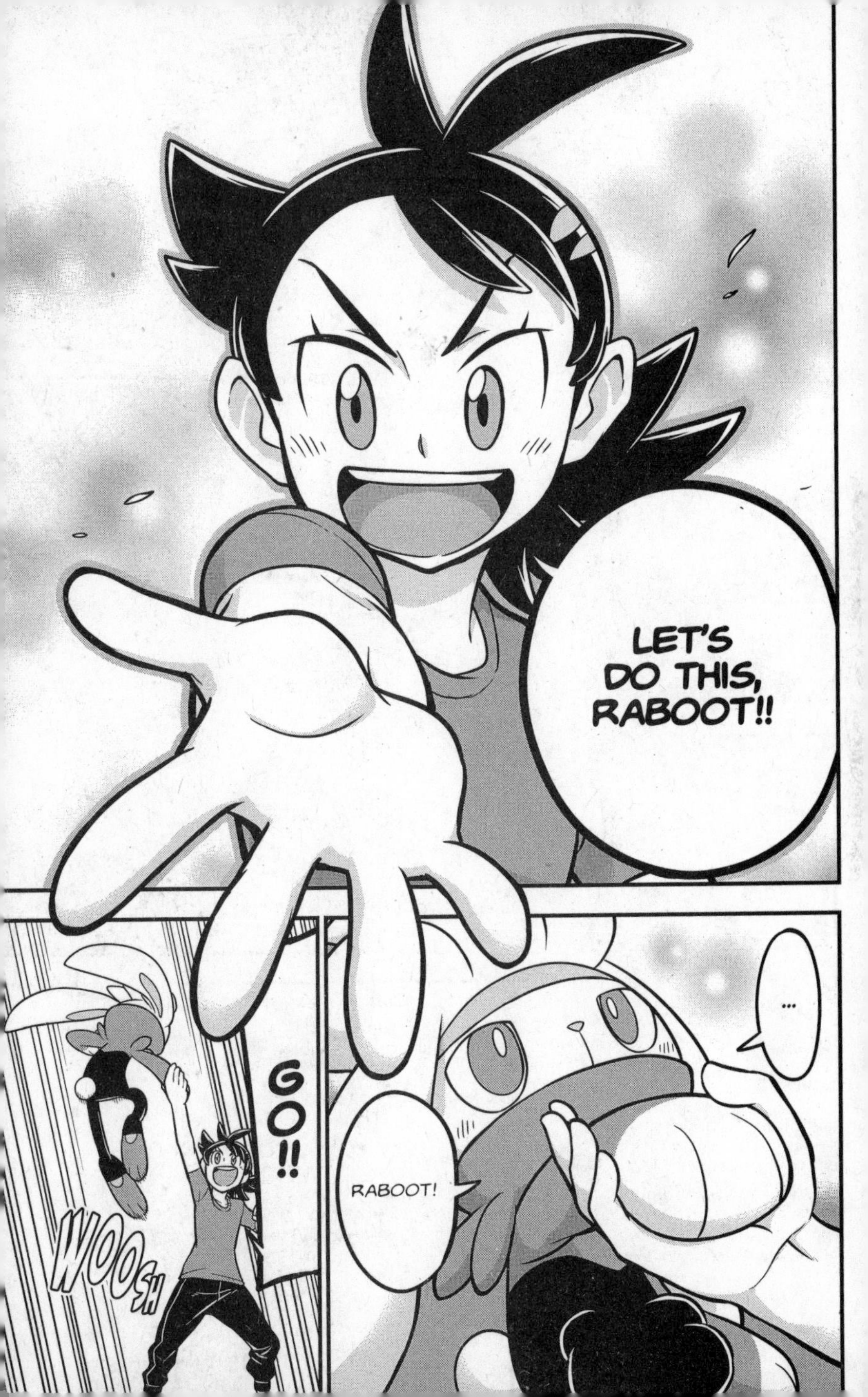
LET'S DO THIS, RABOOT!!
...
RABOOT!
GO!!
WOOSH

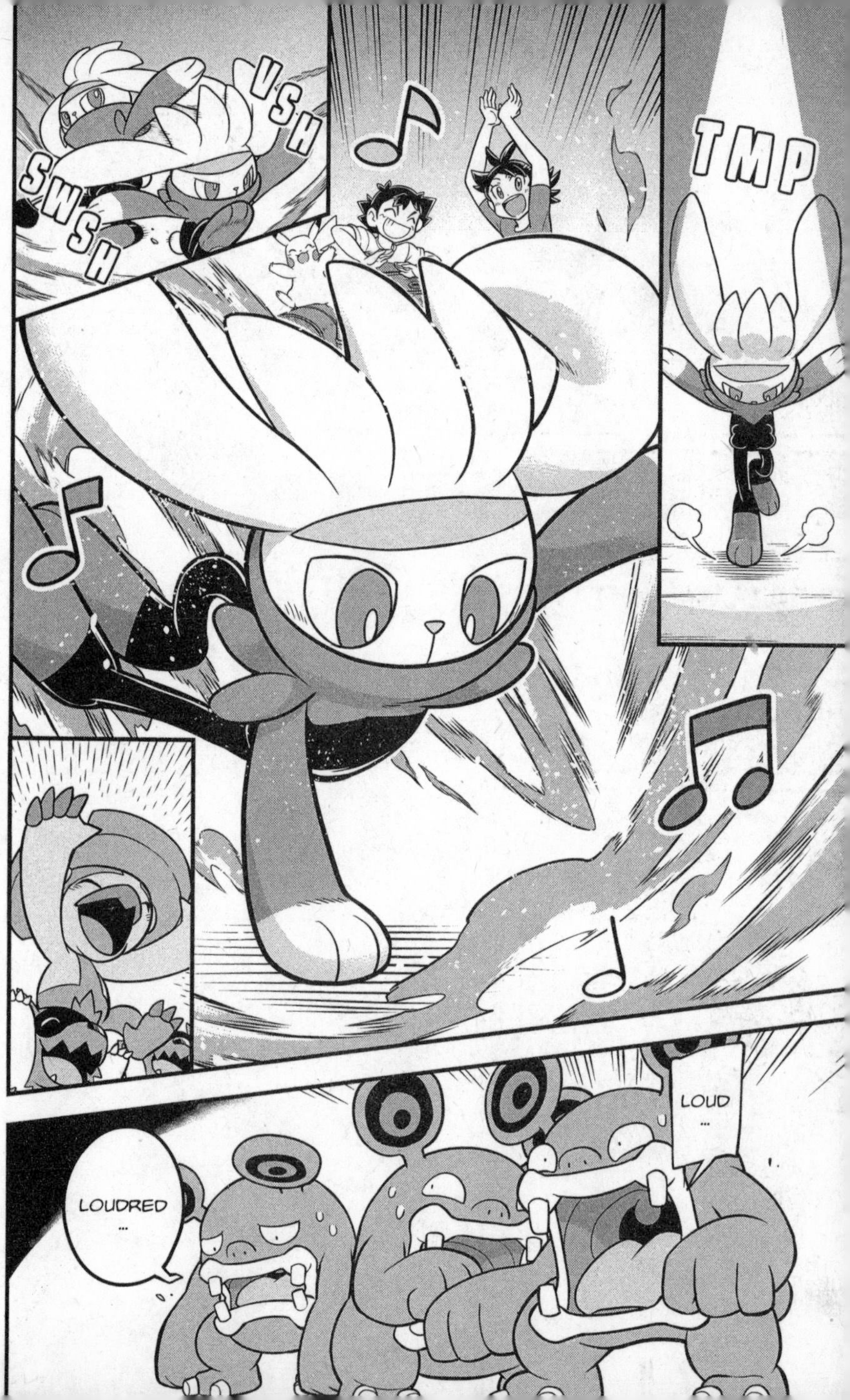
TMP
VSH
SWSH
LOUD...
LOUDRED...

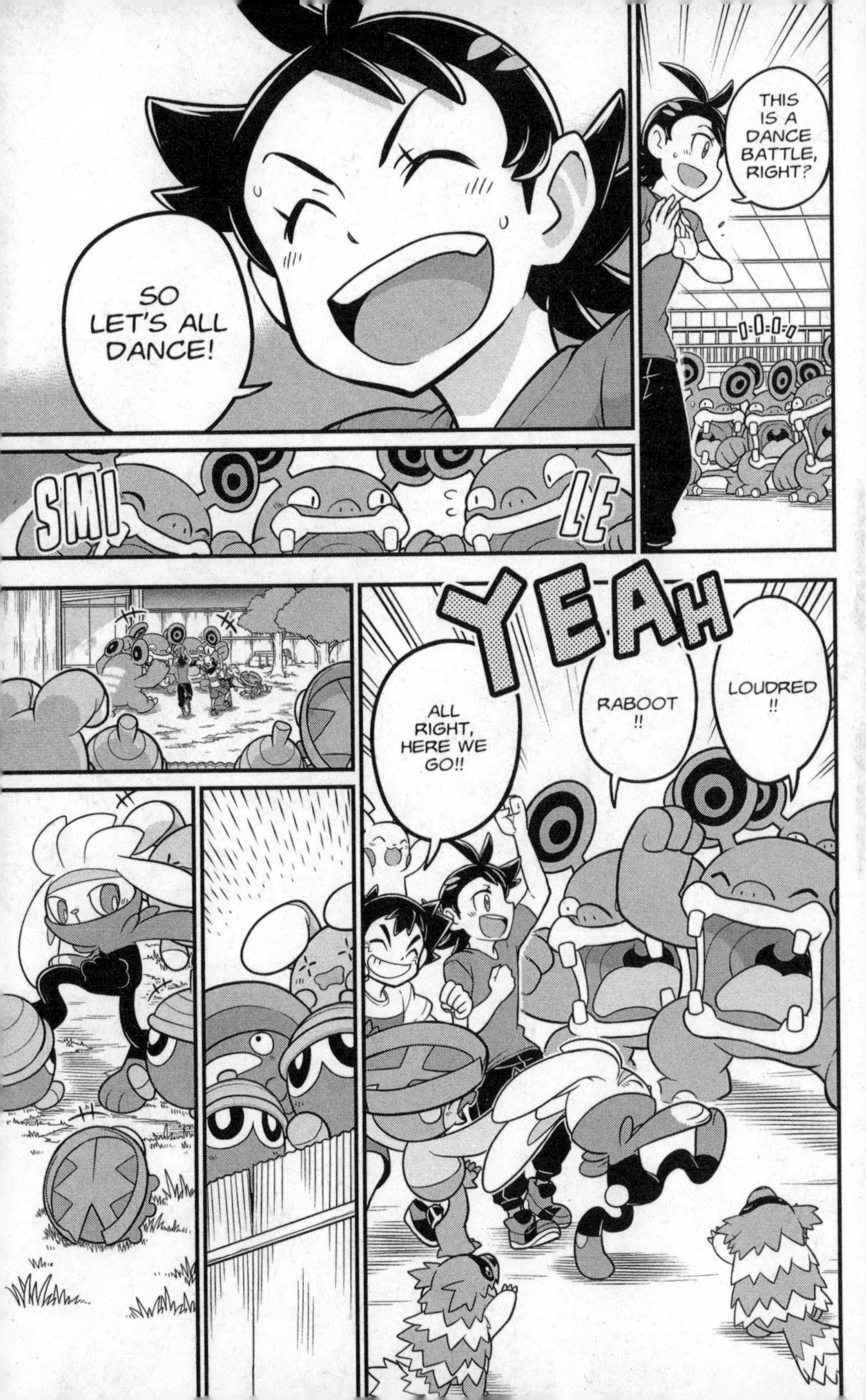
THIS IS A DANCE BATTLE, RIGHT?
SO LET'S ALL DANCE!
SMILE
YEAH
LOUDRED!!
RABOOT!!
ALL RIGHT, HERE WE GO!!

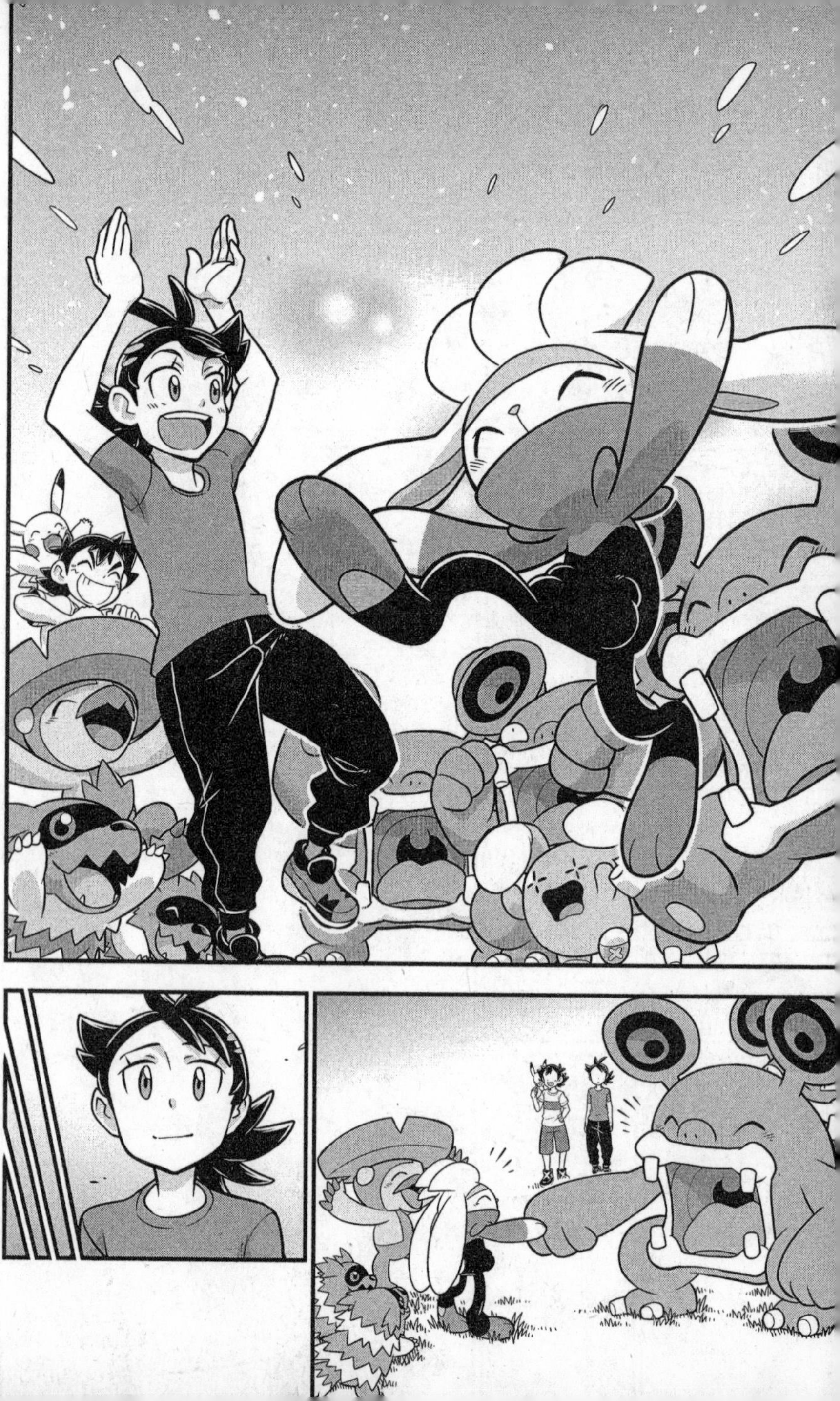

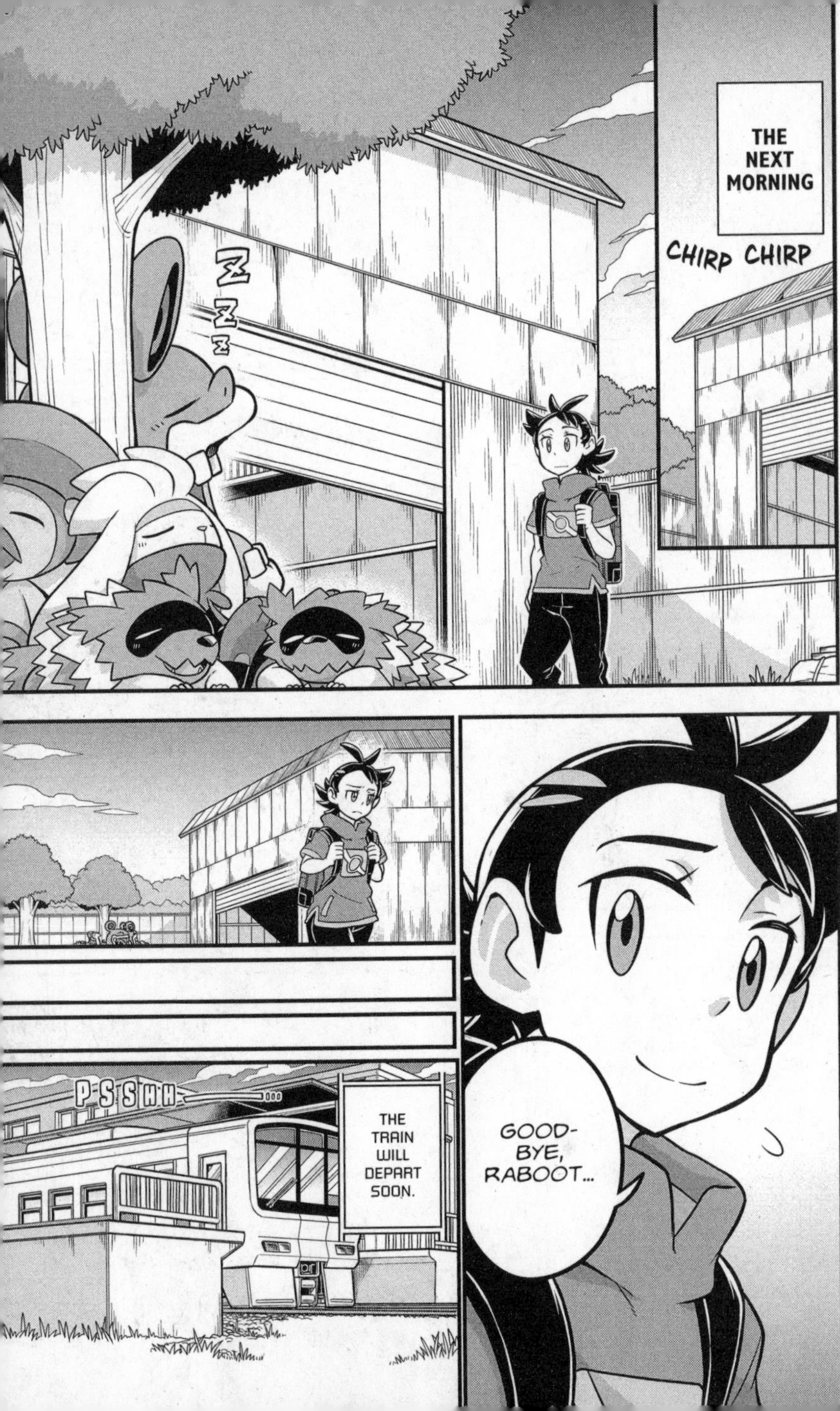
THE NEXT MORNING
CHIRP CHIRP
ZZZ
GOOD-BYE, RABOOT...
PSSHH
THE TRAIN WILL DEPART SOON.

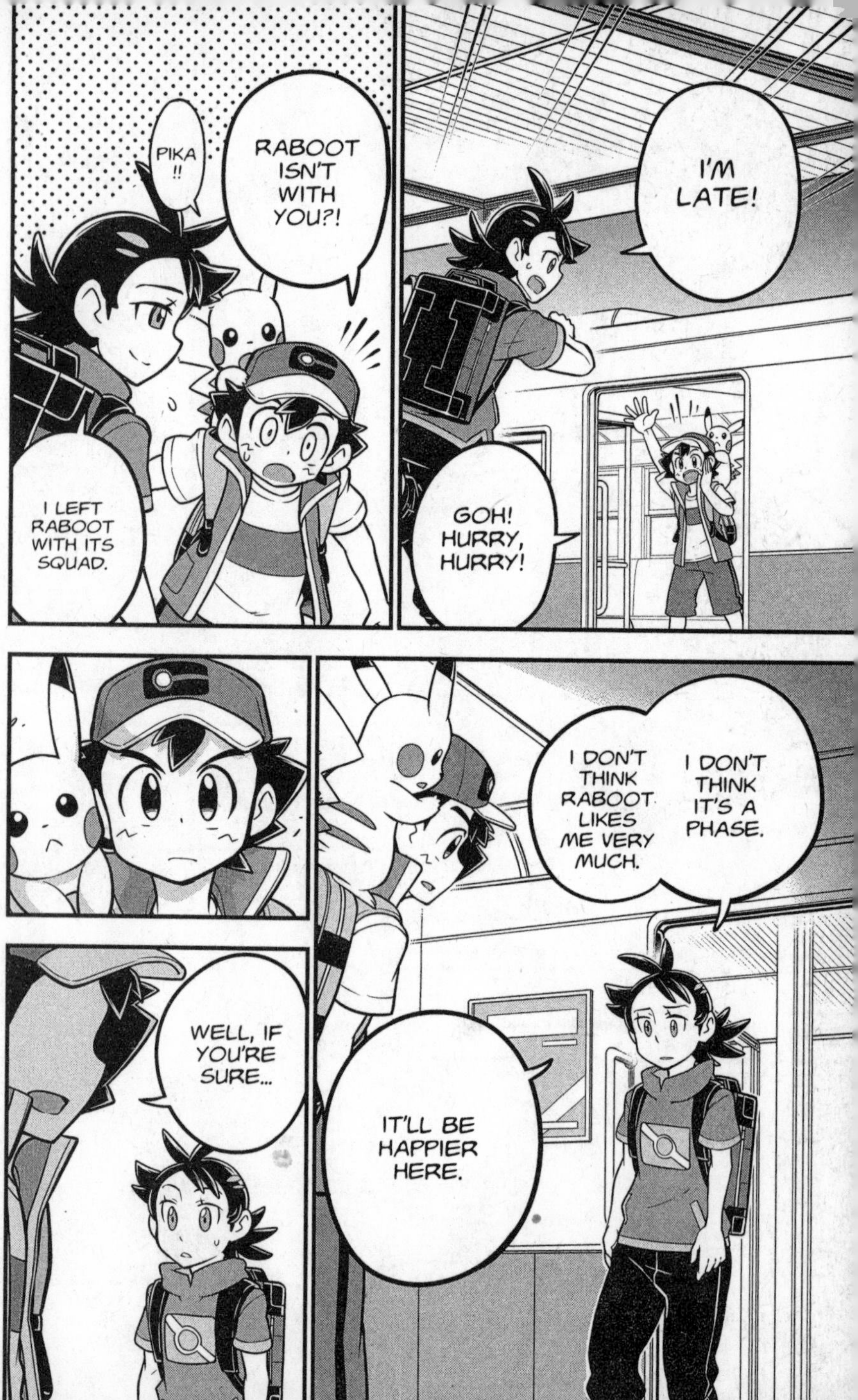
I'M LATE!
GOH! HURRY, HURRY!
RABOOT ISN'T WITH YOU?!
PIKA !!
I LEFT RABOOT WITH ITS SQUAD.
I DON'T THINK RABOOT LIKES ME VERY MUCH. I DON'T THINK IT'S A PHASE.
IT'LL BE HAPPIER HERE.
WELL, IF YOU'RE SURE...

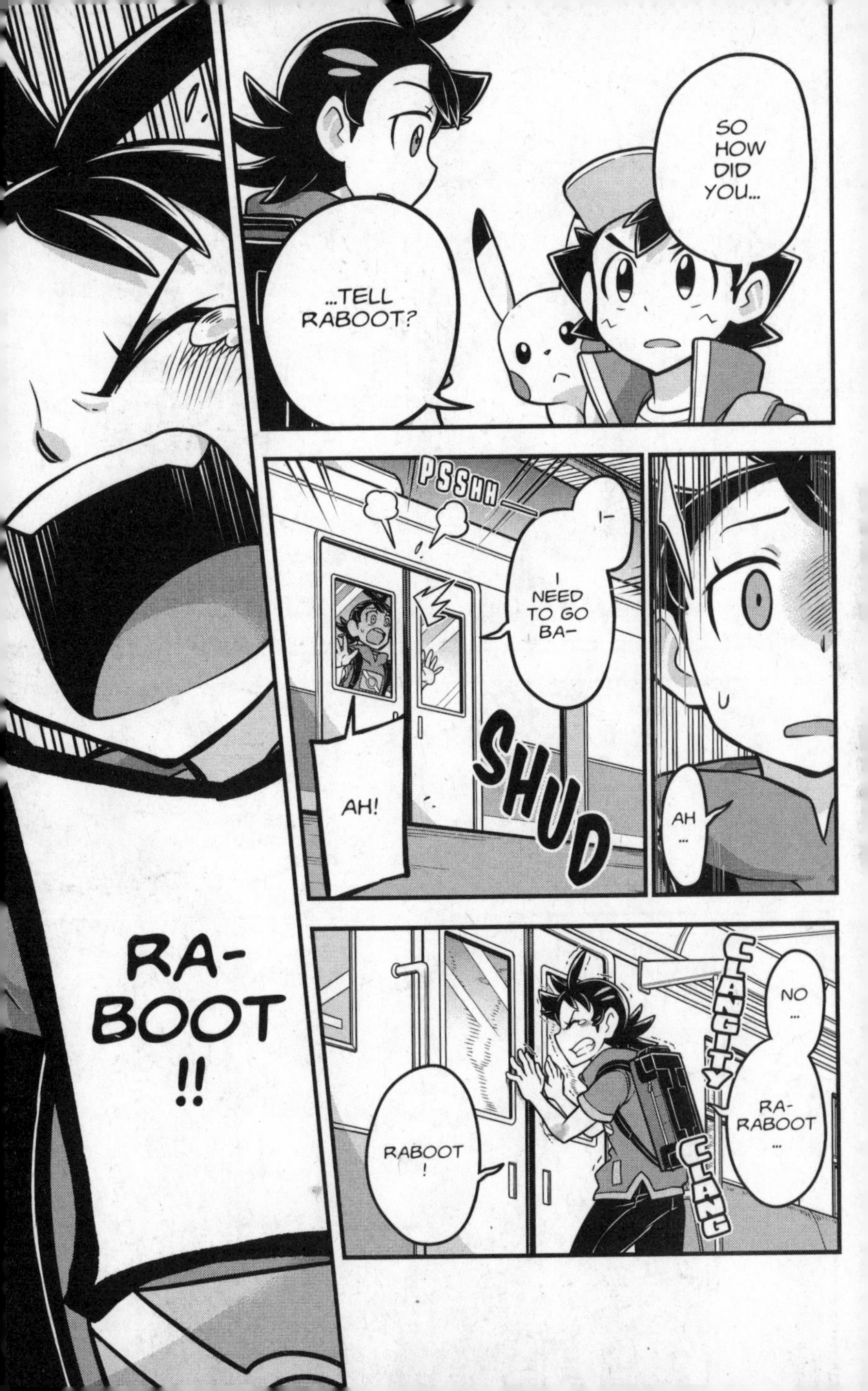
SO HOW DID YOU...
...TELL RABOOT?
AH ...
PSSHH
I– I NEED TO GO BA–
AH!
SHUD
NO ... RA-RABOOT ...
CLANGITY CLANG
RABOOT !
RA-BOOT !!

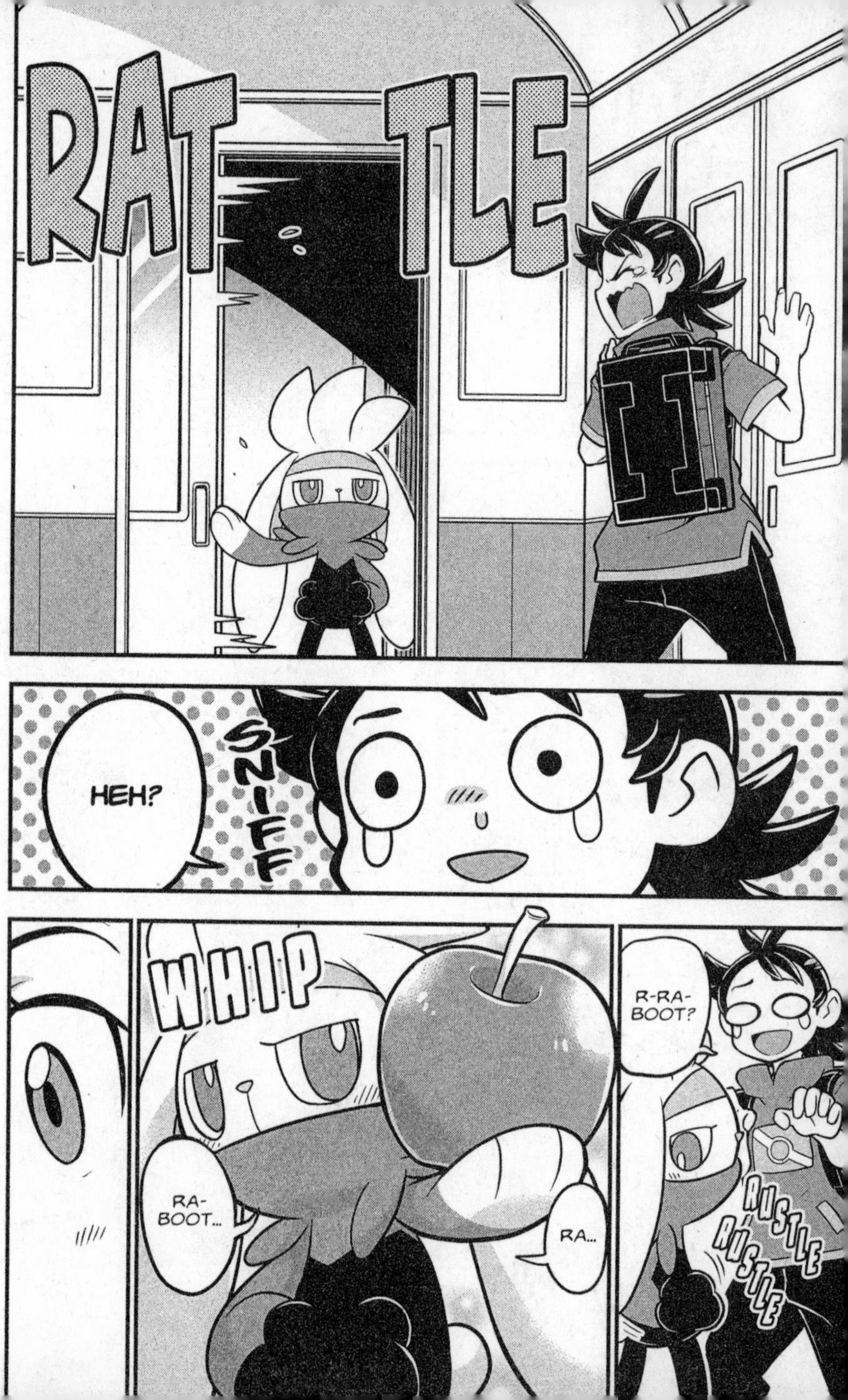
RATTLE
SNIFF
HEH?
R-RA-BOOT?
RUSTLE RUSTLE
WHIP
RA...
RA-BOOT...

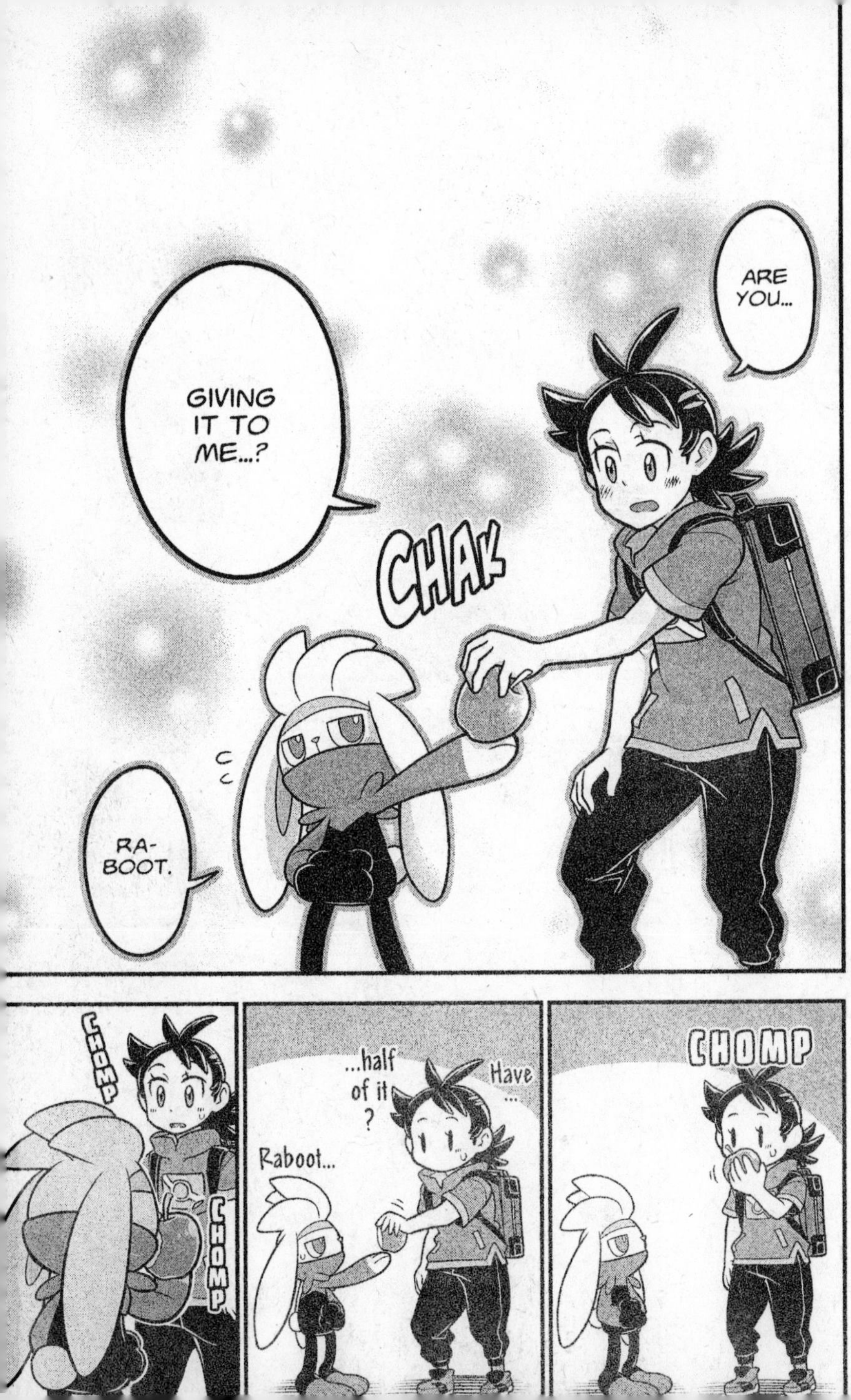
ARE YOU...
GIVING IT TO ME...?
CHAK
RA-BOOT.
CHOMP
Have ...
...half of it ?
Raboot...
CHOMP
CHOMP

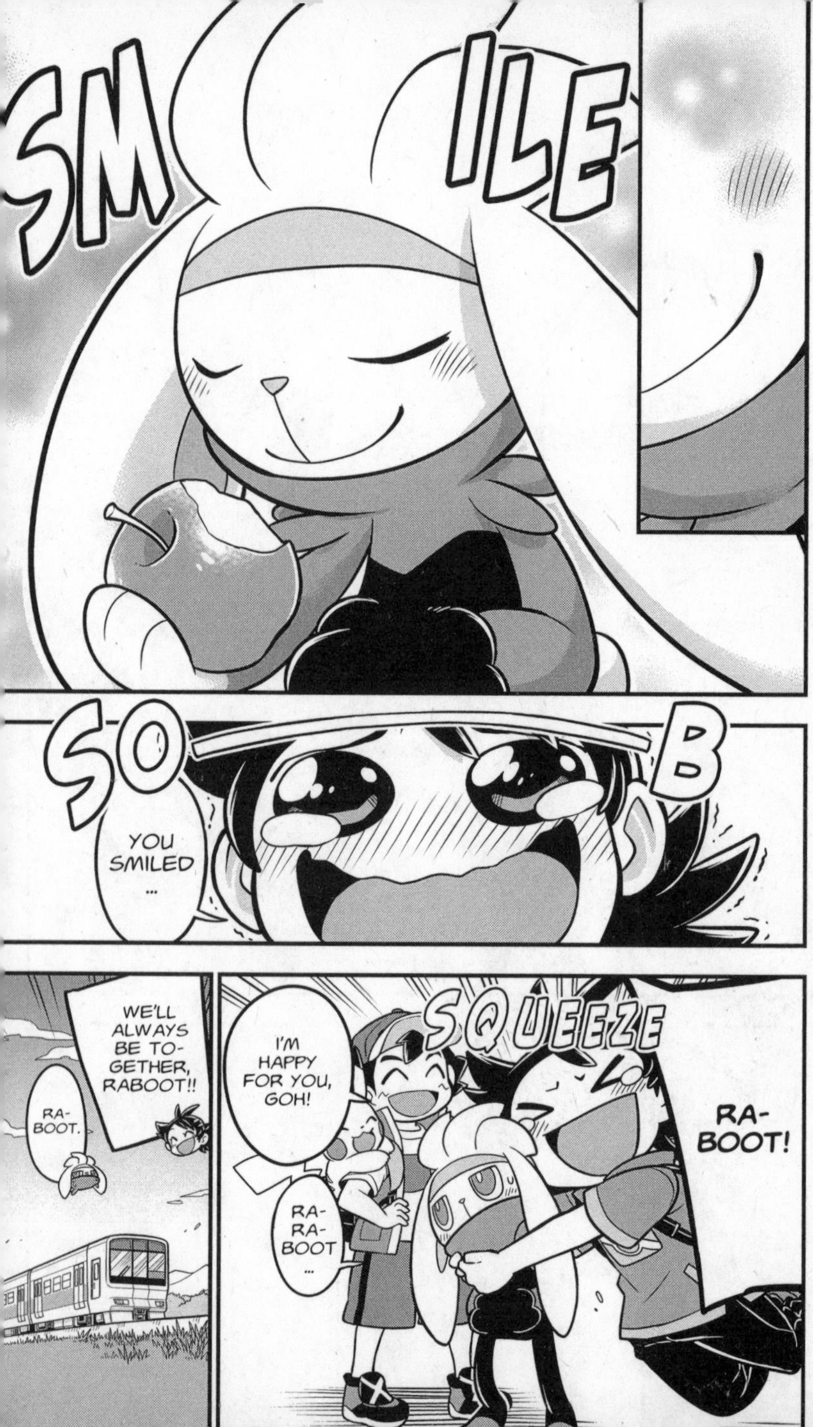
SMILE
SOB
YOU SMILED ...
SQUEEZE
RA-BOOT!
I'M HAPPY FOR YOU, GOH!
RA-RA-BOOT ...
WE'LL ALWAYS BE TO-GETHER, RABOOT!!
RA-BOOT.

Chapter 8
Caring for a Mystery!

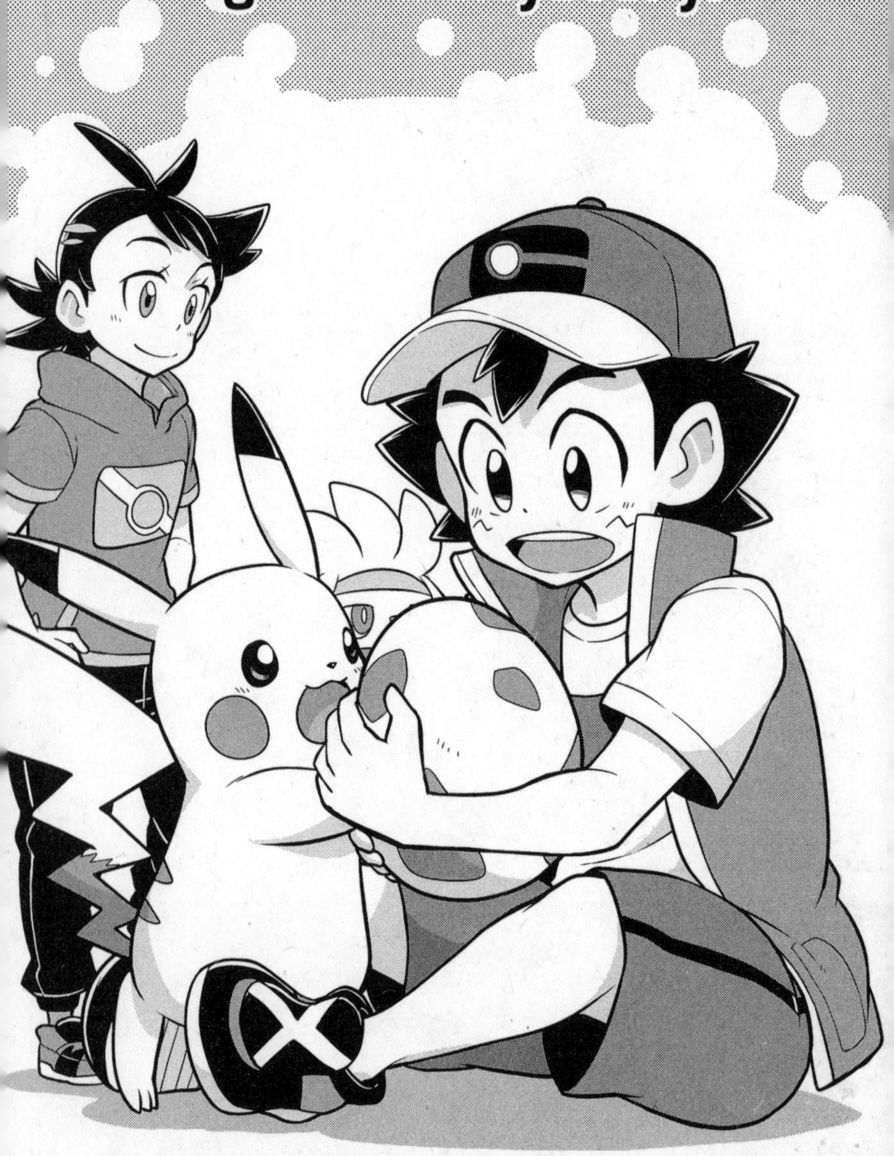

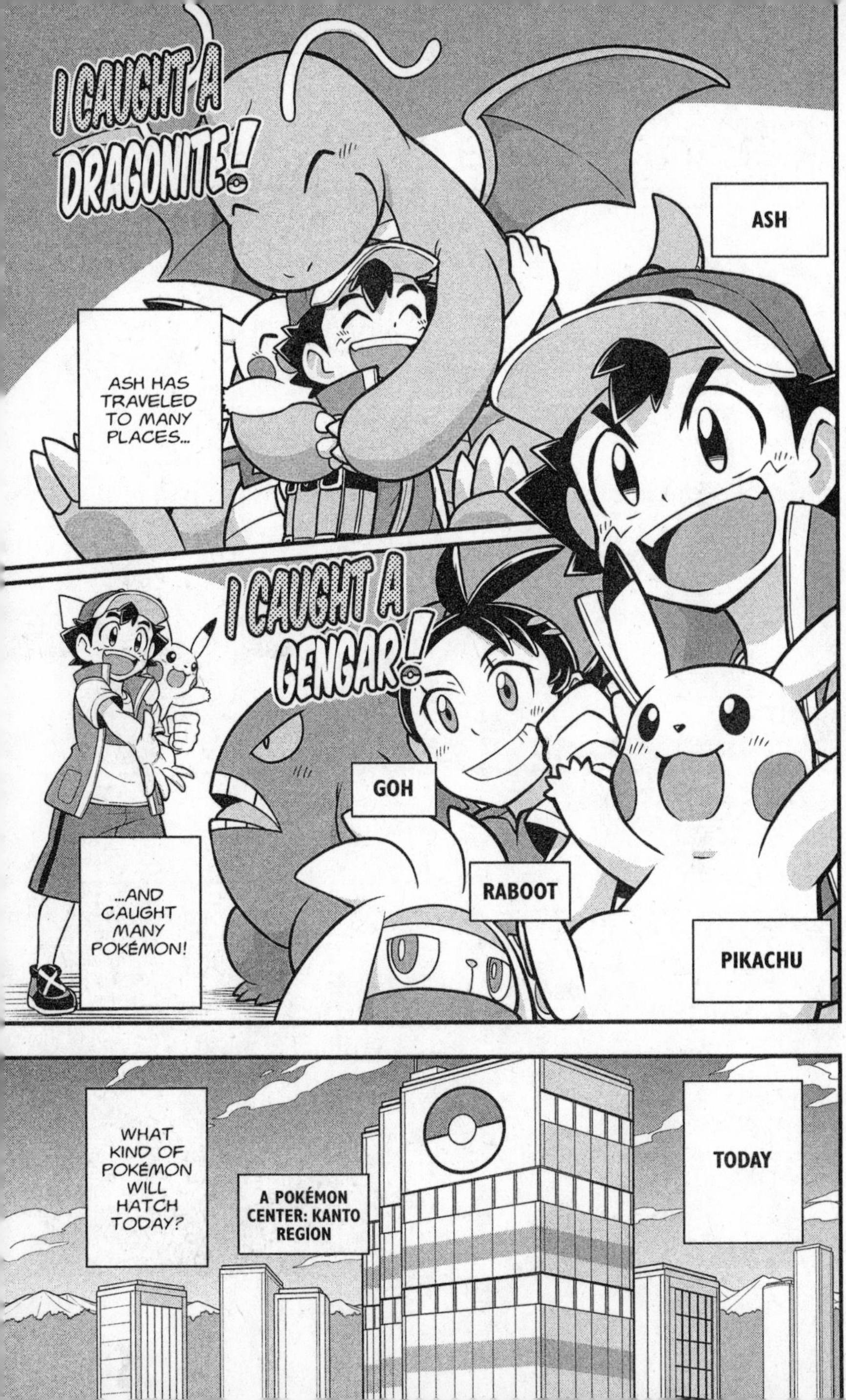
ASH
I CAUGHT A DRAGONITE!
ASH HAS TRAVELED TO MANY PLACES...
I CAUGHT A GENGAR!
GOH
RABOOT
PIKACHU
...AND CAUGHT MANY POKÉMON!
TODAY
A POKÉMON CENTER: KANTO REGION
WHAT KIND OF POKÉMON WILL HATCH TODAY?

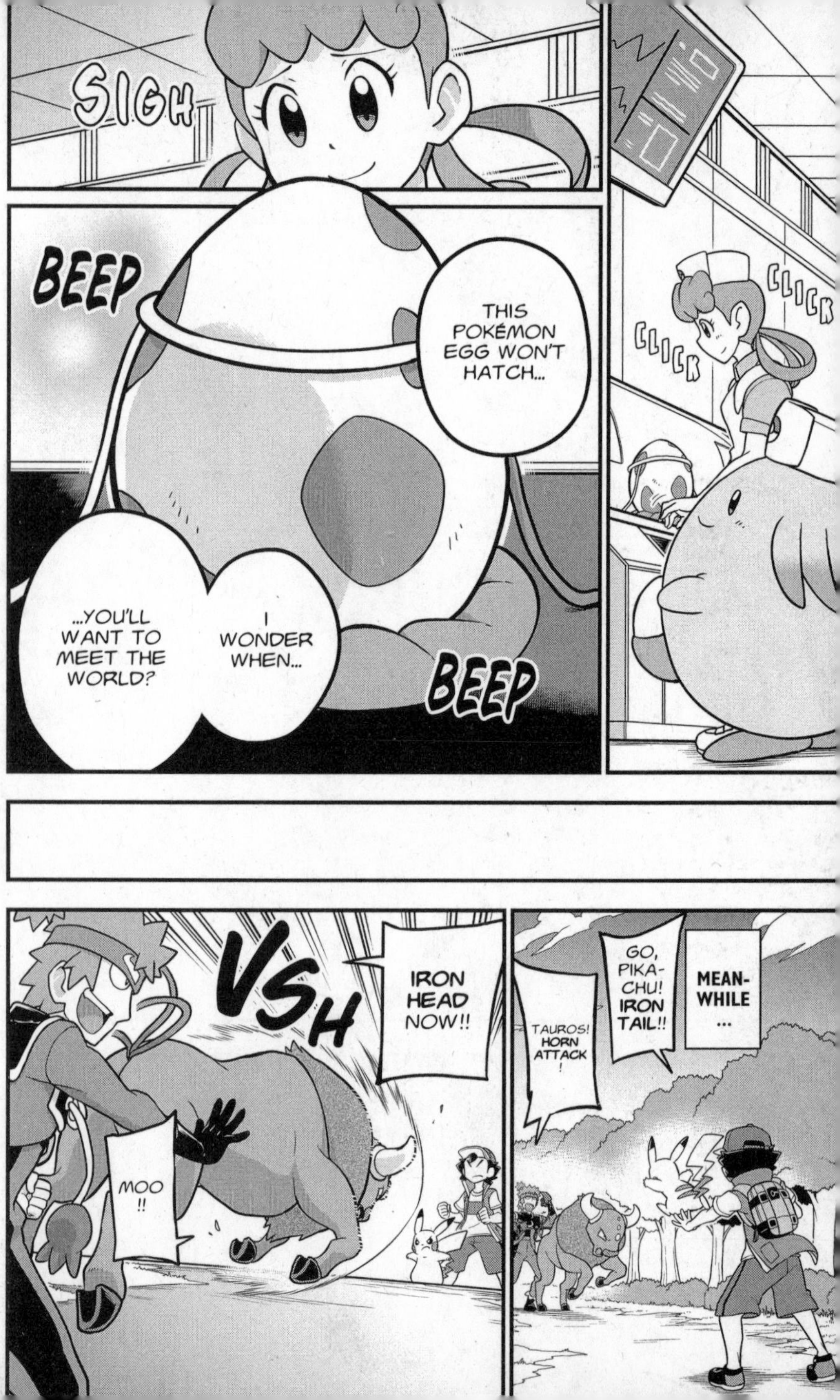
CLICK
CLICK
SIGH
BEEP
THIS POKÉMON EGG WON'T HATCH...
I WONDER WHEN...
...YOU'LL WANT TO MEET THE WORLD?
BEEP
MEAN-WHILE...
GO, PIKA-CHU! IRON TAIL!!
TAUROS! HORN ATTACK!
IRON HEAD NOW!!
VSH
MOO!!

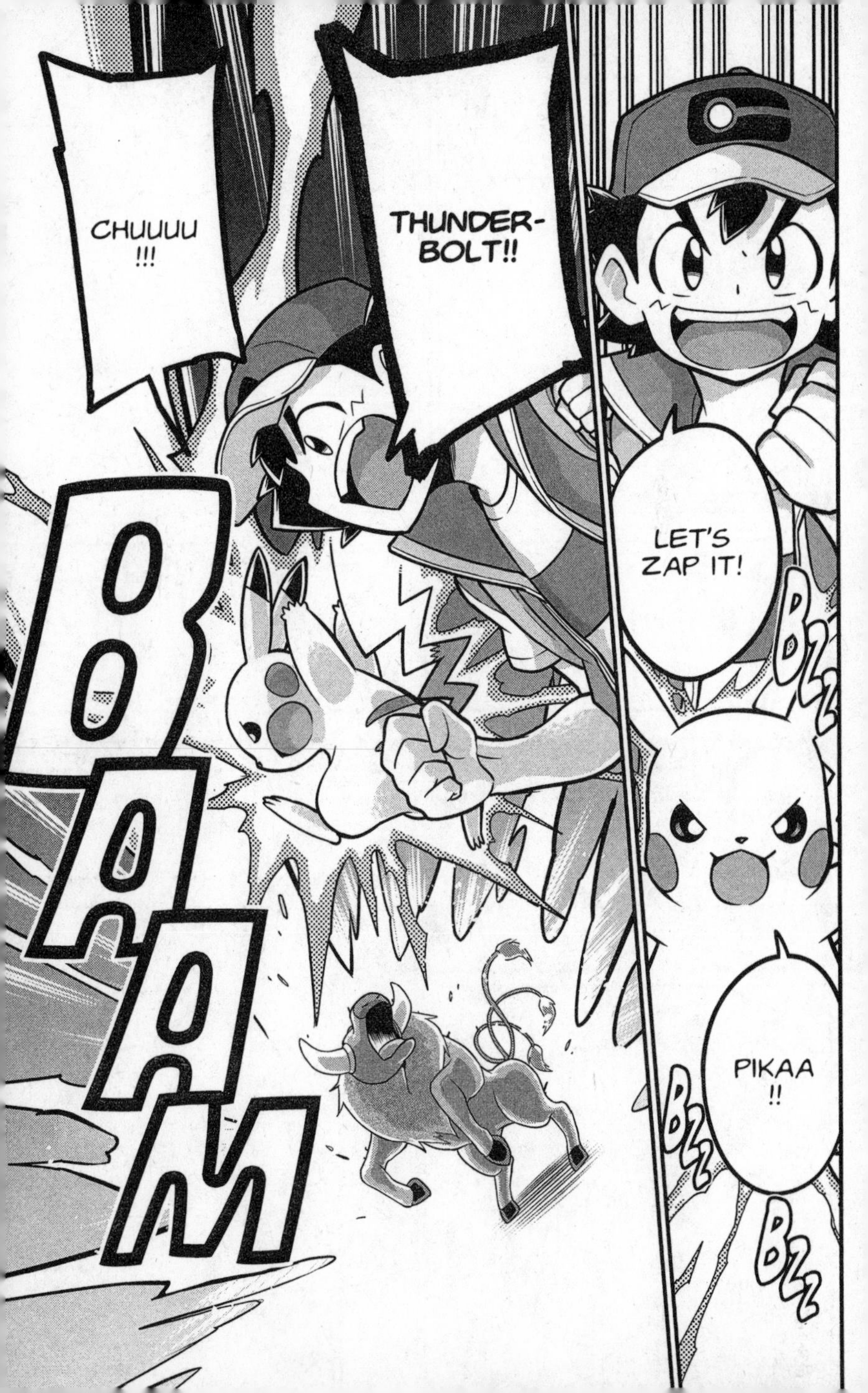
LET'S ZAP IT!
BZZ
PIKAA !!
BZZ
BZZ
THUNDER-BOLT!!
CHUUUU !!!
BOOM

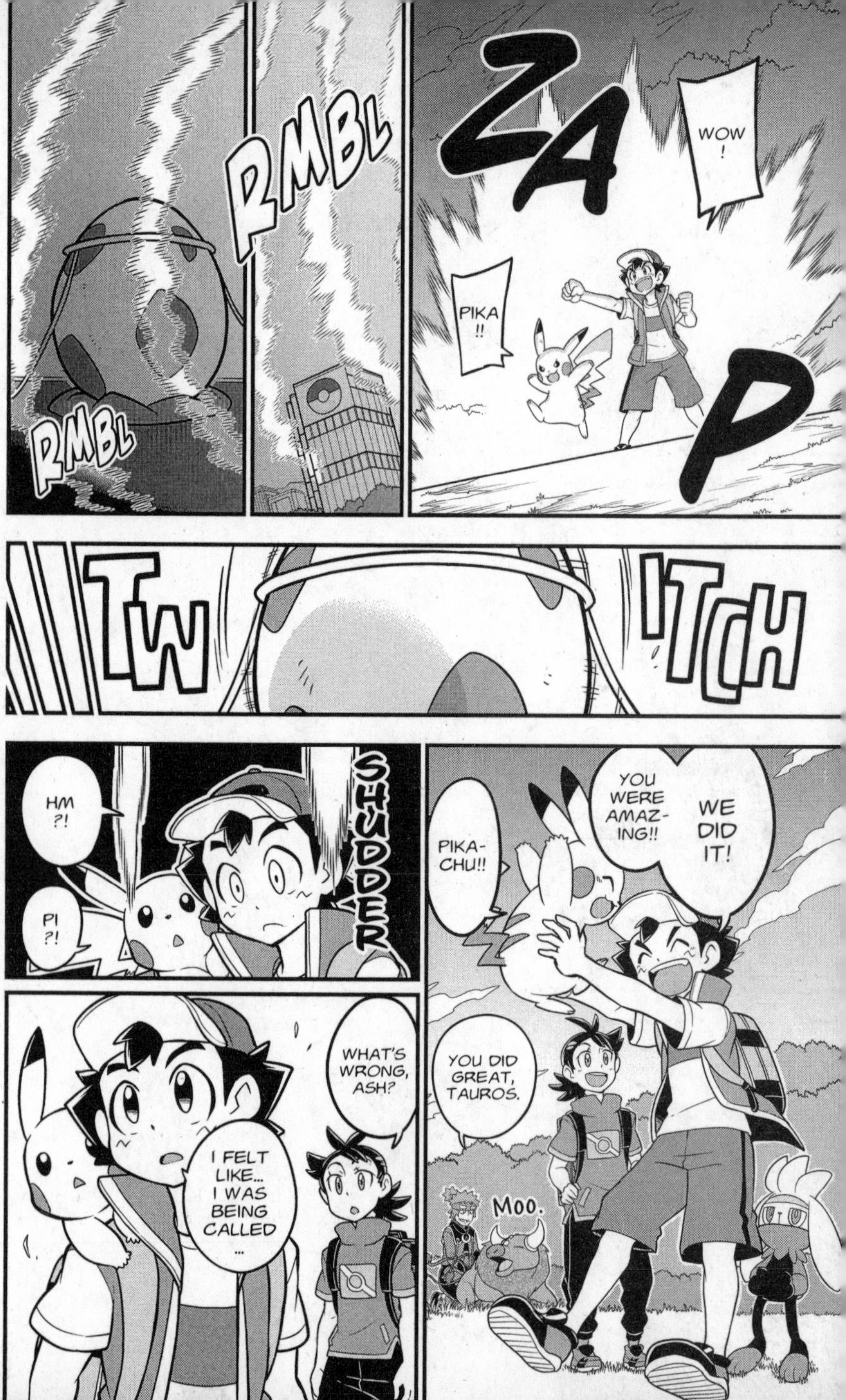
ZAP
WOW!
PIKA!!
RMBL
RMBL
TWITCH
WE DID IT!
YOU WERE AMAZING!!
PIKACHU!!
YOU DID GREAT, TAUROS.
Moo.
SHUDDER
HM?!
PI?!
WHAT'S WRONG, ASH?
I FELT LIKE... I WAS BEING CALLED...

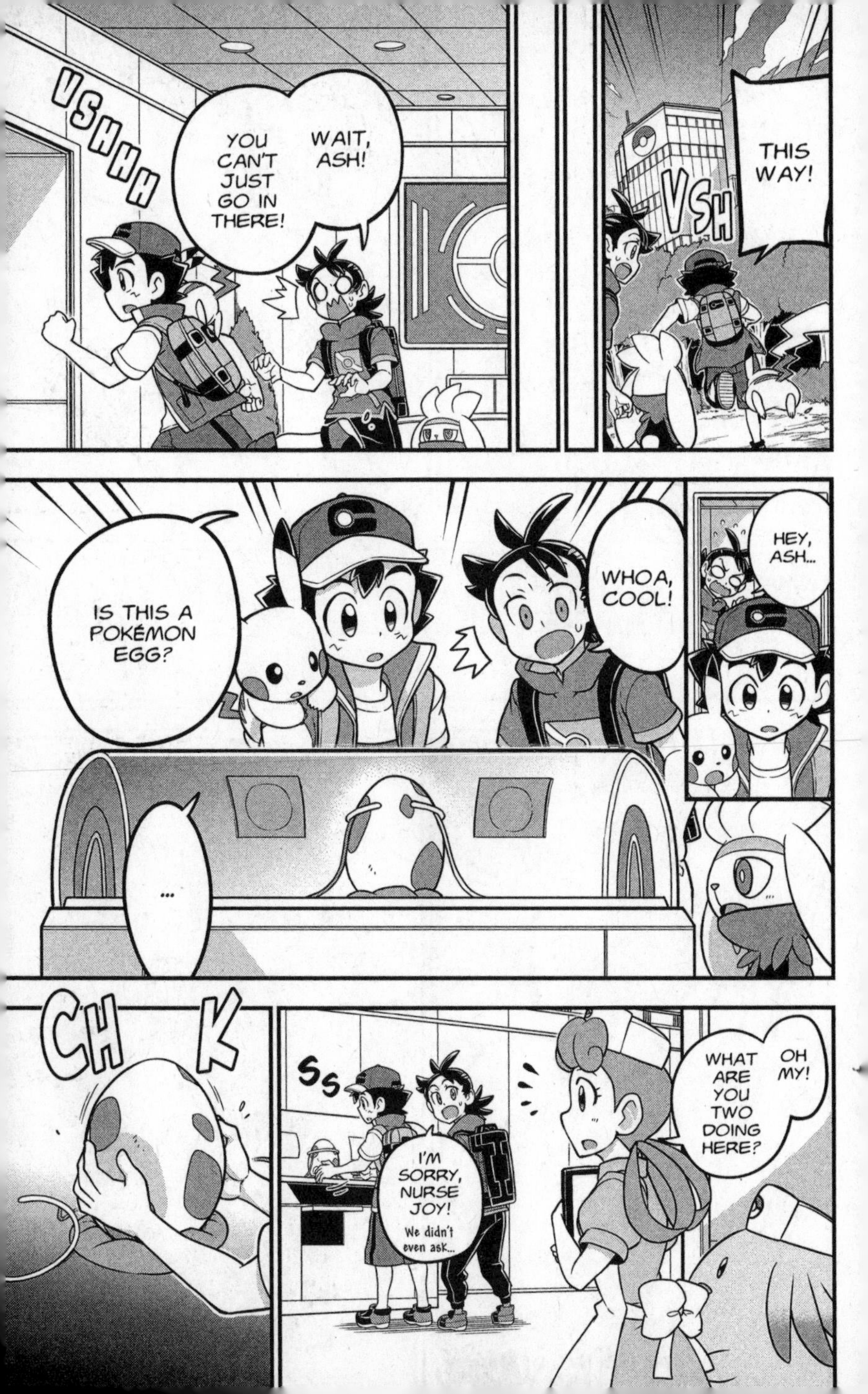
THIS WAY!
VSH
WAIT, ASH!
YOU CAN'T JUST GO IN THERE!
VSHHH
HEY, ASH...
WHOA, COOL!
IS THIS A POKÉMON EGG?
...
OH MY!
WHAT ARE YOU TWO DOING HERE?
SS
I'M SORRY, NURSE JOY!
We didn't even ask...
CH K

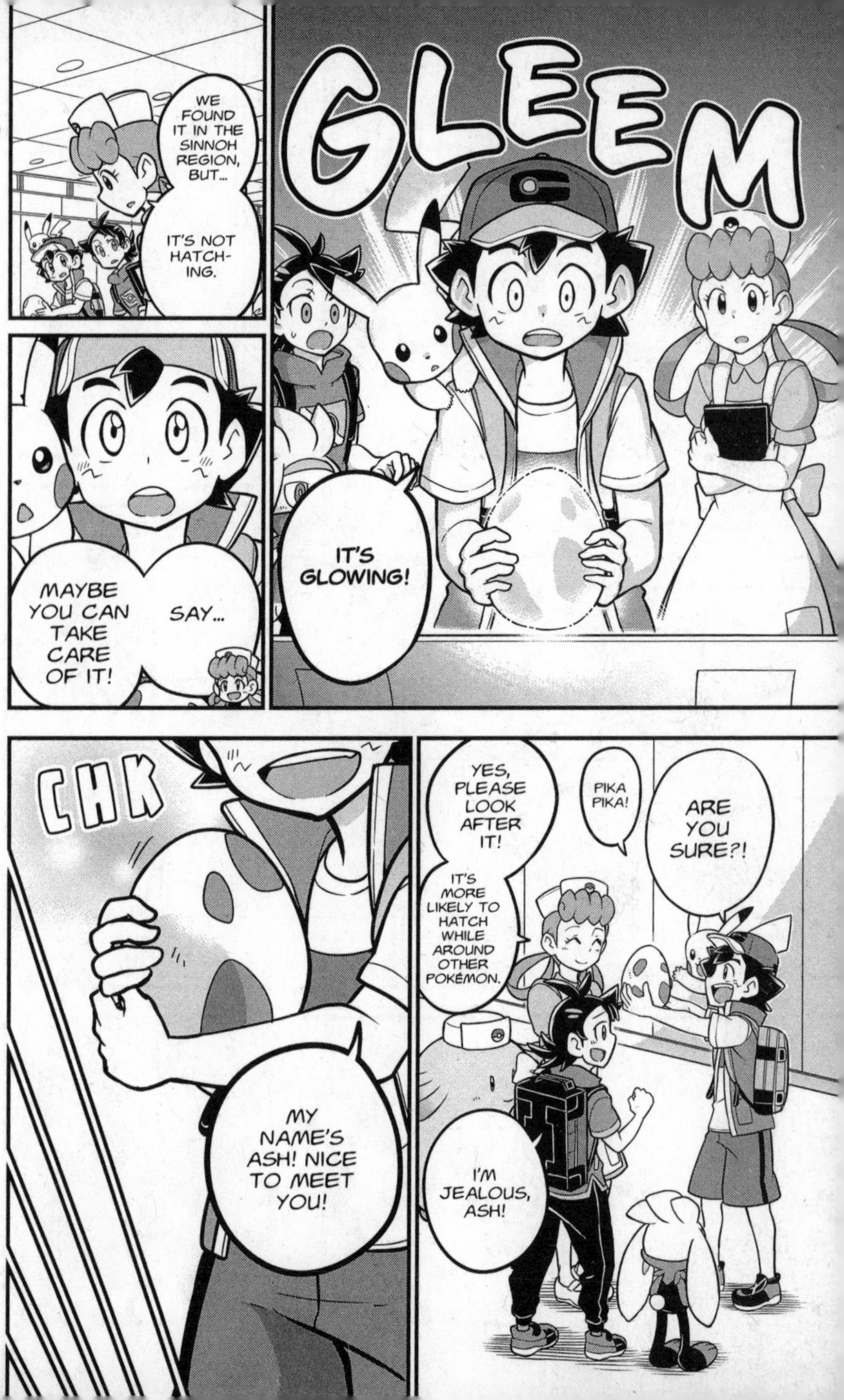
GLEEM
IT'S GLOWING!
WE FOUND IT IN THE SINNOH REGION, BUT...
IT'S NOT HATCHING.
SAY...
MAYBE YOU CAN TAKE CARE OF IT!
ARE YOU SURE?!
PIKA PIKA!
YES, PLEASE LOOK AFTER IT!
IT'S MORE LIKELY TO HATCH WHILE AROUND OTHER POKÉMON.
I'M JEALOUS, ASH!
CHK
MY NAME'S ASH! NICE TO MEET YOU!

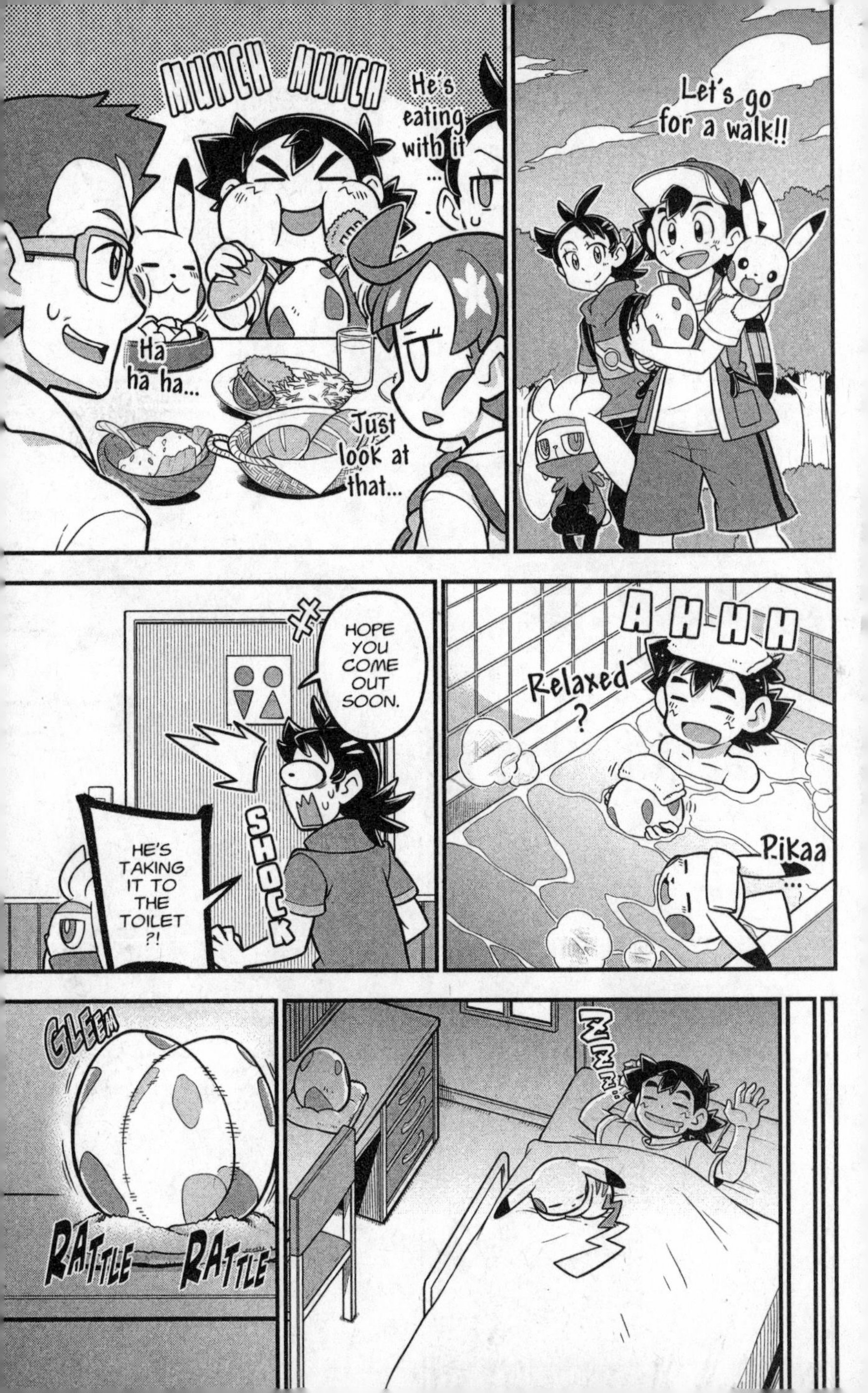
Let's go for a walk!!
MUNCH MUNCH
He's eating with it...
Just look at that...
Ha ha ha...
AHHH
Relaxed?
Pikaa...
HOPE YOU COME OUT SOON.
SHOCK
HE'S TAKING IT TO THE TOILET?!
Zzz...
GLEEM
RATTLE RATTLE

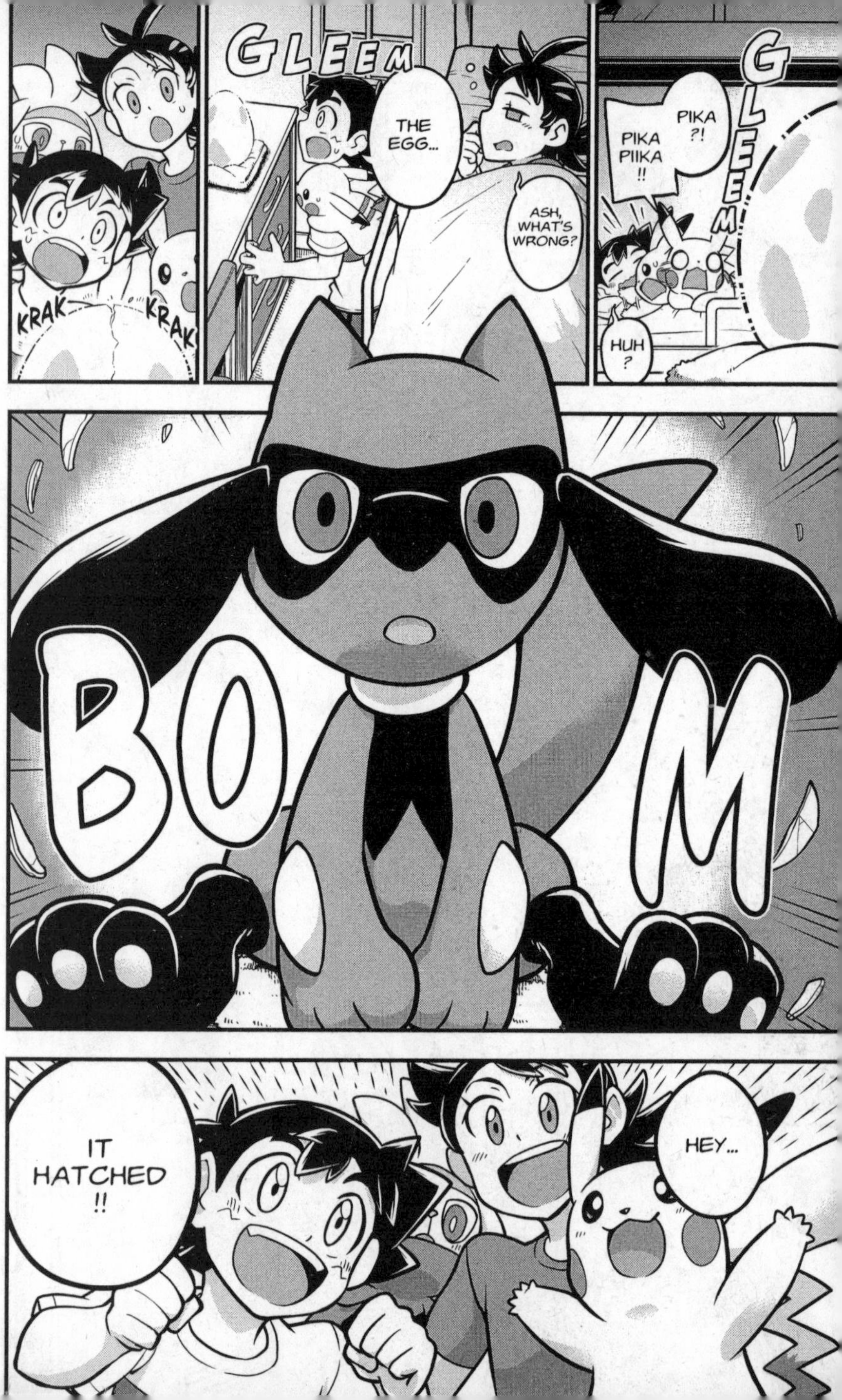
GLEEM
PIKA ?!
PIKA PIIKA !!
HUH ?
GLEEM
THE EGG...
ASH, WHAT'S WRONG?
KRAK KRAK
BOOM
HEY...
IT HATCHED !!

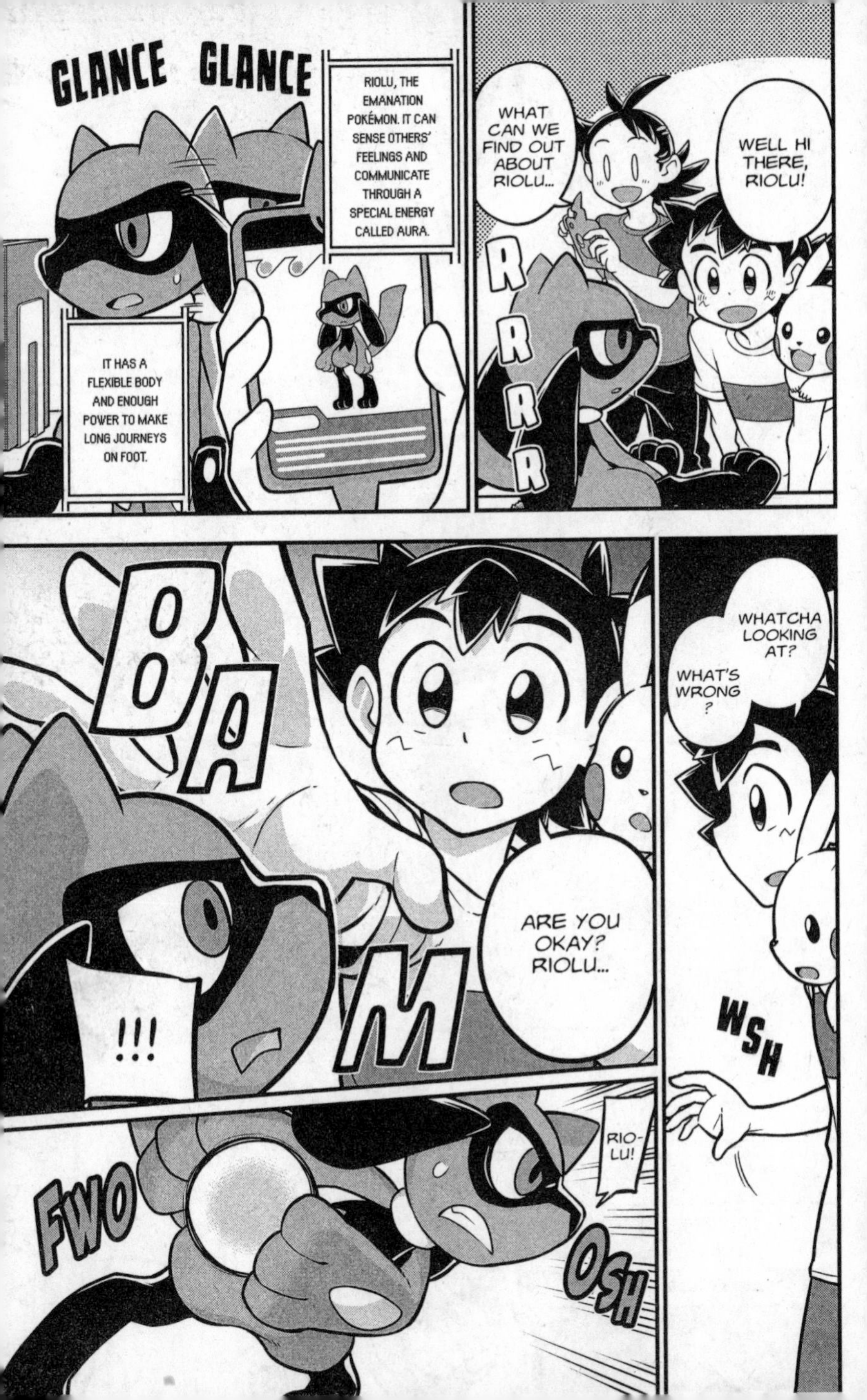
WELL HI THERE, RIOLU!
WHAT CAN WE FIND OUT ABOUT RIOLU...
RRRR
GLANCE GLANCE
RIOLU, THE EMANATION POKÉMON. IT CAN SENSE OTHERS' FEELINGS AND COMMUNICATE THROUGH A SPECIAL ENERGY CALLED AURA.
IT HAS A FLEXIBLE BODY AND ENOUGH POWER TO MAKE LONG JOURNEYS ON FOOT.
WHATCHA LOOKING AT?
WHAT'S WRONG?
WSH
BAM
ARE YOU OKAY? RIOLU...
!!!
RIO-LU!
FWOOSH

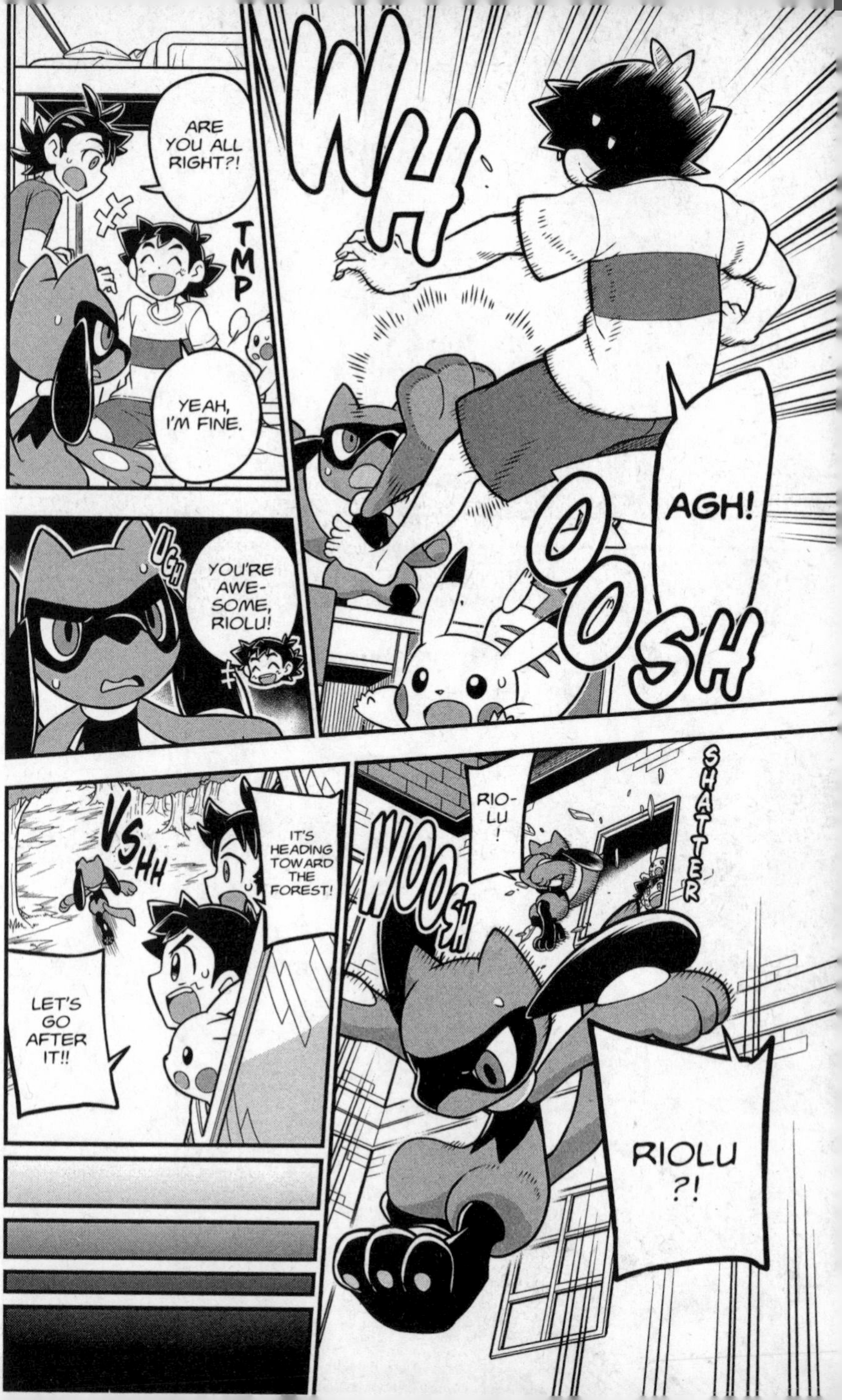
WH
OOSH
AGH!
ARE YOU ALL RIGHT?!
TMP
YEAH, I'M FINE.
UGH
YOU'RE AWESOME, RIOLU!
SHATTER
RIO-LU!
WOOSH
RIOLU ?!
VSHH
IT'S HEADING TOWARD THE FOREST!
LET'S GO AFTER IT!!

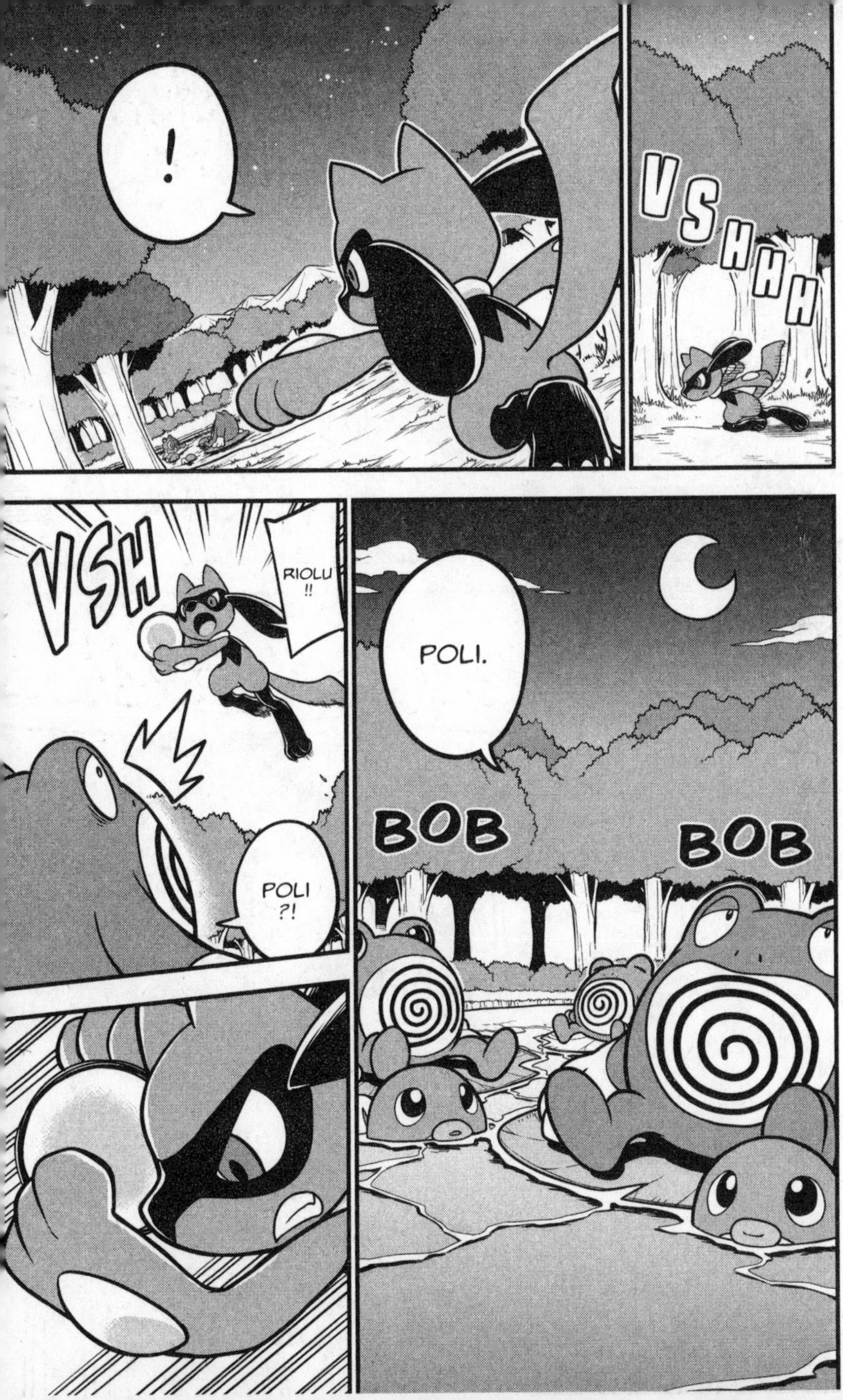
VSHHHH
!
POLI.
BOB
BOB
VSH
RIOLU!!
POLI?!

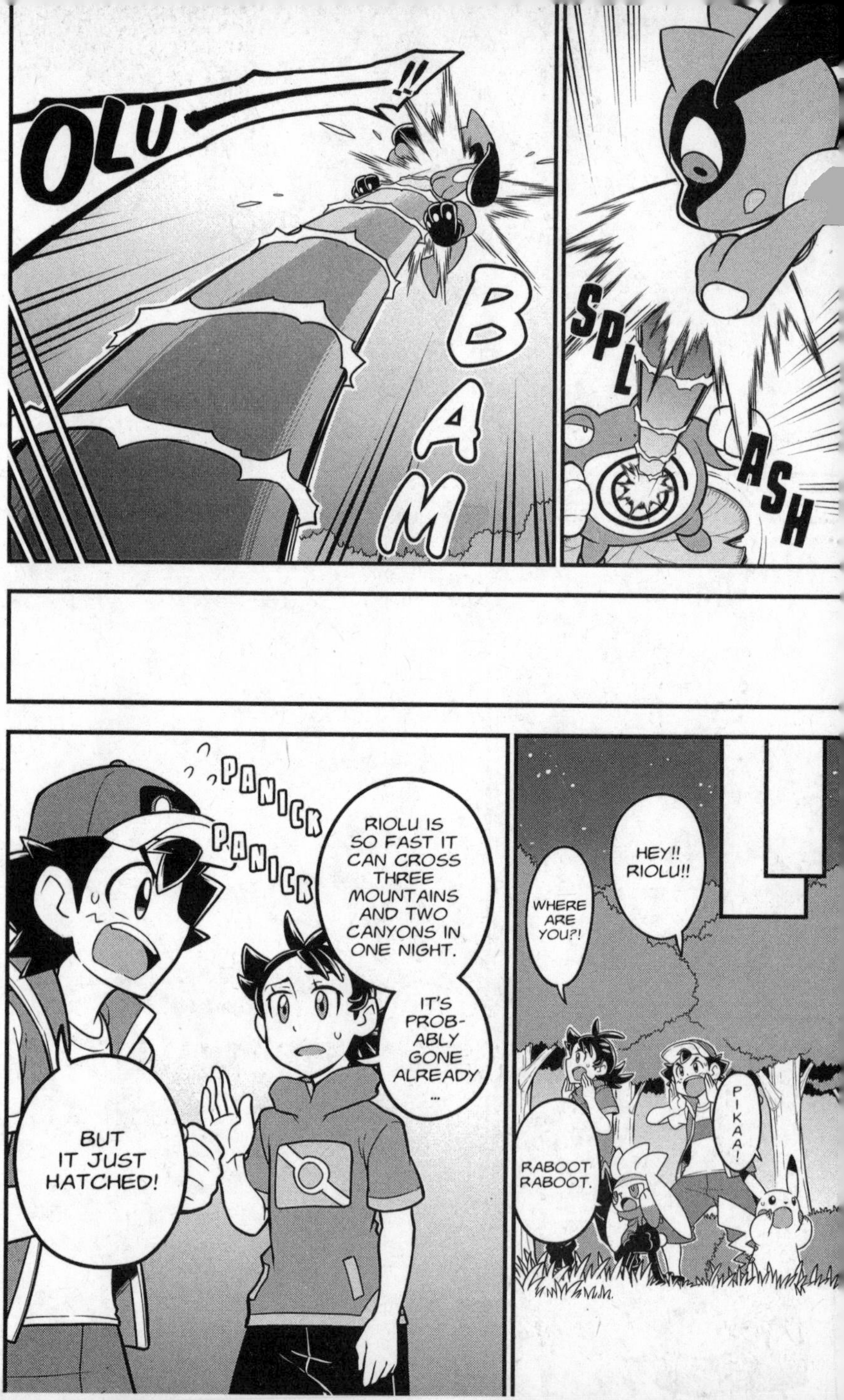
SPLASH
OLU—!!
BAM
HEY!! RIOLU!!
WHERE ARE YOU?!
PIKAA!
RABOOT RABOOT.
PANICK PANICK
RIOLU IS SO FAST IT CAN CROSS THREE MOUNTAINS AND TWO CANYONS IN ONE NIGHT.
IT'S PROBABLY GONE ALREADY...
BUT IT JUST HATCHED!

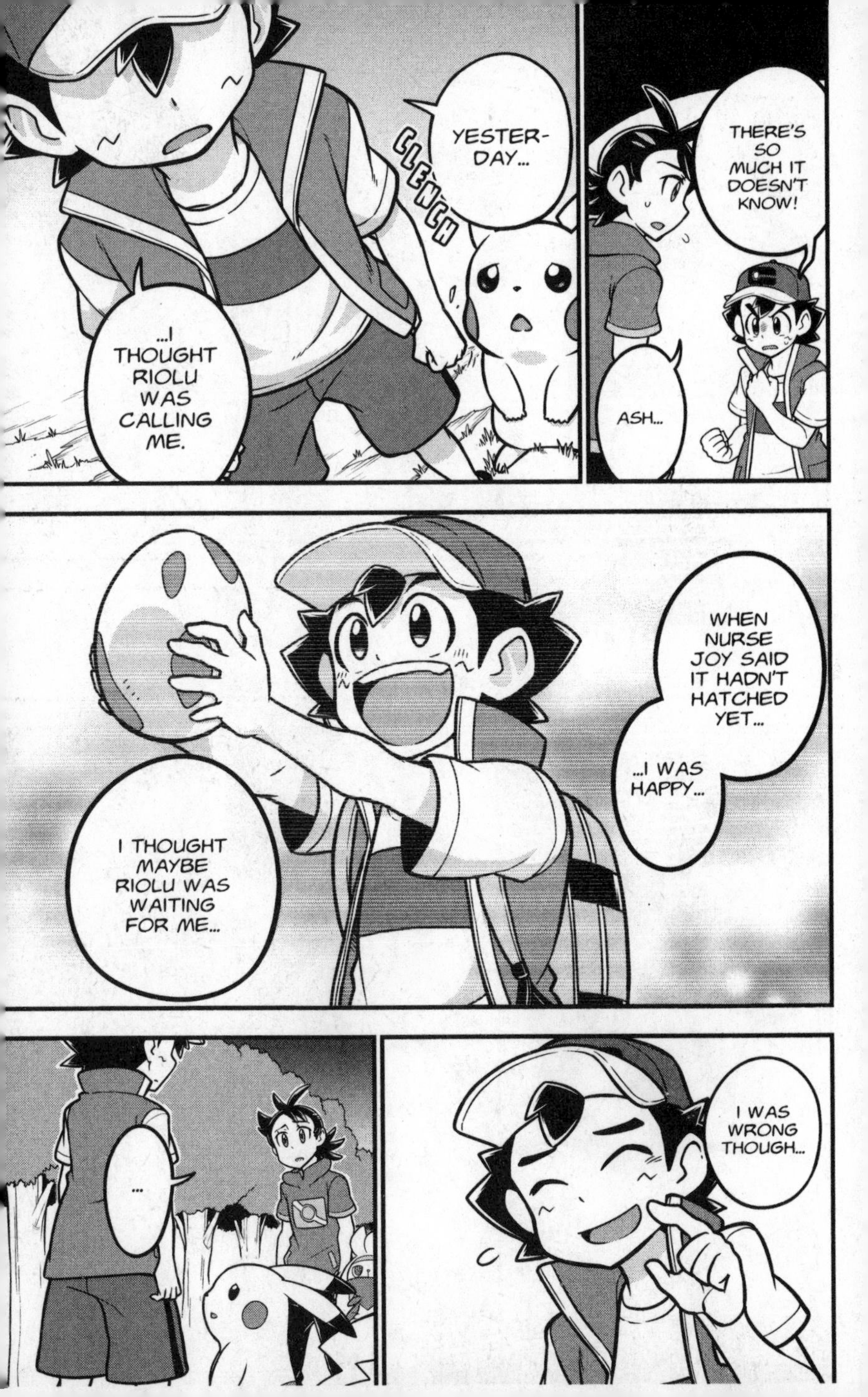
THERE'S SO MUCH IT DOESN'T KNOW!
ASH...
YESTER-DAY...
CLENCH
...I THOUGHT RIOLU WAS CALLING ME.
WHEN NURSE JOY SAID IT HADN'T HATCHED YET...
...I WAS HAPPY...
I THOUGHT MAYBE RIOLU WAS WAITING FOR ME...
I WAS WRONG THOUGH...
...

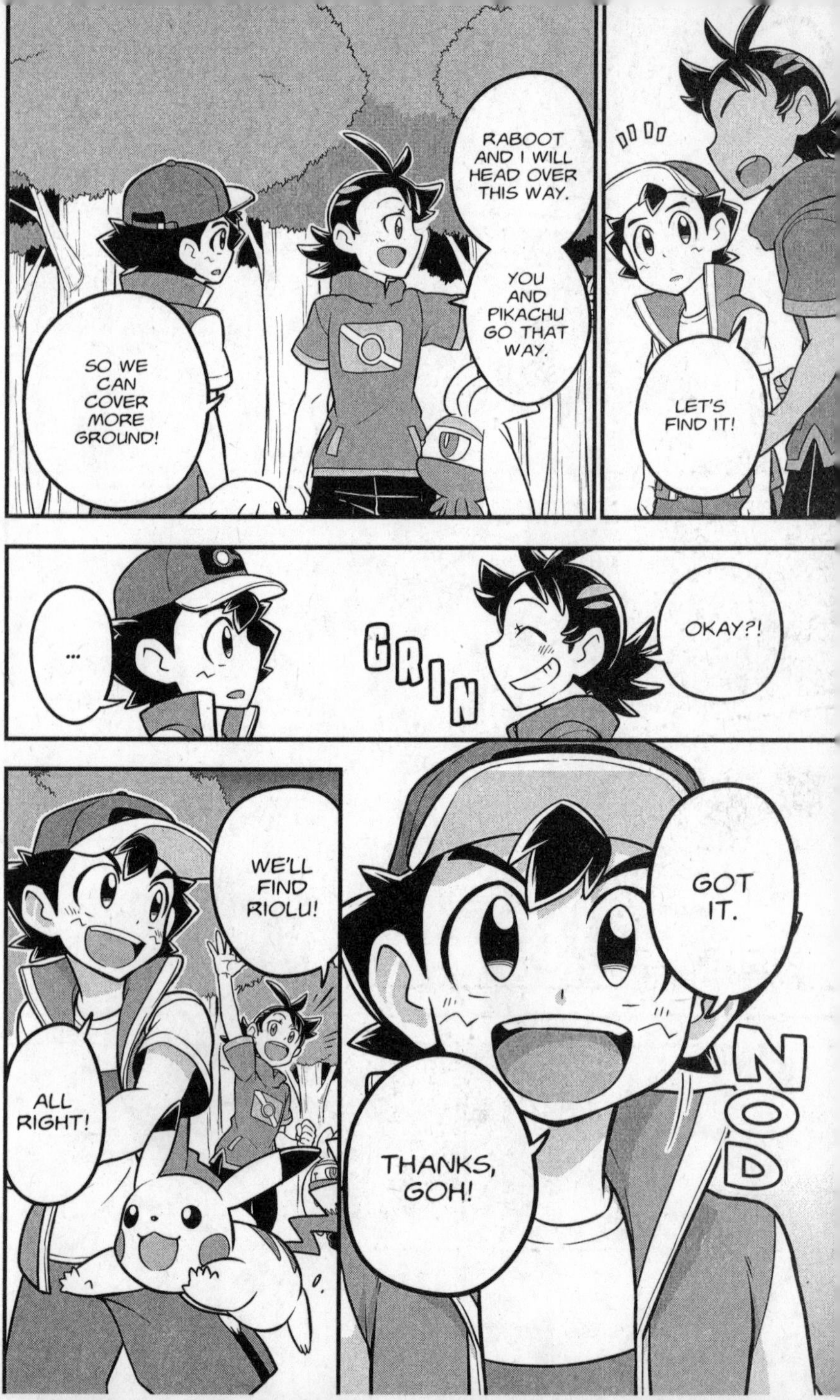

LET'S FIND IT!
RABOOT AND I WILL HEAD OVER THIS WAY.
YOU AND PIKACHU GO THAT WAY.
SO WE CAN COVER MORE GROUND!
OKAY?!
GRIN
...
GOT IT.
NOD
THANKS, GOH!
WE'LL FIND RIOLU!
ALL RIGHT!

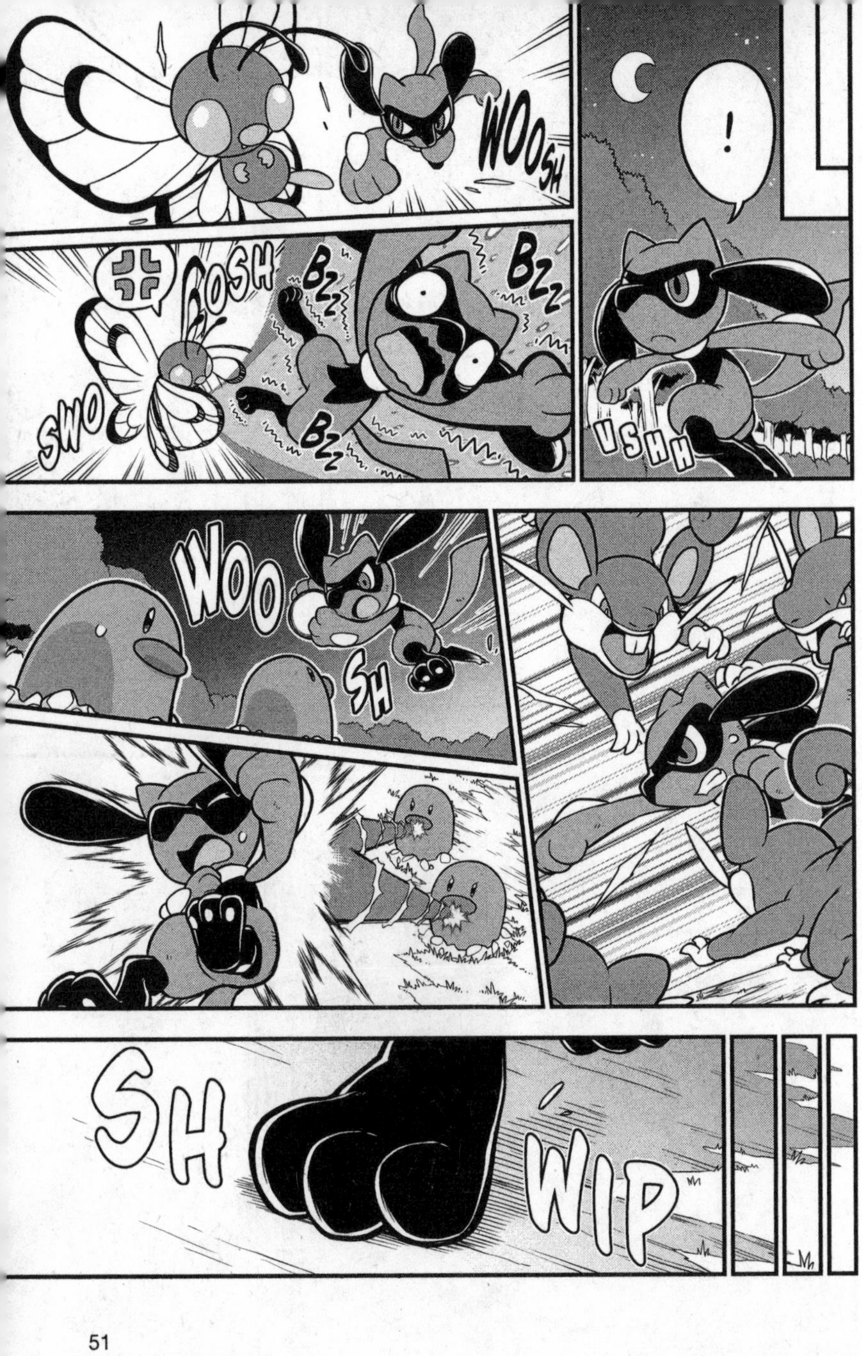

!
VSHH
WOOSH
SWOOSH
BZZ
BZZ
BZZ
WOOSH
SHWIP

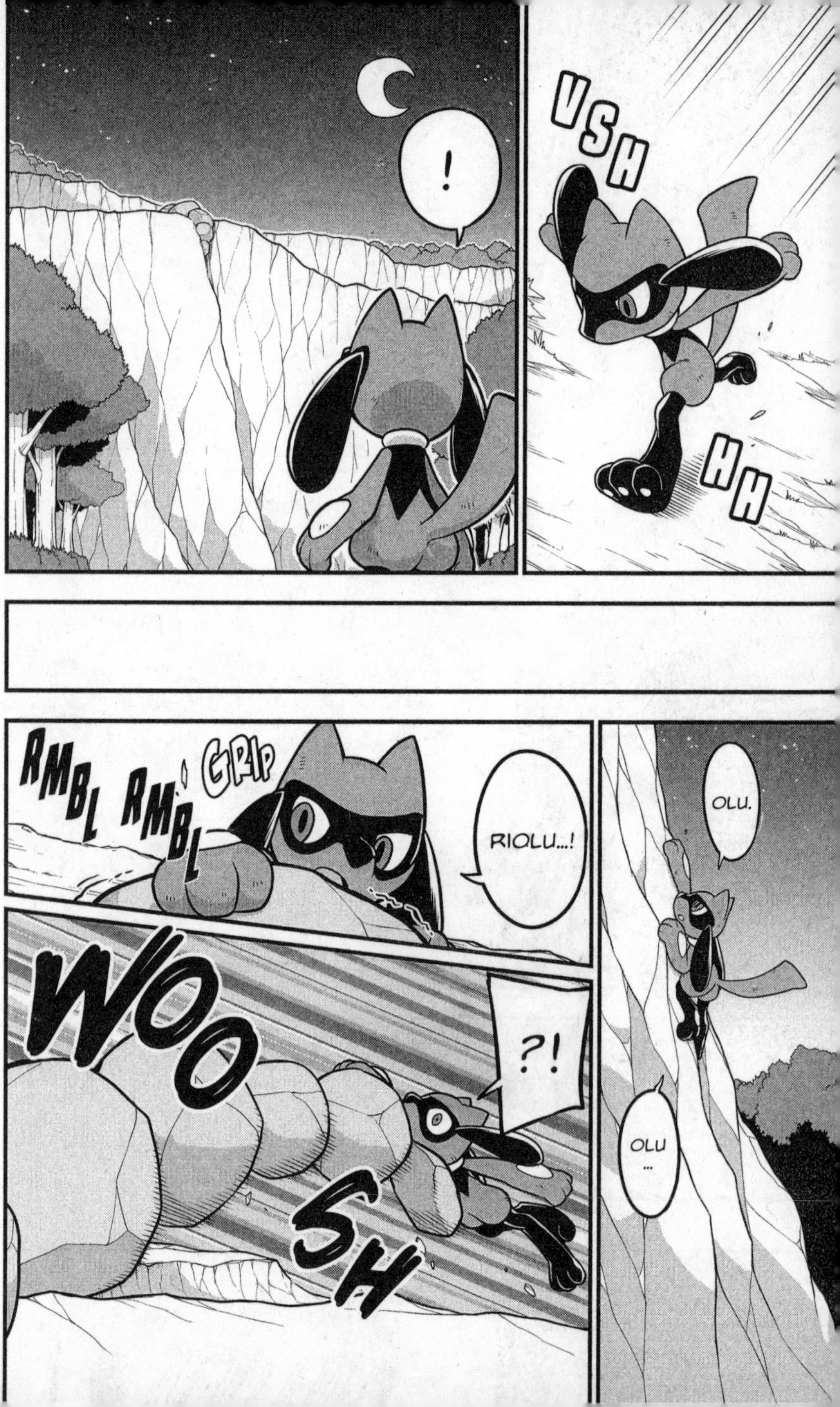
VSH
HH
!
OLU.
OLU
...
RMBL RMBL
GRIP
RIOLU...!
WOOSH
?!

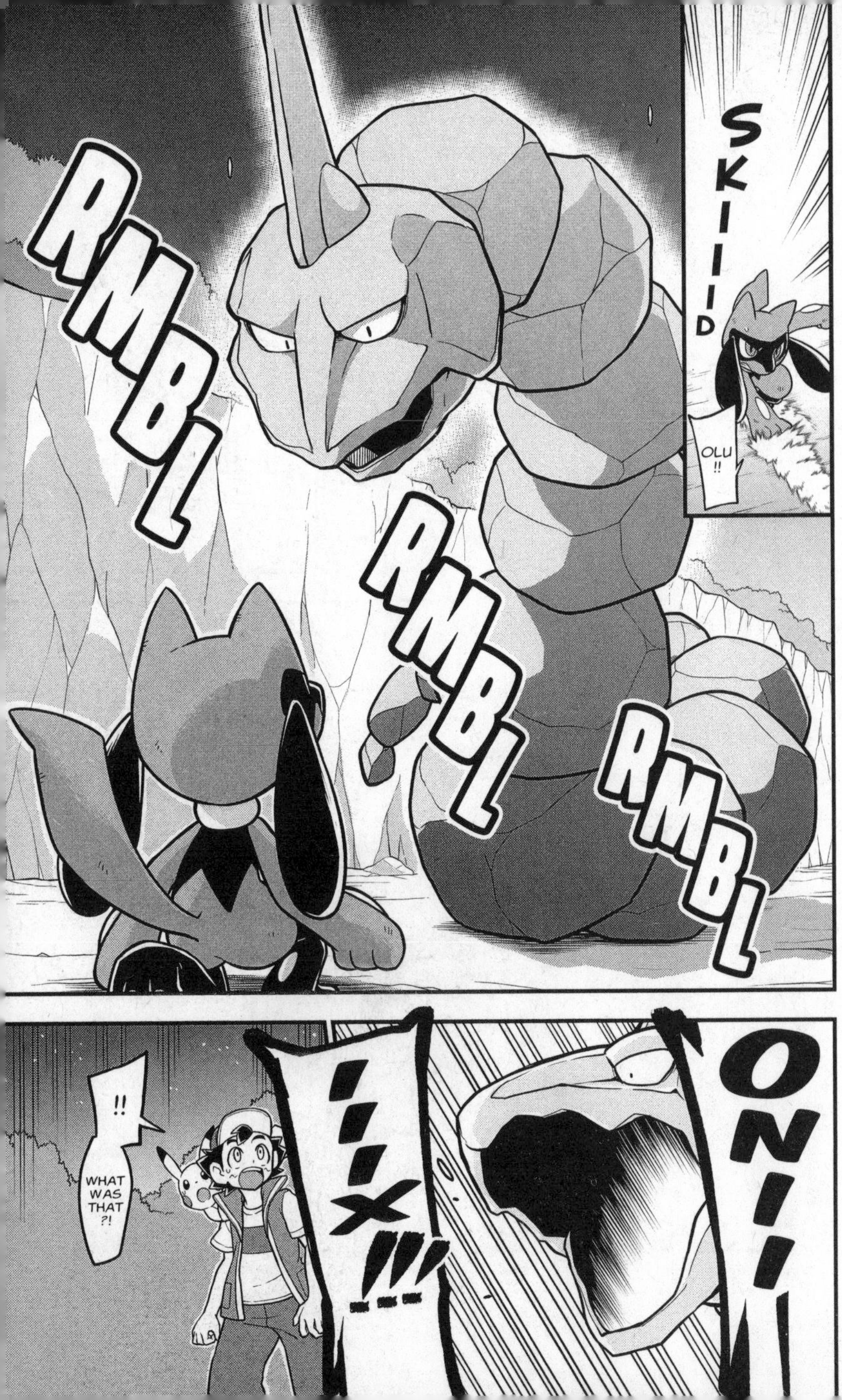
SKIIID
OLU!!
RMBL
RMBL
RMBL
ONIII
IIIX!!!
!!
WHAT WAS THAT?!

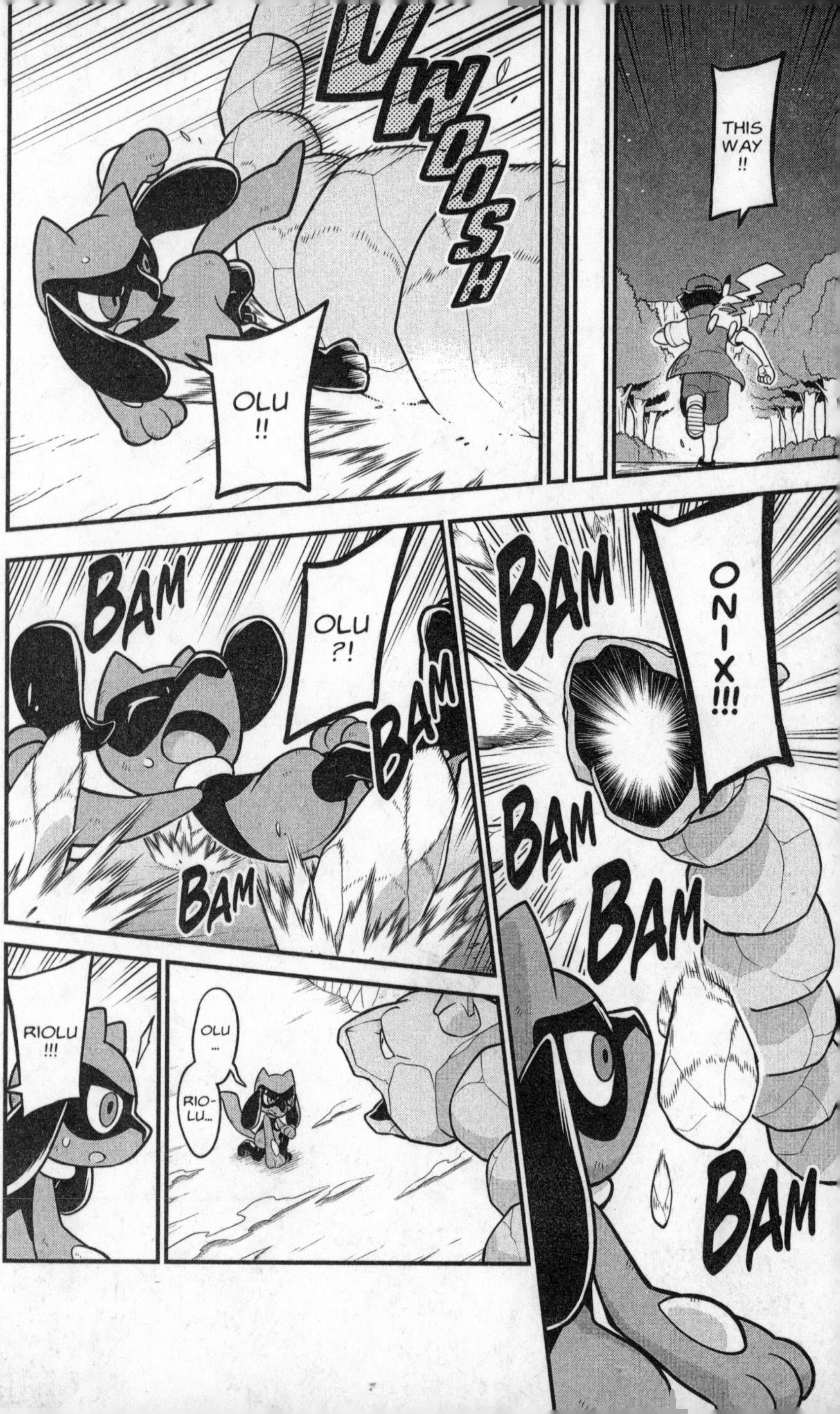
THIS WAY !!
WHOOSH
OLU !!
BAM
ONIX!!!
BAM
BAM
BAM
BAM
BAM
OLU ?!
BAM
BAM
OLU ... RIO-LU...
RIOLU !!!

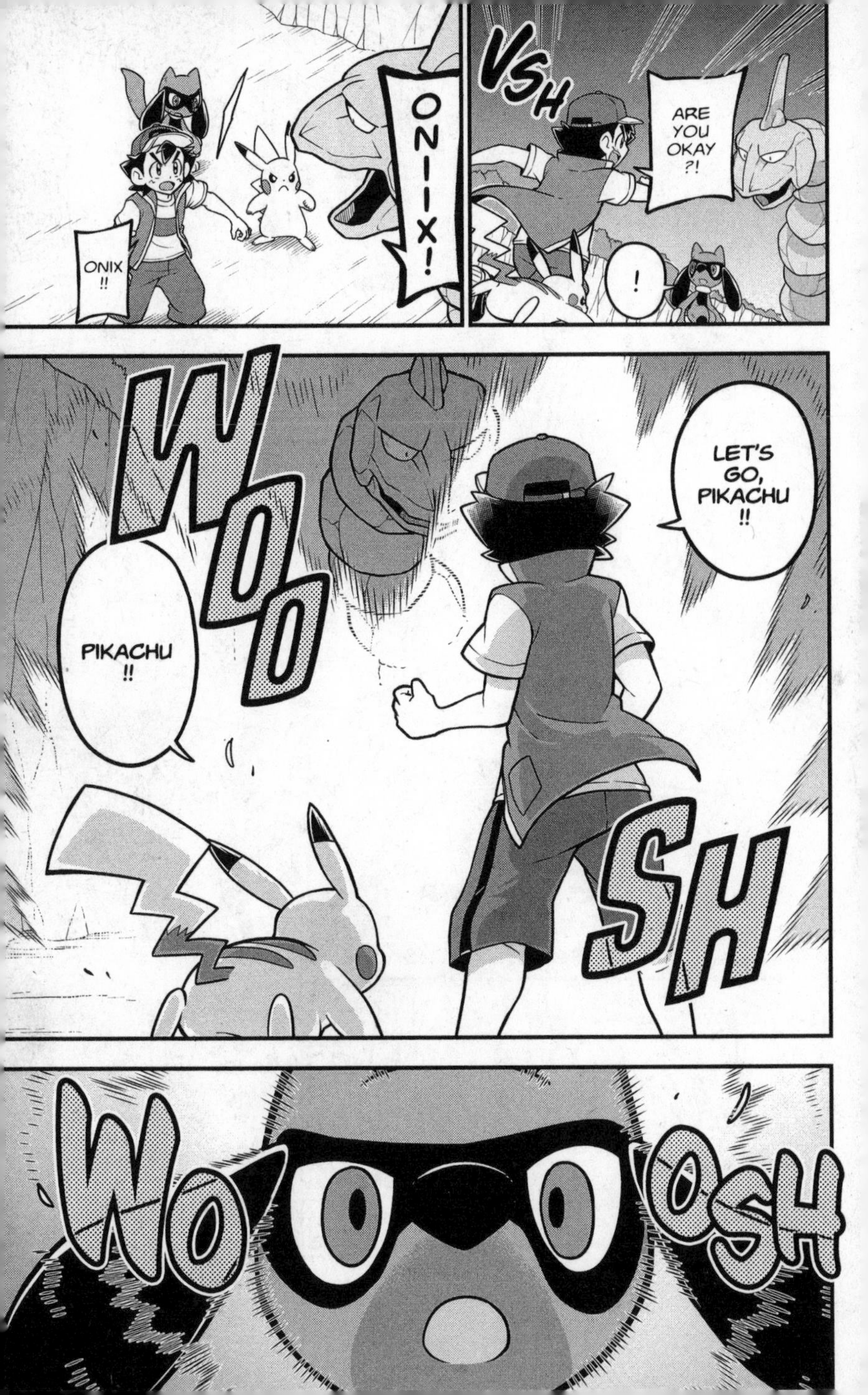
VSH
ARE YOU OKAY ?!
!
ONIIX!
ONIX !!
LET'S GO, PIKACHU !!
WOO
PIKACHU !!
SH
WO OSH

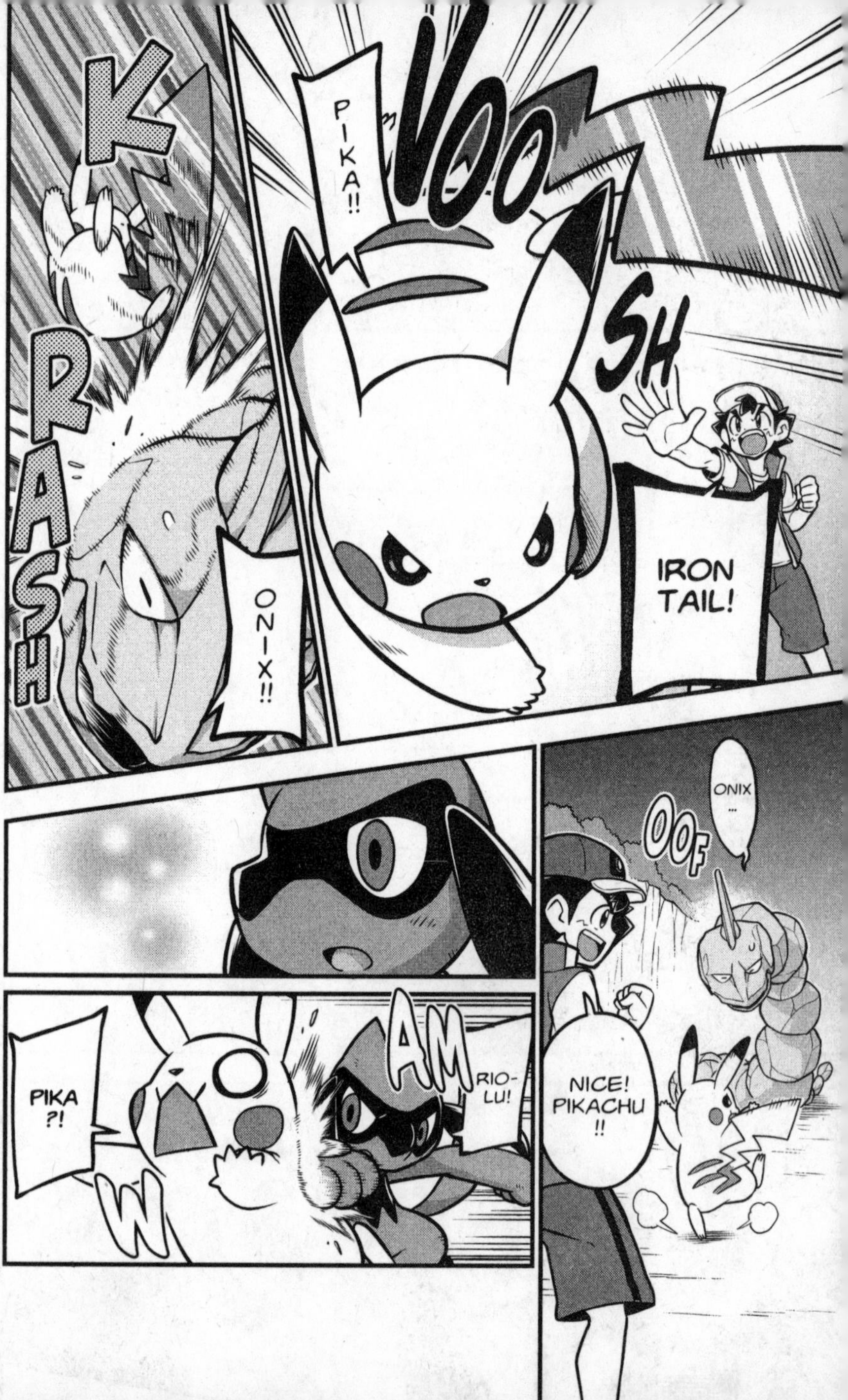

IRON TAIL!
VOO
SH
PIKA!!
KRASH
ONIX!!
ONIX ...
OOF
NICE! PIKACHU !!
RIO-LU!
AM
PIKA ?!
W

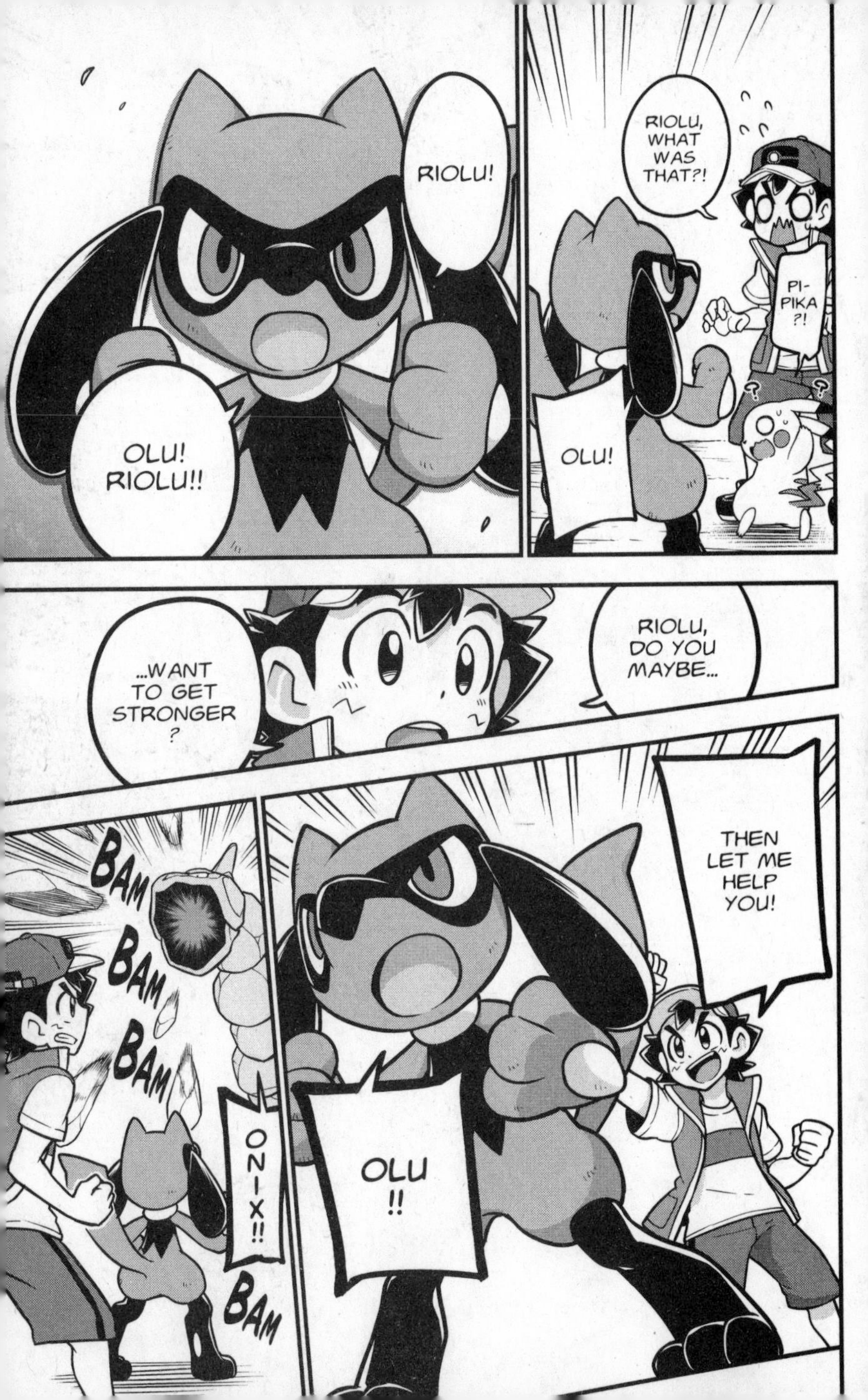
RIOLU, WHAT WAS THAT?!
PI-PIKA?!
OLU!
RIOLU!
OLU! RIOLU!!
RIOLU, DO YOU MAYBE...
...WANT TO GET STRONGER?
THEN LET ME HELP YOU!
OLU!!
BAM
BAM
BAM
ONIX!!
BAM

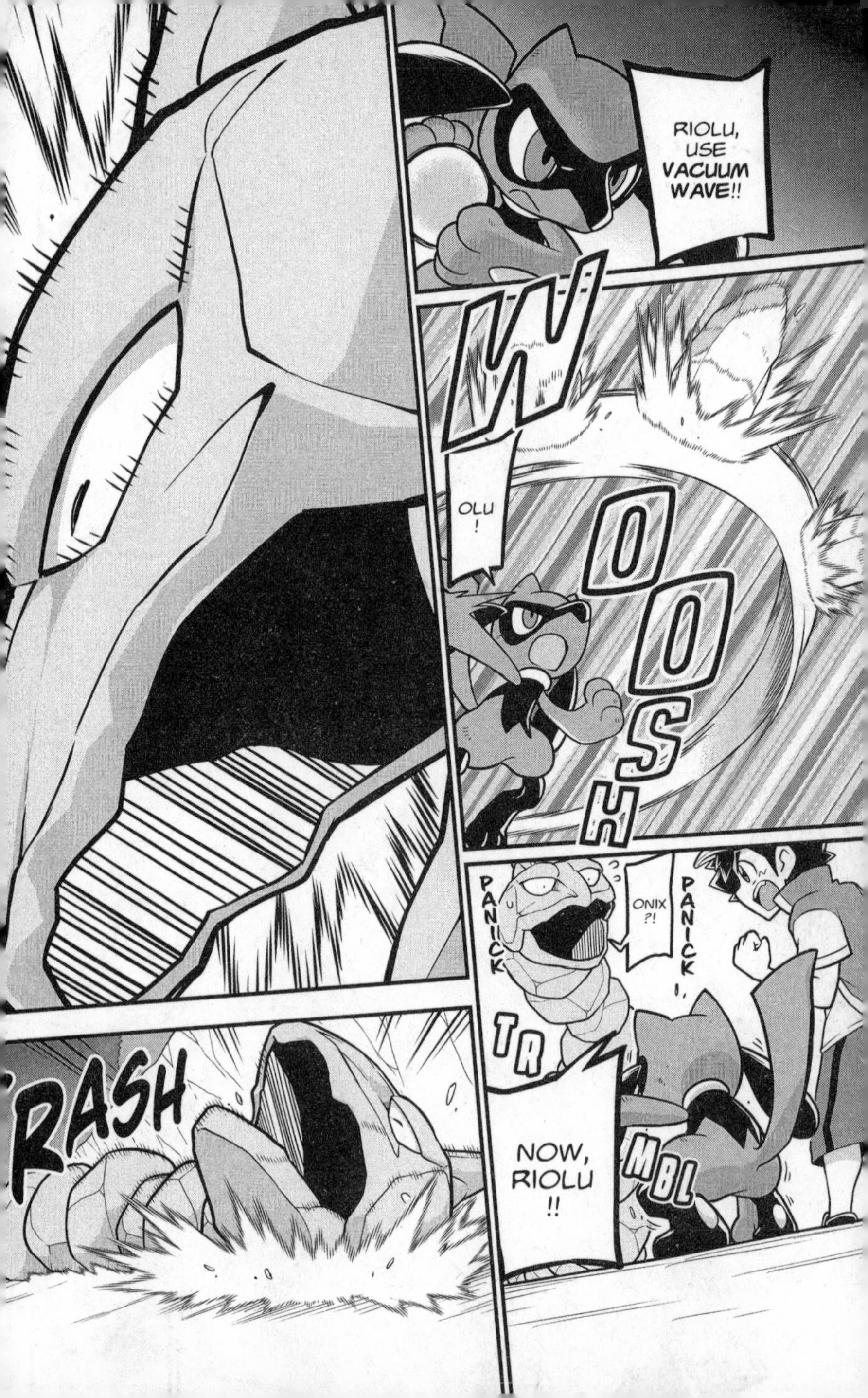
RIOLU, USE VACUUM WAVE!!
WOOOSH
OLU!
PANICK
ONIX?!
PANICK
TR
MBL
NOW, RIOLU!!
RASH

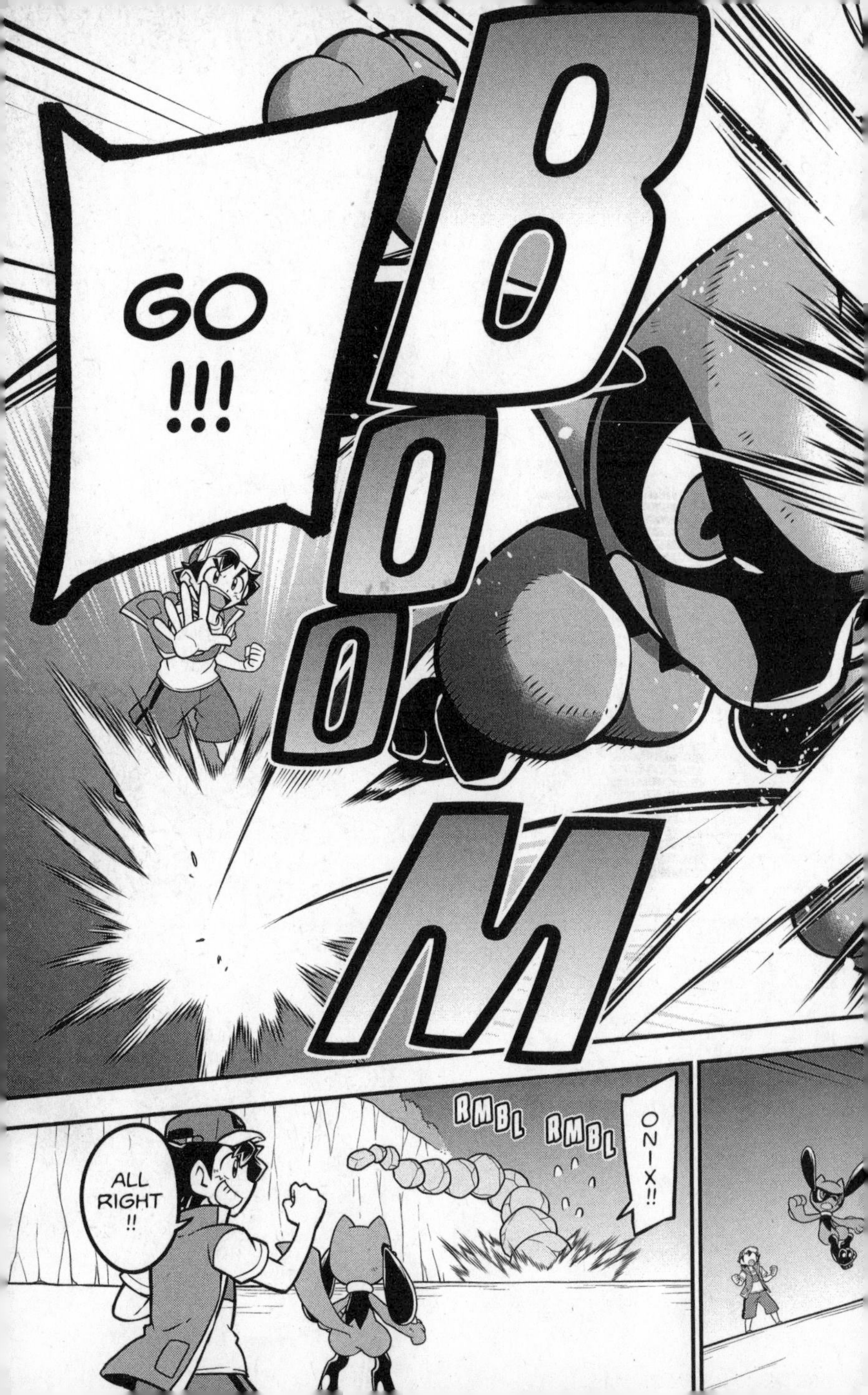
GO!!!
BOOOM
ONIX!!
RMBL RMBL
ALL RIGHT!!

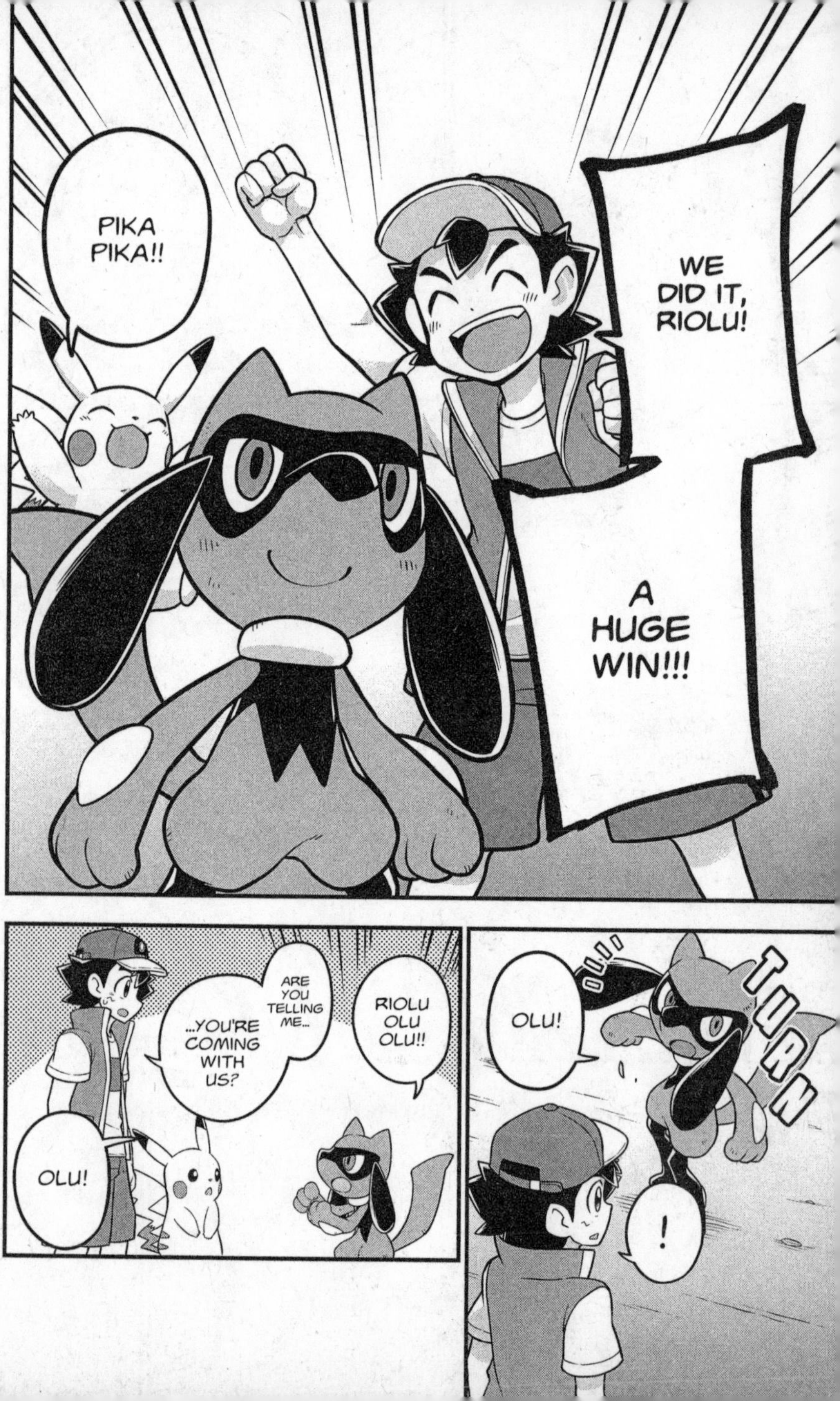
WE DID IT, RIOLU!
A HUGE WIN!!!
PIKA PIKA!!
TURN
OLU!
!
RIOLU OLU OLU!!
ARE YOU TELLING ME...
...YOU'RE COMING WITH US?
OLU!

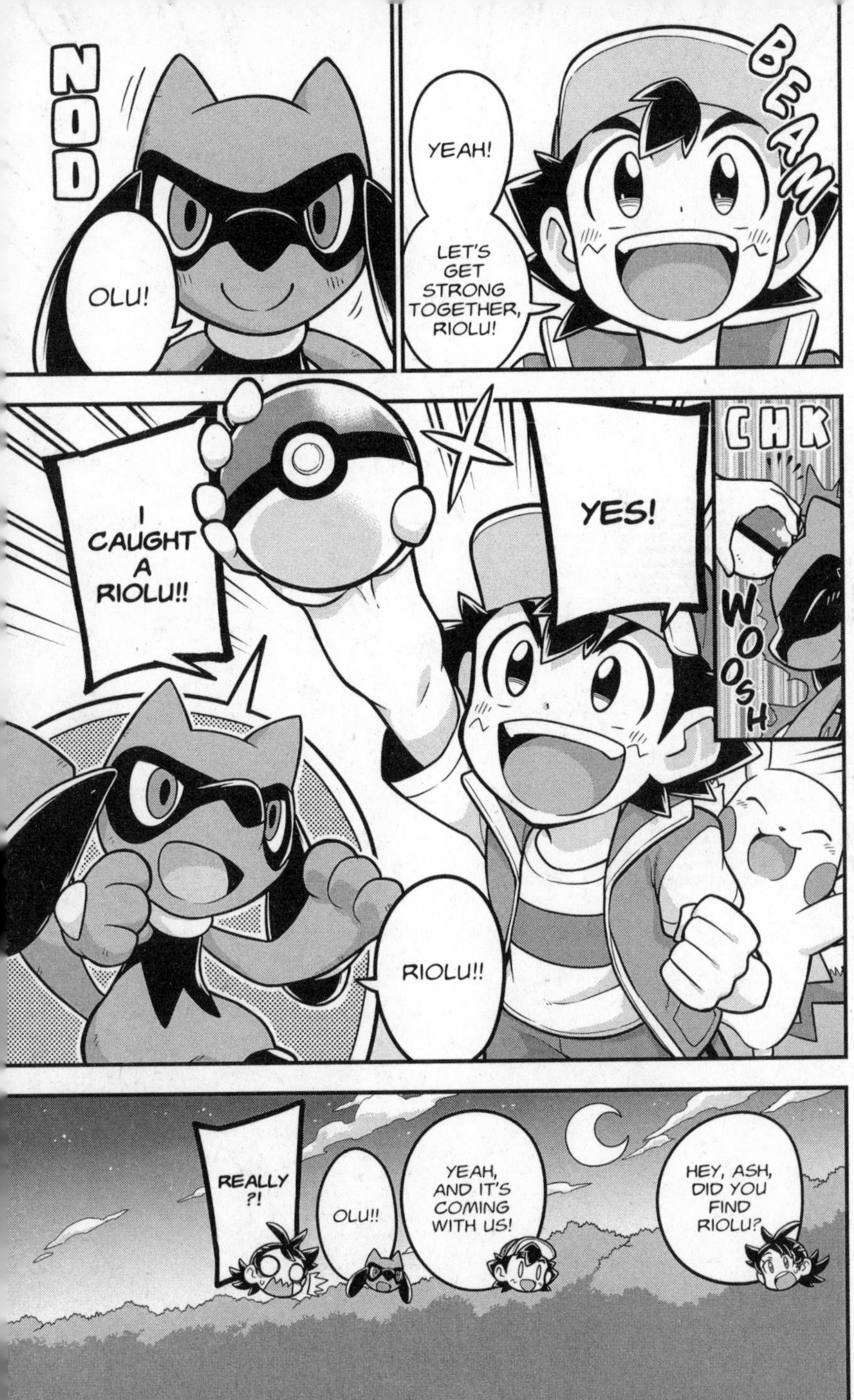
BEAM
YEAH!
LET'S GET STRONG TOGETHER, RIOLU!
NOD
OLU!
CHK
WOOSH
YES!
I CAUGHT A RIOLU!!
RIOLU!!
HEY, ASH, DID YOU FIND RIOLU?
YEAH, AND IT'S COMING WITH US!
OLU!!
REALLY?!

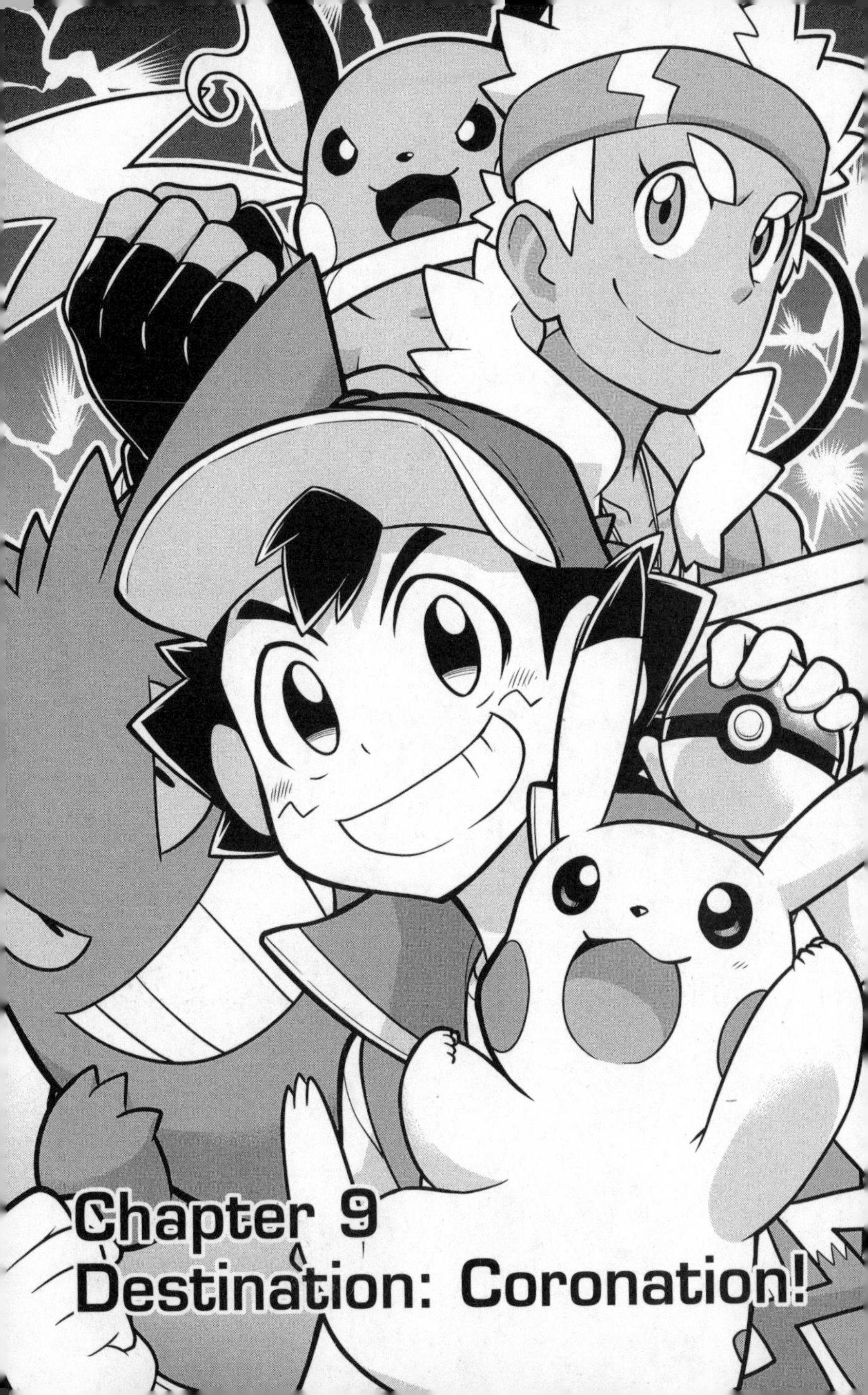
Chapter 9
Destination: Coronation!

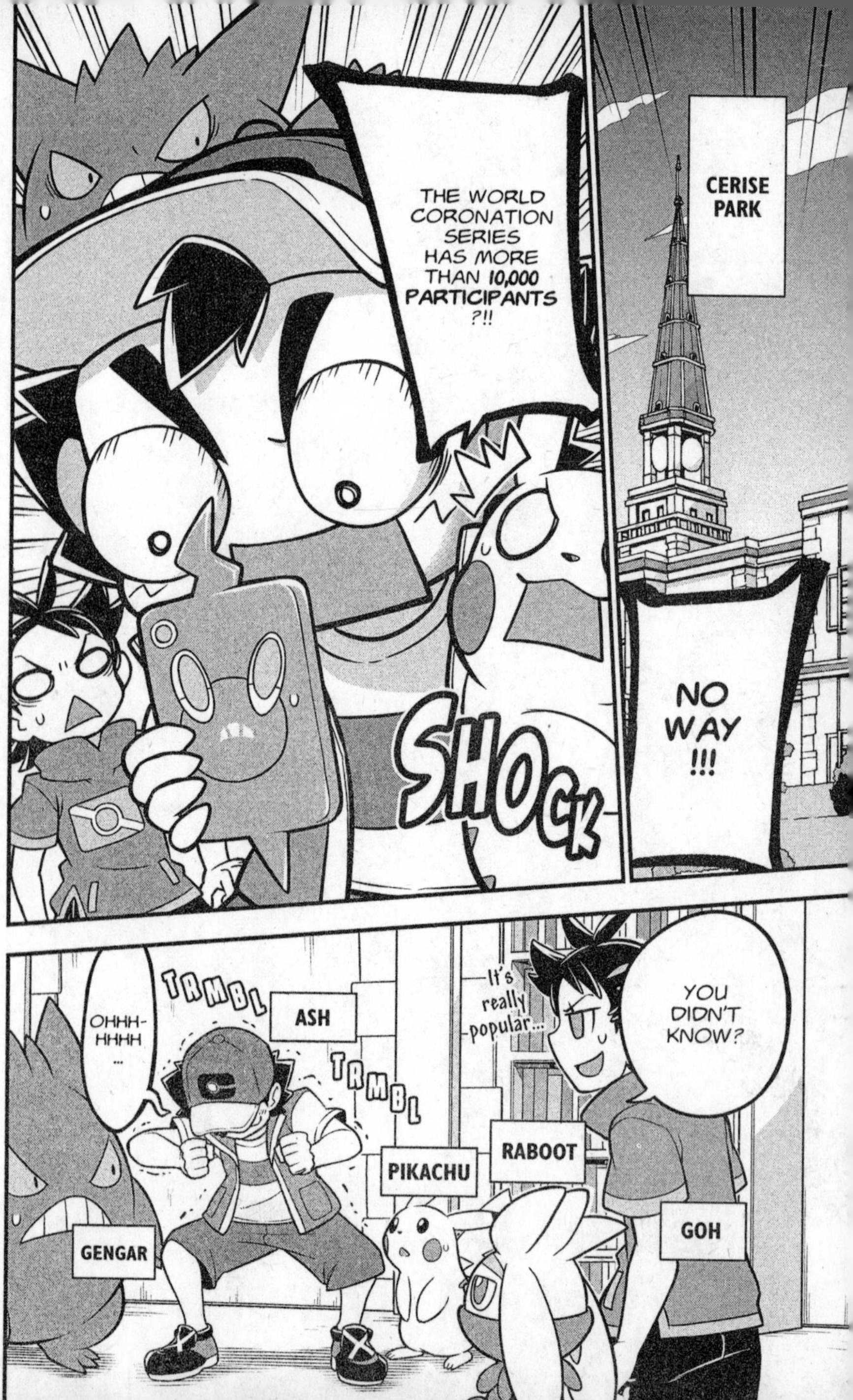
CERISE PARK
NO WAY!!!
THE WORLD CORONATION SERIES HAS MORE THAN 10,000 PARTICIPANTS?!!
SHOCK
YOU DIDN'T KNOW?
It's really popular...
RABOOT
GOH
PIKACHU
TRMBL
TRMBL
ASH
OHHH-HHHH...
GENGAR

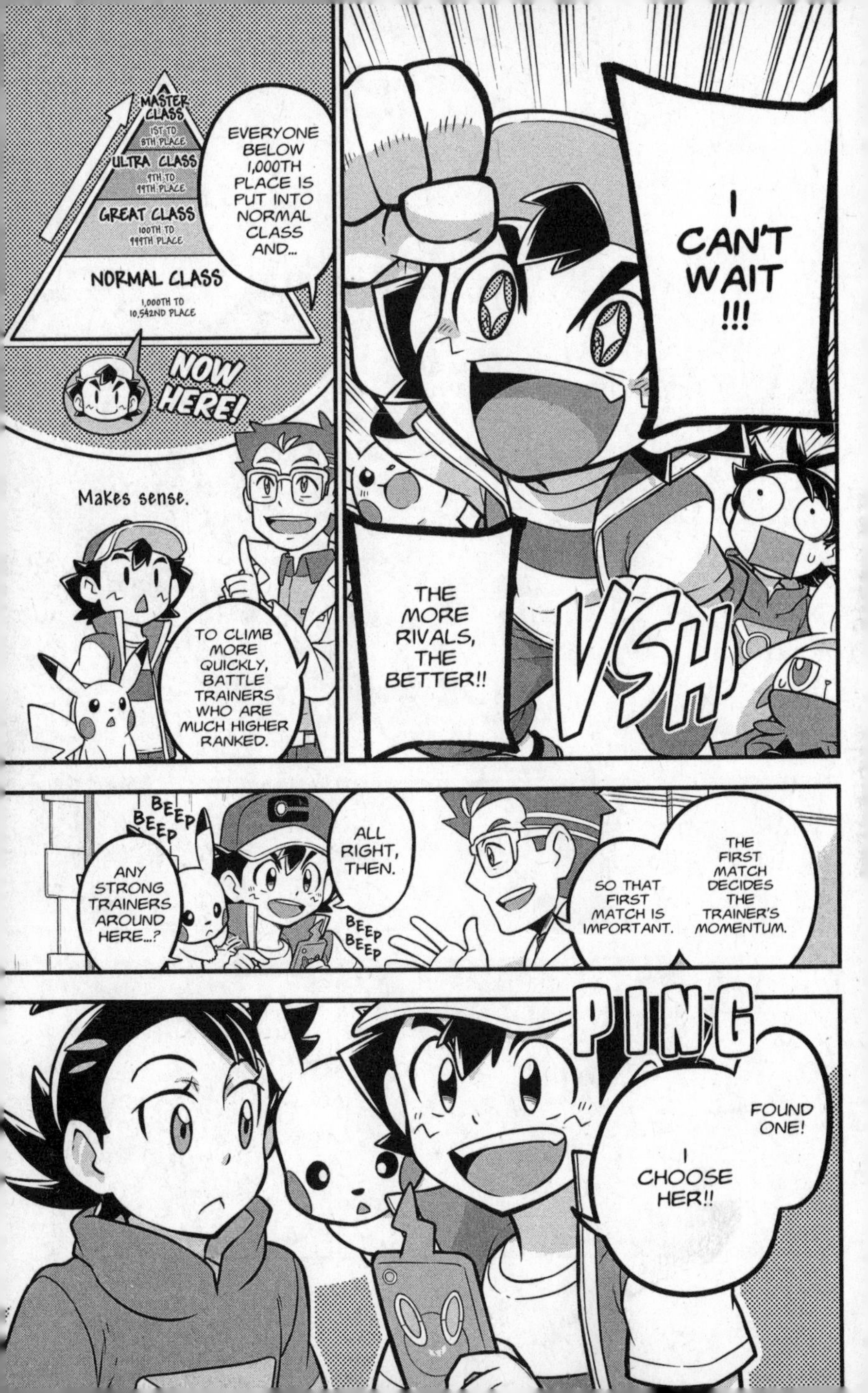

I CAN'T WAIT!!!
THE MORE RIVALS, THE BETTER!!
VSH
EVERYONE BELOW 1,000TH PLACE IS PUT INTO NORMAL CLASS AND...
MASTER CLASS
1ST TO 8TH PLACE
ULTRA CLASS
9TH TO 99TH PLACE
GREAT CLASS
100TH TO 999TH PLACE
NORMAL CLASS
1,000TH TO 10,542ND PLACE
NOW HERE!
Makes sense.
TO CLIMB MORE QUICKLY, BATTLE TRAINERS WHO ARE MUCH HIGHER RANKED.
THE FIRST MATCH DECIDES THE TRAINER'S MOMENTUM.
SO THAT FIRST MATCH IS IMPORTANT.
BEEP BEEP
ALL RIGHT, THEN.
BEEP BEEP
ANY STRONG TRAINERS AROUND HERE...?
PING
FOUND ONE!
I CHOOSE HER!!

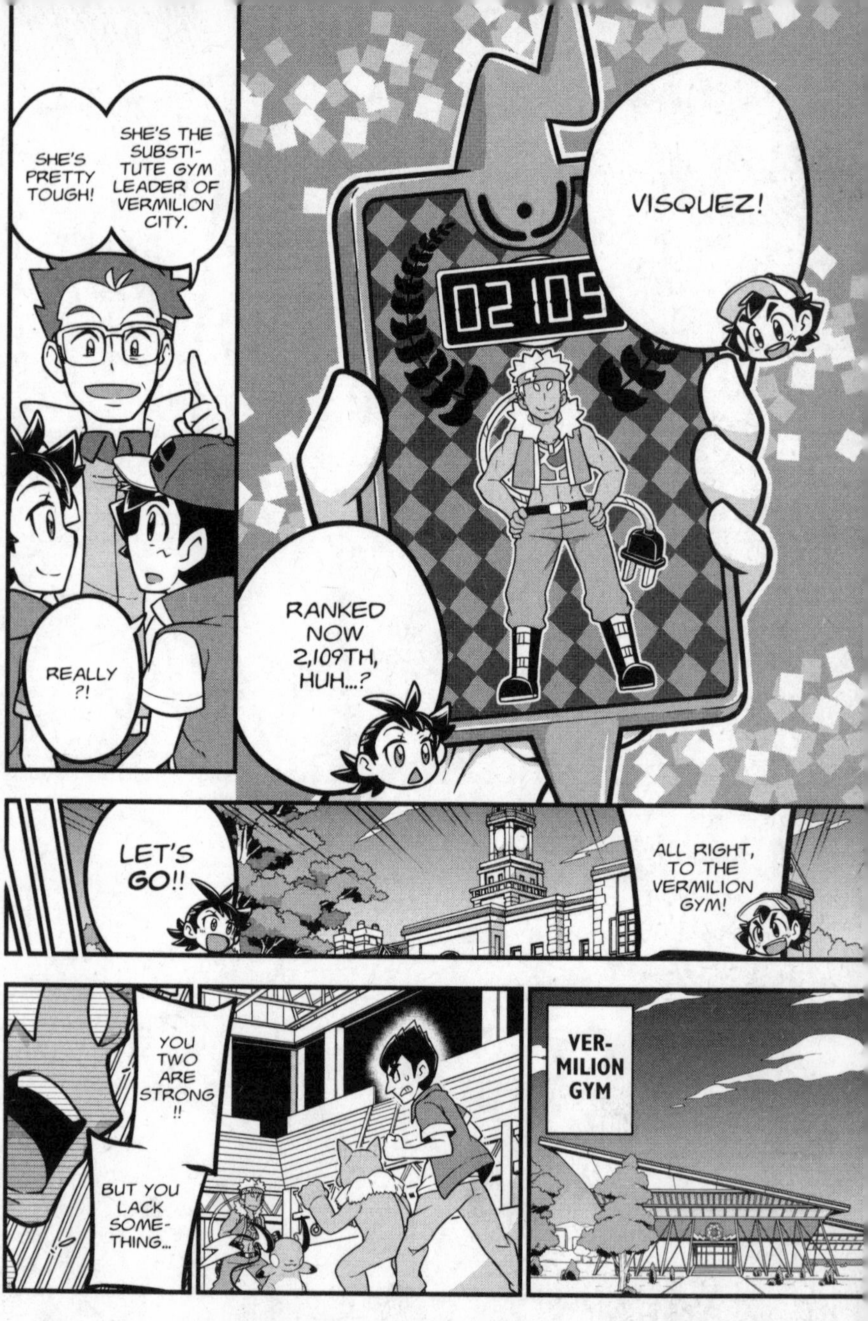
VISQUEZ!
RANKED NOW 2,109TH, HUH...?
SHE'S THE SUBSTI-TUTE GYM LEADER OF VERMILION CITY.
SHE'S PRETTY TOUGH!
REALLY ?!
ALL RIGHT, TO THE VERMILION GYM!
LET'S GO!!
VER-MILION GYM
YOU TWO ARE STRONG !!
BUT YOU LACK SOME-THING...

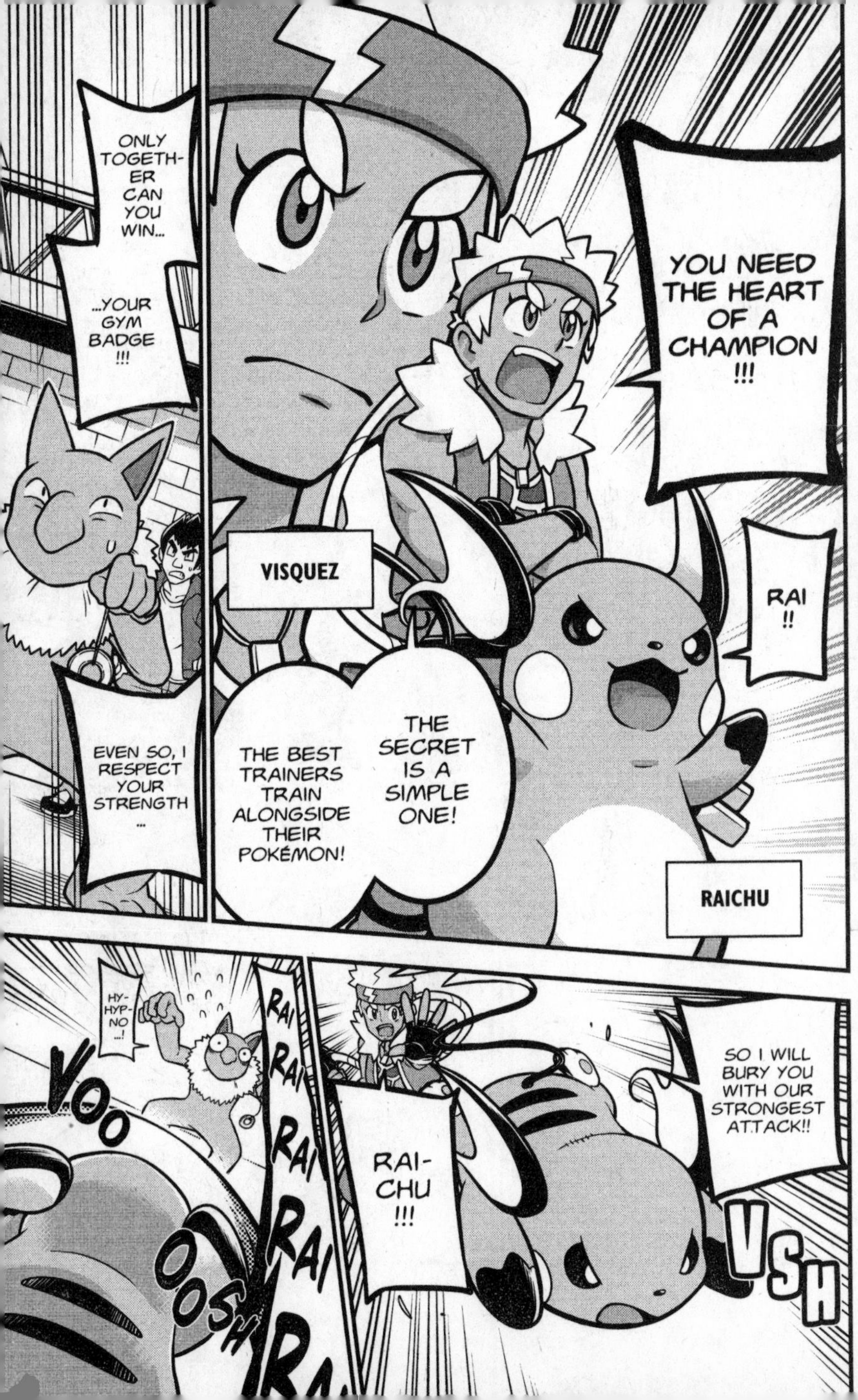
YOU NEED THE HEART OF A CHAMPION!!!
RAI!!
VISQUEZ
THE SECRET IS A SIMPLE ONE!
THE BEST TRAINERS TRAIN ALONGSIDE THEIR POKÉMON!
RAICHU
ONLY TOGETH-ER CAN YOU WIN...
...YOUR GYM BADGE!!!
EVEN SO, I RESPECT YOUR STRENGTH...
SO I WILL BURY YOU WITH OUR STRONGEST ATTACK!!
VSH
RAI-CHU!!!
RAI RAI RAI RAI RAI
HY-HYP-NO...!
VOOOOSH

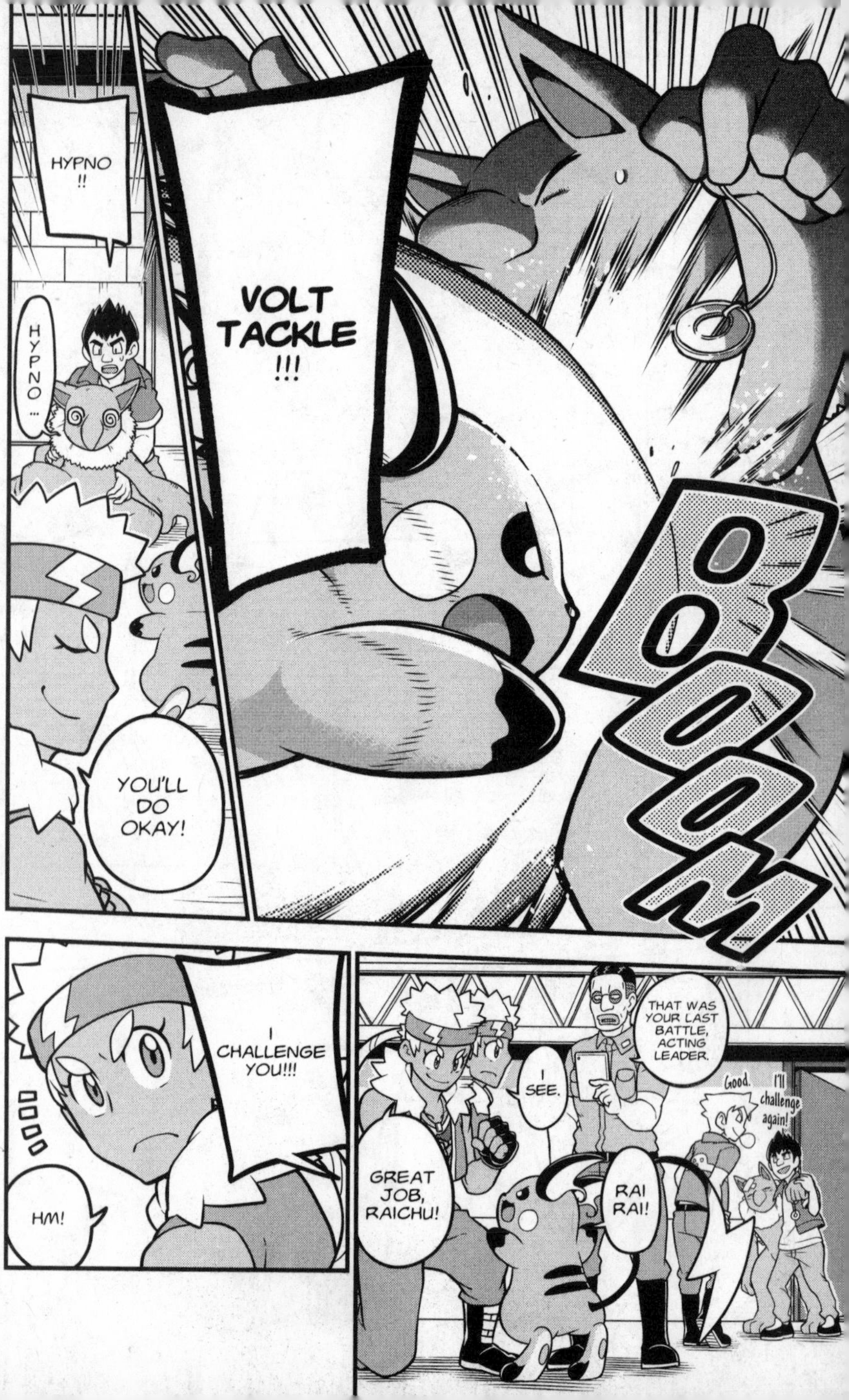
VOLT TACKLE !!!
BOOM
HYPNO !!
HYPNO...
YOU'LL DO OKAY!
THAT WAS YOUR LAST BATTLE, ACTING LEADER.
I SEE.
Good.
I'll challenge again!
RAI RAI!
GREAT JOB, RAICHU!
I CHALLENGE YOU!!!
HM!

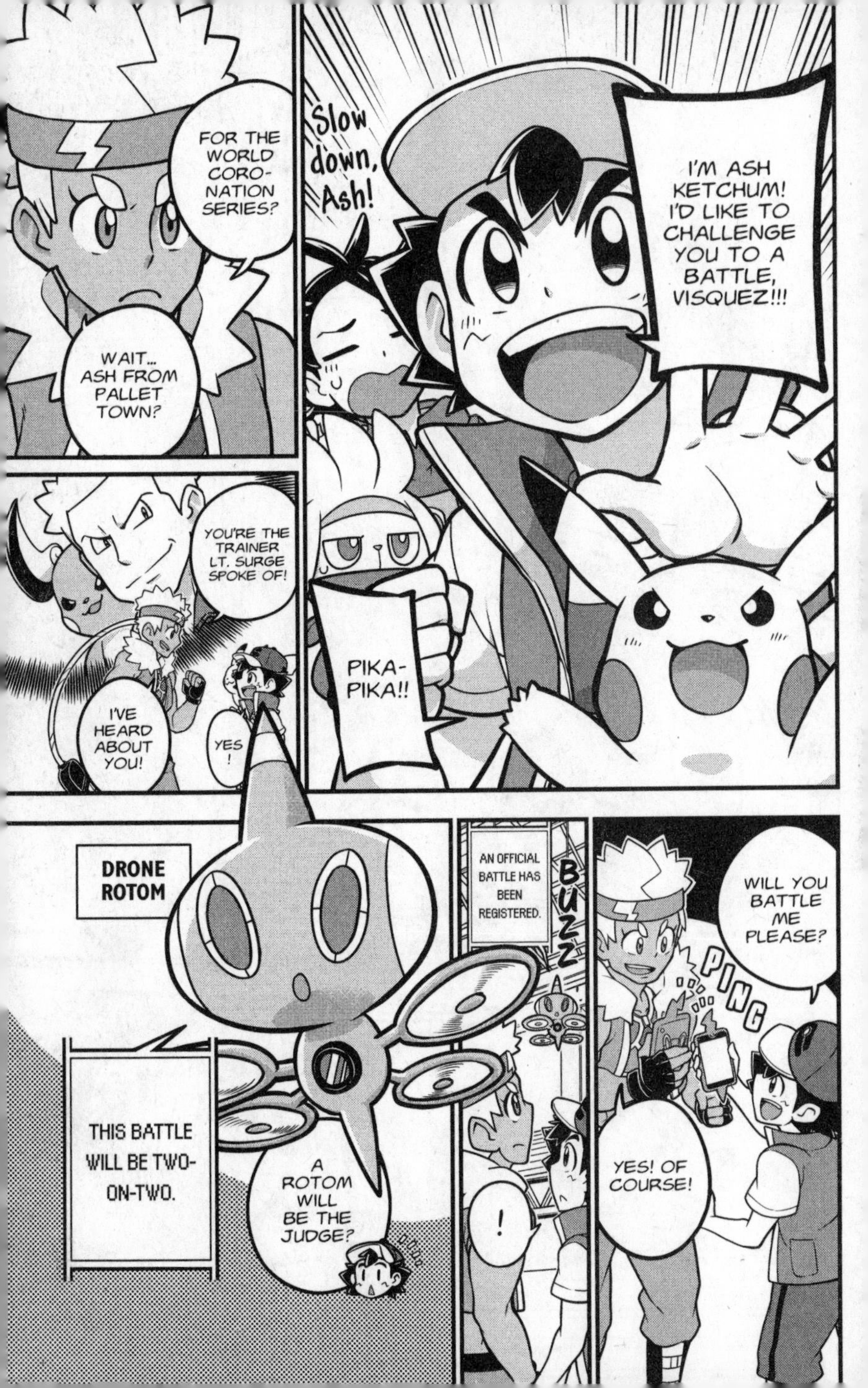

I'M ASH KETCHUM! I'D LIKE TO CHALLENGE YOU TO A BATTLE, VISQUEZ!!!
Slow down, Ash!
PIKA-PIKA!!
FOR THE WORLD CORO-NATION SERIES?
WAIT... ASH FROM PALLET TOWN?
YOU'RE THE TRAINER LT. SURGE SPOKE OF!
YES!
I'VE HEARD ABOUT YOU!
WILL YOU BATTLE ME PLEASE?
PING
YES! OF COURSE!
AN OFFICIAL BATTLE HAS BEEN REGISTERED.
BUZZ
!
DRONE ROTOM
THIS BATTLE WILL BE TWO-ON-TWO.
A ROTOM WILL BE THE JUDGE?

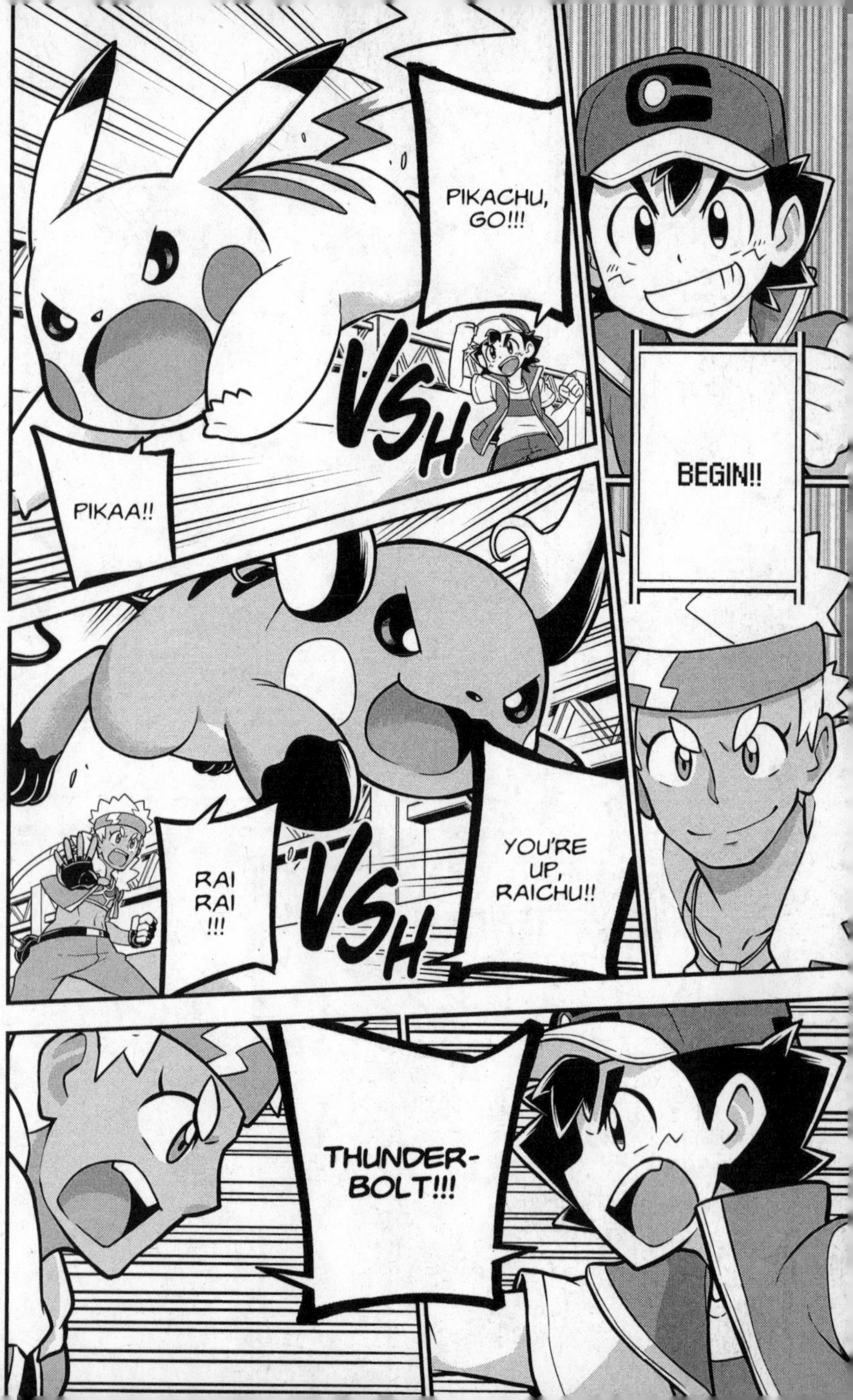
BEGIN!!
PIKACHU, GO!!!
VSH
PIKAA!!
YOU'RE UP, RAICHU!!
VSH
RAI RAI !!!
THUNDER-BOLT!!!

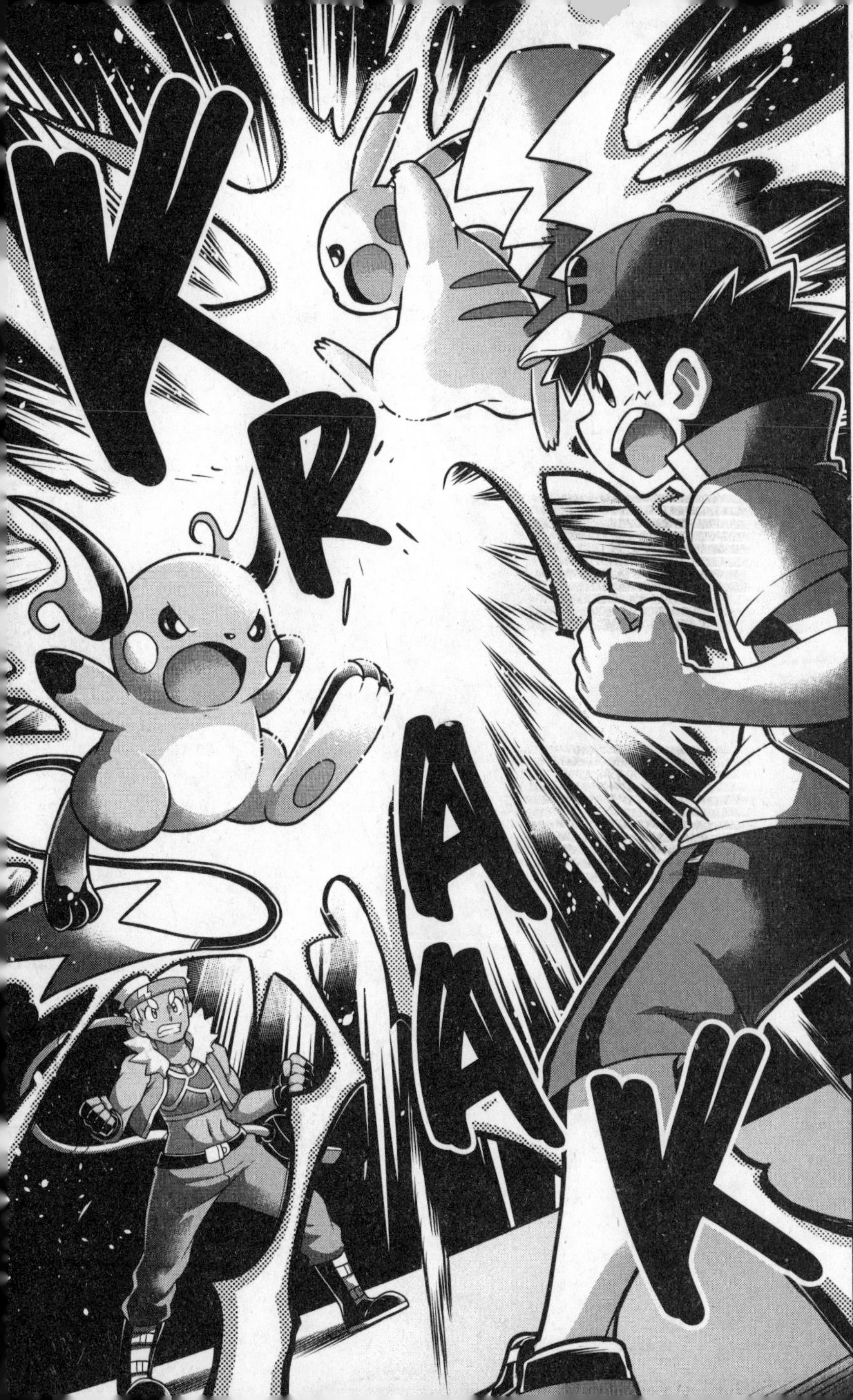
KRAAK

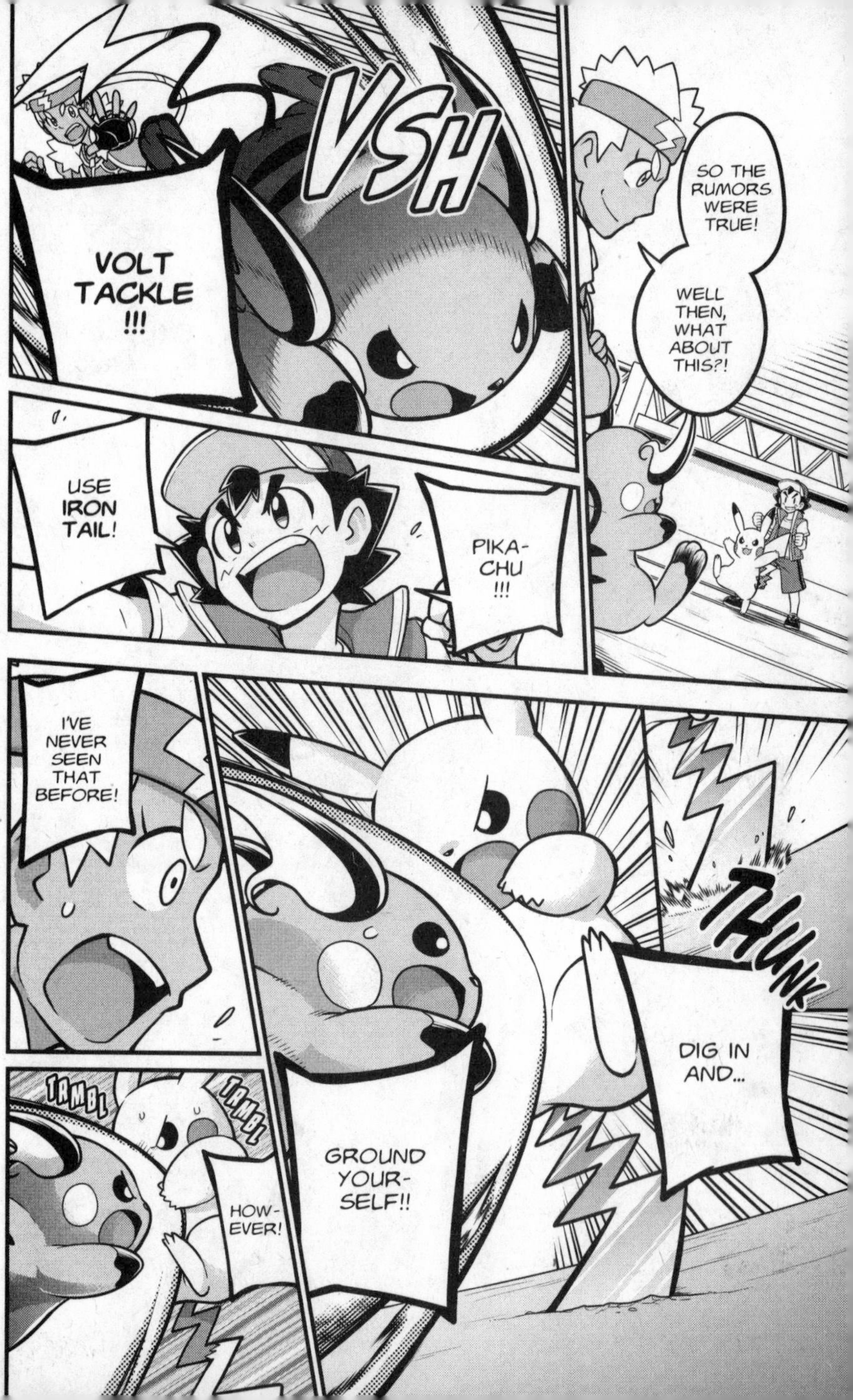
SO THE RUMORS WERE TRUE!
WELL THEN, WHAT ABOUT THIS?!
VSH
VOLT TACKLE !!!
PIKA-CHU !!!
USE IRON TAIL!
THUNK
DIG IN AND...
GROUND YOUR-SELF!!
I'VE NEVER SEEN THAT BEFORE!
TRMBL
TRMBL
HOW-EVER!

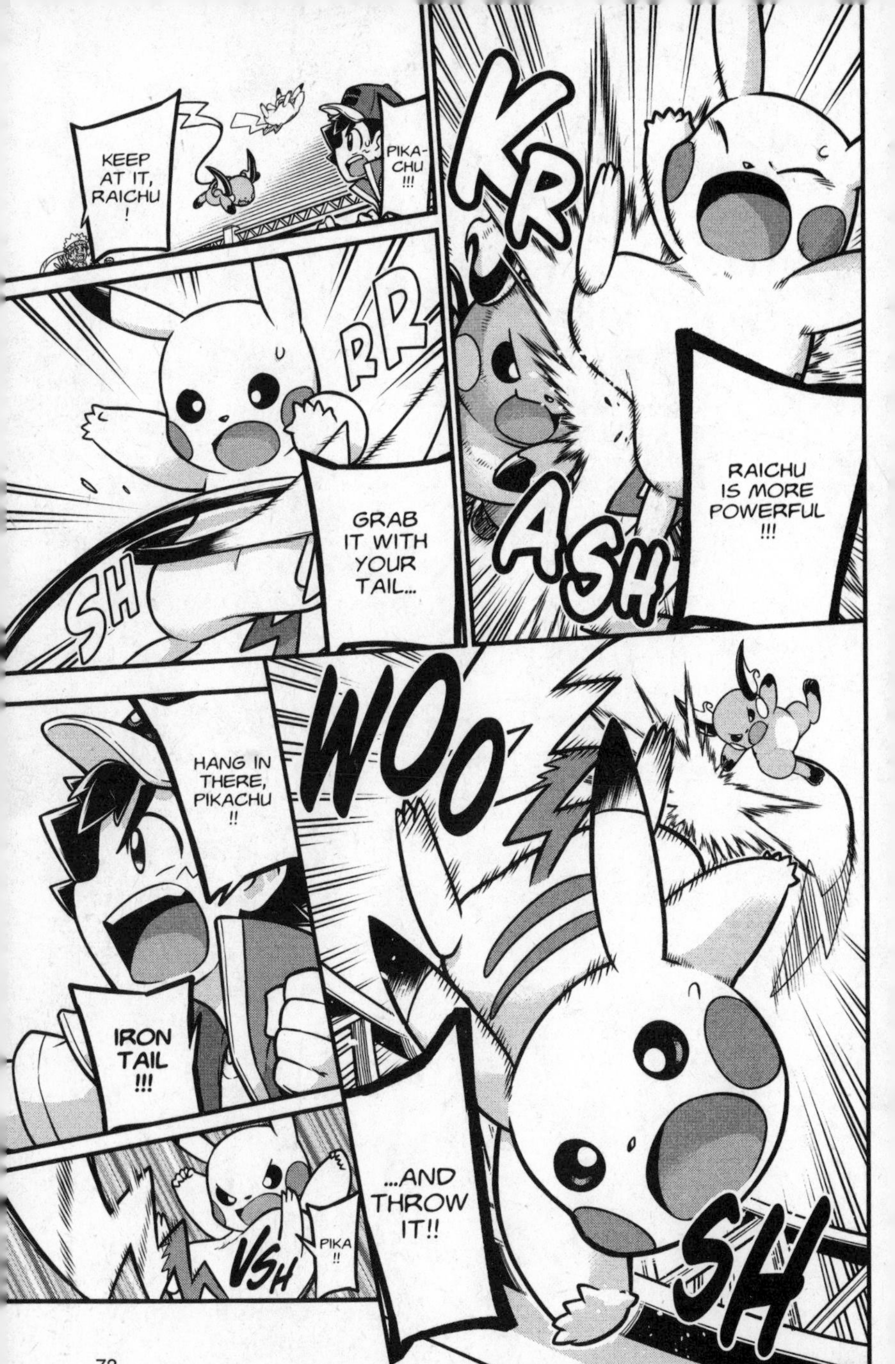
KR
ASH
RAICHU IS MORE POWERFUL!!!
PIKACHU!!!
KEEP AT IT, RAICHU!
RR
GRAB IT WITH YOUR TAIL...
SH
WOO
SH
...AND THROW IT!!
HANG IN THERE, PIKACHU!!
IRON TAIL!!!
PIKA!!
VSH

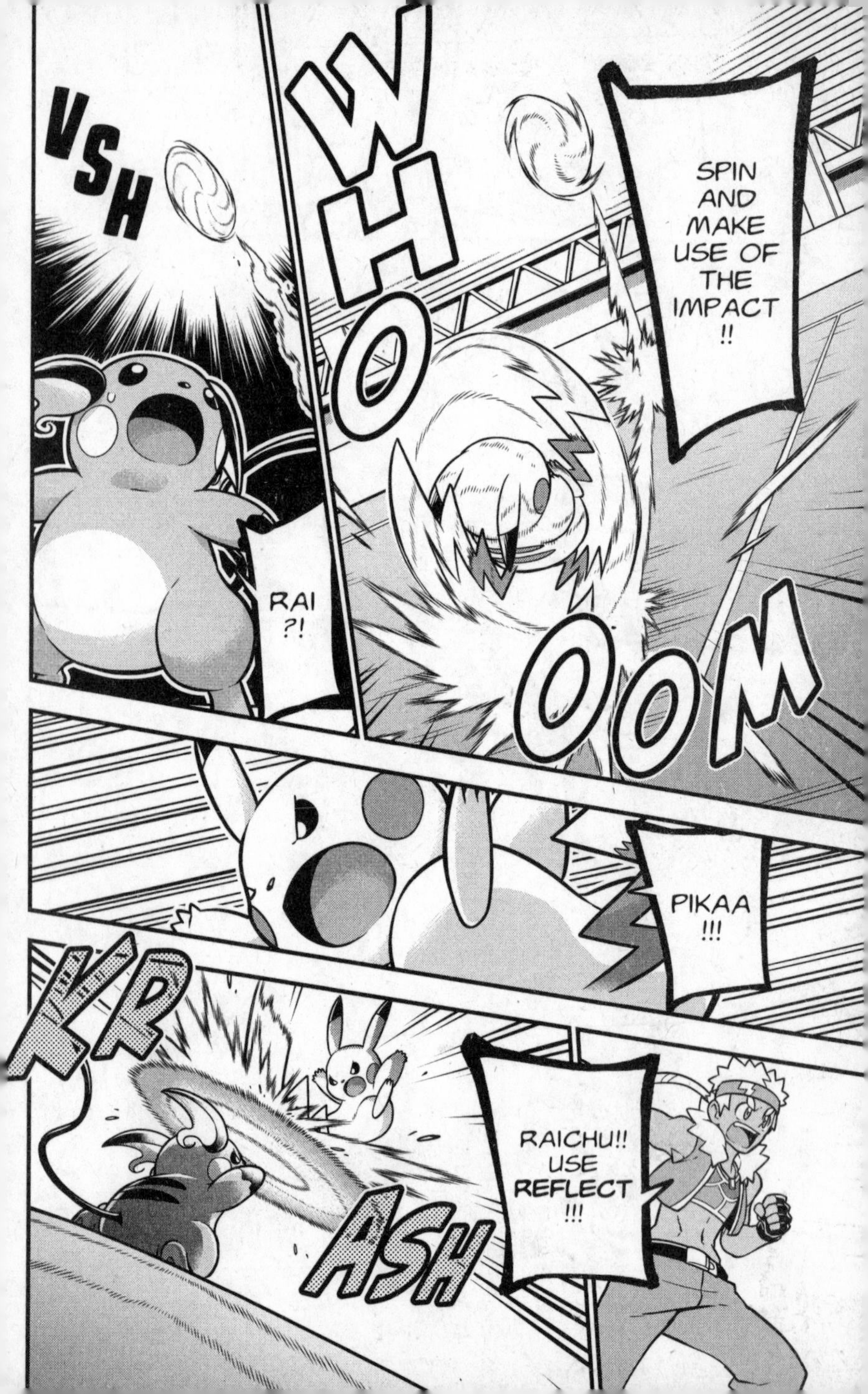
SPIN AND MAKE USE OF THE IMPACT!!
WHOOOM
VSH
RAI?!
PIKAA!!!
RAICHU!! USE REFLECT!!!
KRASH

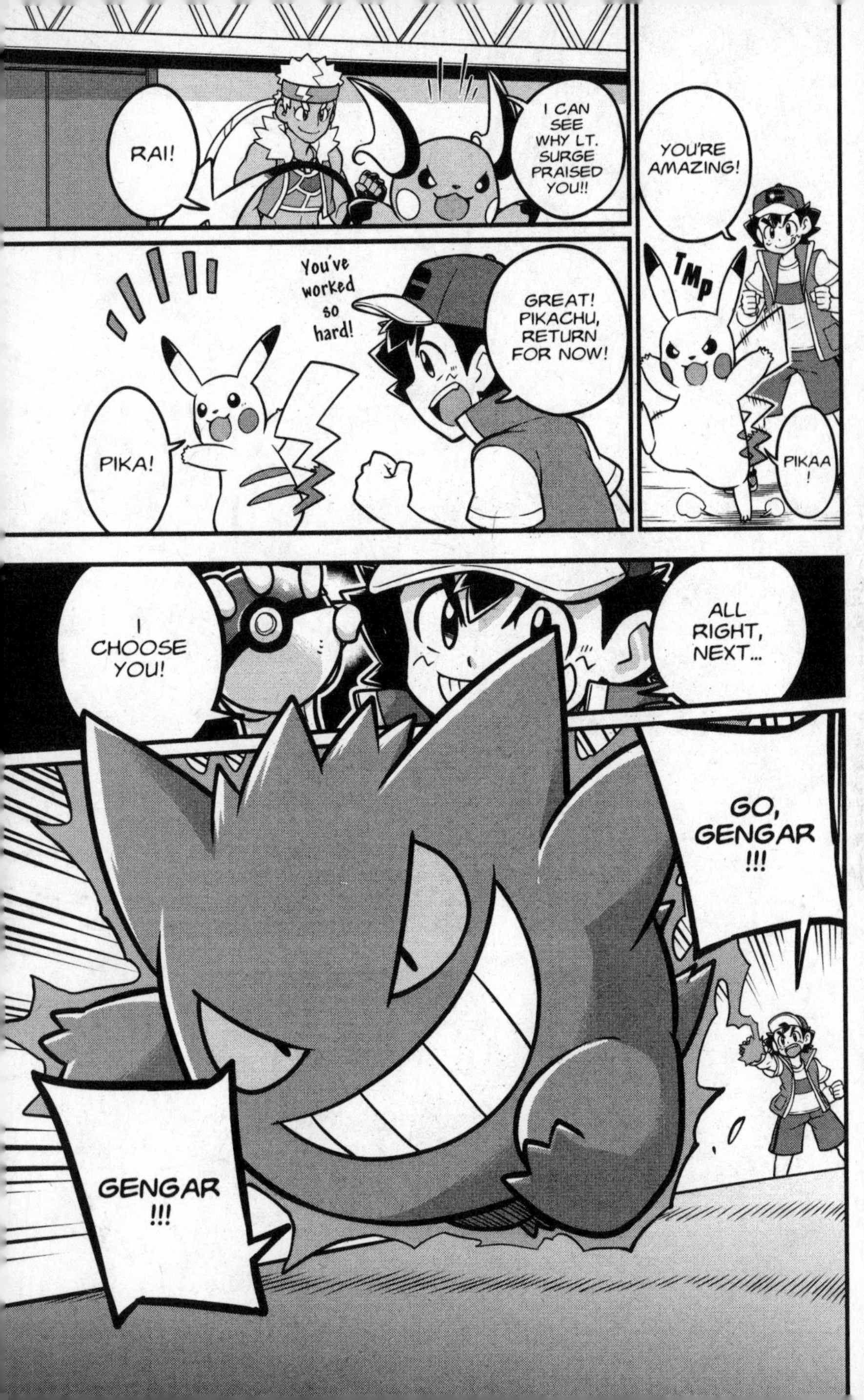
YOU'RE AMAZING!
TMP
PIKAA!
I CAN SEE WHY LT. SURGE PRAISED YOU!!
RAI!
GREAT! PIKACHU, RETURN FOR NOW!
You've worked so hard!
PIKA!
ALL RIGHT, NEXT...
I CHOOSE YOU!
GO, GENGAR!!!
GENGAR!!!

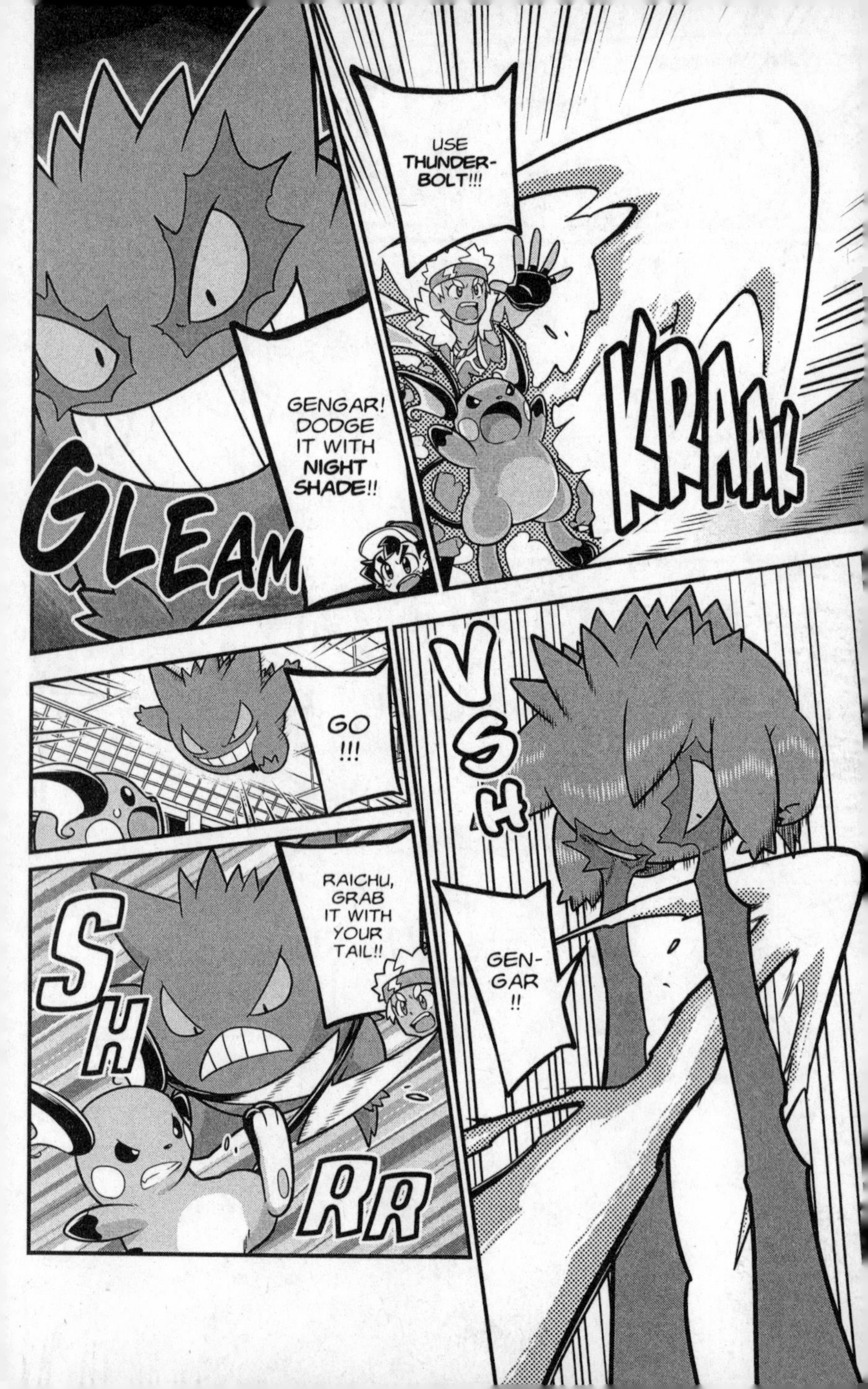
USE THUNDER-BOLT!!!
KRAAK
GENGAR! DODGE IT WITH NIGHT SHADE!!
GLEAM
VSH
GEN-GAR!!
GO!!!
RAICHU, GRAB IT WITH YOUR TAIL!!
SH
RR

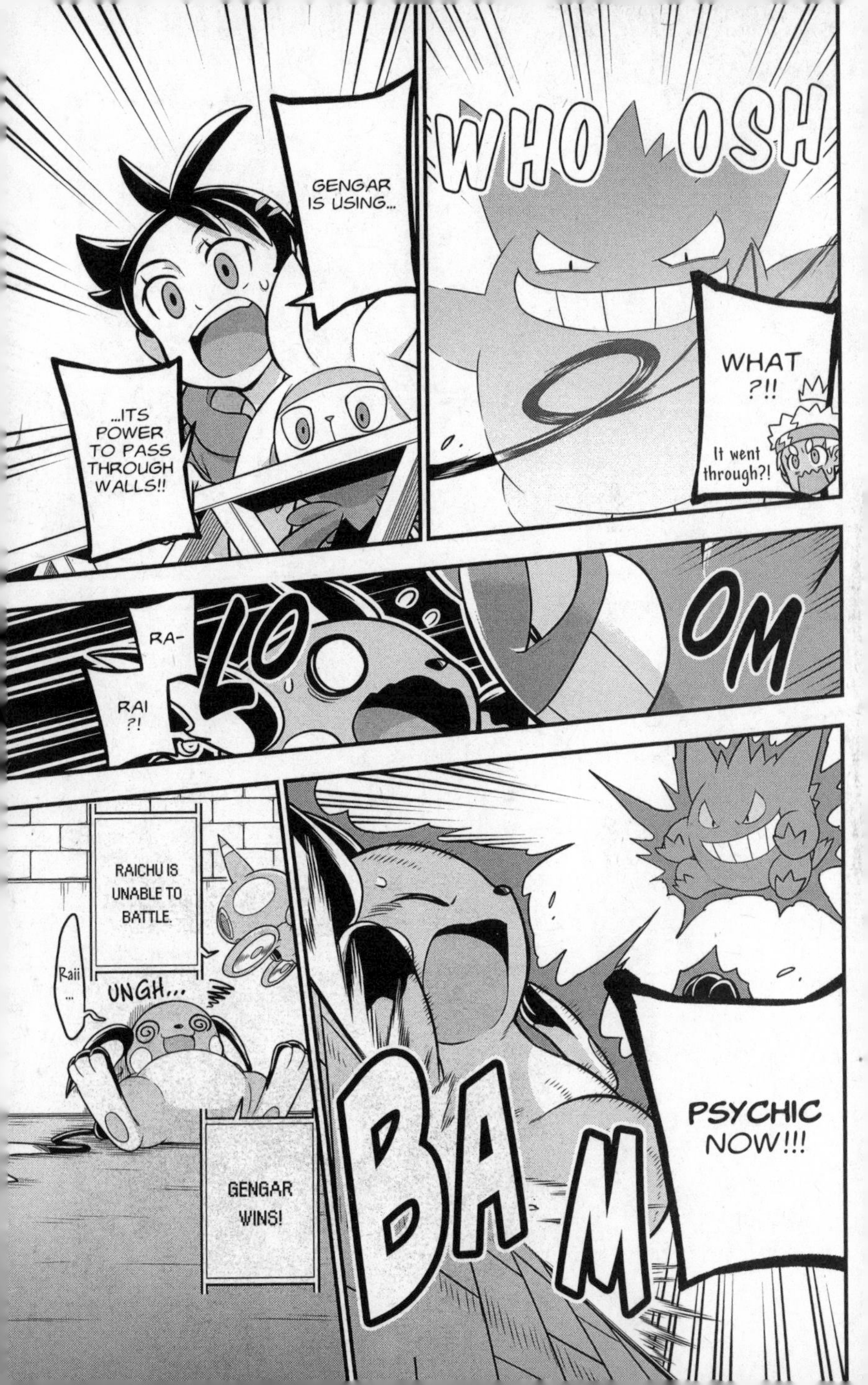
WHOOSH
WHAT?!!
It went through?!
GENGAR IS USING...
...ITS POWER TO PASS THROUGH WALLS!!
LOOM
RA- RAI?!
PSYCHIC NOW!!!
BAM
RAICHU IS UNABLE TO BATTLE.
UNGH...
Raii...
GENGAR WINS!

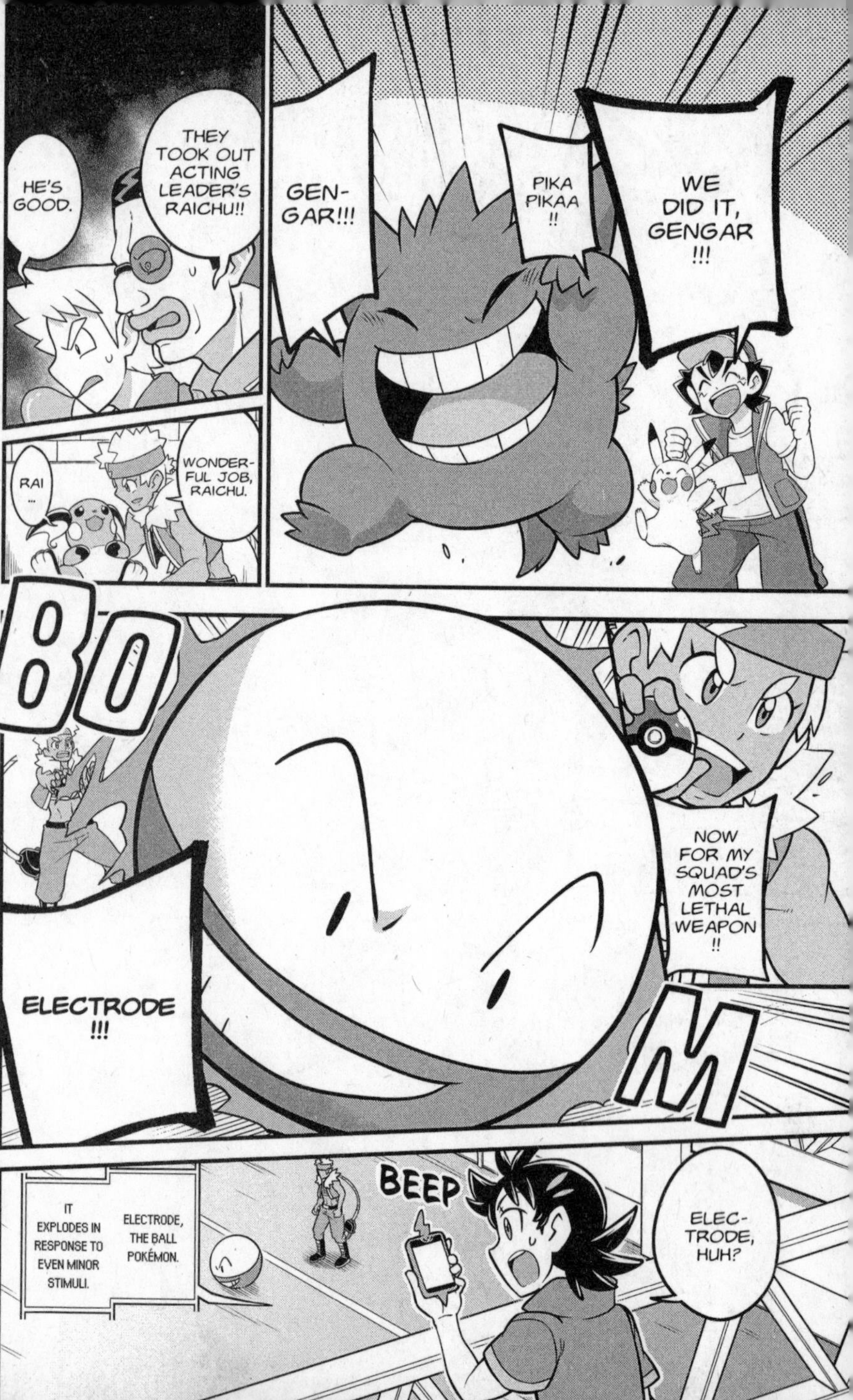
WE DID IT, GENGAR!!!
PIKA PIKAA!!
GEN-GAR!!!
THEY TOOK OUT ACTING LEADER'S RAICHU!!
HE'S GOOD.
WONDER-FUL JOB, RAICHU.
RAI...
BOOM
NOW FOR MY SQUAD'S MOST LETHAL WEAPON!!
ELECTRODE!!!
ELEC-TRODE, HUH?
BEEP
ELECTRODE, THE BALL POKÉMON.
IT EXPLODES IN RESPONSE TO EVEN MINOR STIMULI.

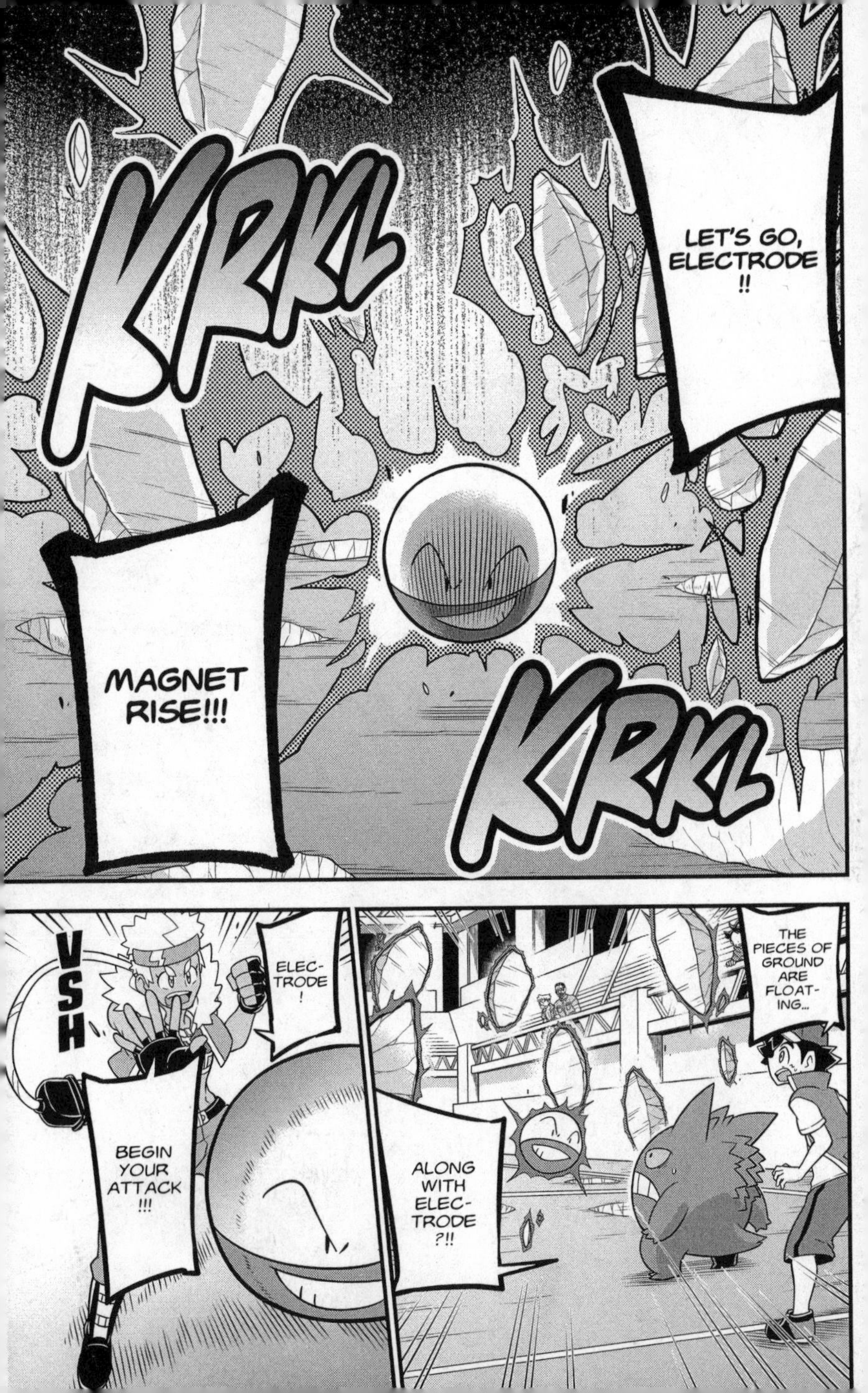
LET'S GO, ELECTRODE !!
KRKL
MAGNET RISE!!!
KRKL
THE PIECES OF GROUND ARE FLOATING...
ALONG WITH ELECTRODE ?!!
ELECTRODE !
VSH
BEGIN YOUR ATTACK !!!

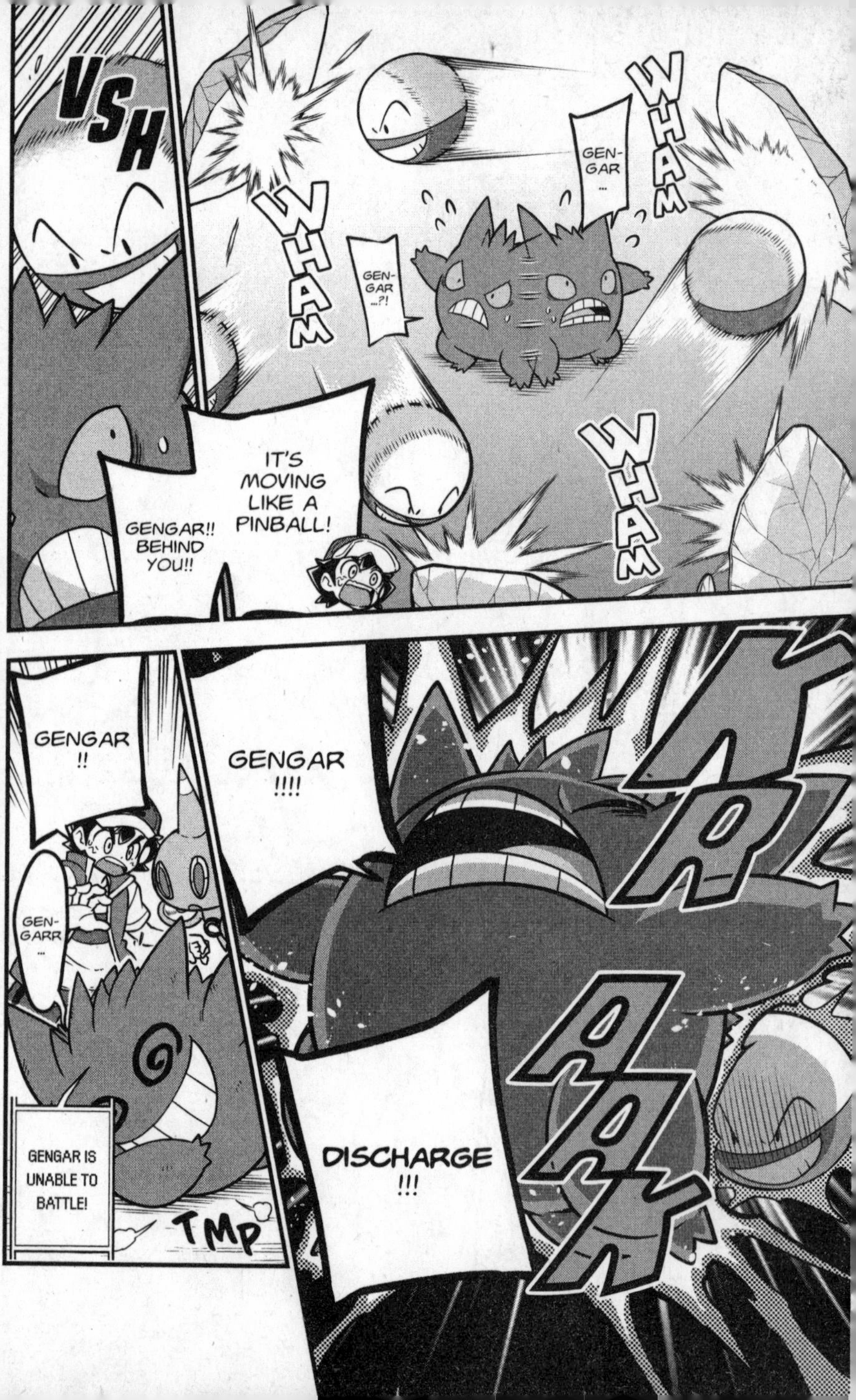
WHAM
GEN-GAR ...
WHAM
GEN-GAR ...?!
VSH
WHAM
IT'S MOVING LIKE A PINBALL!
GENGAR!! BEHIND YOU!!
GENGAR !!!!
DISCHARGE !!!
GENGAR !!
GEN-GARR ...
GENGAR IS UNABLE TO BATTLE!
TMP

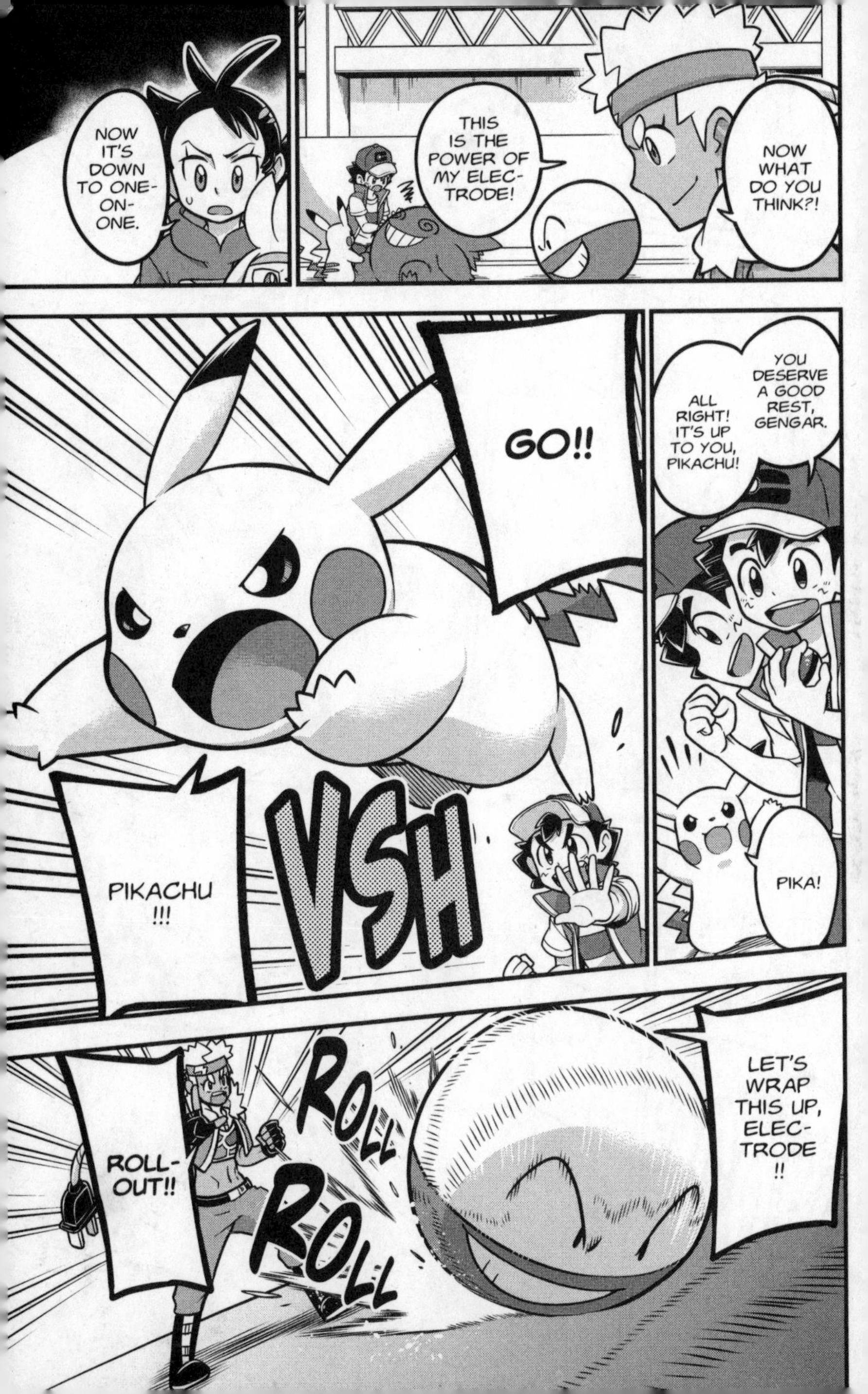
NOW WHAT DO YOU THINK?!
THIS IS THE POWER OF MY ELEC-TRODE!
NOW IT'S DOWN TO ONE-ON-ONE.
YOU DESERVE A GOOD REST, GENGAR.
ALL RIGHT! IT'S UP TO YOU, PIKACHU!
PIKA!
GO!!
PIKACHU!!!
VSH
LET'S WRAP THIS UP, ELEC-TRODE!!
ROLL
ROLL
ROLL-OUT!!

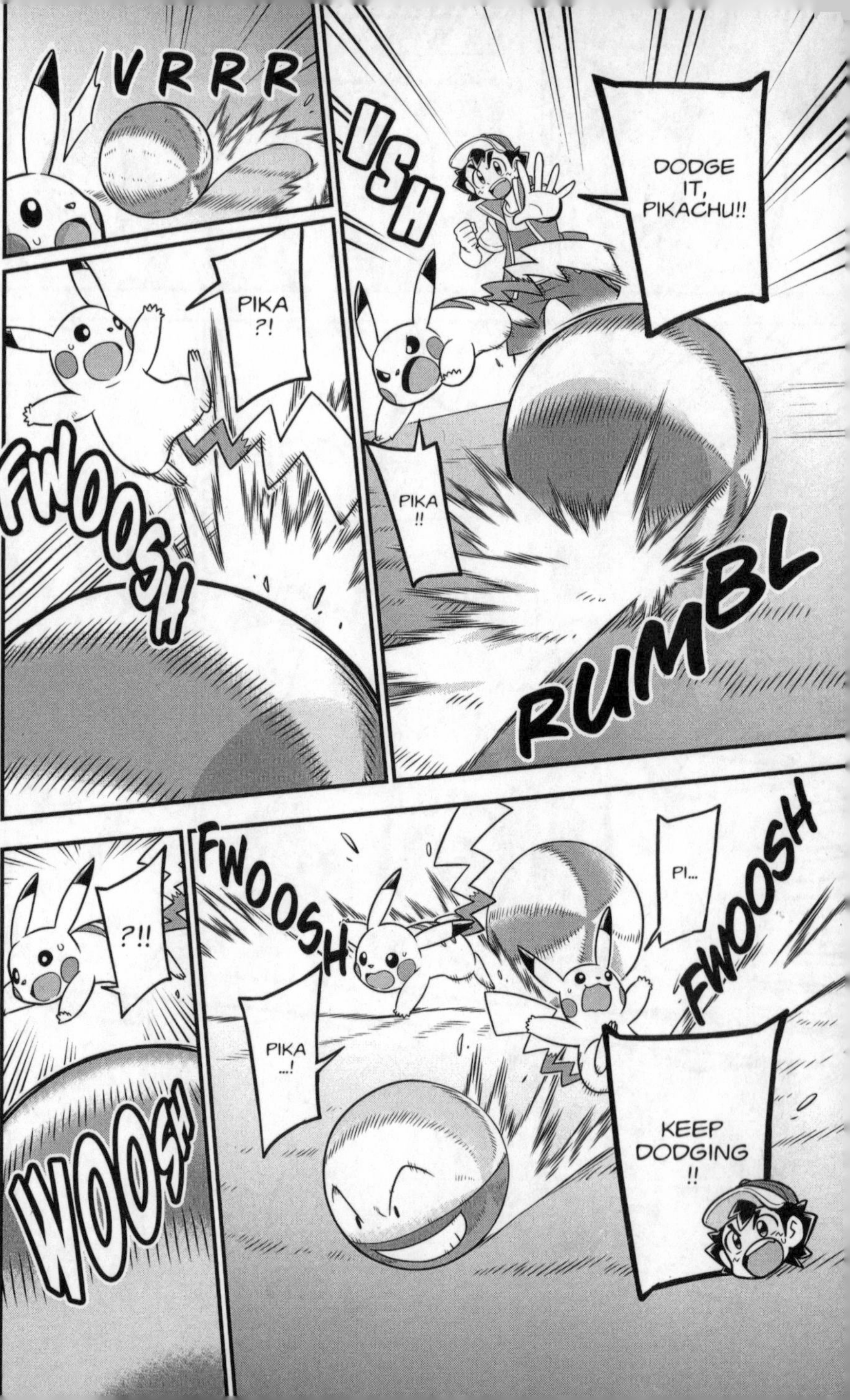
DODGE IT, PIKACHU!!
VSH
PIKA !!
RUMBL
V R R R
PIKA ?!
FWOOSH
FWOOSH
PI...
FWOOSH
KEEP DODGING !!
FWOOSH
PIKA ...!
?!!
WOOSH

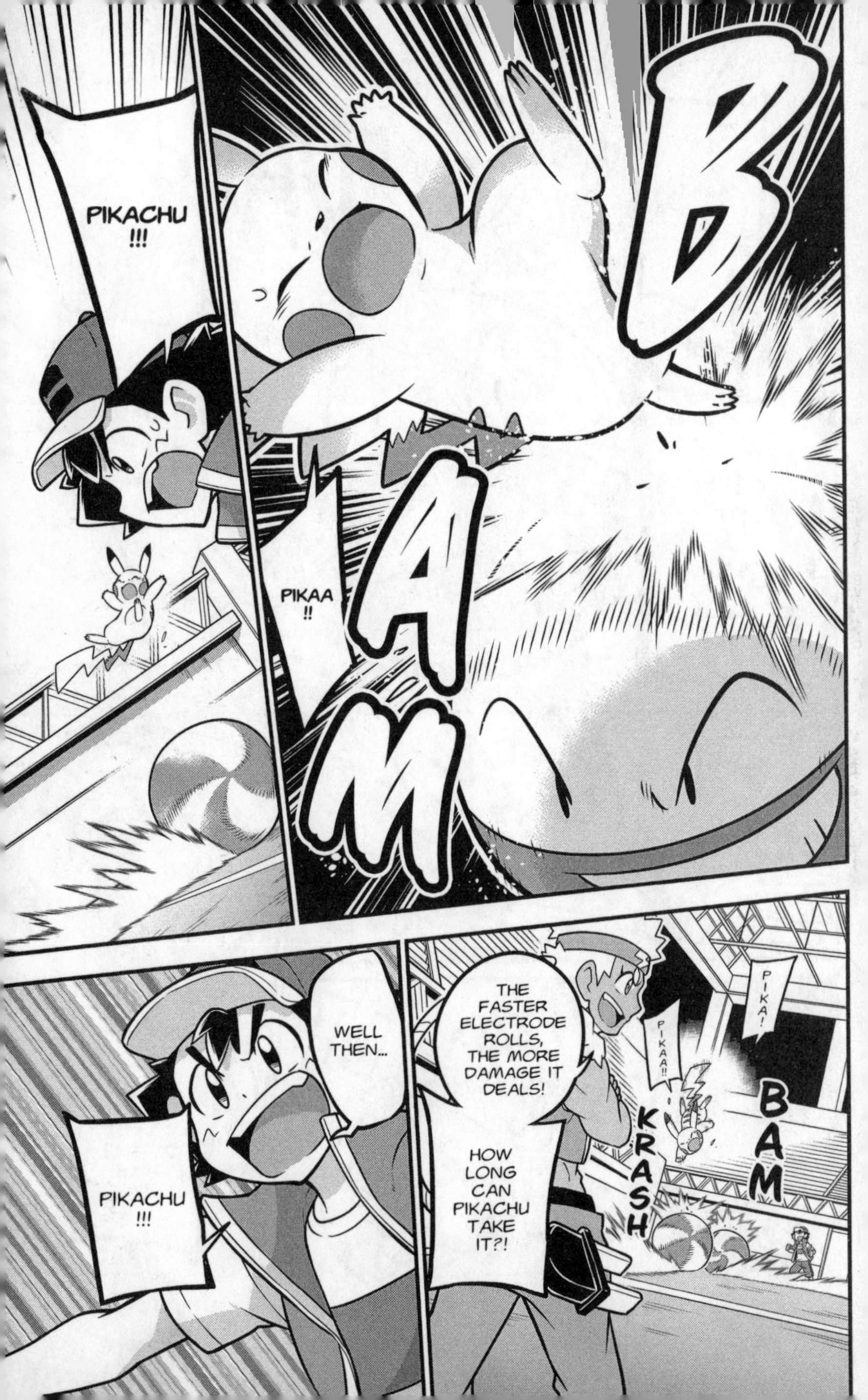
BAM
PIKAA!!
PIKACHU!!!
PIKA!
BAM
PIKAA!!
KRASH
THE FASTER ELECTRODE ROLLS, THE MORE DAMAGE IT DEALS!
HOW LONG CAN PIKACHU TAKE IT?!
WELL THEN...
PIKACHU!!!

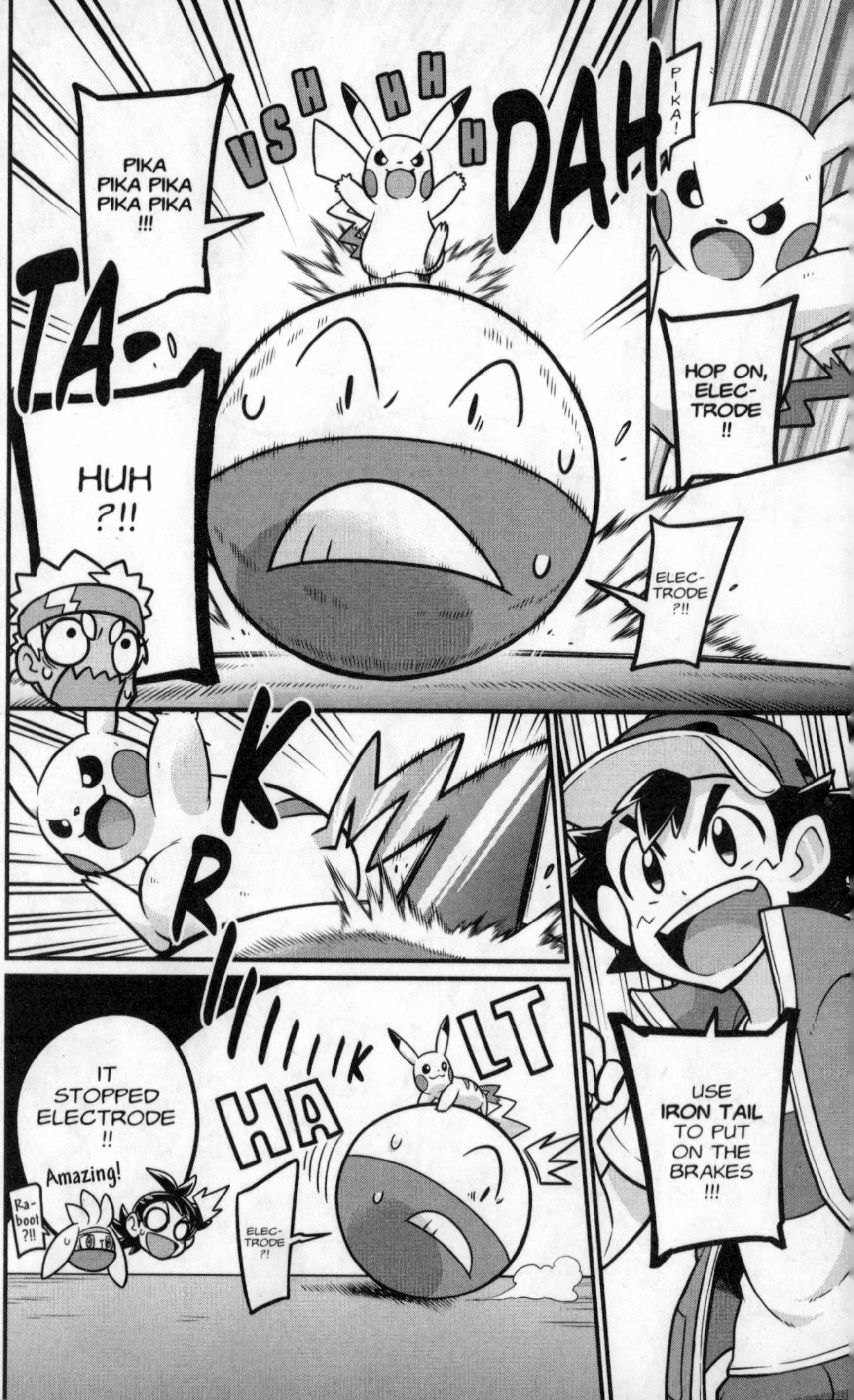
PIKA!
HOP ON, ELEC-TRODE!!
DAH
VSHHHH
PIKA PIKA PIKA PIKA PIKA!!!
ELEC-TRODE?!!
TA-
HUH?!!
USE IRON TAIL TO PUT ON THE BRAKES!!!
KRIIIIIIIK
HALT
ELEC-TRODE?!
IT STOPPED ELECTRODE!!
Amazing!
Ra-boot?!!

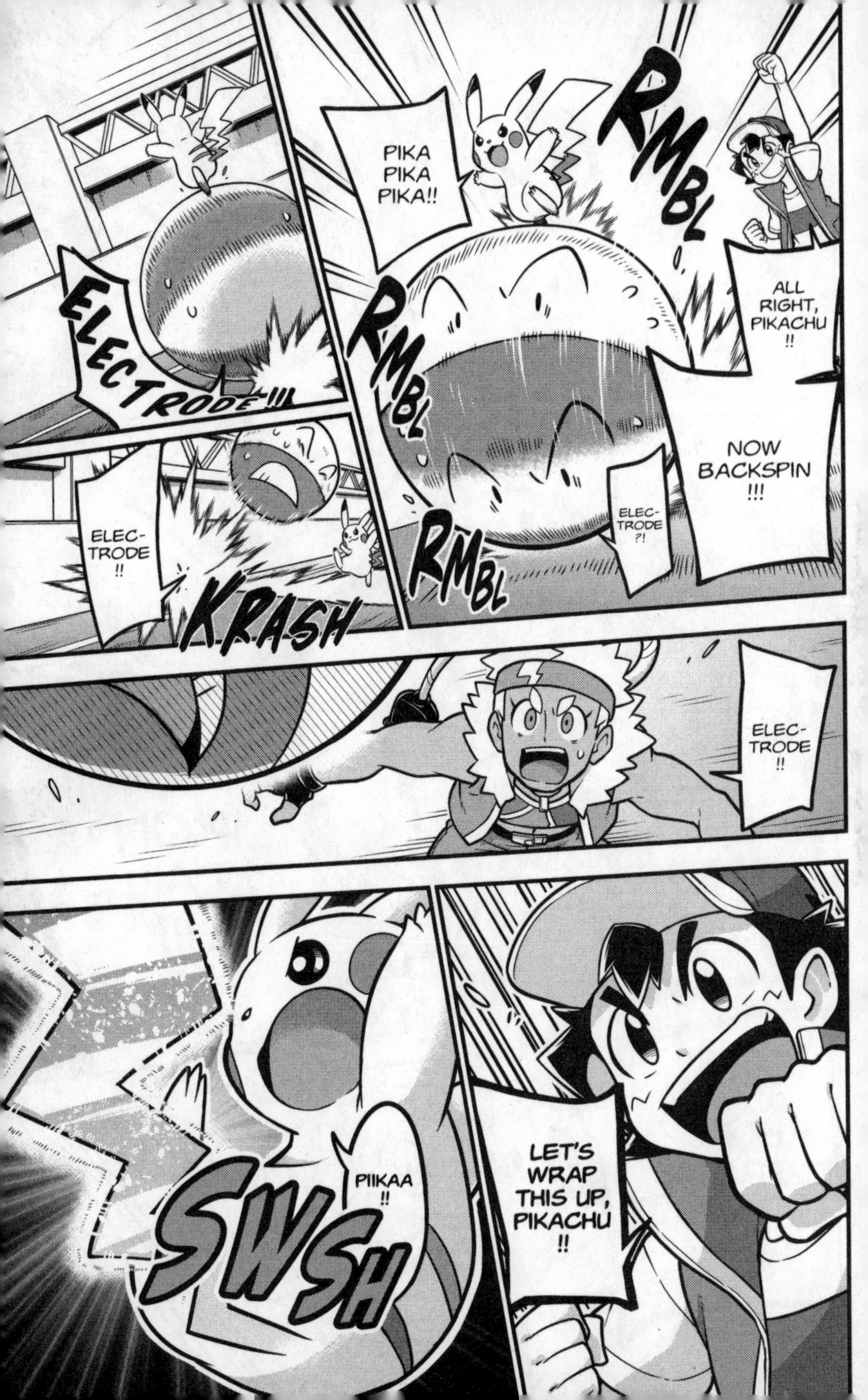

RMBL
ALL RIGHT, PIKACHU!!
NOW BACKSPIN!!!
PIKA PIKA PIKA!!
RMBL
ELECTRODE?!
RMBL
ELECTRODE!!!
ELECTRODE!!
KRASH
ELECTRODE!!
LET'S WRAP THIS UP, PIKACHU!!
PIIKAA!!
SWSH

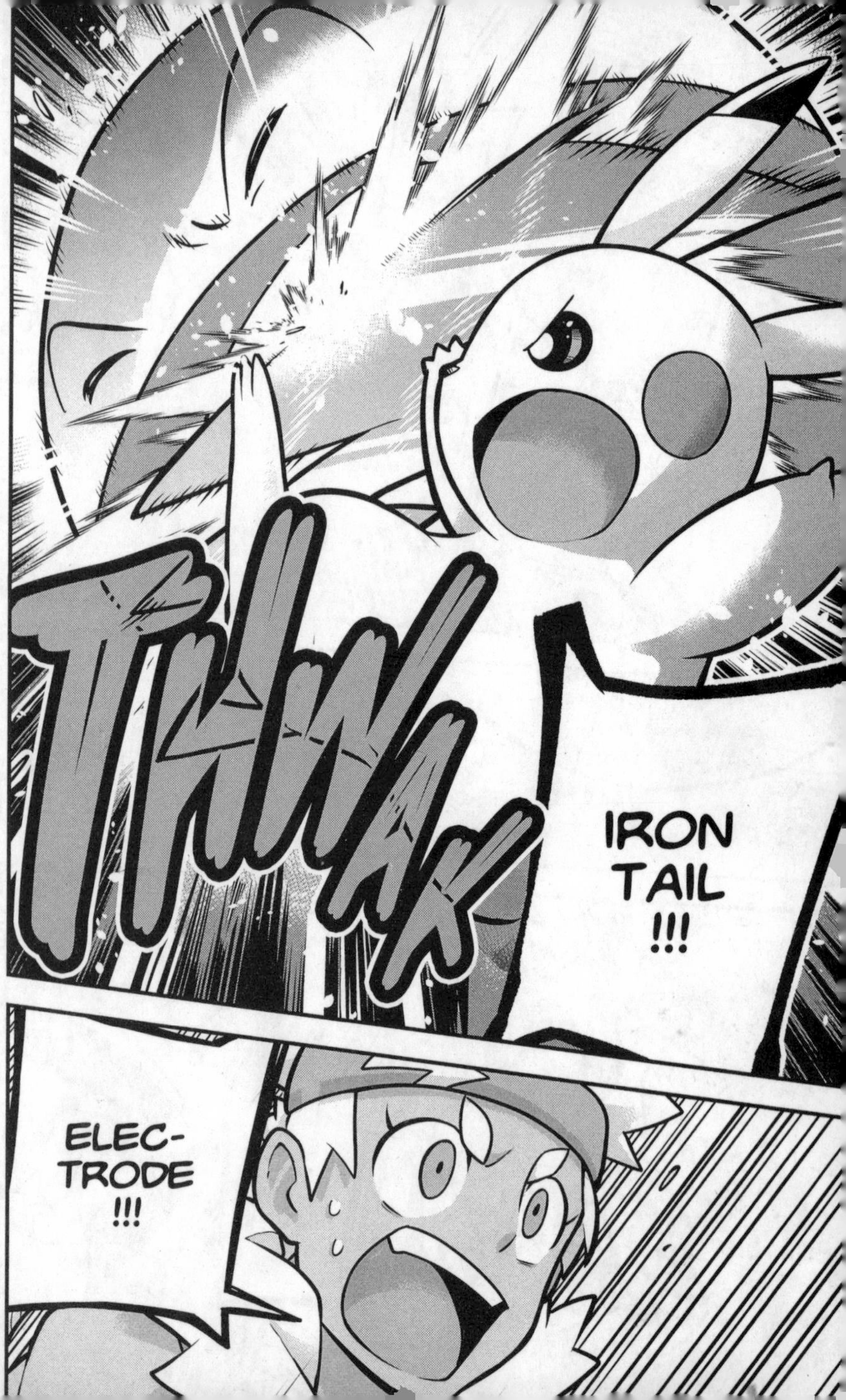
THUNK
IRON TAIL !!!
ELEC-TRODE !!!

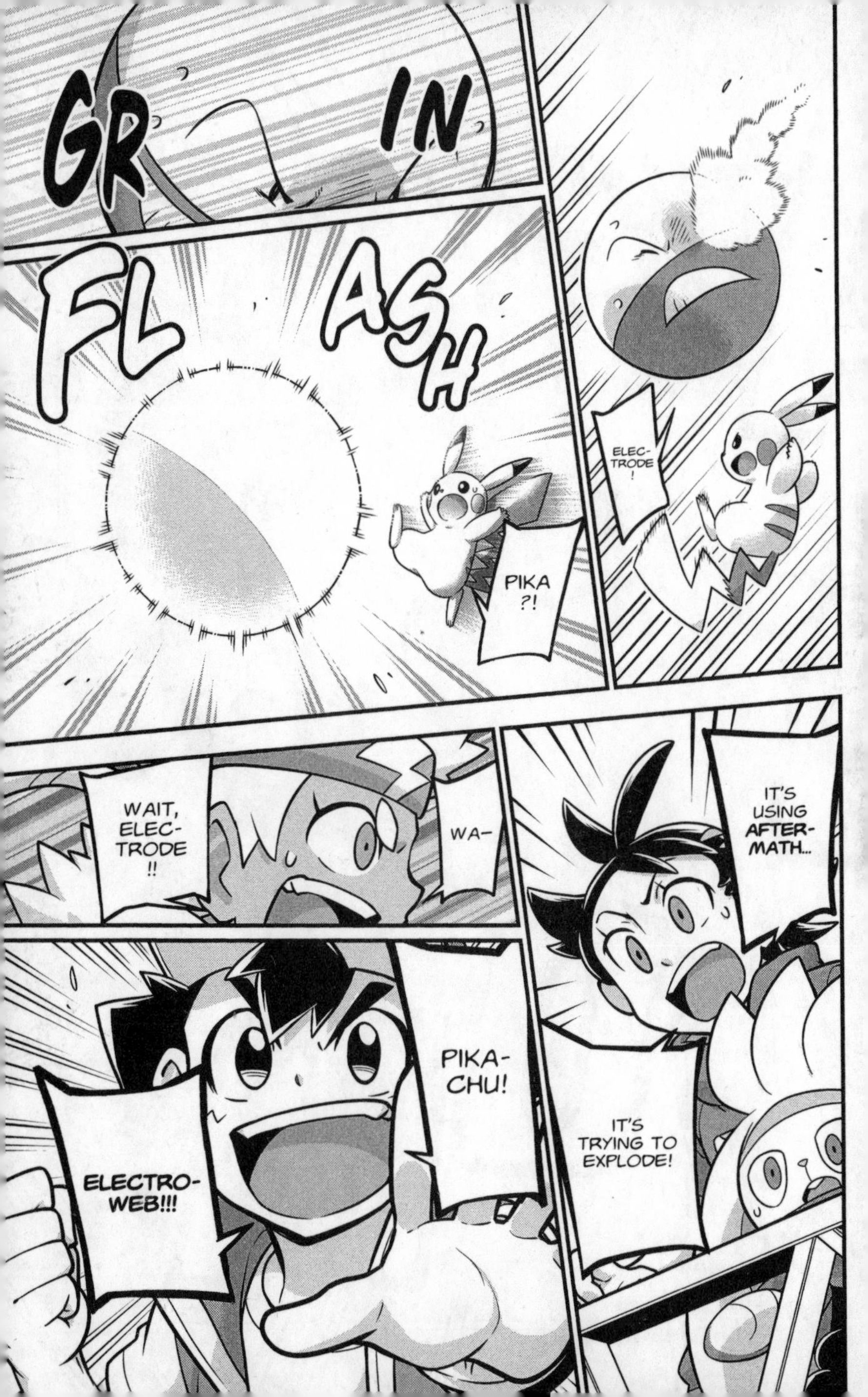
ELECTRODE!
GR IN
FLASH
PIKA ?!
IT'S USING AFTERMATH...
IT'S TRYING TO EXPLODE!
WA-
WAIT, ELECTRODE!!
PIKACHU!
ELECTROWEB!!!

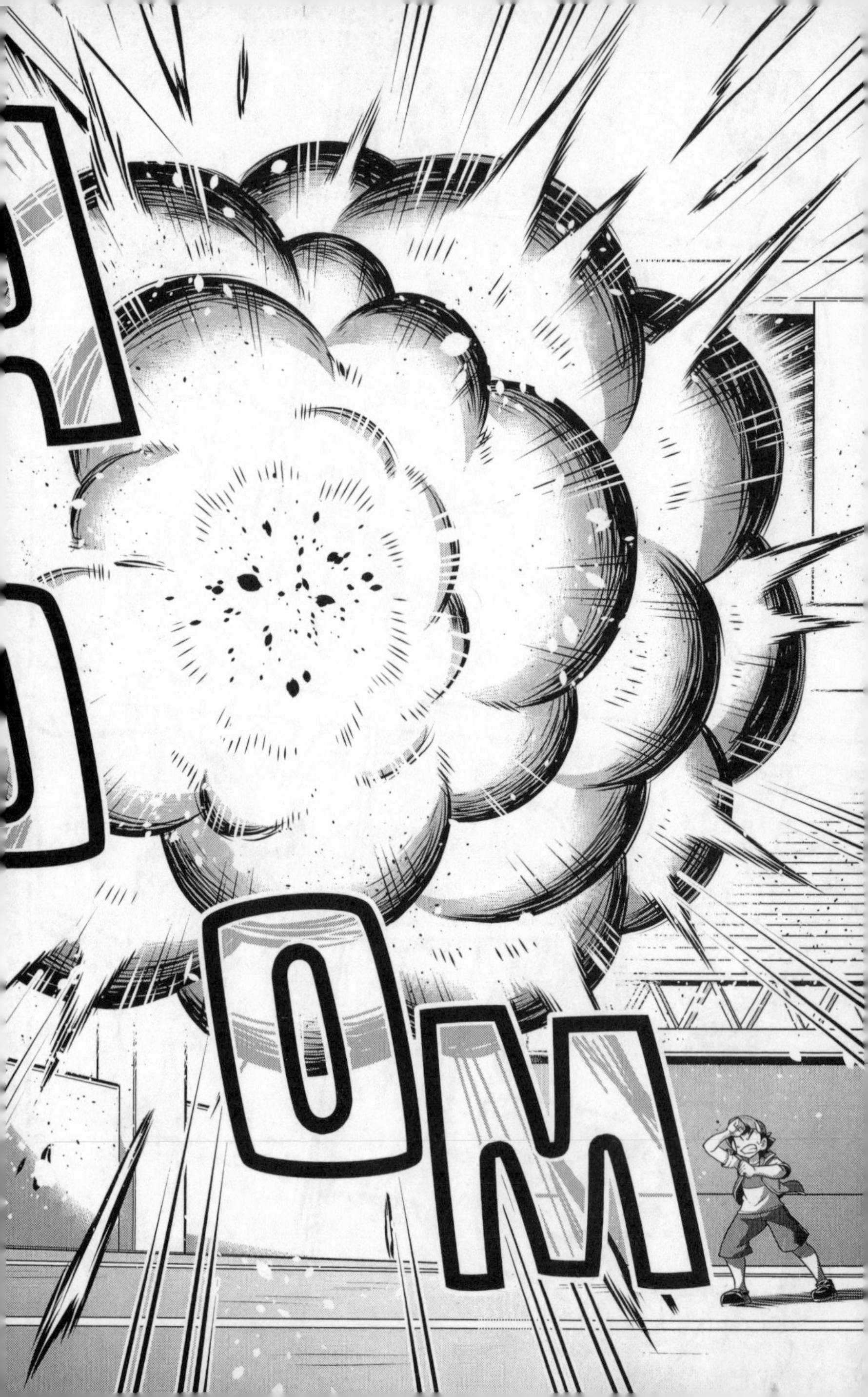
OM

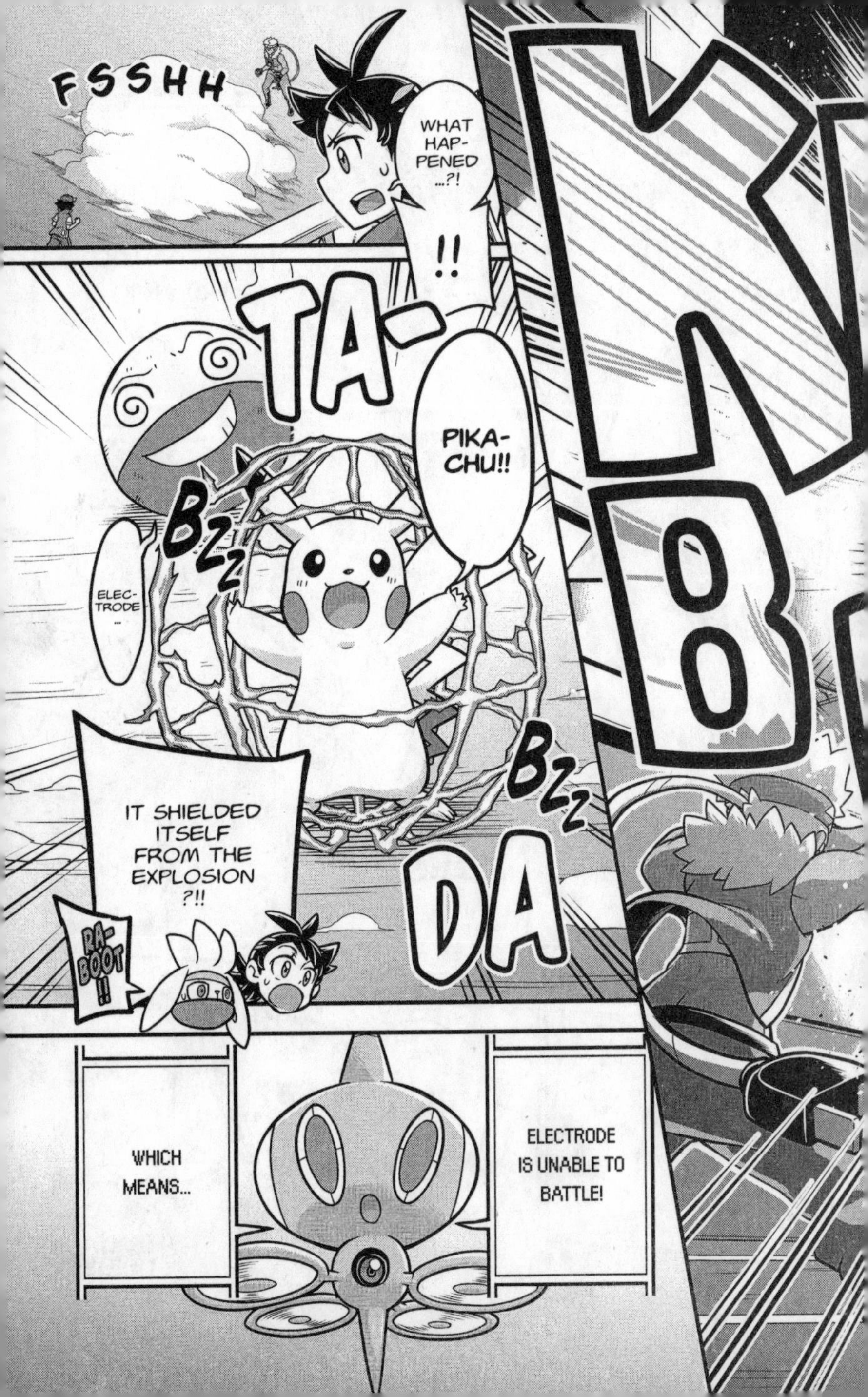
FSSHH
WHAT HAP-PENED ...?!
!!
TA-
PIKA-CHU!!
BZZ
ELEC-TRODE ...
BZZ
DA
IT SHIELDED ITSELF FROM THE EXPLOSION ?!!
RA-BOOT !!
ELECTRODE IS UNABLE TO BATTLE!
WHICH MEANS...

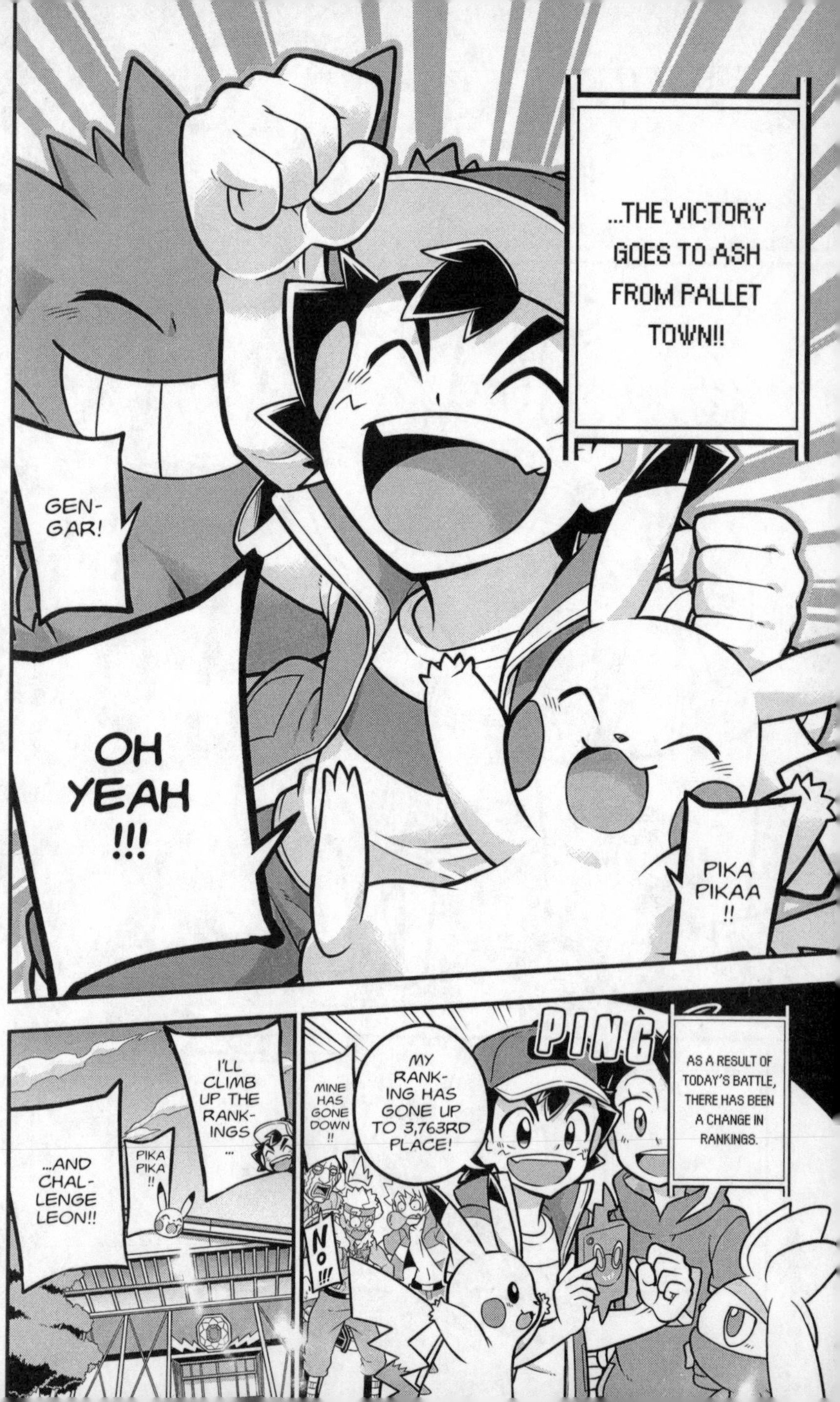
...THE VICTORY GOES TO ASH FROM PALLET TOWN!!
GEN-GAR!
OH YEAH !!!
PIKA PIKAA !!
PING
AS A RESULT OF TODAY'S BATTLE, THERE HAS BEEN A CHANGE IN RANKINGS.
MY RANK-ING HAS GONE UP TO 3,763RD PLACE!
MINE HAS GONE DOWN !!
NO!!!
I'LL CLIMB UP THE RANK-INGS ...
PIKA PIKA !!
...AND CHAL-LENGE LEON!!

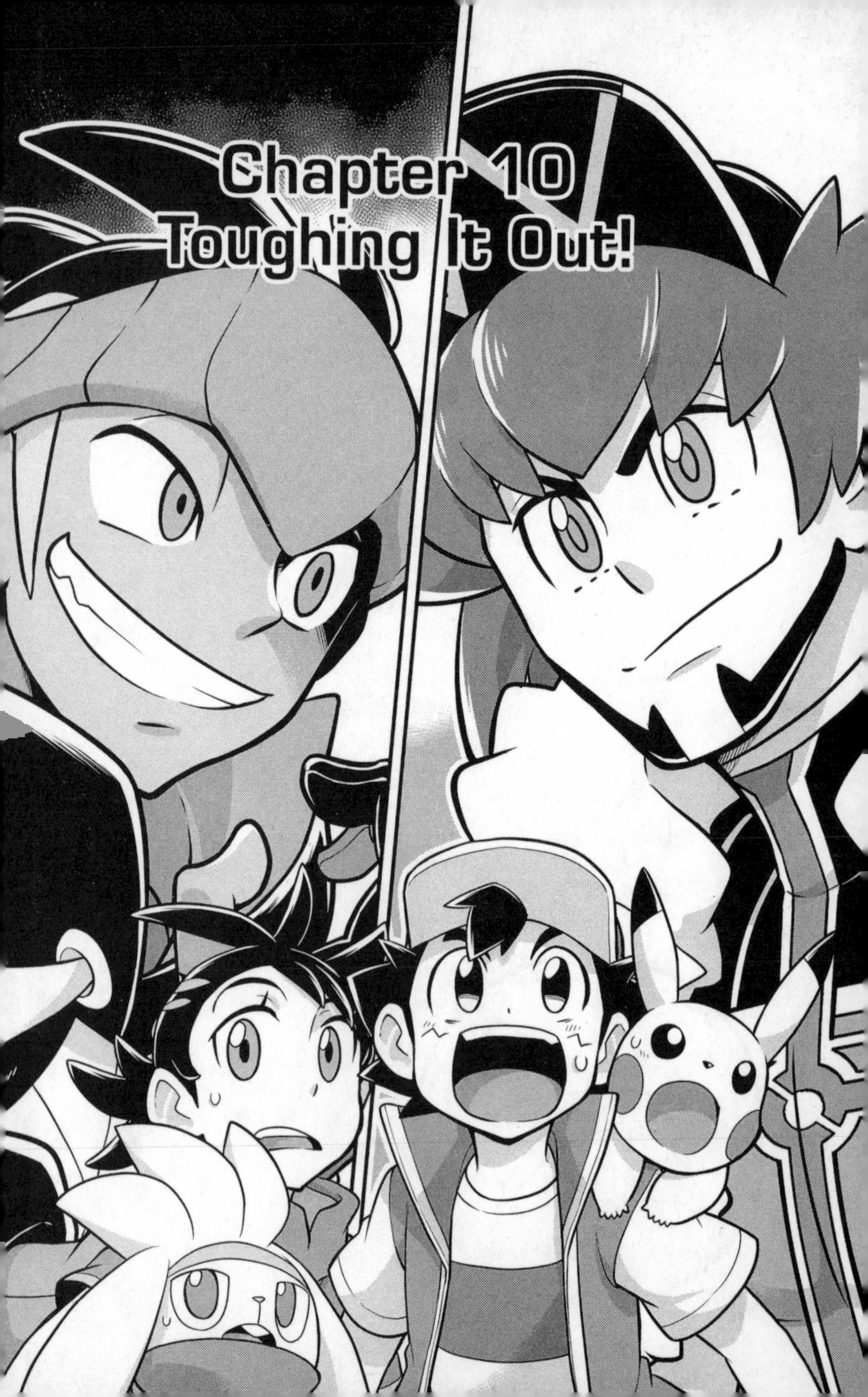
Chapter 10
Toughing It Out!

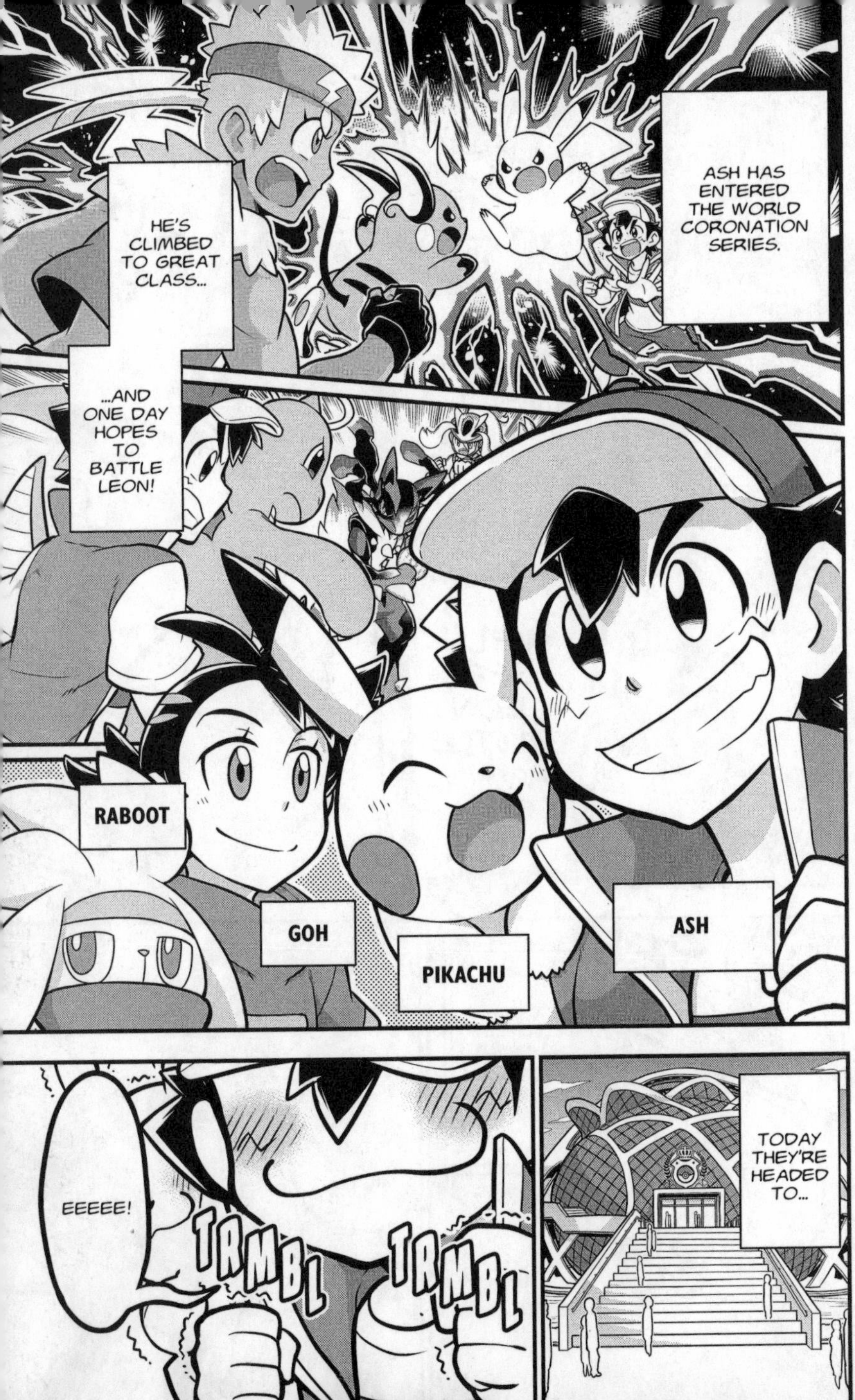
ASH HAS ENTERED THE WORLD CORONATION SERIES.
HE'S CLIMBED TO GREAT CLASS...
...AND ONE DAY HOPES TO BATTLE LEON!
ASH
PIKACHU
GOH
RABOOT
TODAY THEY'RE HEADED TO...
EEEEE!
TRMBL
TRMBL

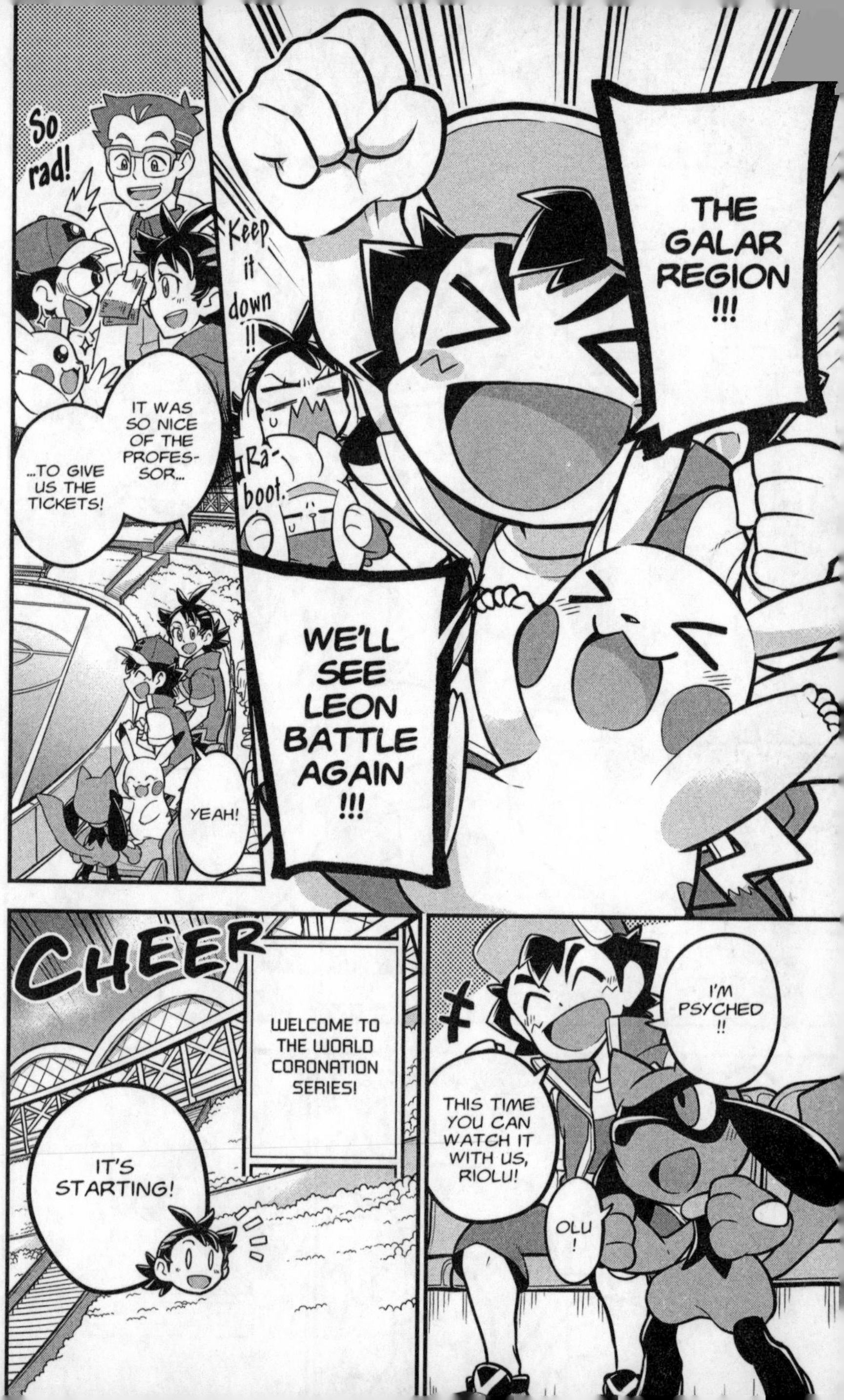
THE GALAR REGION!!!
Keep it down!!
Ra-boot.
WE'LL SEE LEON BATTLE AGAIN!!!
So rad!
IT WAS SO NICE OF THE PROFES-SOR...
...TO GIVE US THE TICKETS!
YEAH!
I'M PSYCHED!!
THIS TIME YOU CAN WATCH IT WITH US, RIOLU!
OLU!
CHEER
WELCOME TO THE WORLD CORONATION SERIES!
IT'S STARTING!

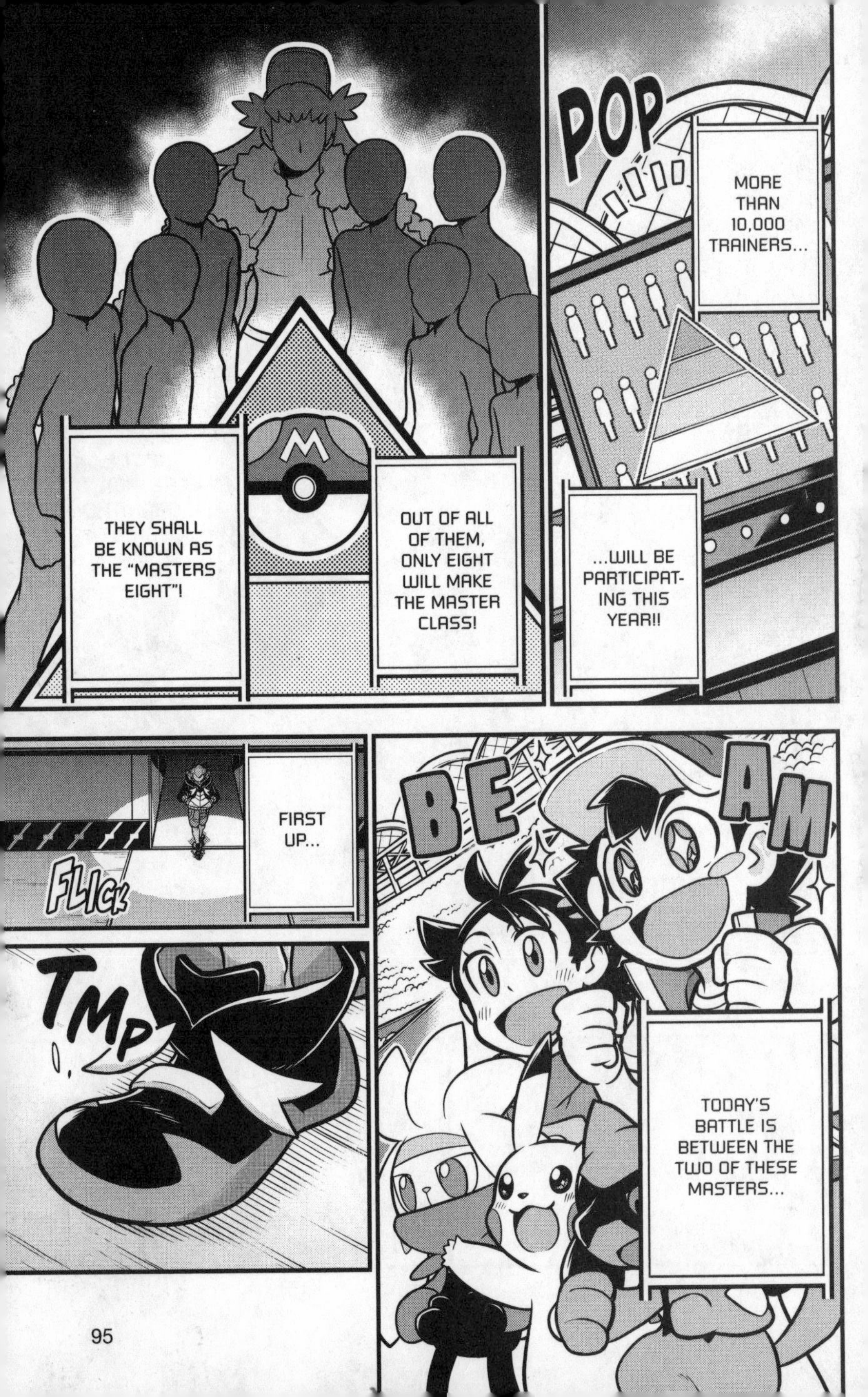
POP
MORE THAN 10,000 TRAINERS...
...WILL BE PARTICIPATING THIS YEAR!!
OUT OF ALL OF THEM, ONLY EIGHT WILL MAKE THE MASTER CLASS!
THEY SHALL BE KNOWN AS THE "MASTERS EIGHT"!
BE AM
TODAY'S BATTLE IS BETWEEN THE TWO OF THESE MASTERS...
FIRST UP...
FLICK
TMP

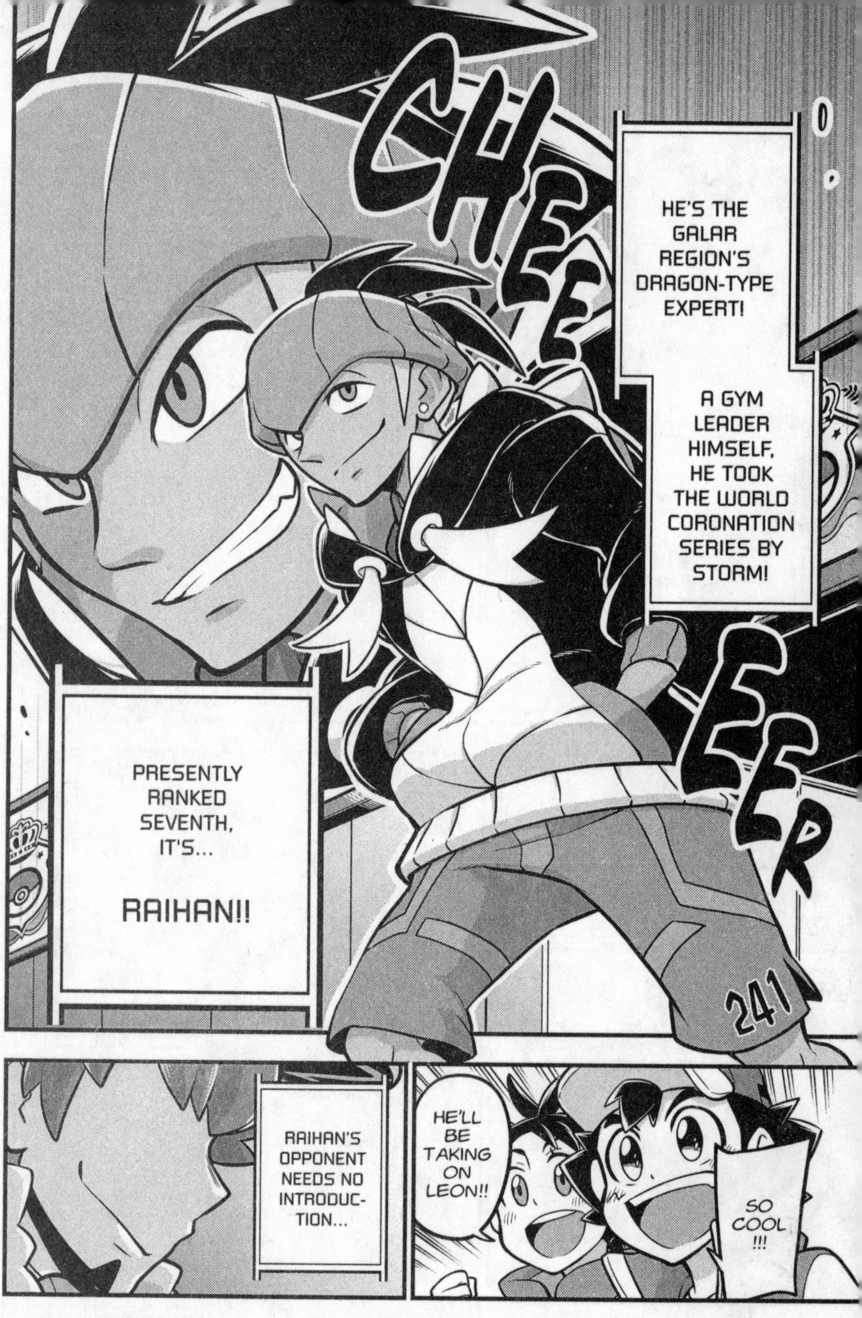
HE'S THE GALAR REGION'S DRAGON-TYPE EXPERT!
A GYM LEADER HIMSELF, HE TOOK THE WORLD CORONATION SERIES BY STORM!
CHEEEEER
PRESENTLY RANKED SEVENTH, IT'S...
RAIHAN!!
241
HE'LL BE TAKING ON LEON!!
SO COOL!!!
RAIHAN'S OPPONENT NEEDS NO INTRODUC-TION...

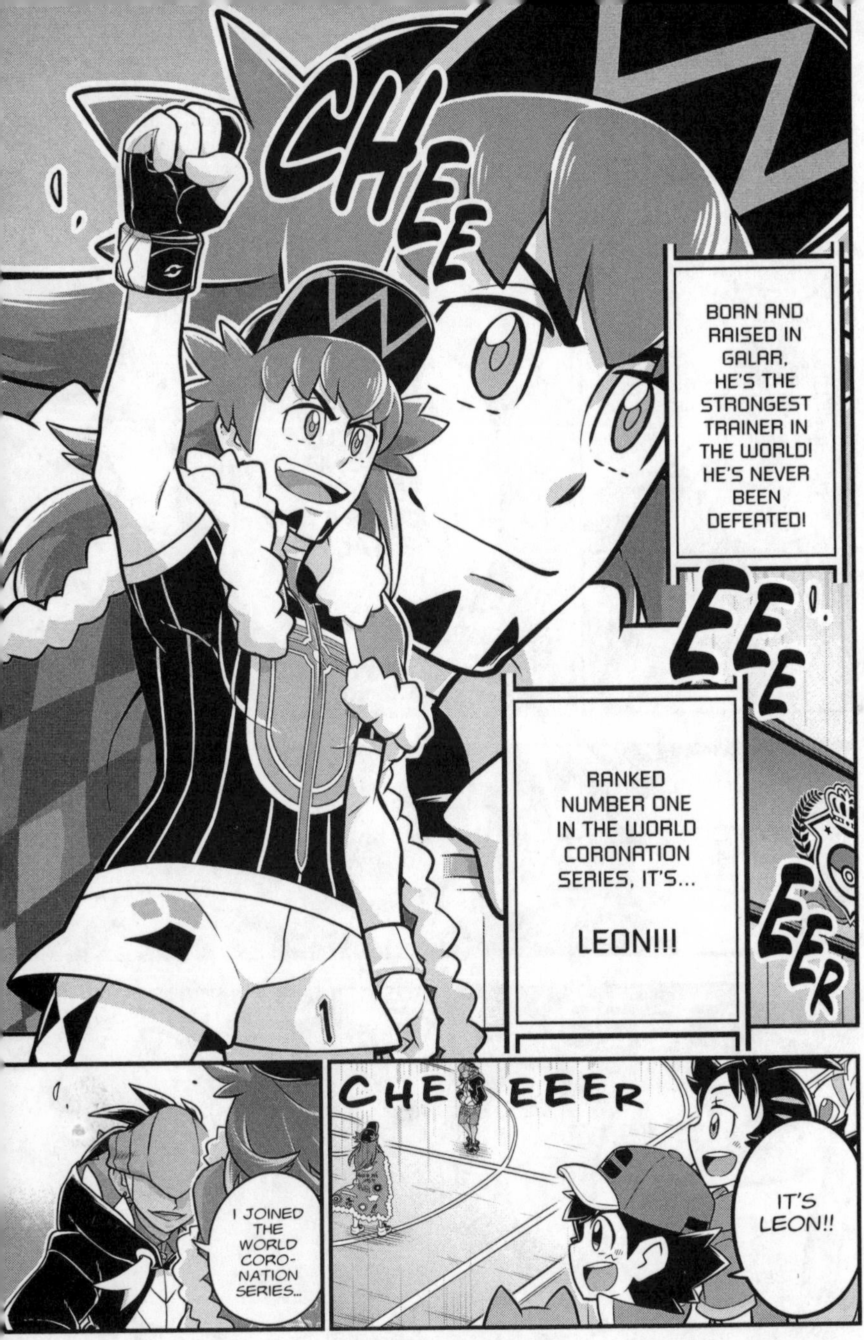
CHEEEEEEEER
BORN AND RAISED IN GALAR, HE'S THE STRONGEST TRAINER IN THE WORLD! HE'S NEVER BEEN DEFEATED!
RANKED NUMBER ONE IN THE WORLD CORONATION SERIES, IT'S...
LEON!!!
CHEEEEER
IT'S LEON!!
I JOINED THE WORLD CORO-NATION SERIES...

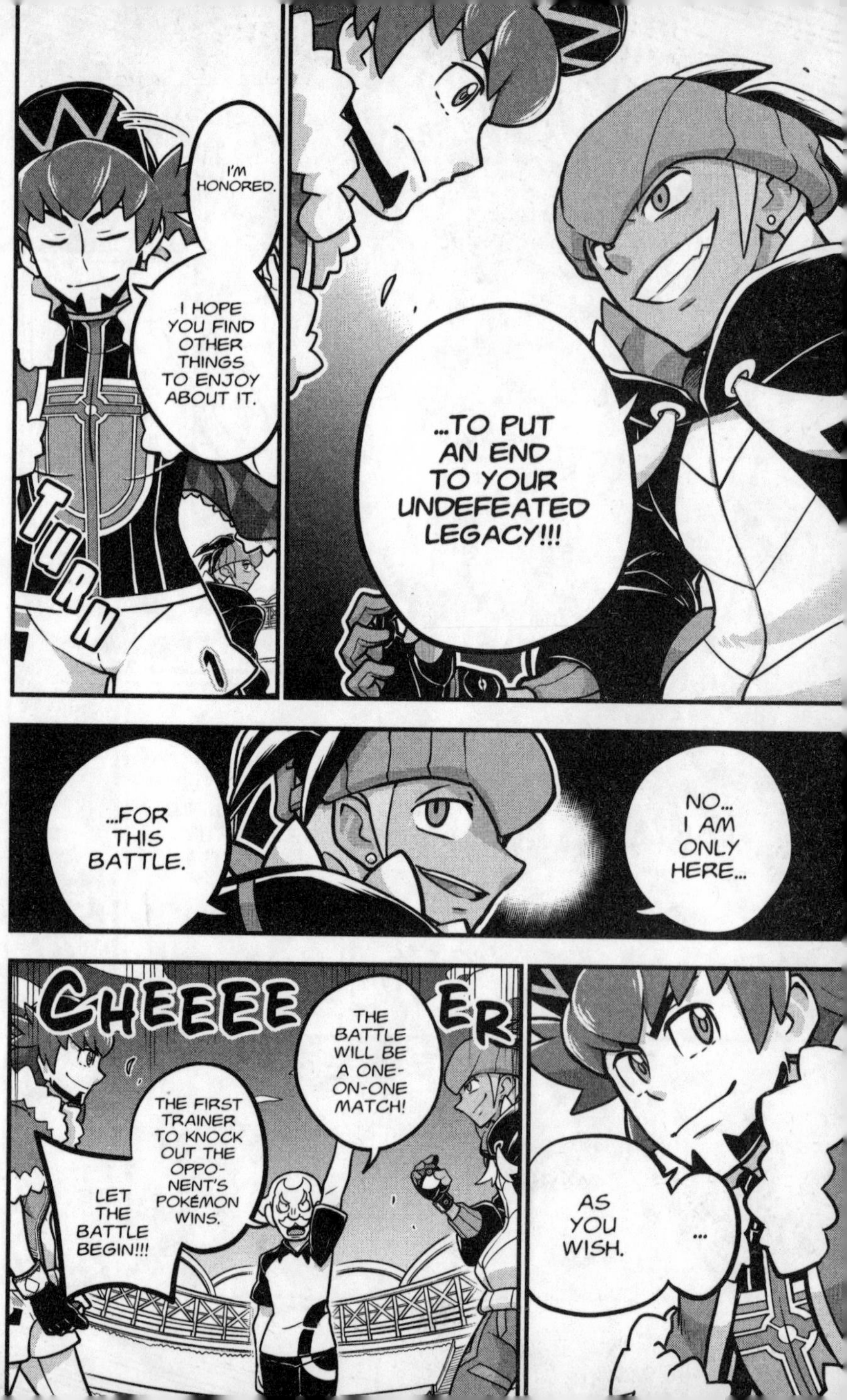
...TO PUT AN END TO YOUR UNDEFEATED LEGACY!!!
I'M HONORED.
I HOPE YOU FIND OTHER THINGS TO ENJOY ABOUT IT.
TURN
NO... I AM ONLY HERE...
...FOR THIS BATTLE.
AS YOU WISH.
...
CHEEEEER
THE BATTLE WILL BE A ONE-ON-ONE MATCH!
THE FIRST TRAINER TO KNOCK OUT THE OPPONENT'S POKÉMON WINS.
LET THE BATTLE BEGIN!!!

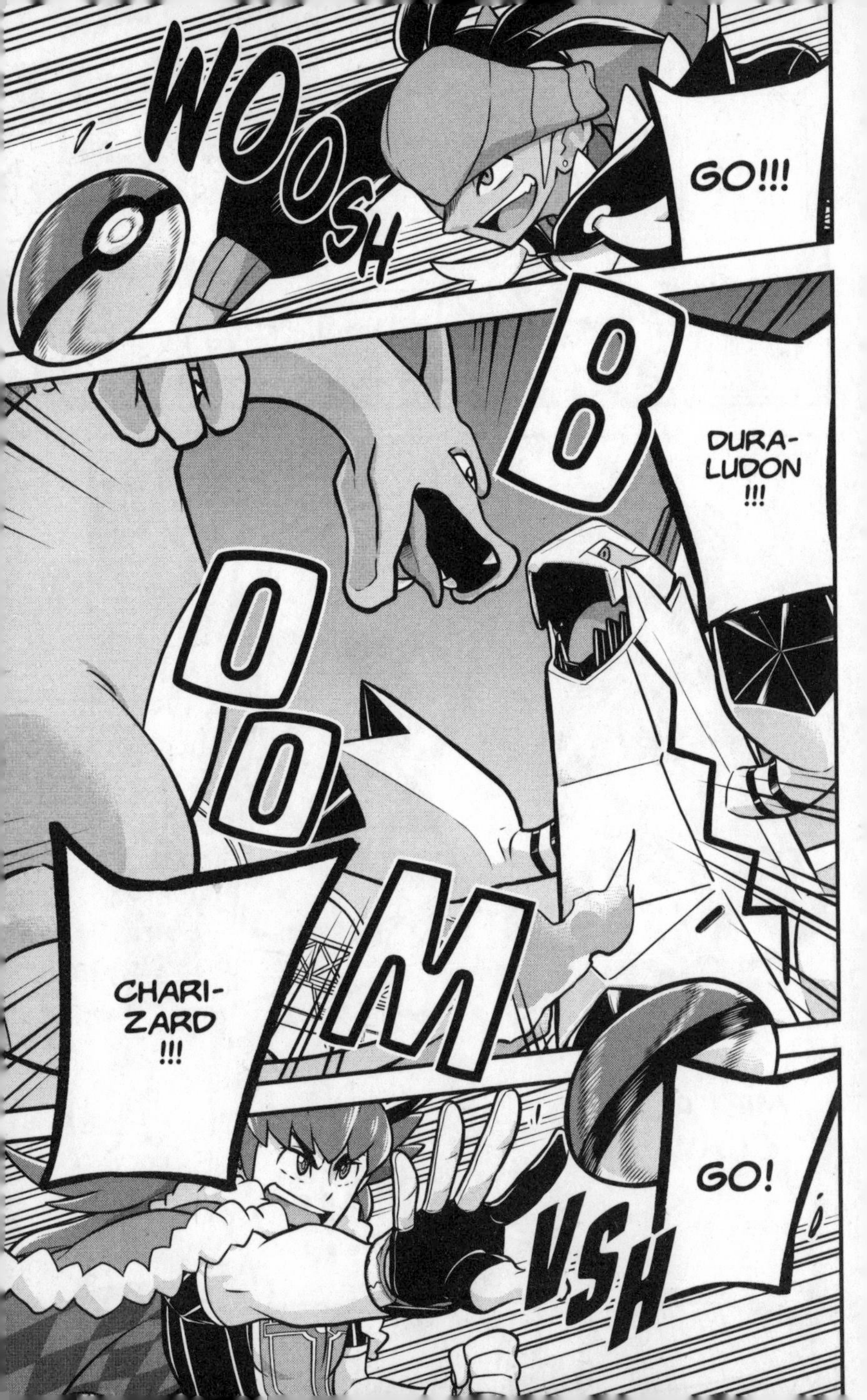
GO!!!
WOOSH
DURA-LUDON!!!
BOOM
CHARI-ZARD!!!
GO!
VSH

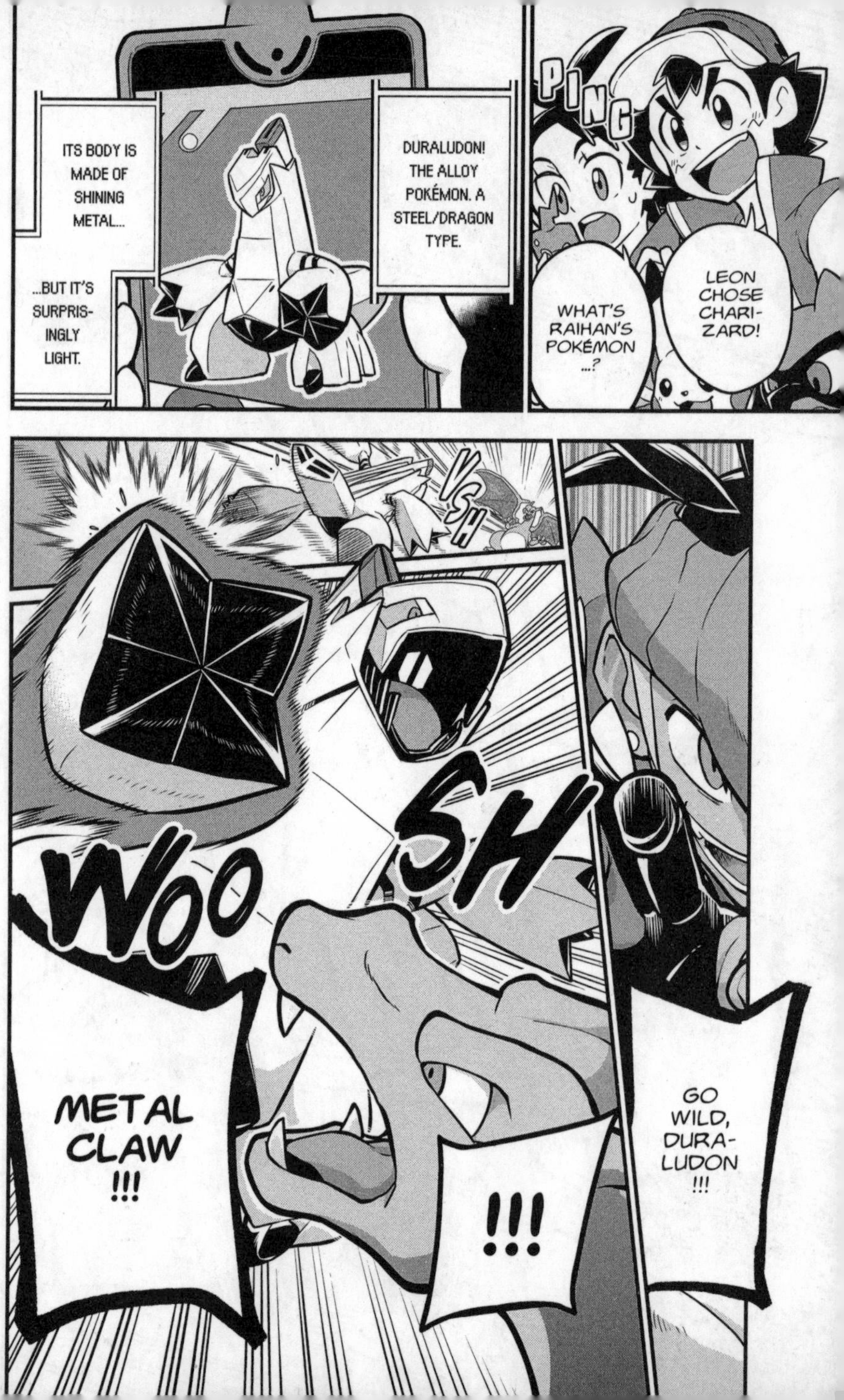
PING
LEON CHOSE CHARI-ZARD!
WHAT'S RAIHAN'S POKÉMON ...?
DURALUDON! THE ALLOY POKÉMON. A STEEL/DRAGON TYPE.
ITS BODY IS MADE OF SHINING METAL...
...BUT IT'S SURPRIS-INGLY LIGHT.
GO WILD, DURA-LUDON !!!
VSH
WOOSH
!!!
METAL CLAW !!!

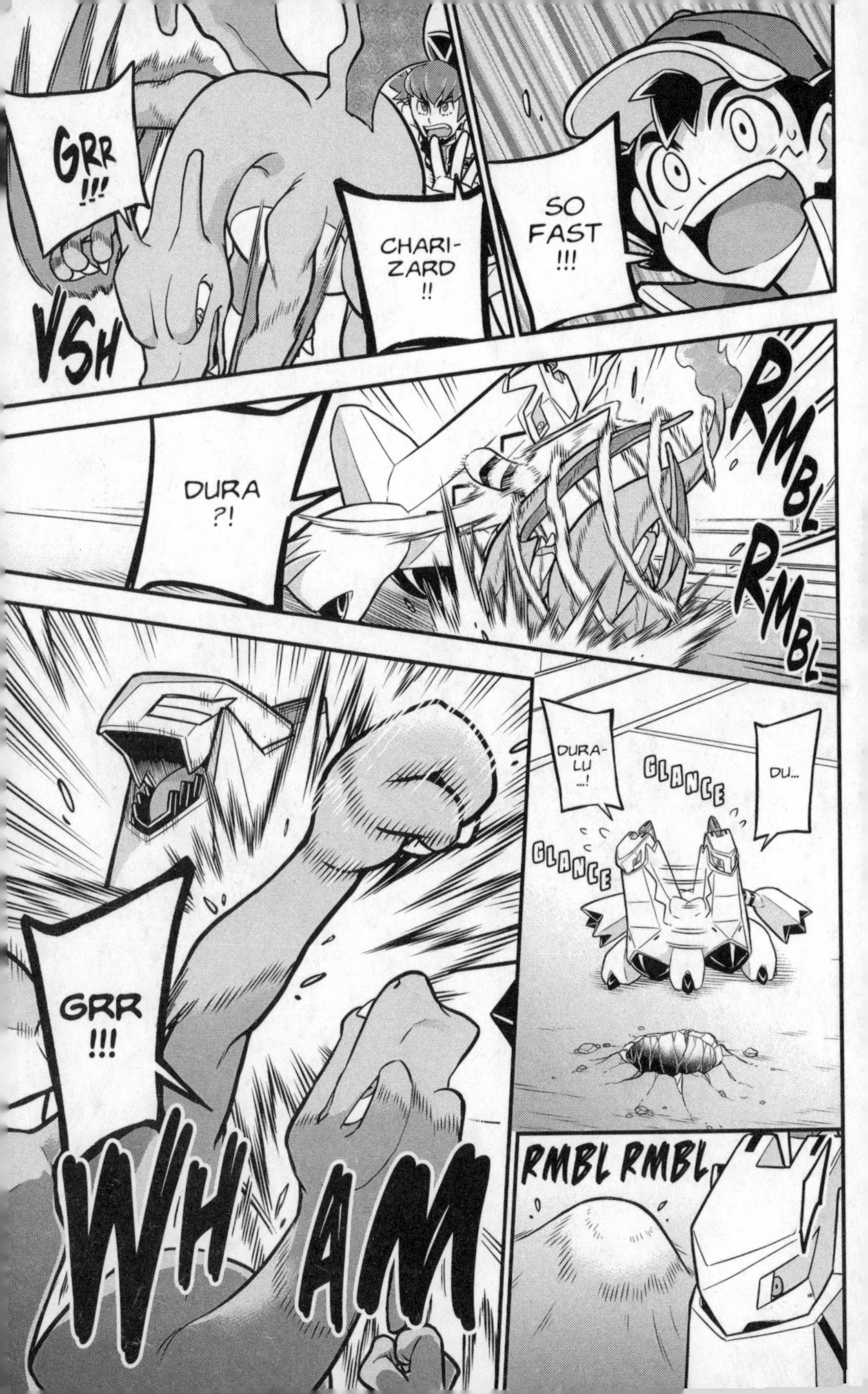
SO FAST !!!
CHARI-ZARD !!
GRR !!!
VSH
RMBL
RMBL
DURA ?!
DU...
GLANCE
DURA-LU ...!
GLANCE
RMBL RMBL
GRR !!!
WHAM

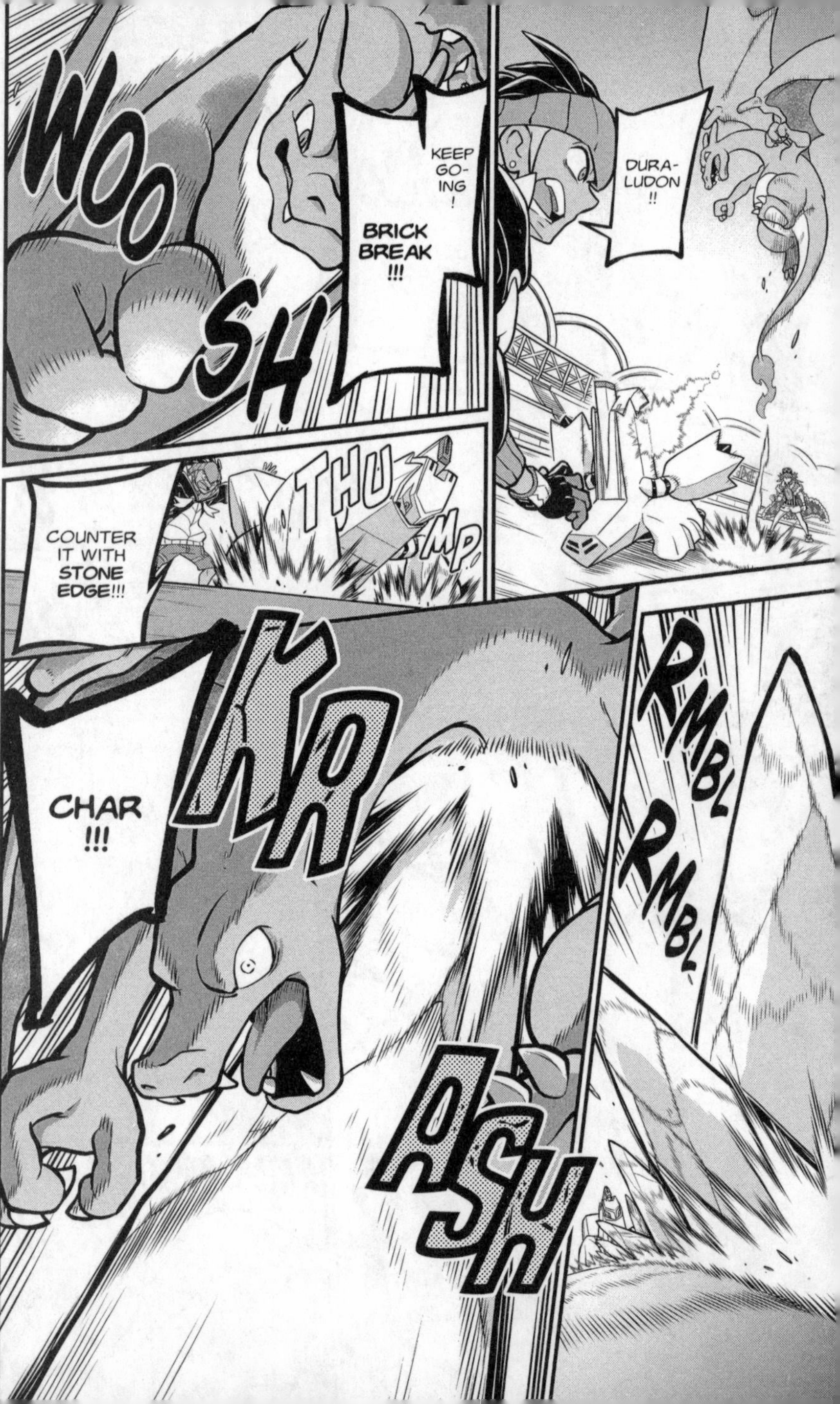
DURA-LUDON!!
WOOSH
KEEP GO-ING!
BRICK BREAK!!!
THUMP
COUNTER IT WITH STONE EDGE!!!
RMBL RMBL
KRASH
CHAR!!!

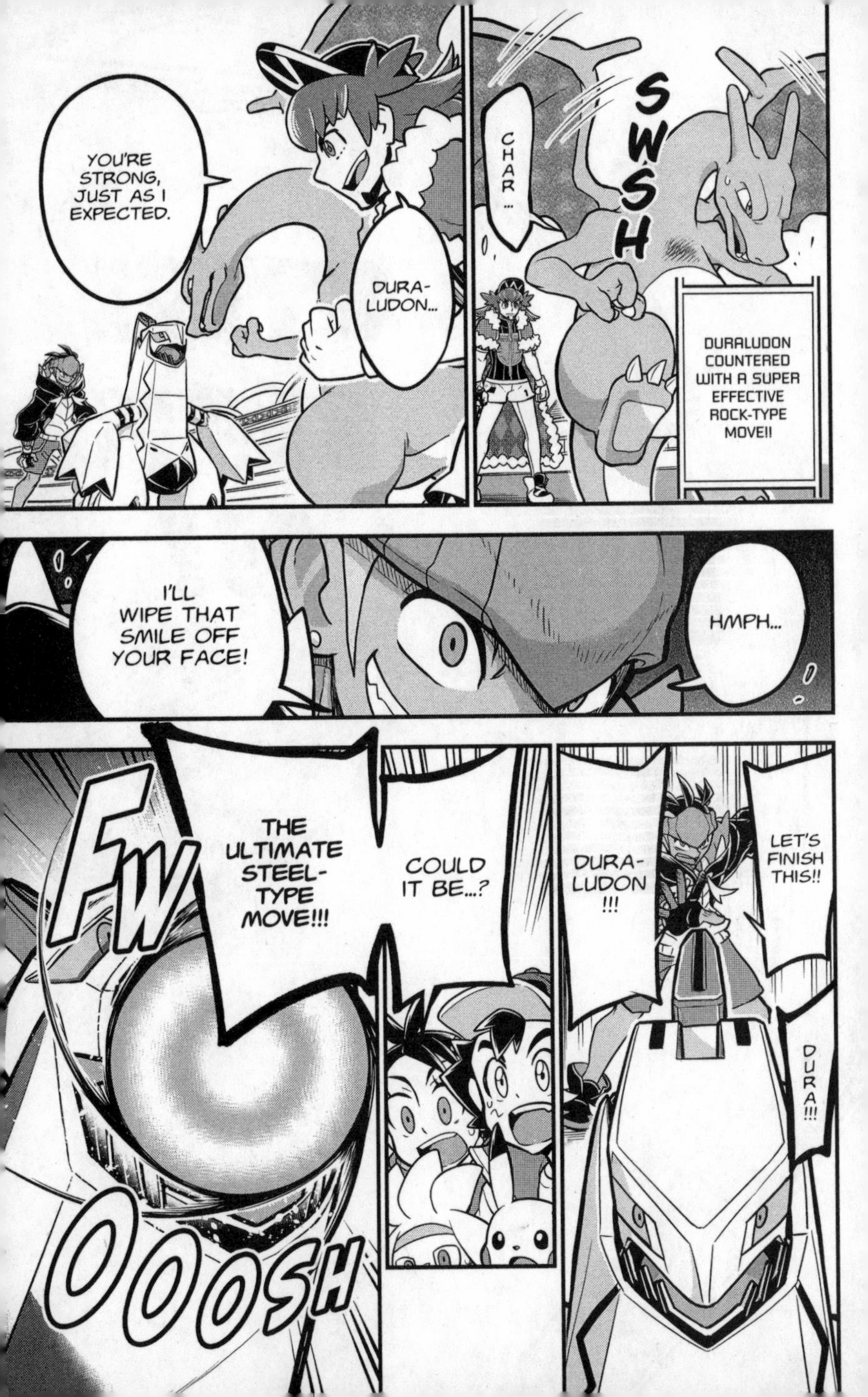
SWSH
CHAR...
DURALUDON COUNTERED WITH A SUPER EFFECTIVE ROCK-TYPE MOVE!!
DURA-LUDON...
YOU'RE STRONG, JUST AS I EXPECTED.
HMPH...
I'LL WIPE THAT SMILE OFF YOUR FACE!
DURA!!!
LET'S FINISH THIS!!
DURA-LUDON!!!
COULD IT BE...?
THE ULTIMATE STEEL-TYPE MOVE!!!
FWOOOSH

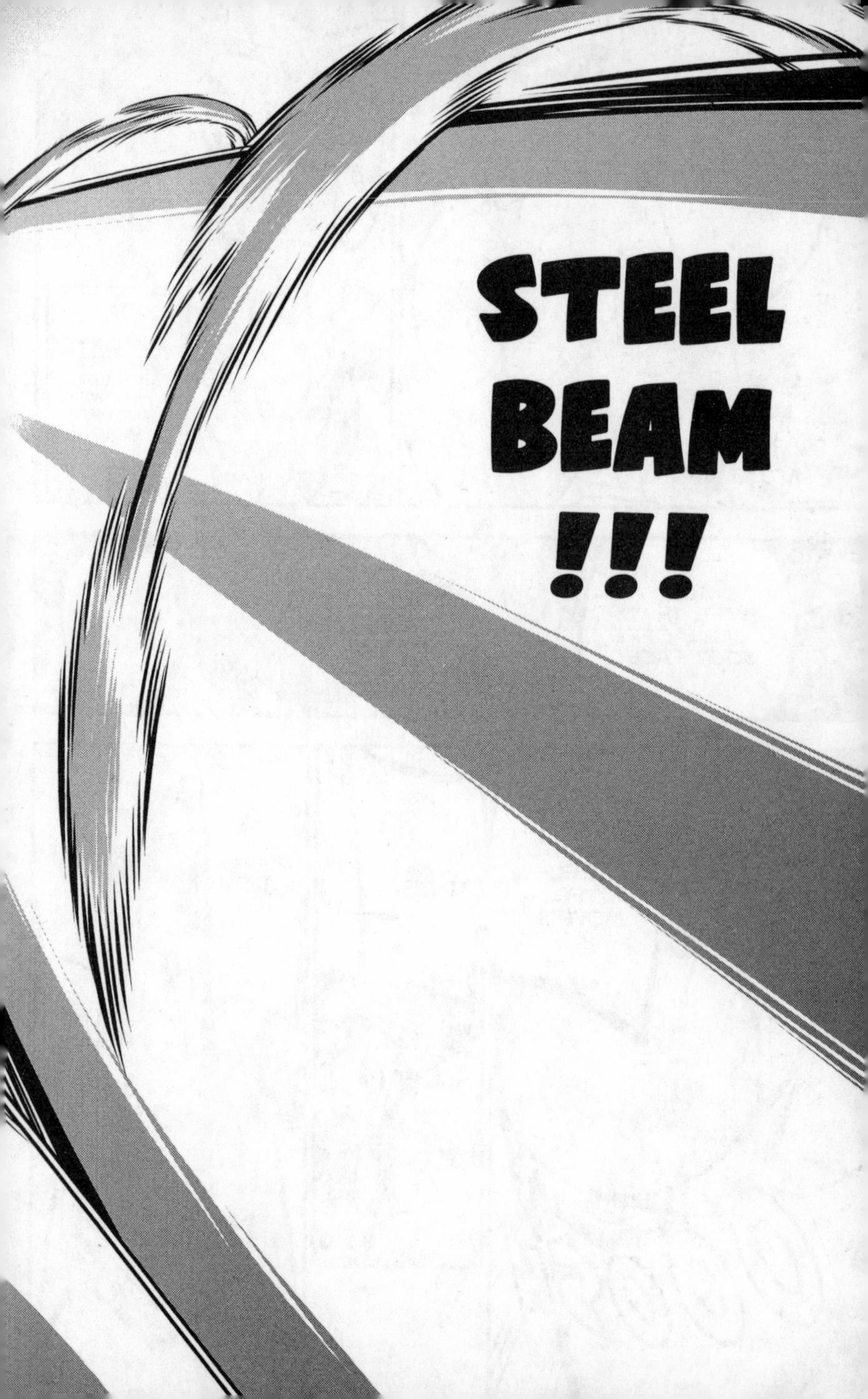
STEEL BEAM !!!

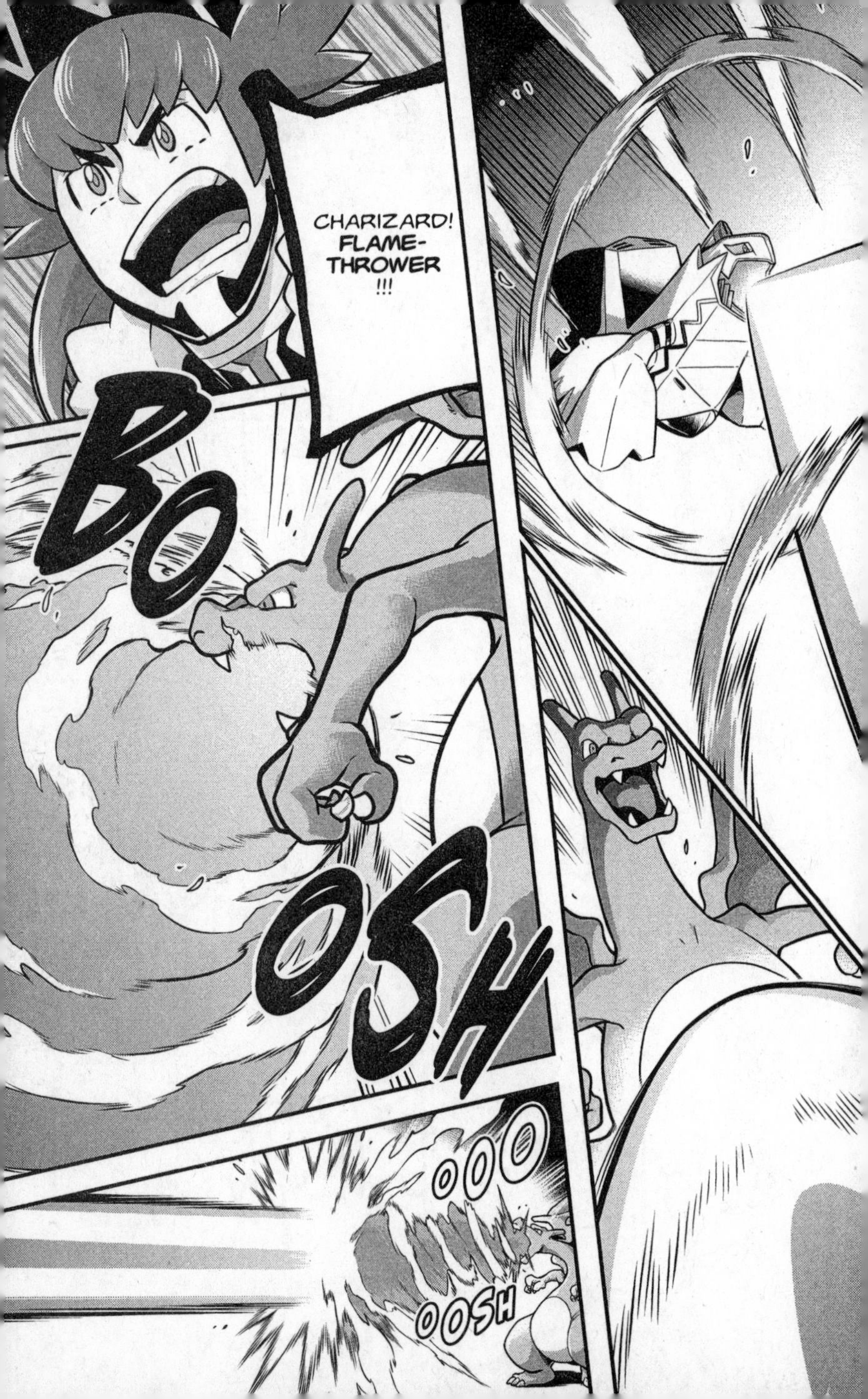
CHARIZARD! FLAME-THROWER !!!
BOOSH
OOOO
OOSH

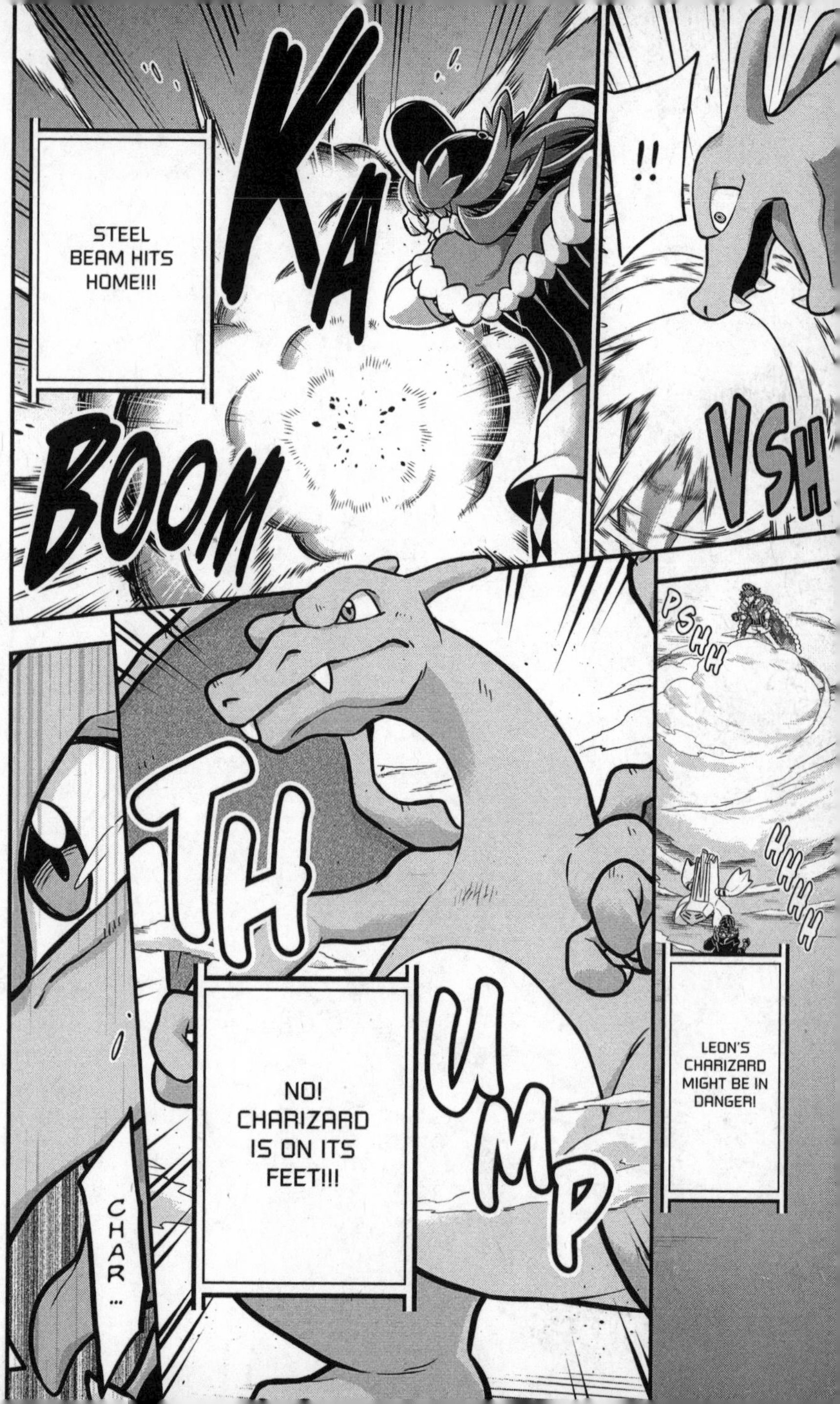
!!
VSH
STEEL BEAM HITS HOME!!!
KA
BOOM
PSHH
HHHHH
LEON'S CHARIZARD MIGHT BE IN DANGER!
THUMP
NO! CHARIZARD IS ON ITS FEET!!!
CHAR...

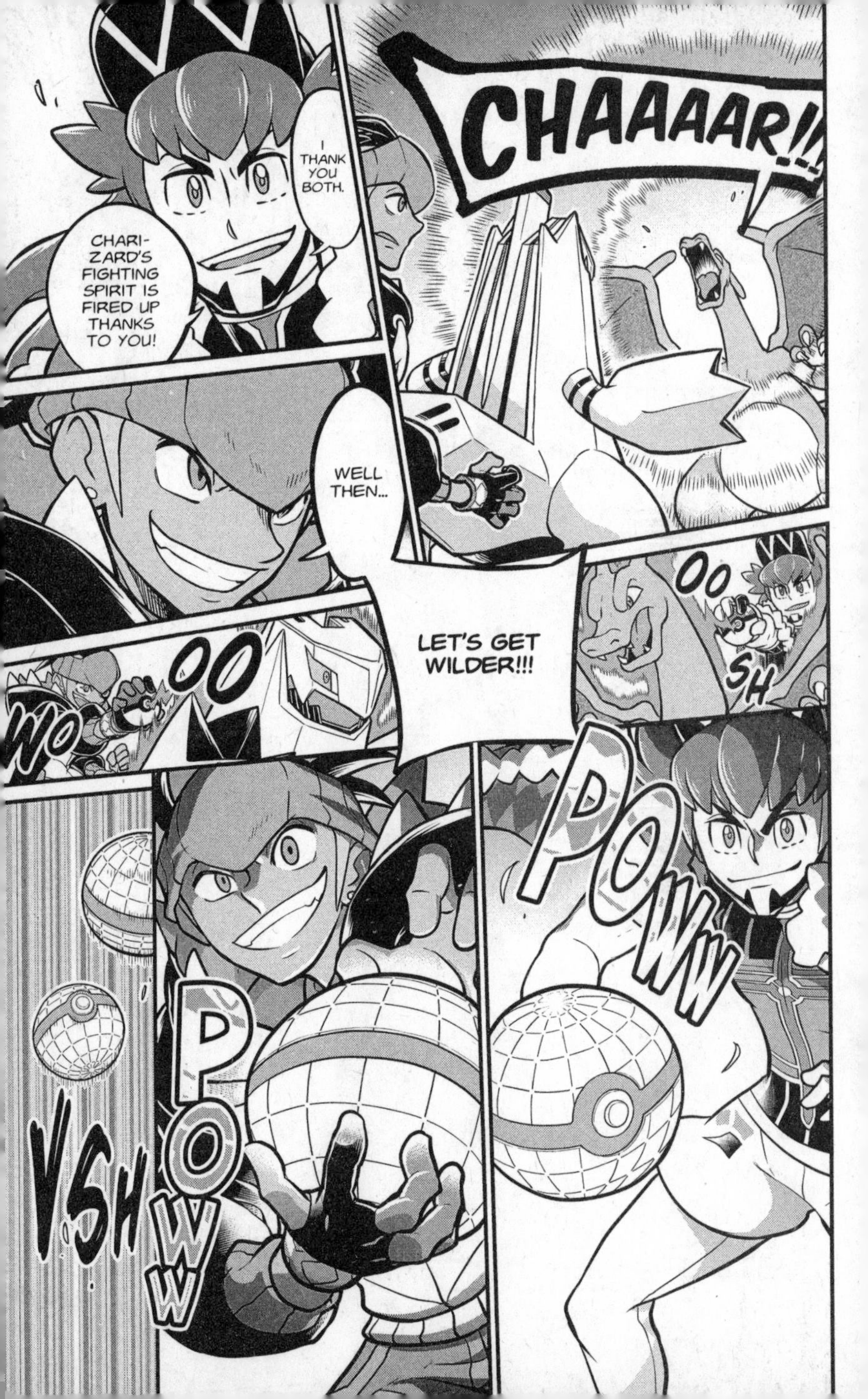
CHAAAAR!!!
I THANK YOU BOTH.
CHARI-ZARD'S FIGHTING SPIRIT IS FIRED UP THANKS TO YOU!
WELL THEN...
LET'S GET WILDER!!!
OO SH
WOOO
POWW
POWWW
V.SH

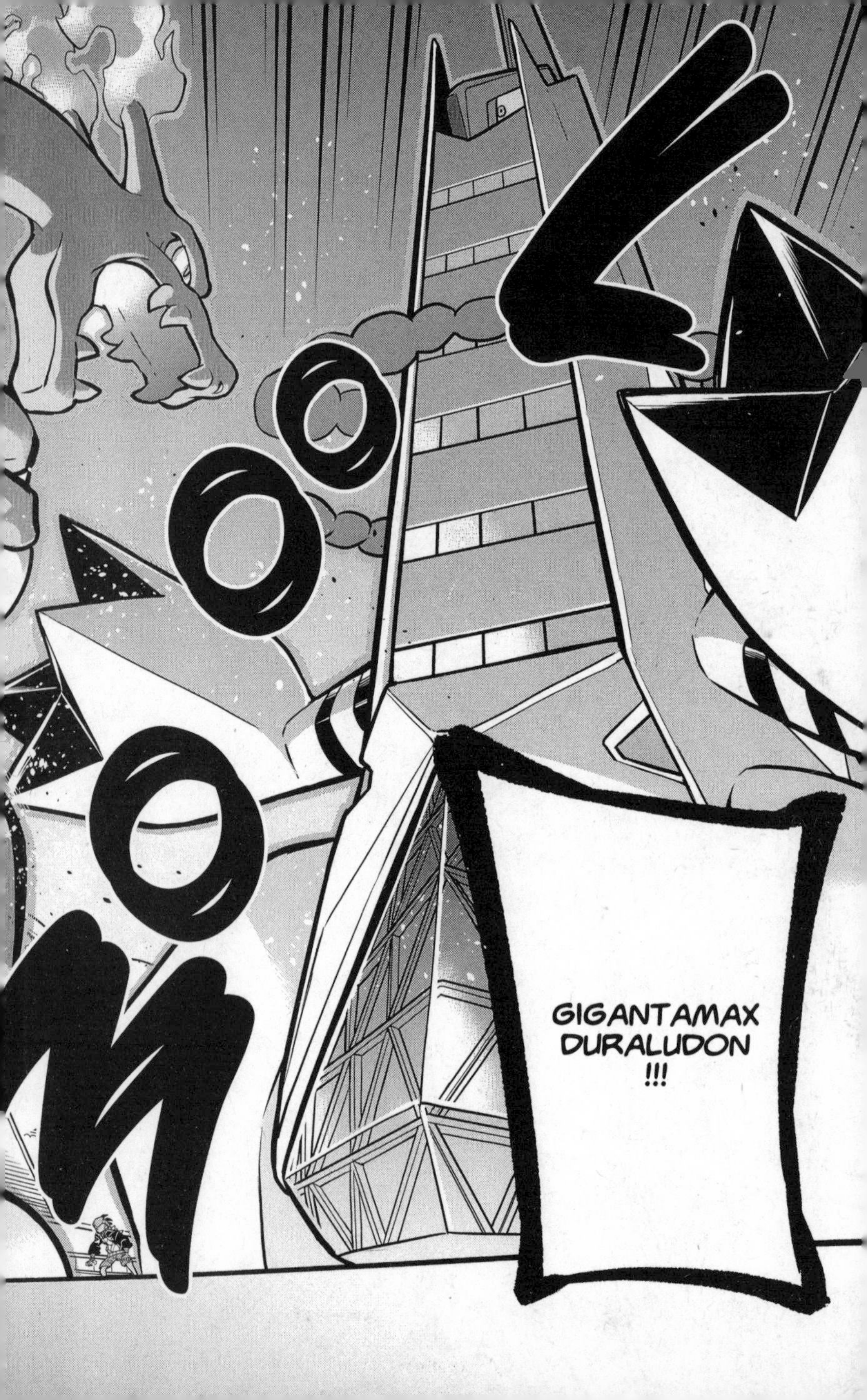
GIGANTAMAX DURALUDON !!!

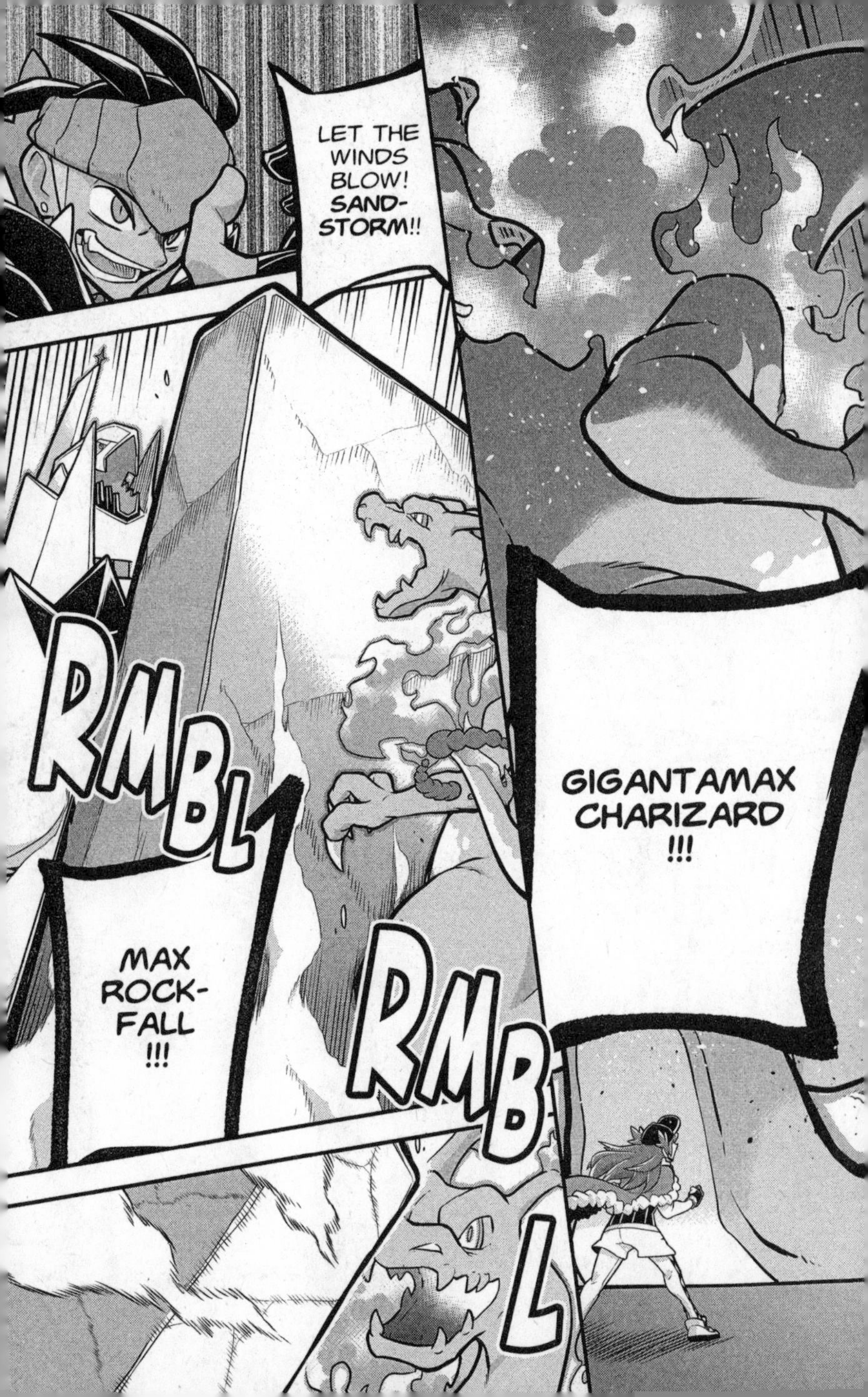
LET THE WINDS BLOW! SANDSTORM!!
GIGANTAMAX CHARIZARD !!!
RMBL
MAX ROCK-FALL !!!
RMBL

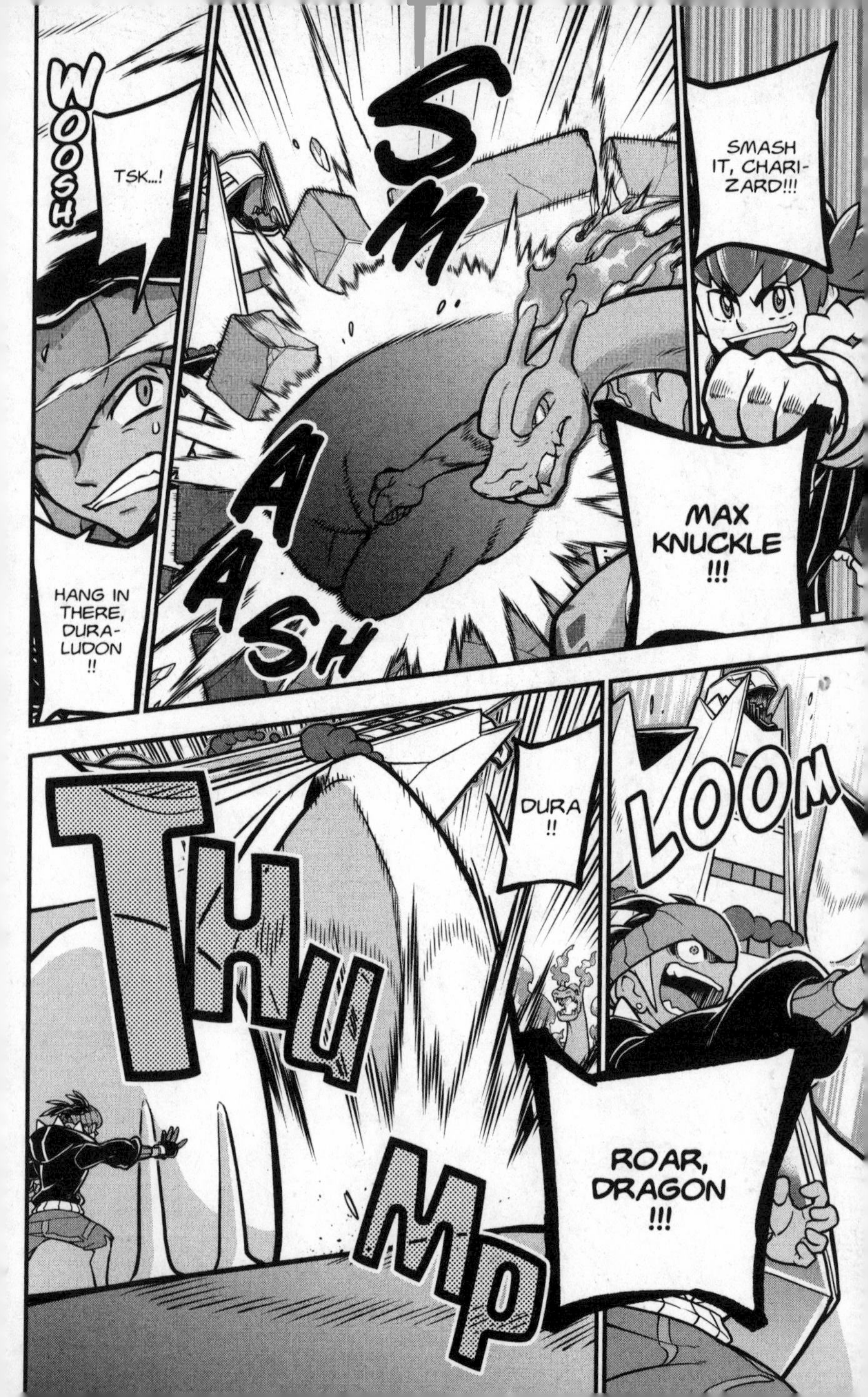
SMASH IT, CHARI-ZARD!!!
MAX KNUCKLE !!!
SMAAASH
WOOSH
TSK...!
HANG IN THERE, DURA-LUDON !!
LOOM
ROAR, DRAGON !!!
DURA !!
THUMP

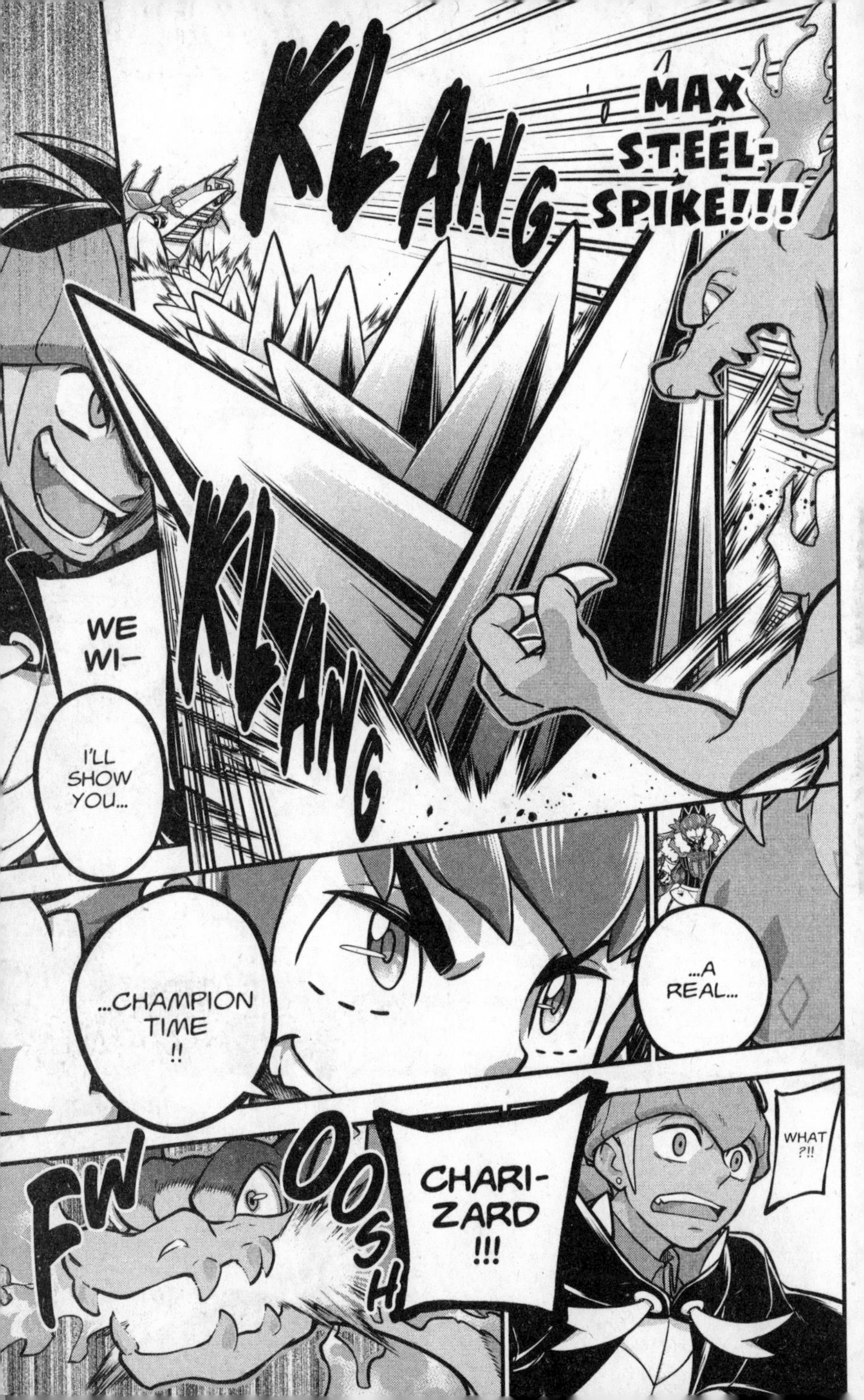
MAX STEEL-SPIKE!!!
KLANG
KLANG
WE WI-
I'LL SHOW YOU...
...A REAL...
...CHAMPION TIME !!
WHAT ?!!
CHARI-ZARD !!!
FWOOOSH

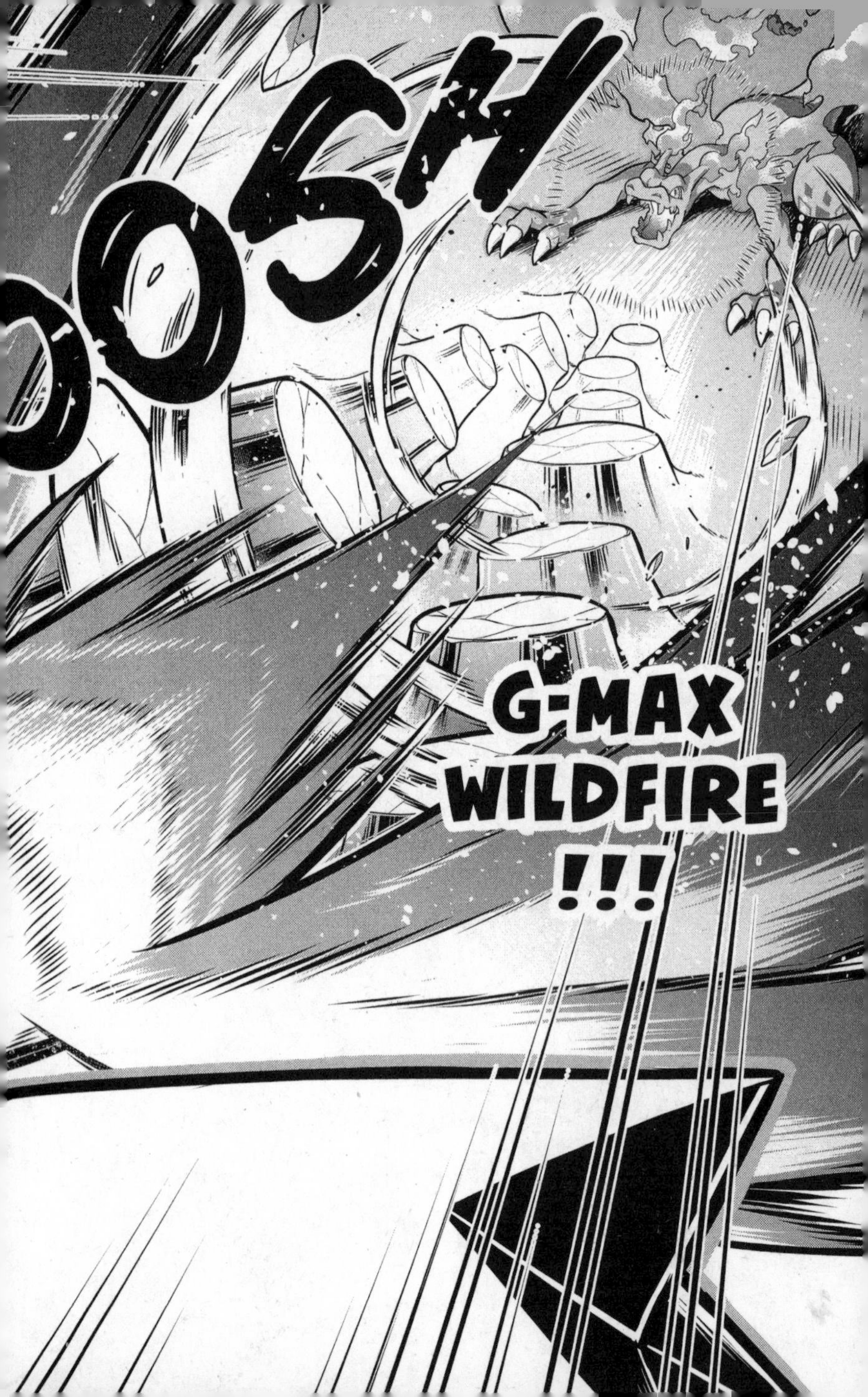
FOOSH
G-MAX WILDFIRE !!!

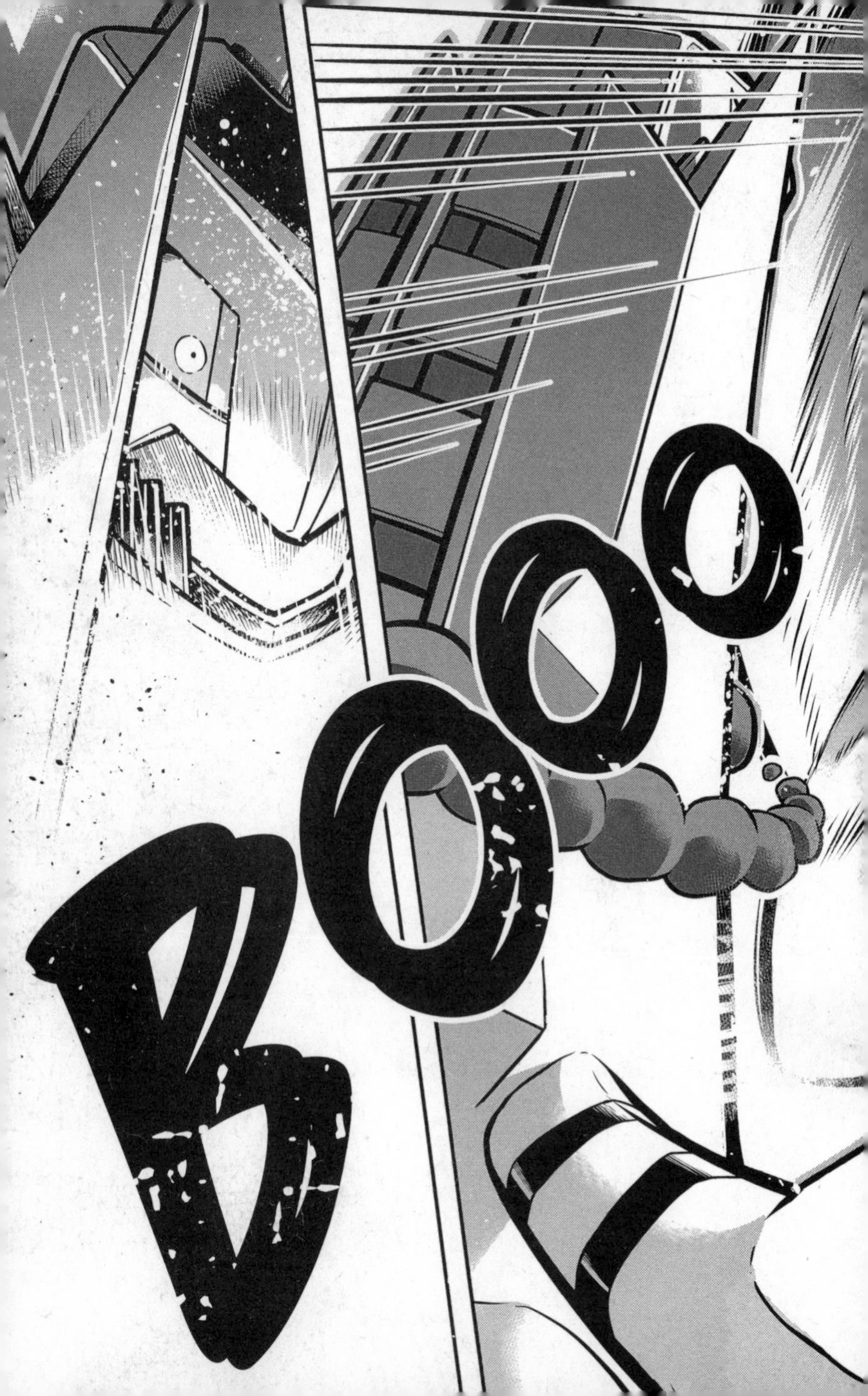
BOOOO

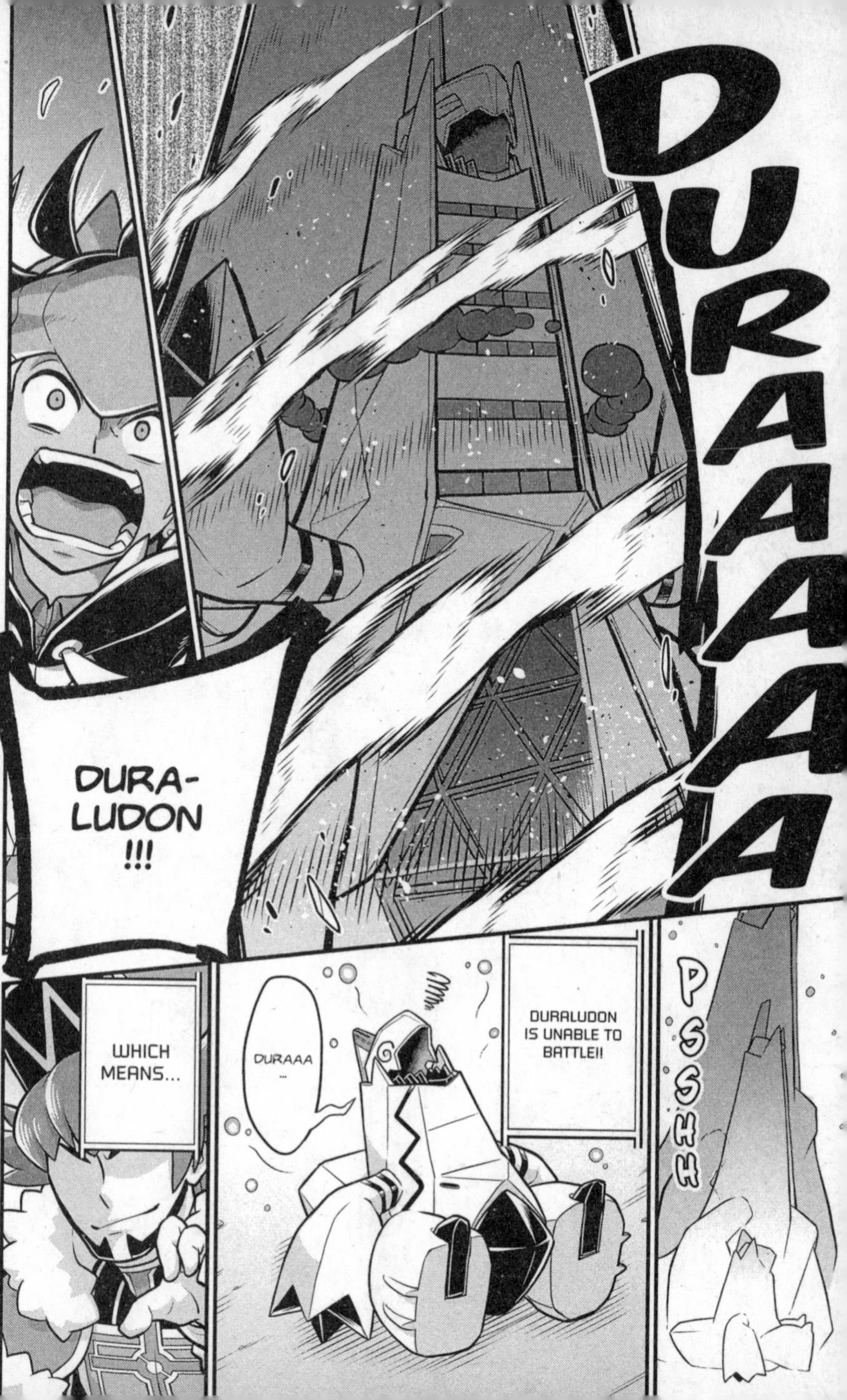
DURAAAAA
DURA-
LUDON
!!!
PSSHH
DURALUDON IS UNABLE TO BATTLE!!
DURAAA
...
WHICH MEANS...

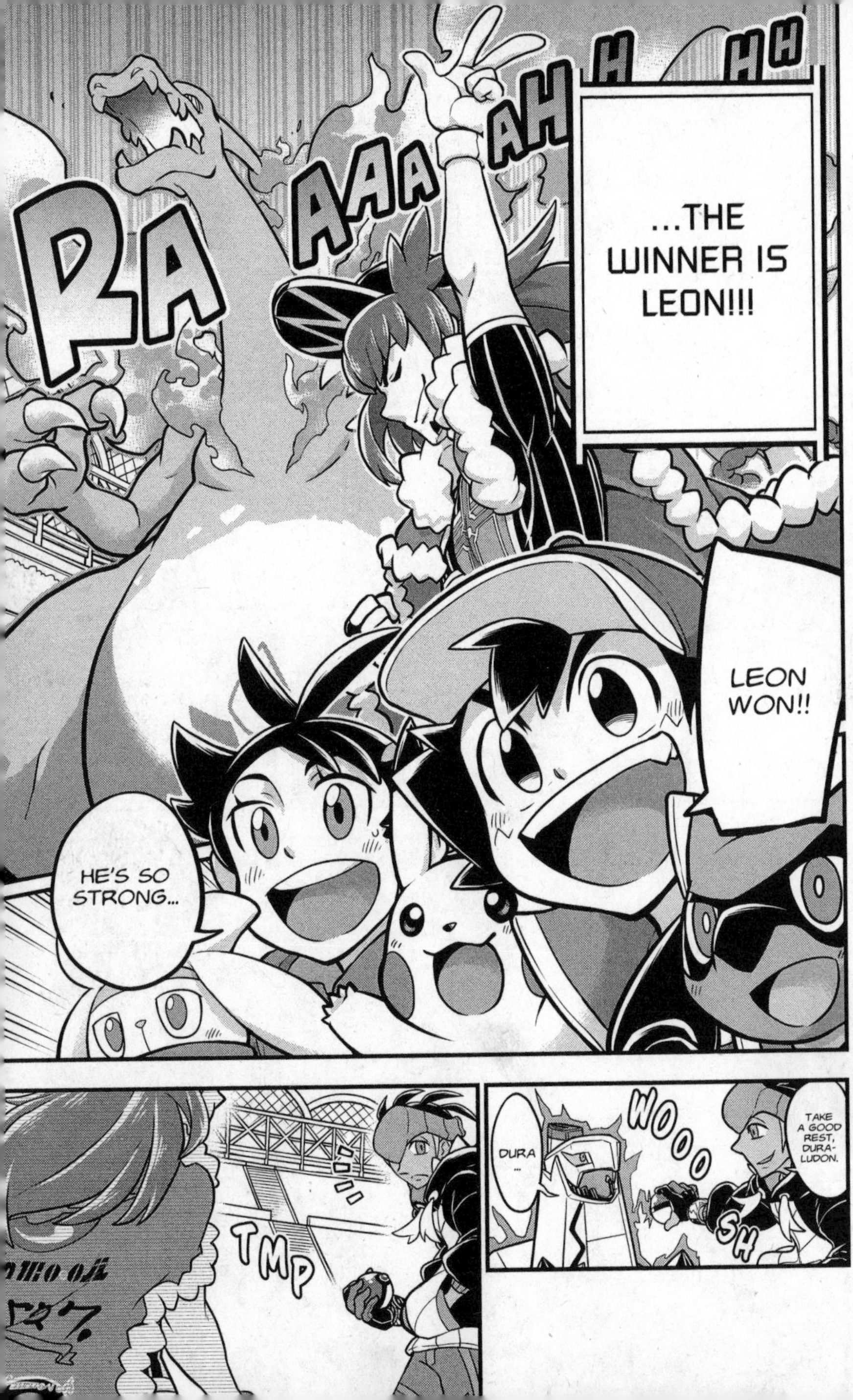
RAAAAAHHHHH
...THE WINNER IS LEON!!!
LEON WON!!
HE'S SO STRONG...
TAKE A GOOD REST, DURA-LUDON.
WOOOSH
DURA...
TMP

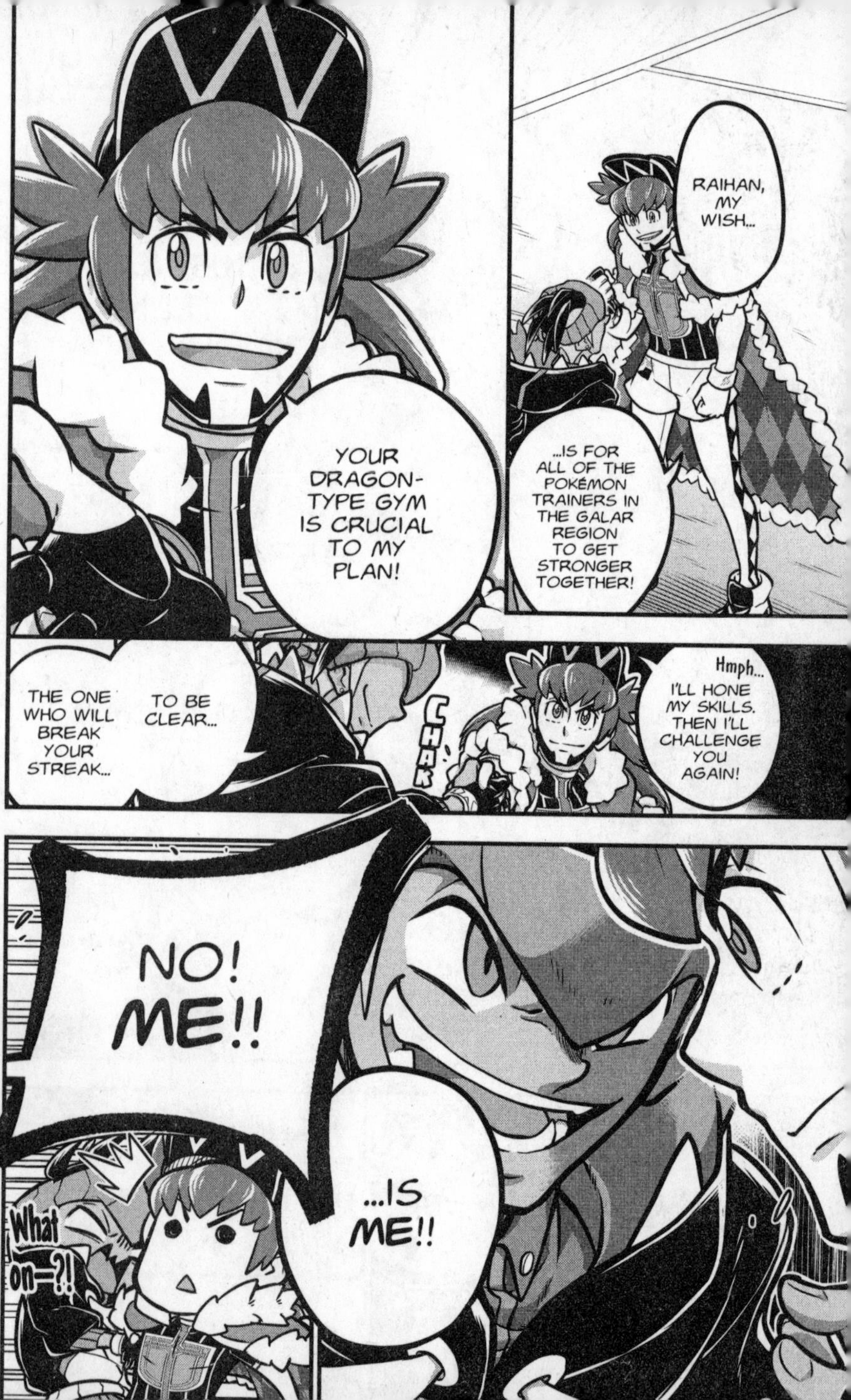
RAIHAN, MY WISH...
...IS FOR ALL OF THE POKÉMON TRAINERS IN THE GALAR REGION TO GET STRONGER TOGETHER!
YOUR DRAGON-TYPE GYM IS CRUCIAL TO MY PLAN!
Hmph...
I'LL HONE MY SKILLS. THEN I'LL CHALLENGE YOU AGAIN!
CHAK
TO BE CLEAR...
THE ONE WHO WILL BREAK YOUR STREAK...
NO! ME!!
...IS ME!!
What on—?!

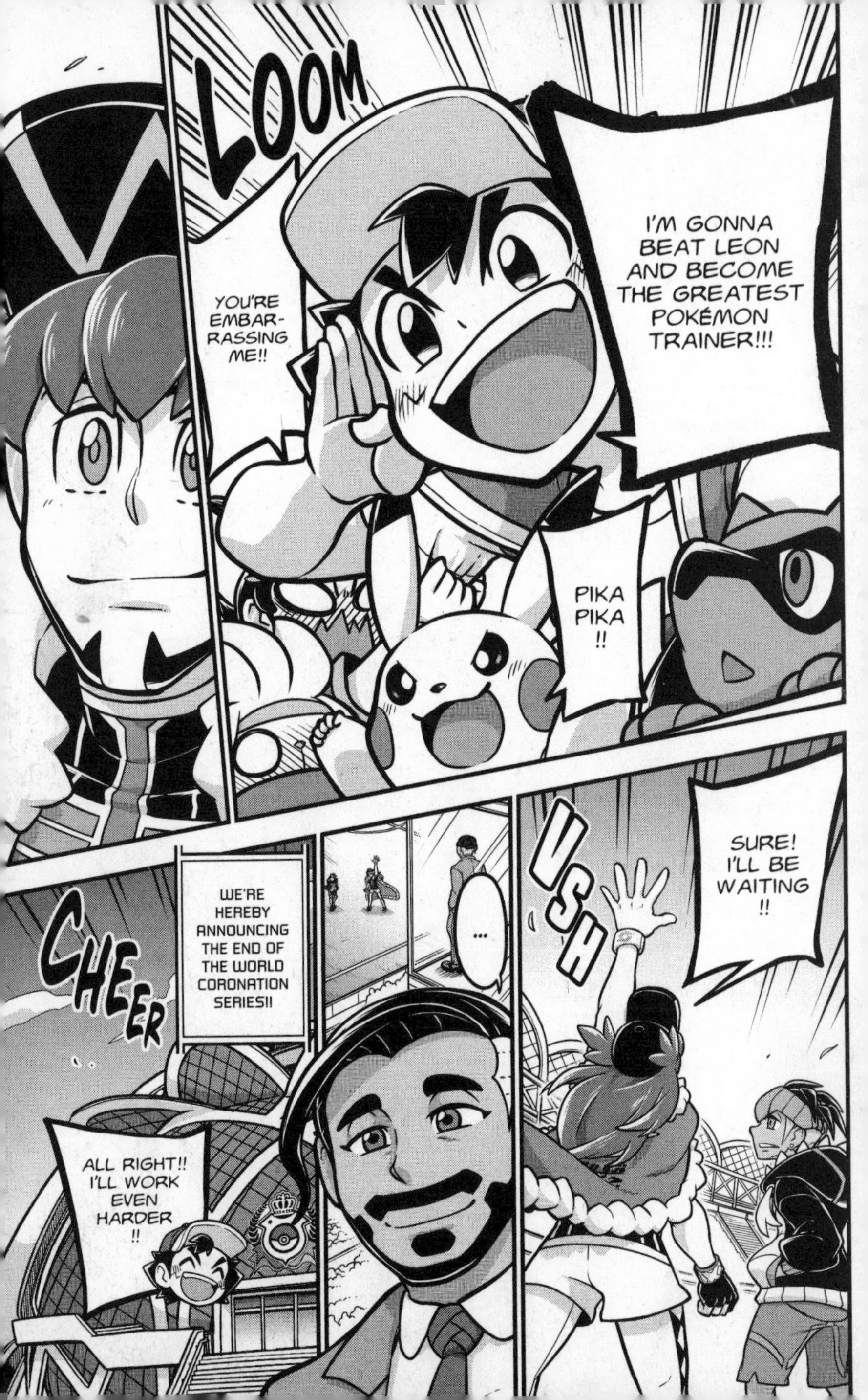
I'M GONNA BEAT LEON AND BECOME THE GREATEST POKÉMON TRAINER!!!
YOU'RE EMBARRASSING ME!!
PIKA PIKA !!
LOOM
SURE! I'LL BE WAITING !!
VSH
...
WE'RE HEREBY ANNOUNCING THE END OF THE WORLD CORONATION SERIES!!
CHEER
ALL RIGHT!! I'LL WORK EVEN HARDER !!

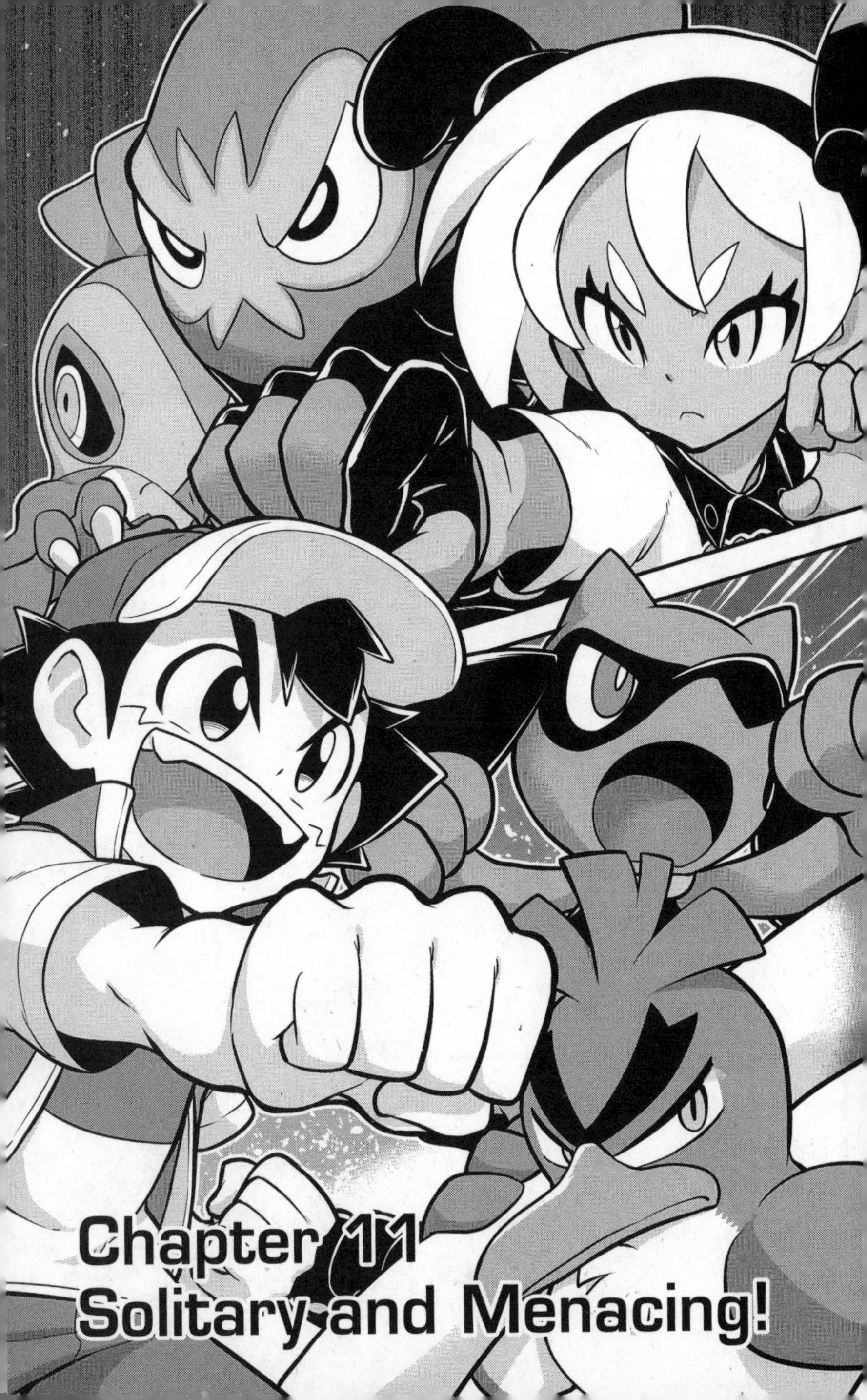
Chapter 11
Solitary and Menacing!

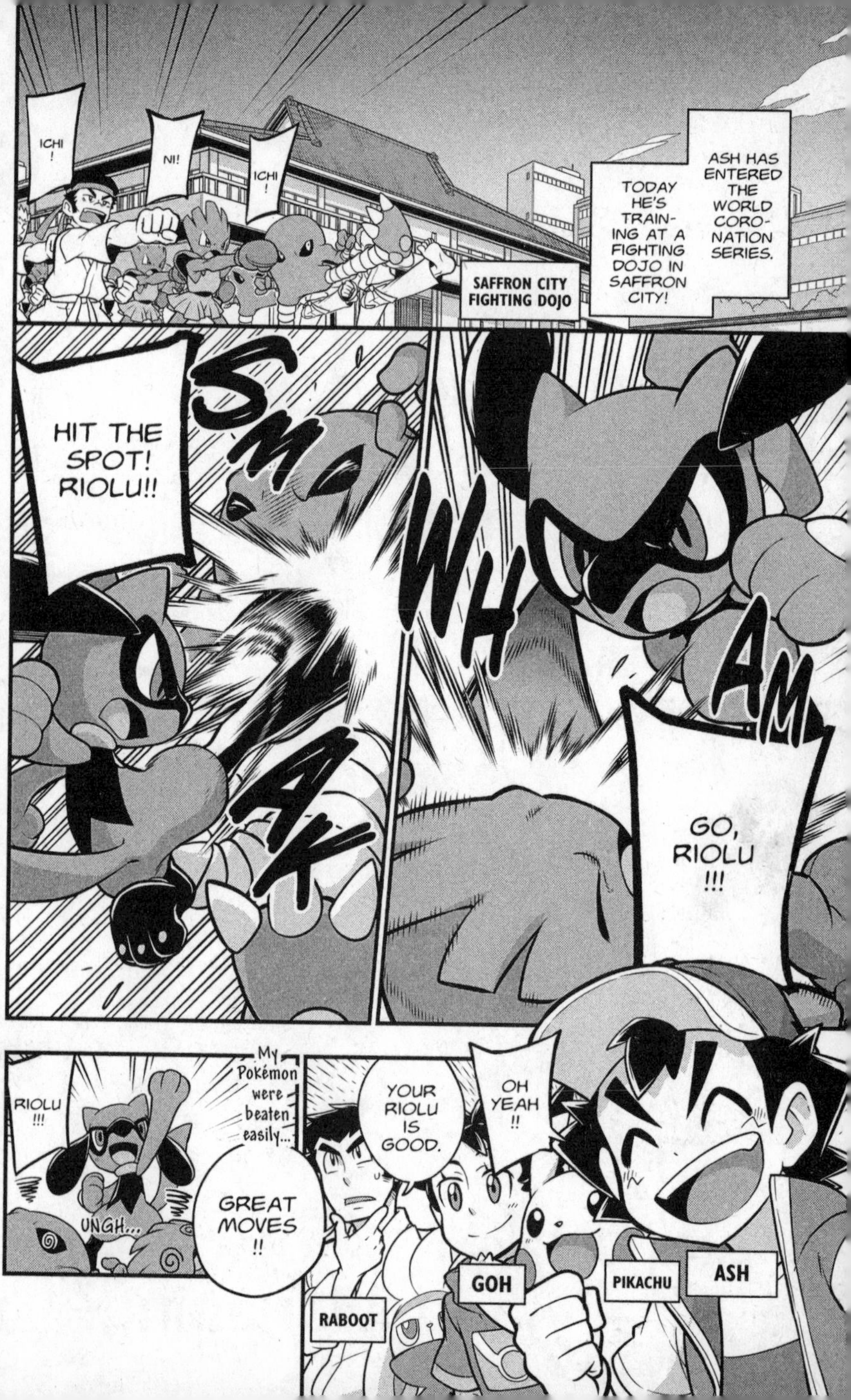

ASH HAS ENTERED THE WORLD CORONATION SERIES.
TODAY HE'S TRAINING AT A FIGHTING DOJO IN SAFFRON CITY!
SAFFRON CITY FIGHTING DOJO
ICHI!
NI!
ICHI!
WHAM
GO, RIOLU!!!
SMAAK
HIT THE SPOT! RIOLU!!
OH YEAH!!
ASH
PIKACHU
YOUR RIOLU IS GOOD.
GOH
RABOOT
My Pokémon were beaten easily...
GREAT MOVES!!
RIOLU!!!
UNGH...

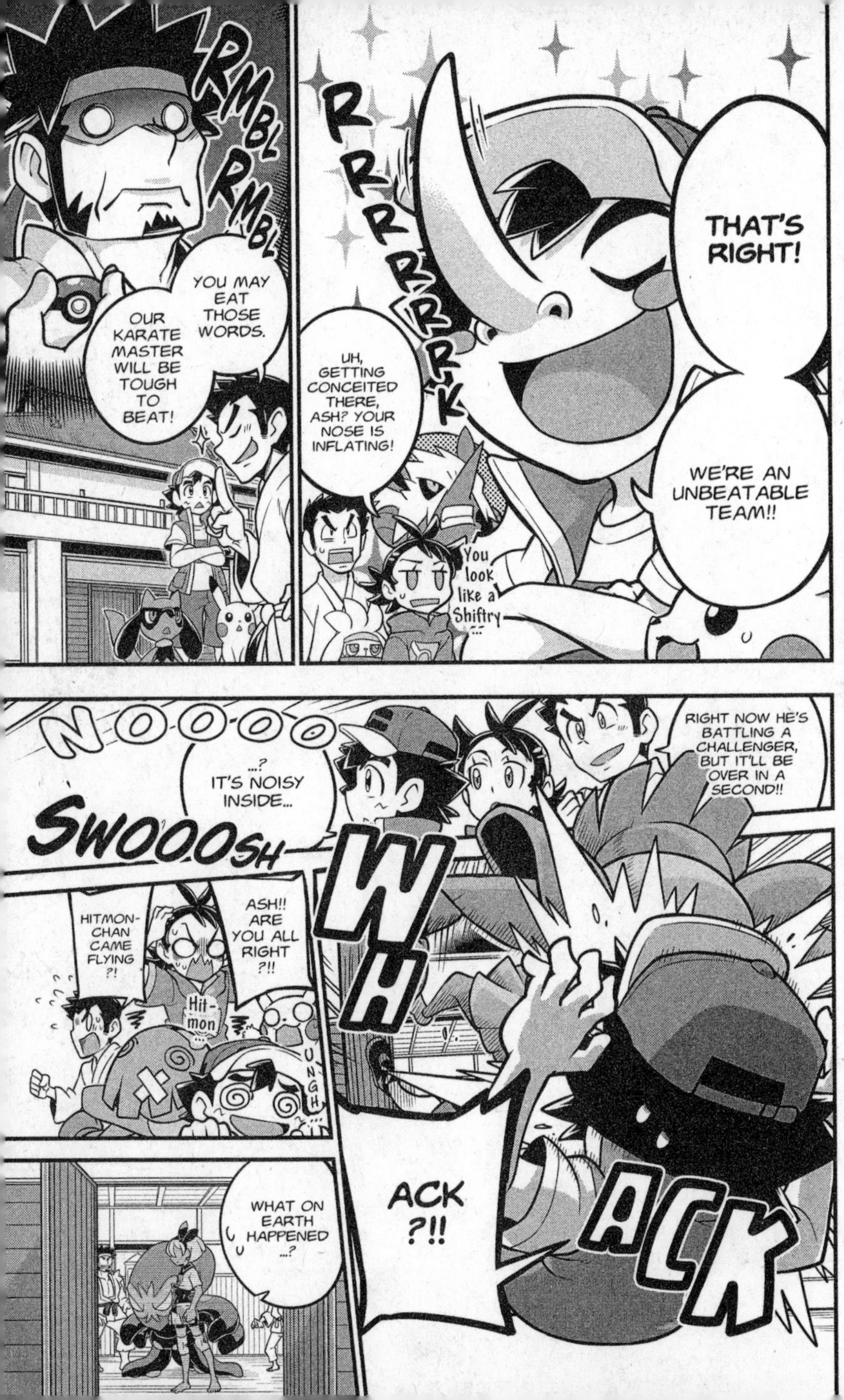
THAT'S RIGHT!
WE'RE AN UNBEATABLE TEAM!!
RRRRRRRK
UH, GETTING CONCEITED THERE, ASH? YOUR NOSE IS INFLATING!
You look like a Shiftry...
RMBL RMBL
YOU MAY EAT THOSE WORDS.
OUR KARATE MASTER WILL BE TOUGH TO BEAT!
RIGHT NOW HE'S BATTLING A CHALLENGER, BUT IT'LL BE OVER IN A SECOND!!
...? IT'S NOISY INSIDE...
NOOOO
SWOOOSH
WHH
ACK ?!!
ACK
ASH!! ARE YOU ALL RIGHT ?!!
HITMON-CHAN CAME FLYING ?!
Hit-mon...
UNGH...
WHAT ON EARTH HAPPENED ...?

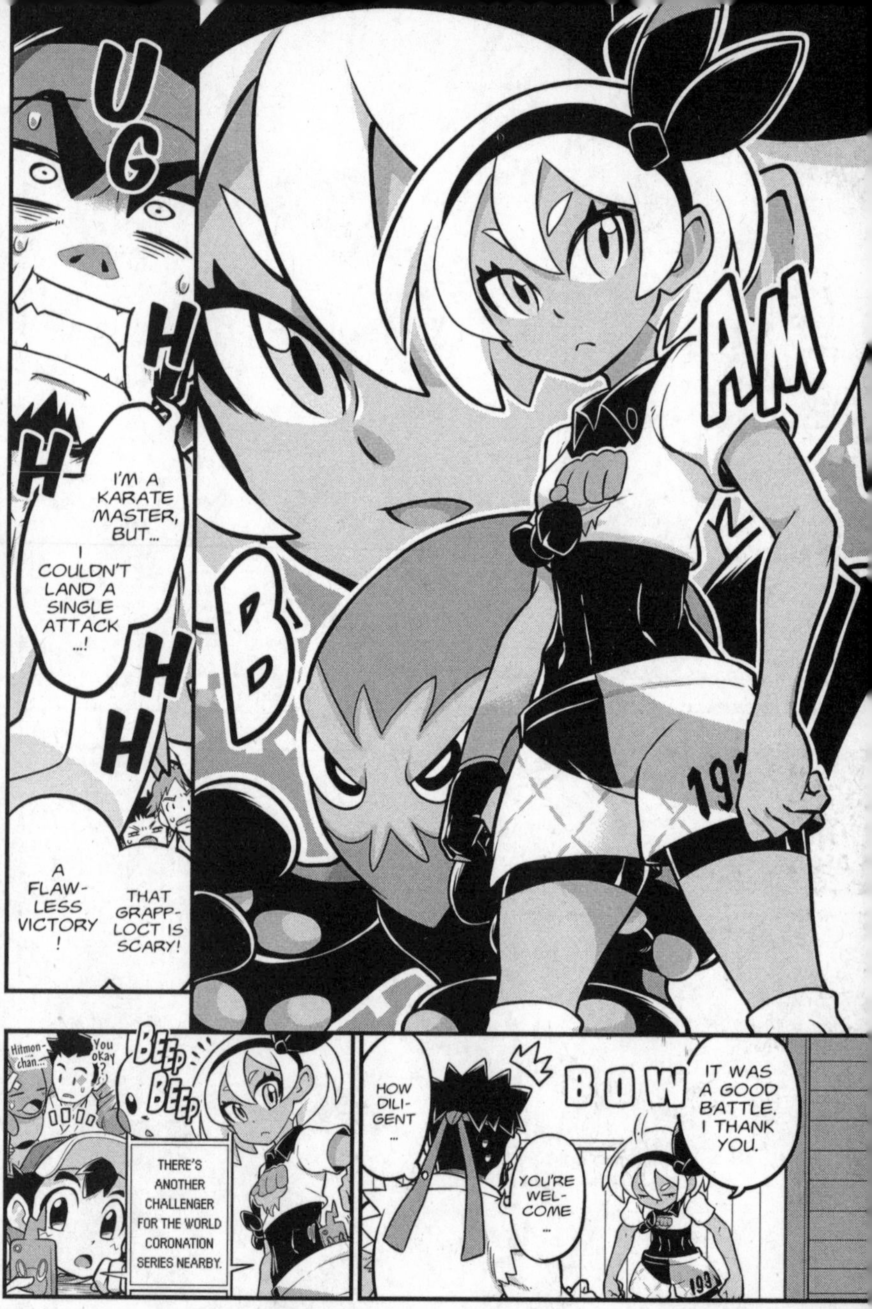
BAM
UGH
HHHHHH
I'M A KARATE MASTER, BUT... I COULDN'T LAND A SINGLE ATTACK...!
THAT GRAPPLOCT IS SCARY!
A FLAWLESS VICTORY!
IT WAS A GOOD BATTLE. I THANK YOU.
BOW
HOW DILIGENT...
YOU'RE WELCOME...
BEEP BEEP
You okay?
Hitmon-chan...
THERE'S ANOTHER CHALLENGER FOR THE WORLD CORONATION SERIES NEARBY.

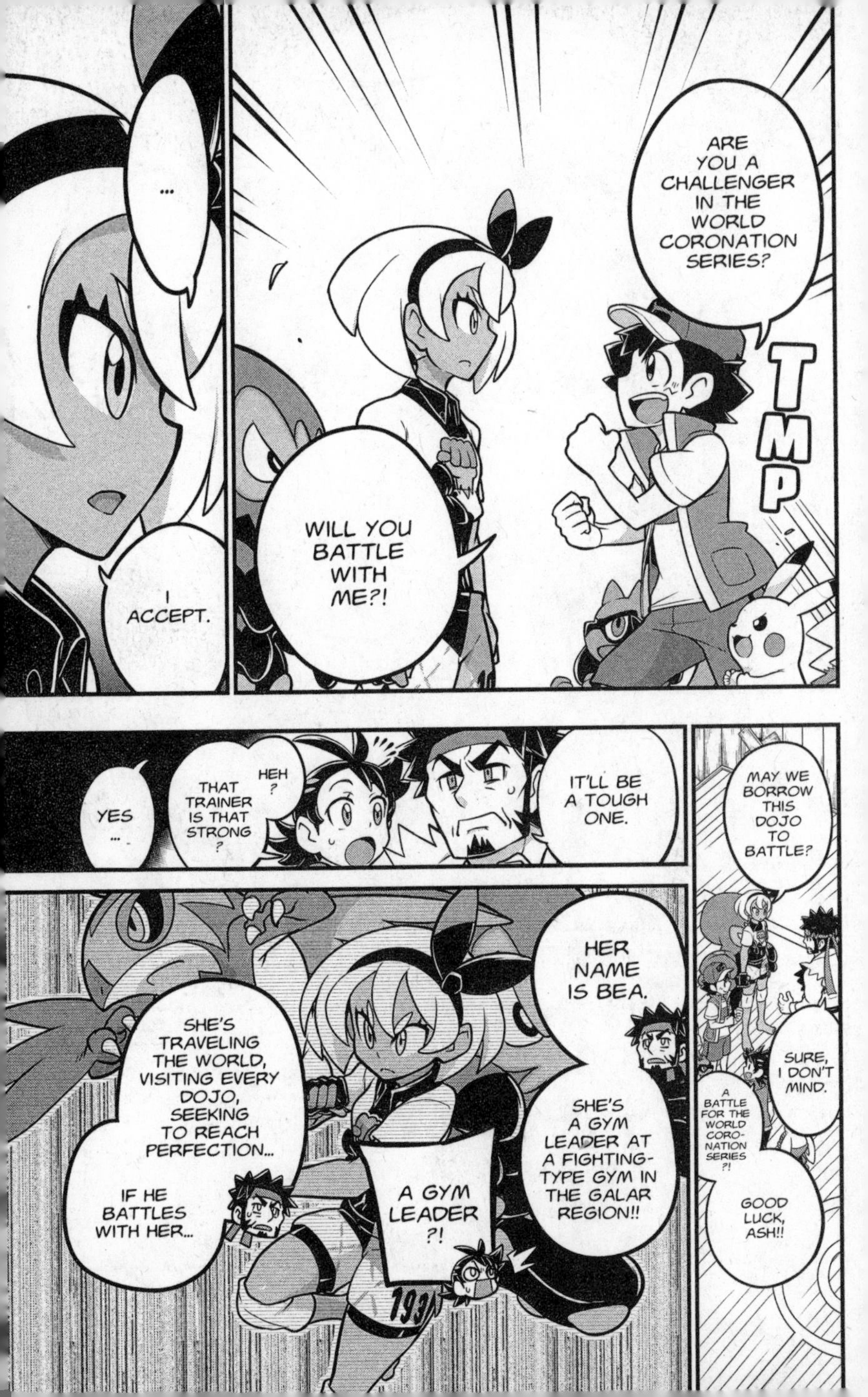
ARE YOU A CHALLENGER IN THE WORLD CORONATION SERIES?
TMP
WILL YOU BATTLE WITH ME?!
...
I ACCEPT.
MAY WE BORROW THIS DOJO TO BATTLE?
SURE, I DON'T MIND.
A BATTLE FOR THE WORLD CORO-NATION SERIES?!
GOOD LUCK, ASH!!
IT'LL BE A TOUGH ONE.
HEH?
THAT TRAINER IS THAT STRONG?
YES...
HER NAME IS BEA.
SHE'S A GYM LEADER AT A FIGHTING-TYPE GYM IN THE GALAR REGION!!
SHE'S TRAVELING THE WORLD, VISITING EVERY DOJO, SEEKING TO REACH PERFECTION...
A GYM LEADER?!
IF HE BATTLES WITH HER...

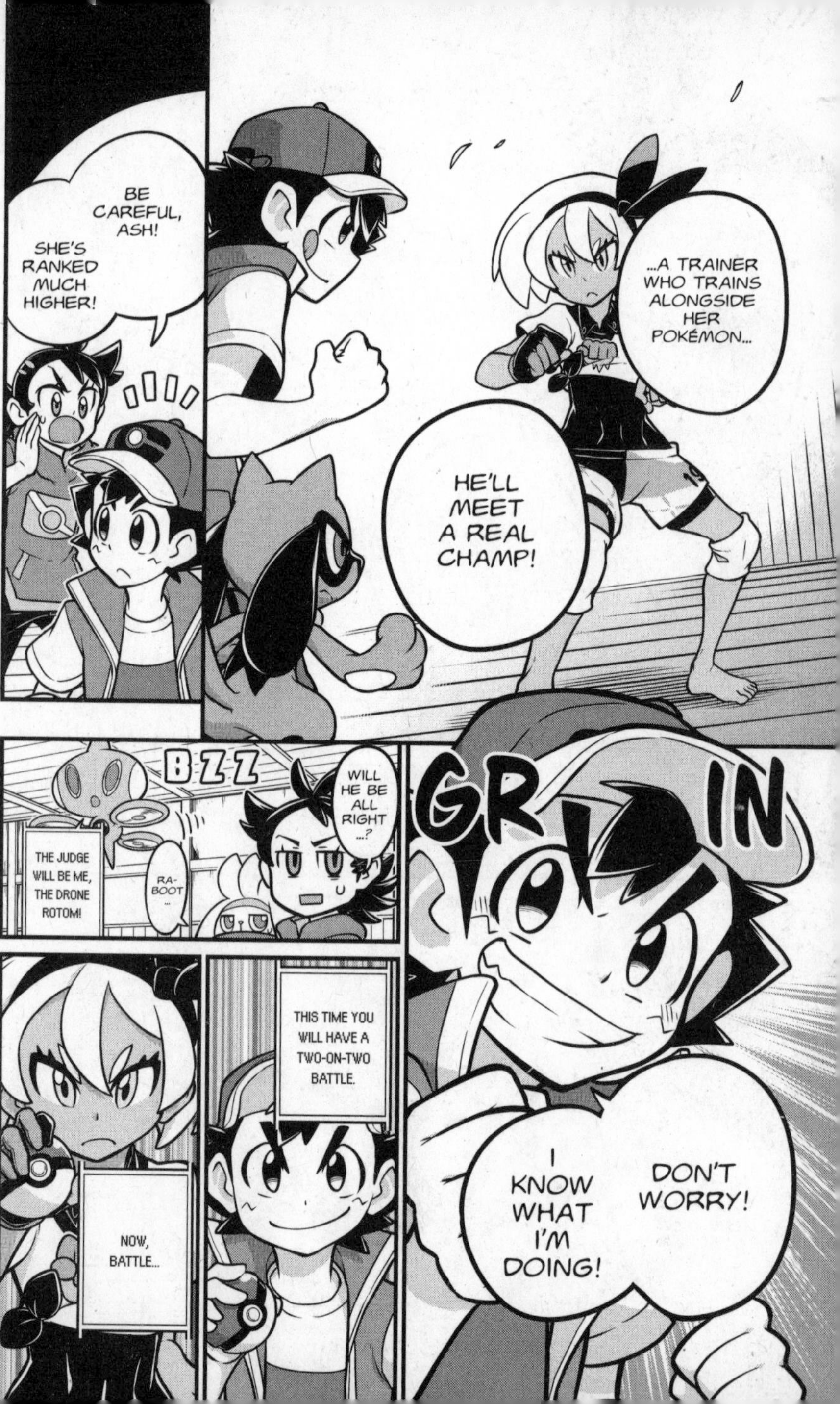
...A TRAINER WHO TRAINS ALONGSIDE HER POKÉMON...
HE'LL MEET A REAL CHAMP!
BE CAREFUL, ASH!
SHE'S RANKED MUCH HIGHER!
GRIN
DON'T WORRY!
I KNOW WHAT I'M DOING!
BZZ
WILL HE BE ALL RIGHT ...?
THE JUDGE WILL BE ME, THE DRONE ROTOM!
RA-BOOT ...
THIS TIME YOU WILL HAVE A TWO-ON-TWO BATTLE.
NOW, BATTLE...

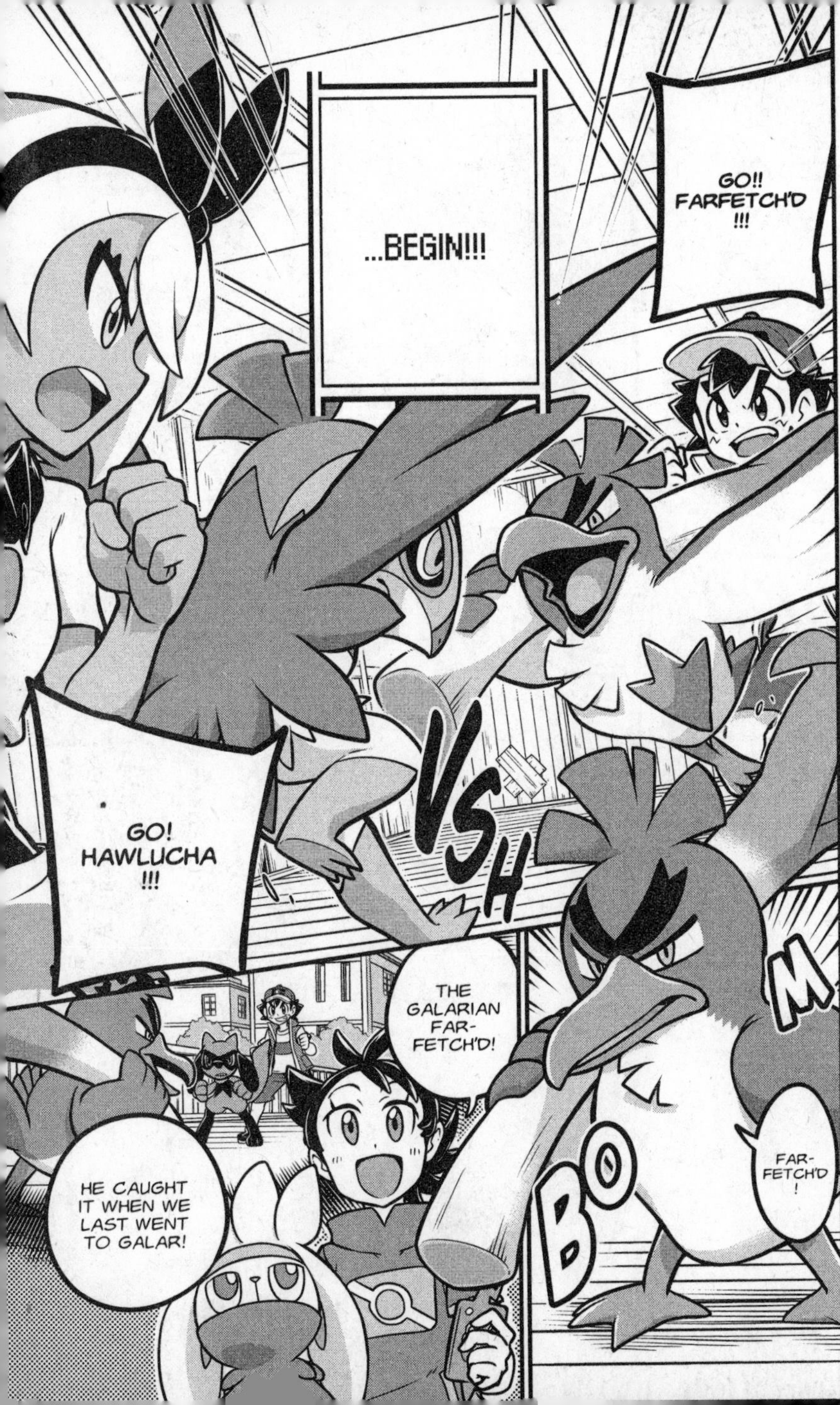
GO!! FARFETCH'D !!!
...BEGIN!!!
GO! HAWLUCHA !!!
VSH
BOM
FAR-FETCH'D!
THE GALARIAN FAR-FETCH'D!
HE CAUGHT IT WHEN WE LAST WENT TO GALAR!

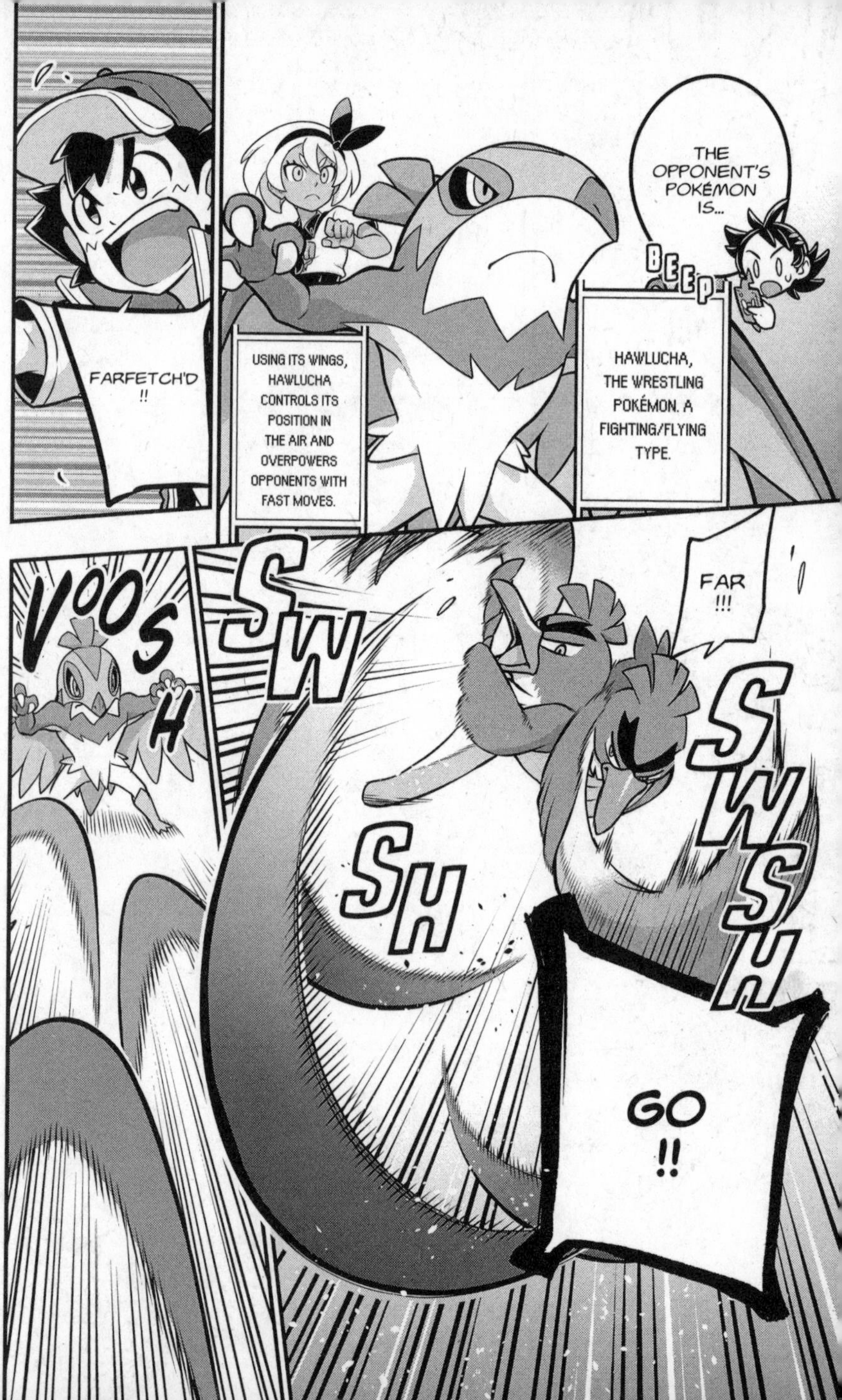
THE OPPONENT'S POKÉMON IS...
BEEP
HAWLUCHA, THE WRESTLING POKÉMON. A FIGHTING/FLYING TYPE.
USING ITS WINGS, HAWLUCHA CONTROLS ITS POSITION IN THE AIR AND OVERPOWERS OPPONENTS WITH FAST MOVES.
FARFETCH'D !!
FAR !!!
SWSH
SH
GO !!
SW
VOOSH

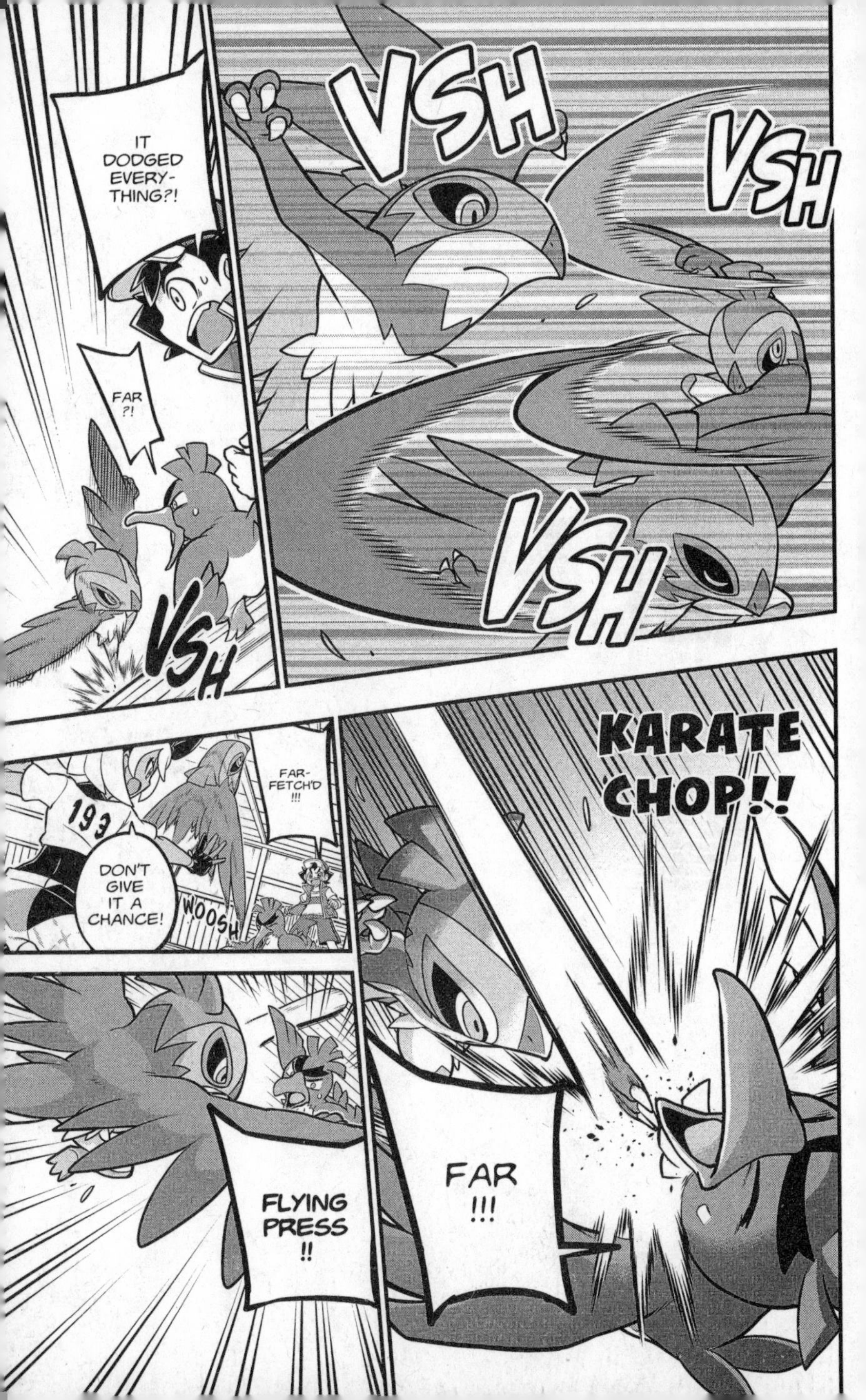
VSH
VSH
VSH
IT DODGED EVERY-THING?!
FAR ?!
VSH
KARATE CHOP!!
FAR !!!
FAR-FETCH'D !!!
193
DON'T GIVE IT A CHANCE!
WOOSH
FLYING PRESS !!

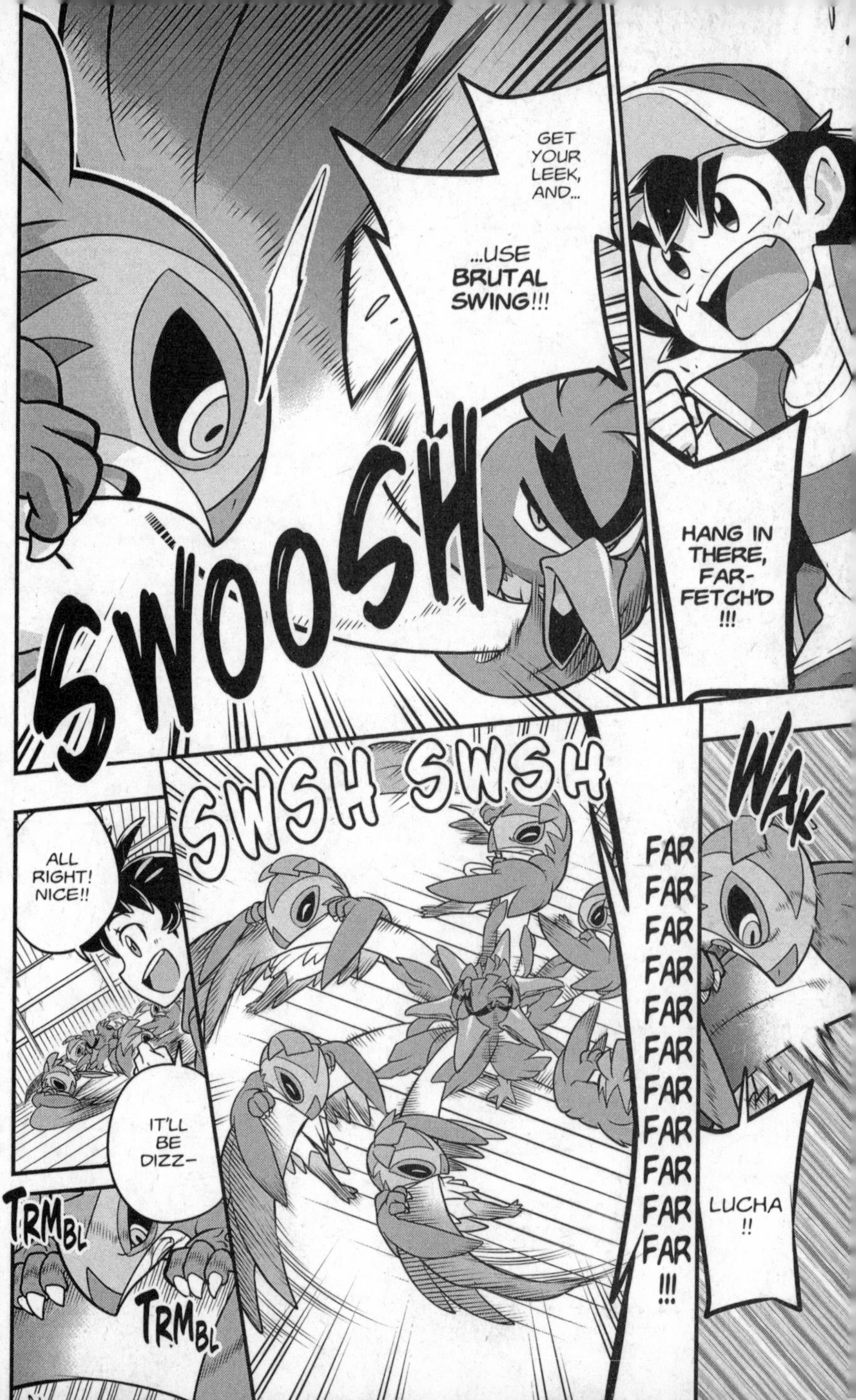
GET YOUR LEEK, AND...
...USE BRUTAL SWING!!!
HANG IN THERE, FAR-FETCH'D!!!
SWOOSH
WAK
LUCHA!!
FAR FAR FAR FAR FAR FAR FAR FAR FAR FAR FAR FAR!!!
SWSH SWSH
ALL RIGHT! NICE!!
IT'LL BE DIZZ–
TRMBL
TRMBL

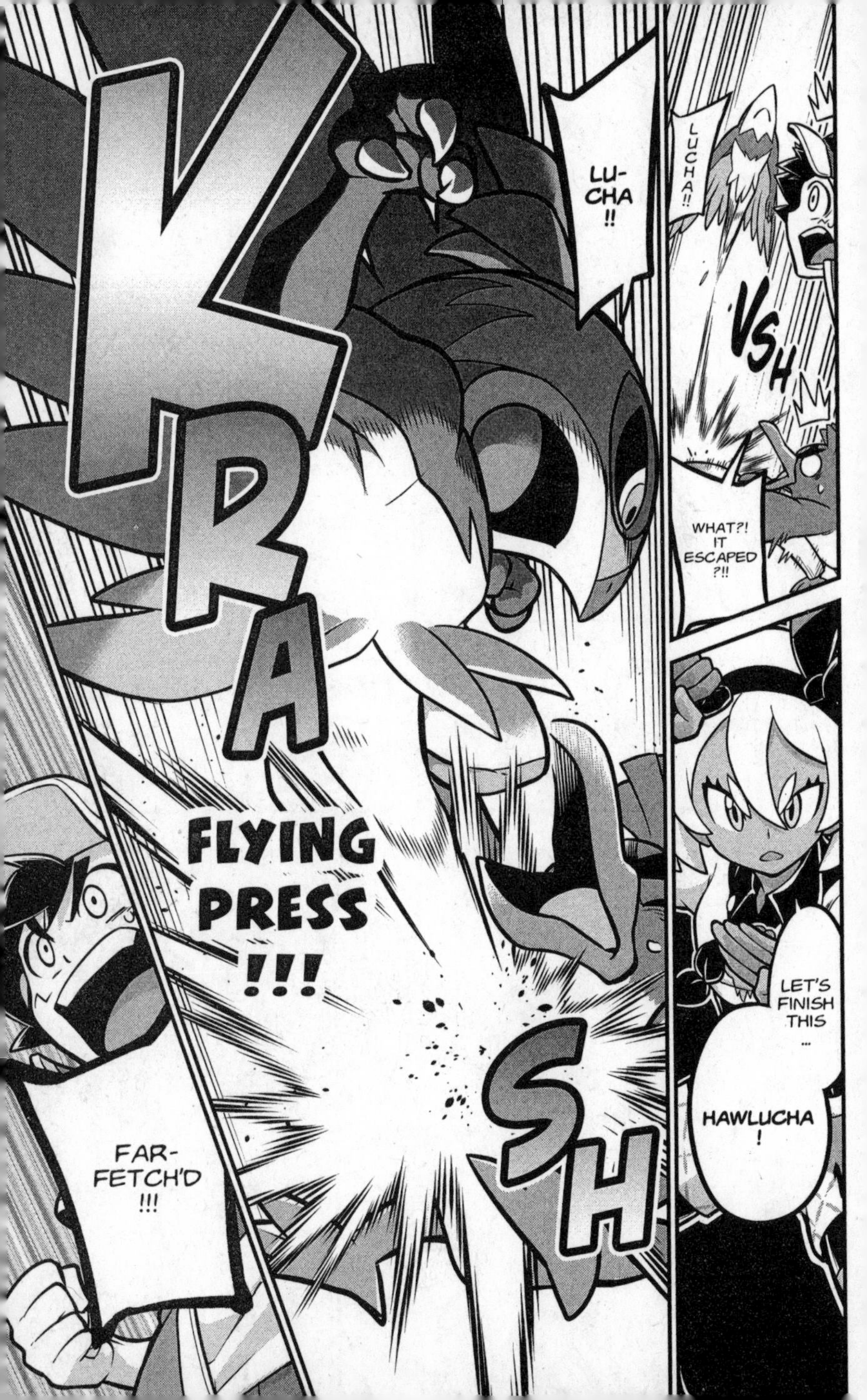

LUCHA!!
VSH
WHAT?! IT ESCAPED?!!
LET'S FINISH THIS...
HAWLUCHA!
LU-CHA!!
KRA
FLYING PRESS!!!
SH
FAR-FETCH'D!!!

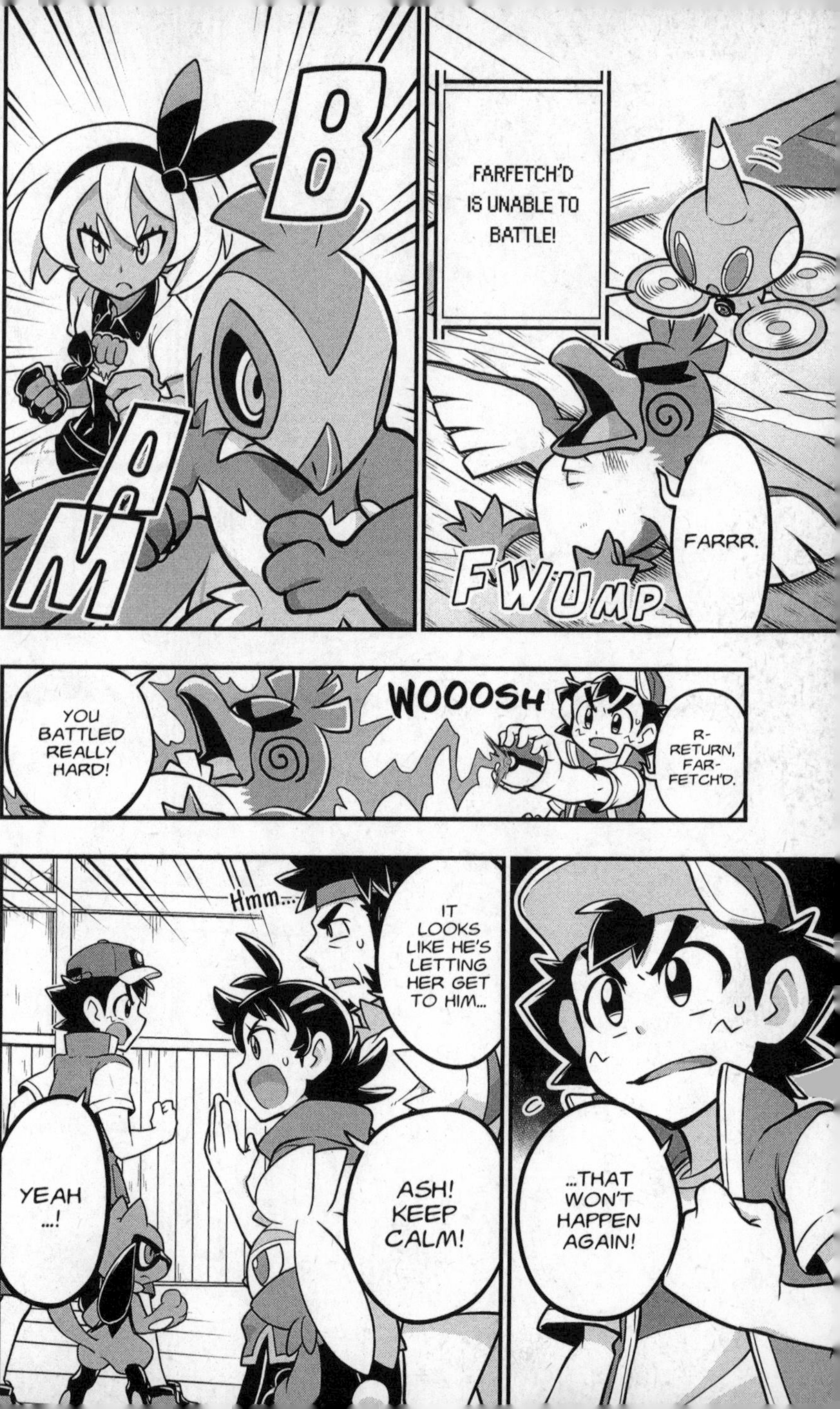
FARFETCH'D IS UNABLE TO BATTLE!
FWUMP
FARRR.
BAM
R-RETURN, FAR-FETCH'D.
WOOOSH
YOU BATTLED REALLY HARD!
...THAT WON'T HAPPEN AGAIN!
IT LOOKS LIKE HE'S LETTING HER GET TO HIM...
Hmm...
ASH! KEEP CALM!
YEAH ...!

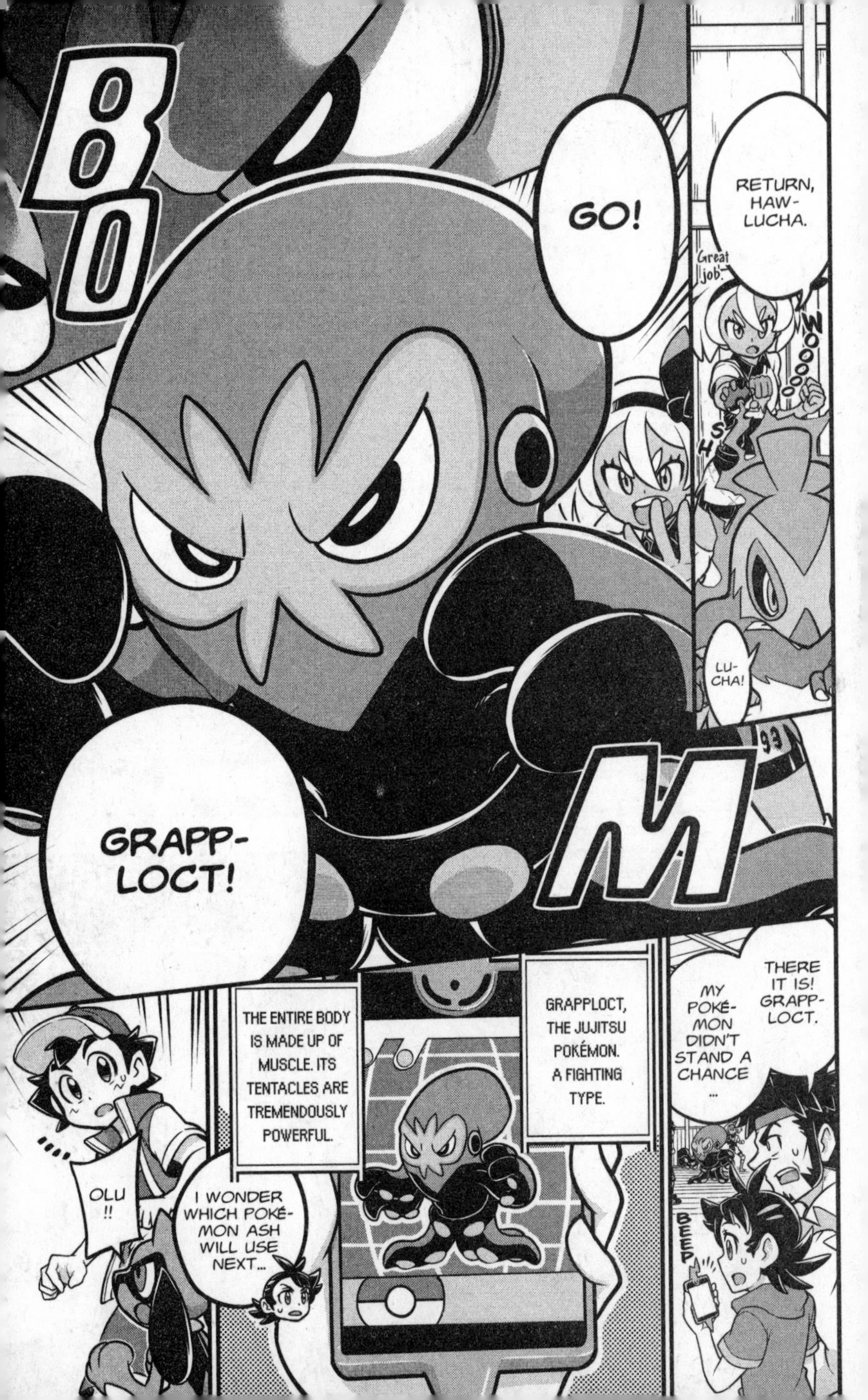
RETURN, HAW-LUCHA.
Great job.
WOOOOOSH
LU-CHA!
GO!
BOO
M
GRAPP-LOCT!
THERE IT IS! GRAPP-LOCT.
MY POKÉ-MON DIDN'T STAND A CHANCE ...
BEEP
GRAPPLOCT, THE JUJITSU POKÉMON. A FIGHTING TYPE.
THE ENTIRE BODY IS MADE UP OF MUSCLE. ITS TENTACLES ARE TREMENDOUSLY POWERFUL.
I WONDER WHICH POKÉ-MON ASH WILL USE NEXT...
....
OLU !!

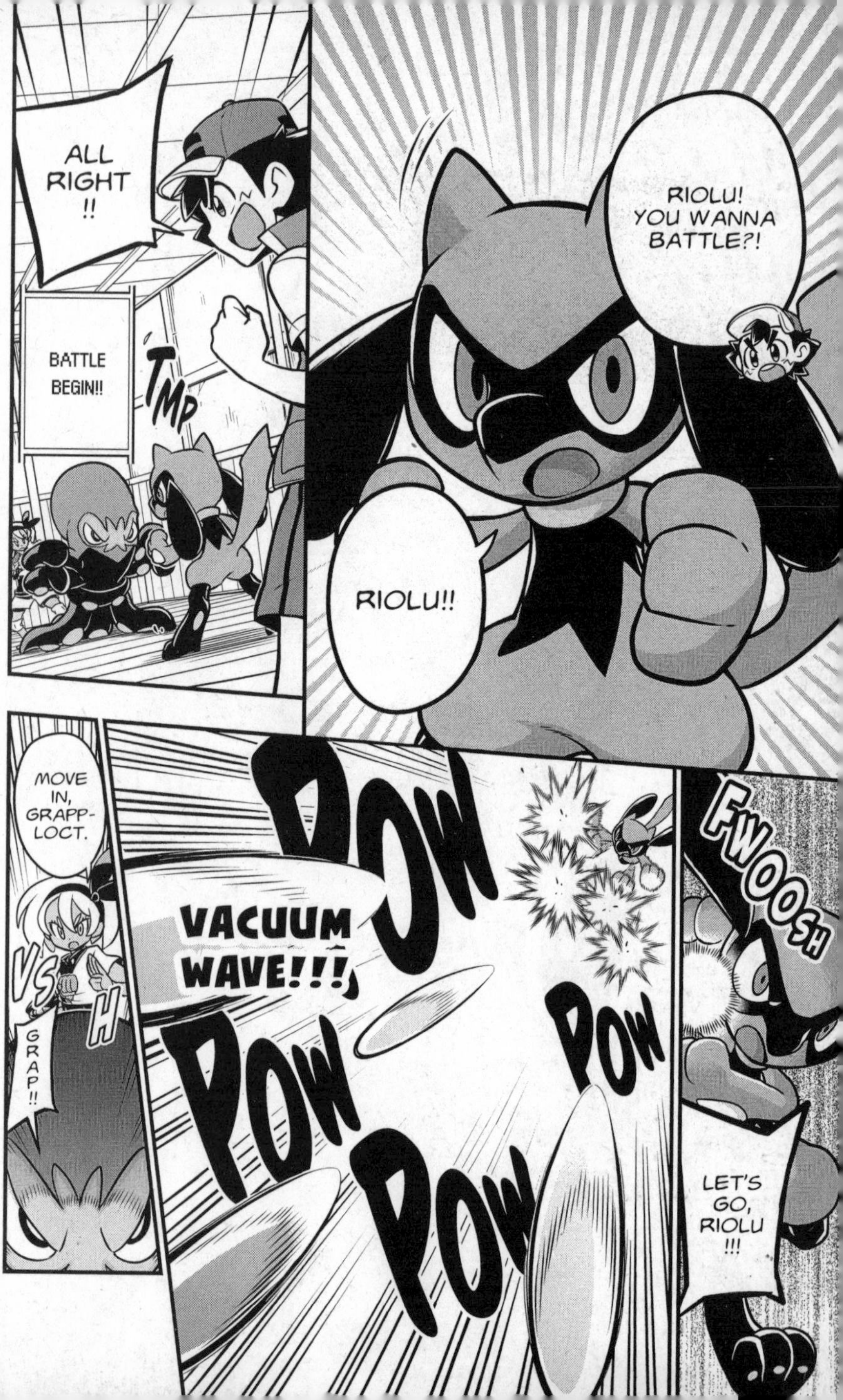
RIOLU! YOU WANNA BATTLE?!
RIOLU!!
ALL RIGHT !!
TMP
BATTLE BEGIN!!
FWOOSH
LET'S GO, RIOLU !!!
POW
POW
POW
POW
VACUUM WAVE!!!
MOVE IN, GRAPP-LOCT.
VSH
GRAP!!

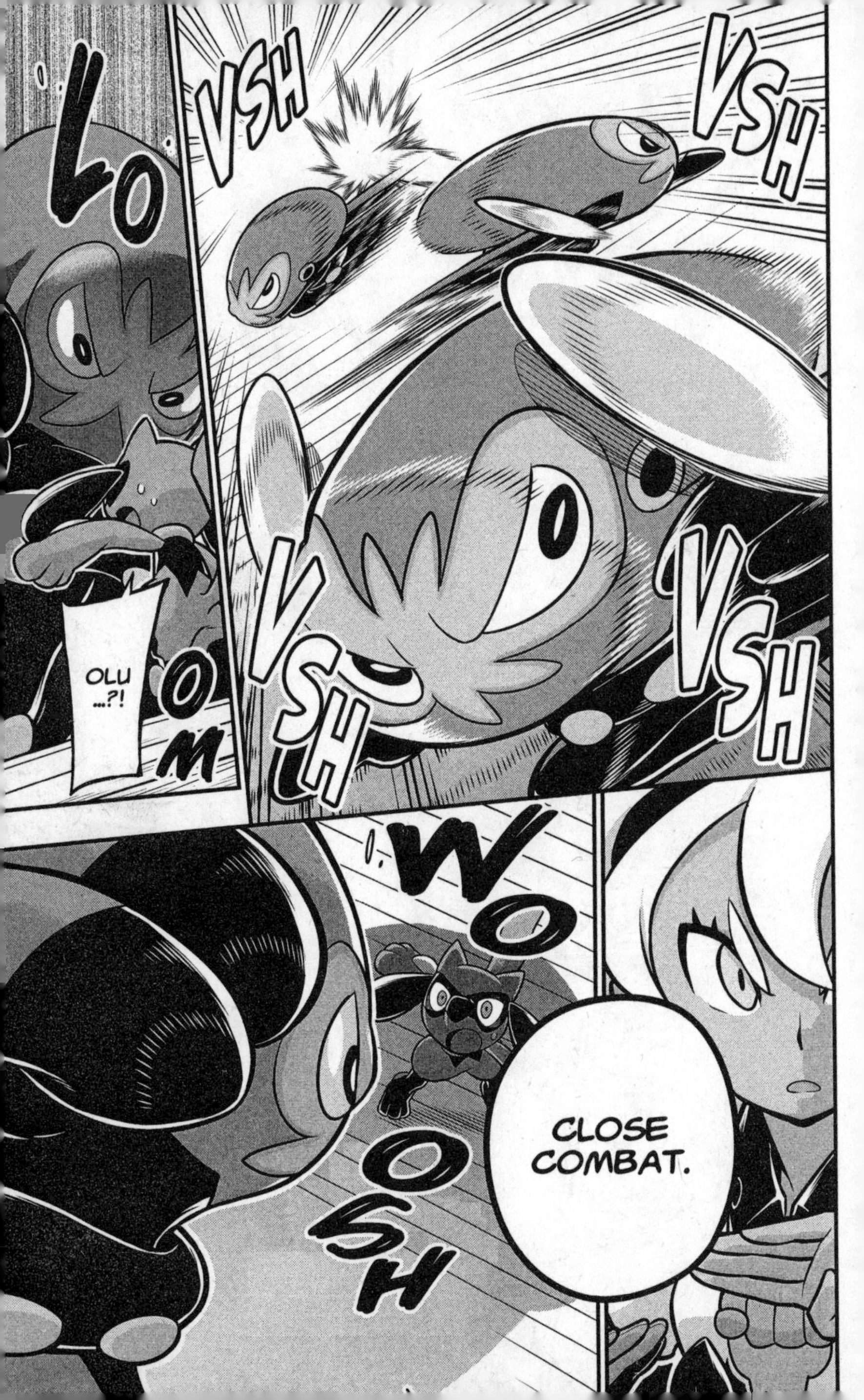
VSH
VSH
VSH
VSH
LO
OLU ...?!
OM
CLOSE COMBAT.
WOOSH

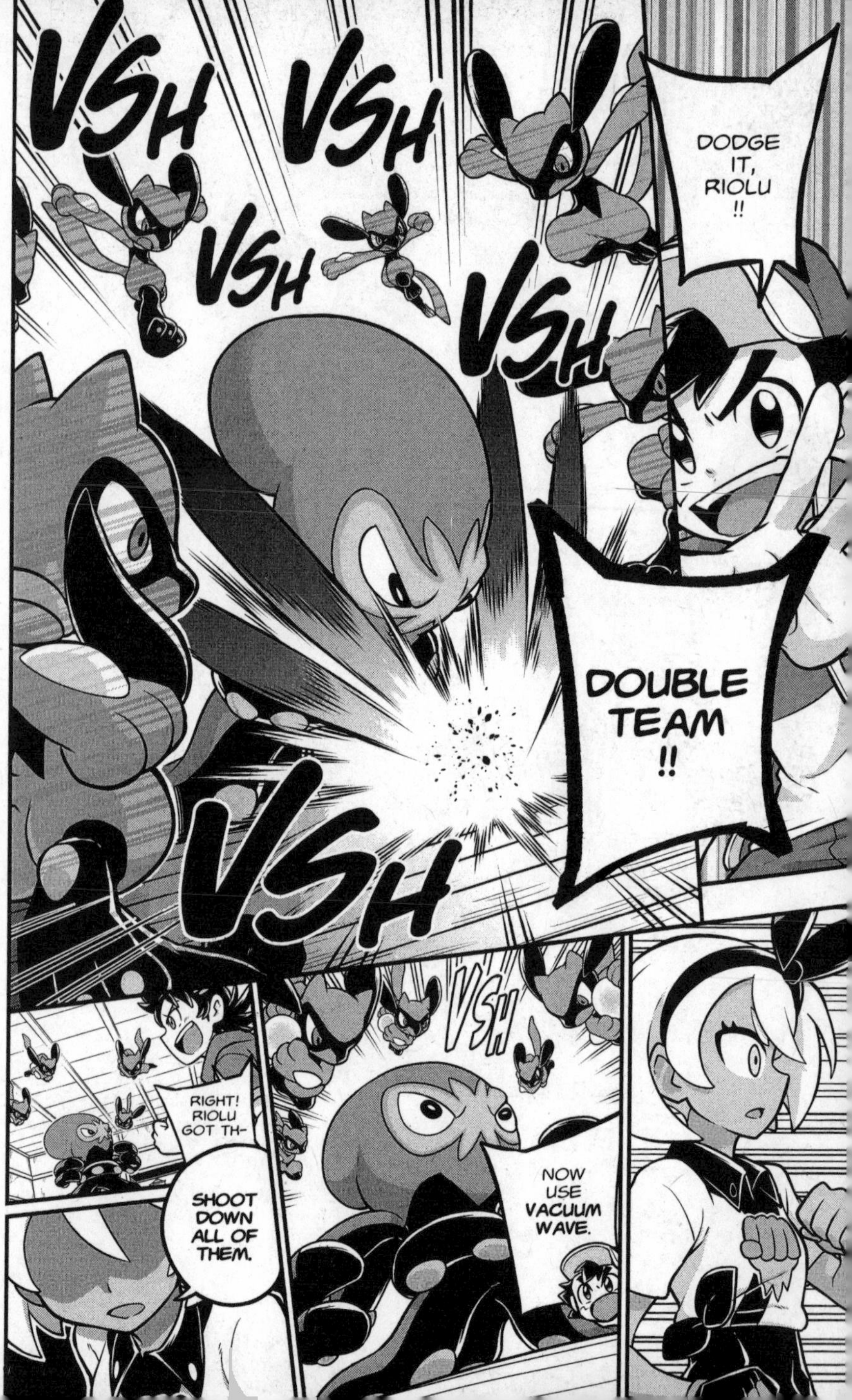
DODGE IT, RIOLU!!
VSH
VSH
VSH
VSH
DOUBLE TEAM!!
VSH
VSH
NOW USE VACUUM WAVE.
RIGHT! RIOLU GOT TH-
SHOOT DOWN ALL OF THEM.

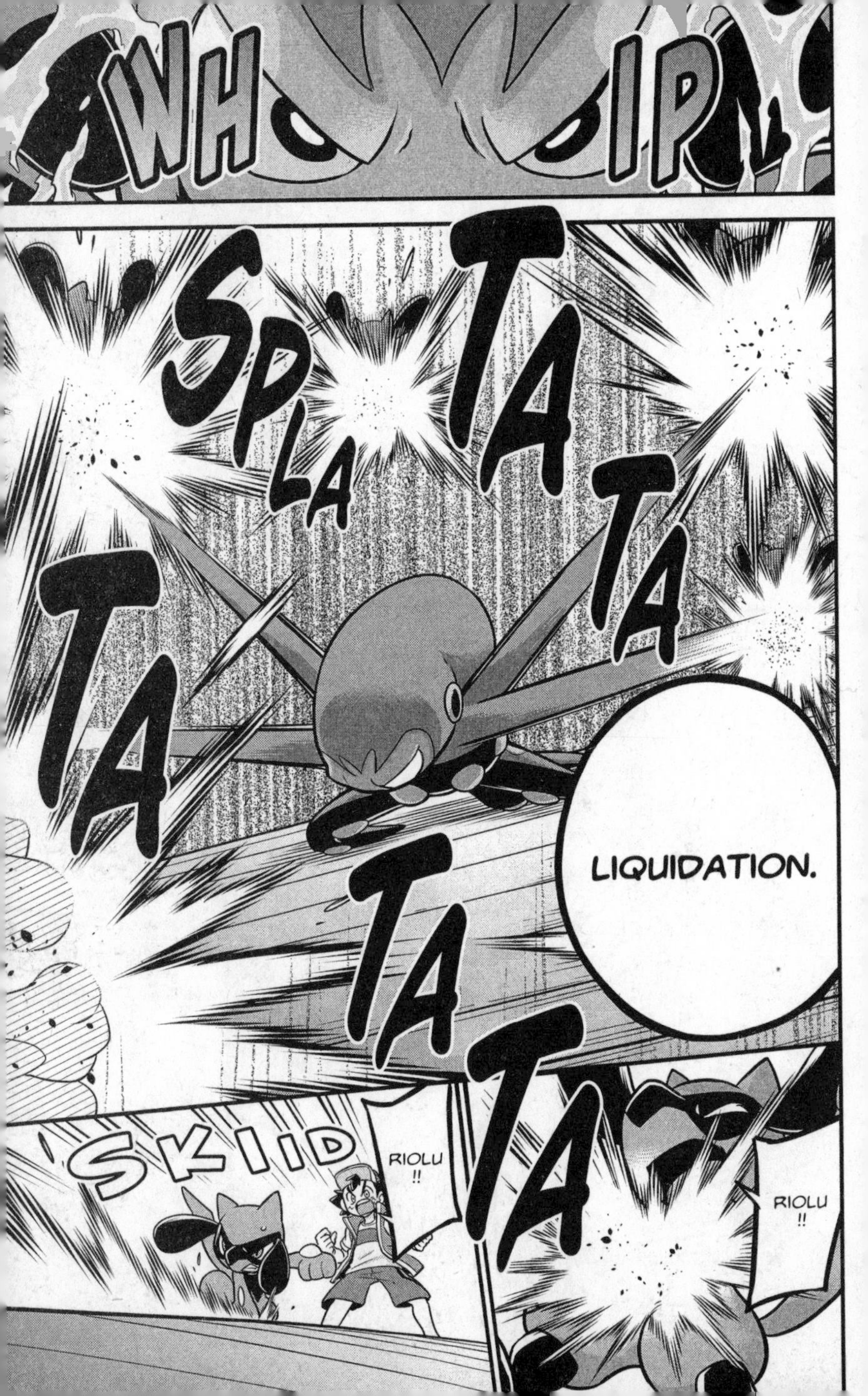
WH IP
SPLA
TA
TA
TA TA
LIQUIDATION.
TA TA TA
RIOLU!!
SKIID
RIOLU!!

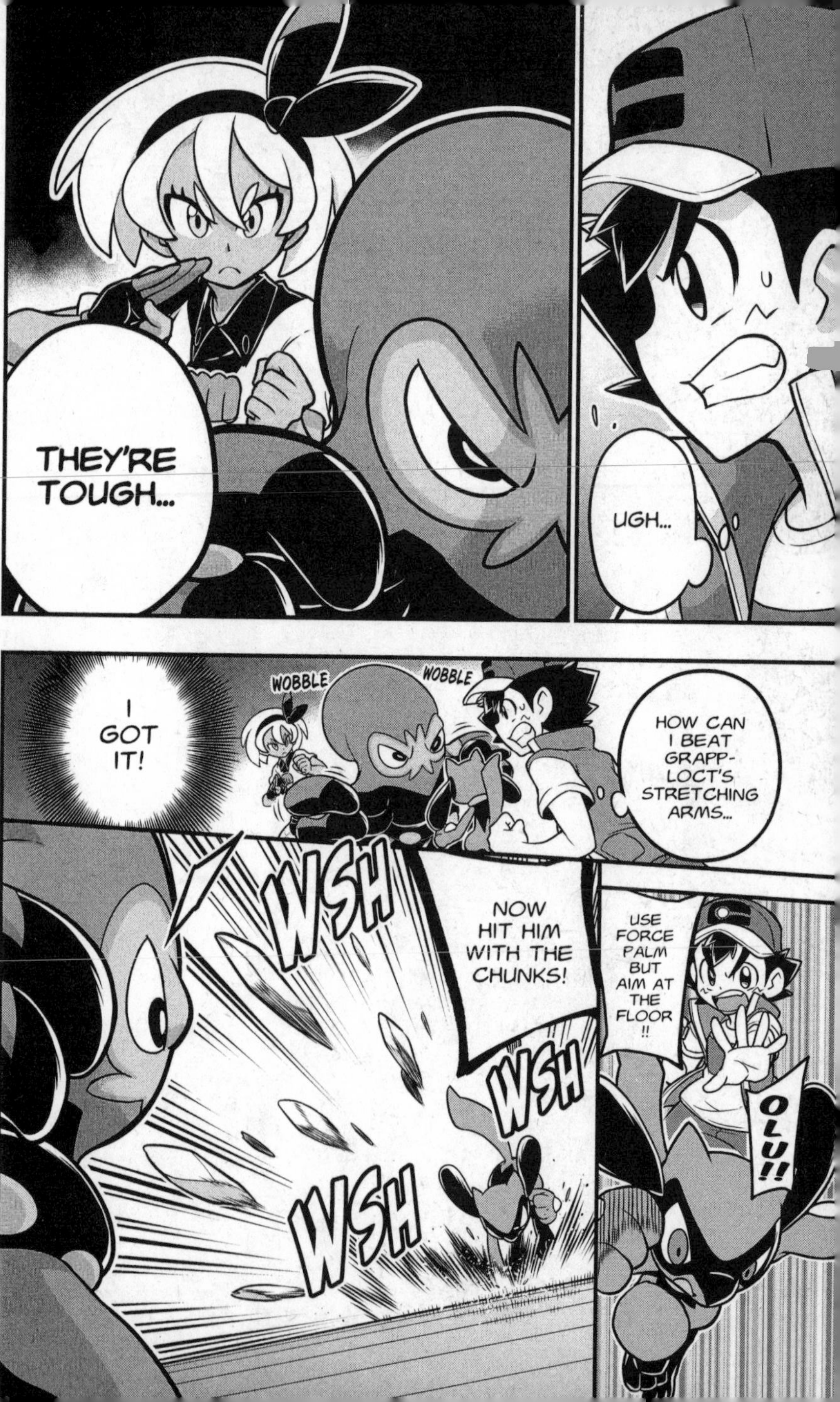
UGH...
THEY'RE TOUGH...
HOW CAN I BEAT GRAPP-LOCT'S STRETCHING ARMS...
WOBBLE
WOBBLE
I GOT IT!
USE FORCE PALM BUT AIM AT THE FLOOR !!
OLU!!
NOW HIT HIM WITH THE CHUNKS!
WSH
WSH
WSH

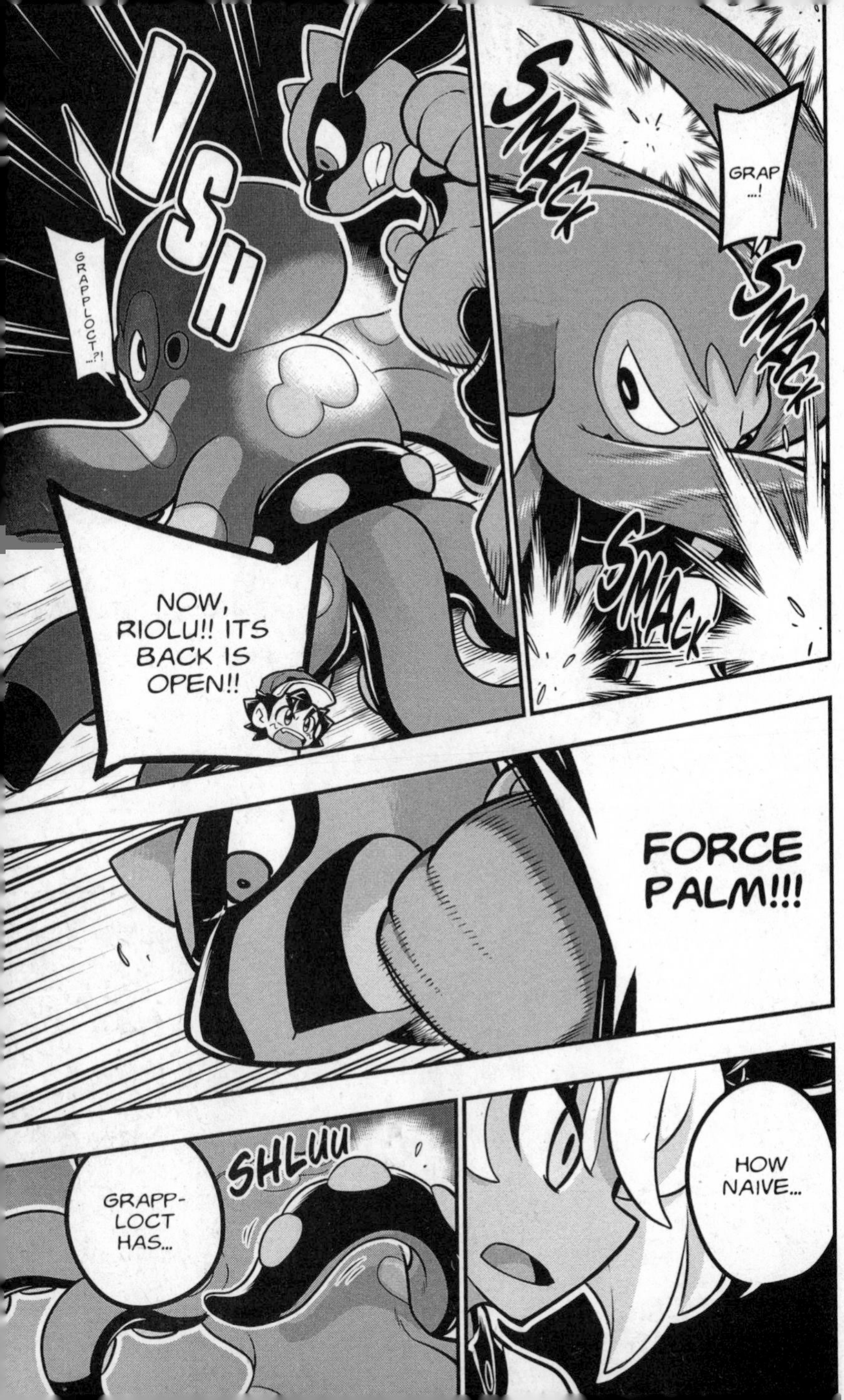
SMACK
GRAP ...!
SMACK
SMACK
VSH
GRAPPLOCT ...?!
NOW, RIOLU!! ITS BACK IS OPEN!!
FORCE PALM!!!
HOW NAIVE...
SHLUU
GRAPP-LOCT HAS...

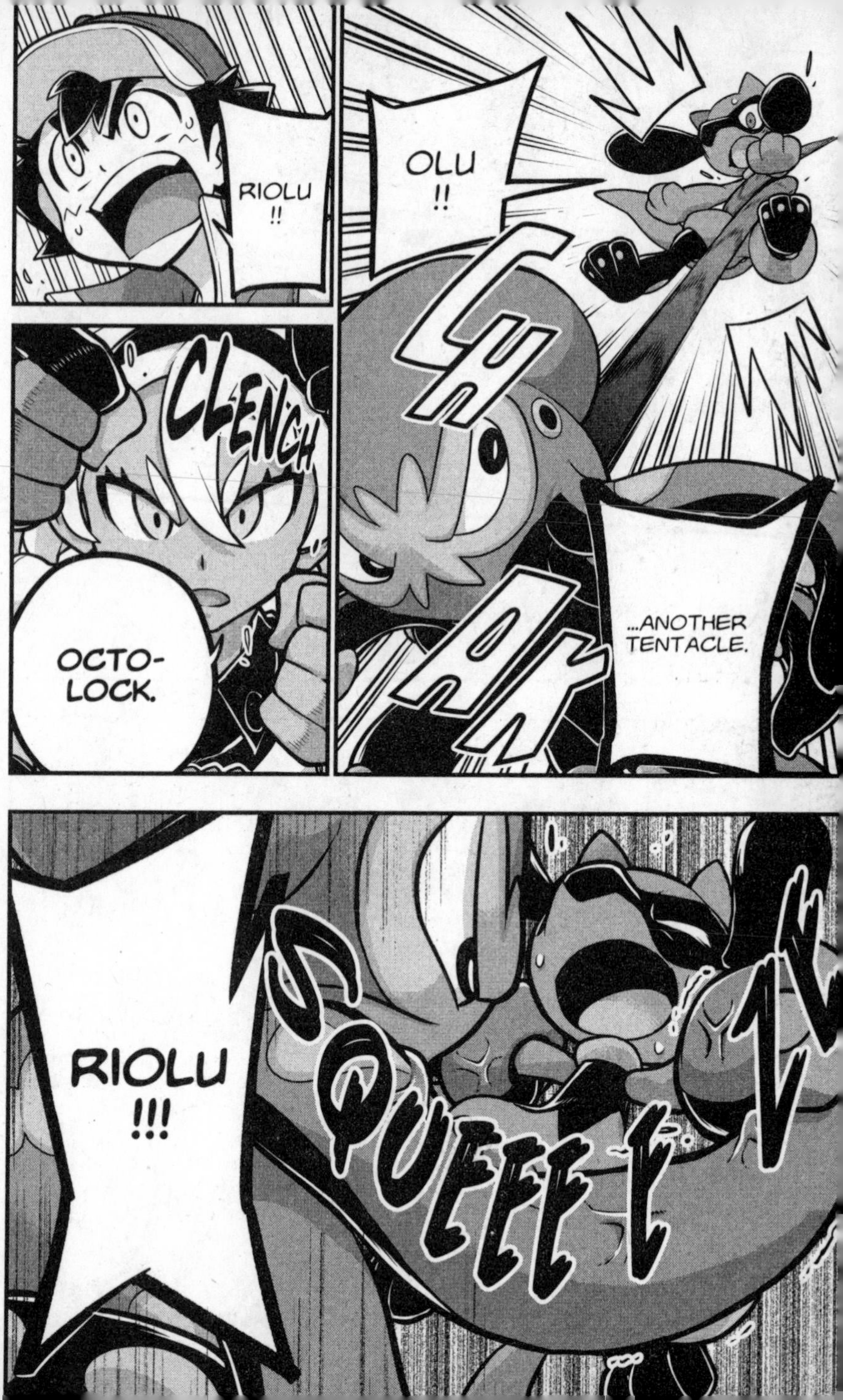
OLU !!
CHAK
...ANOTHER TENTACLE.
RIOLU !!
CLENCH
OCTO-LOCK.
SQUEEEZ
RIOLU !!!

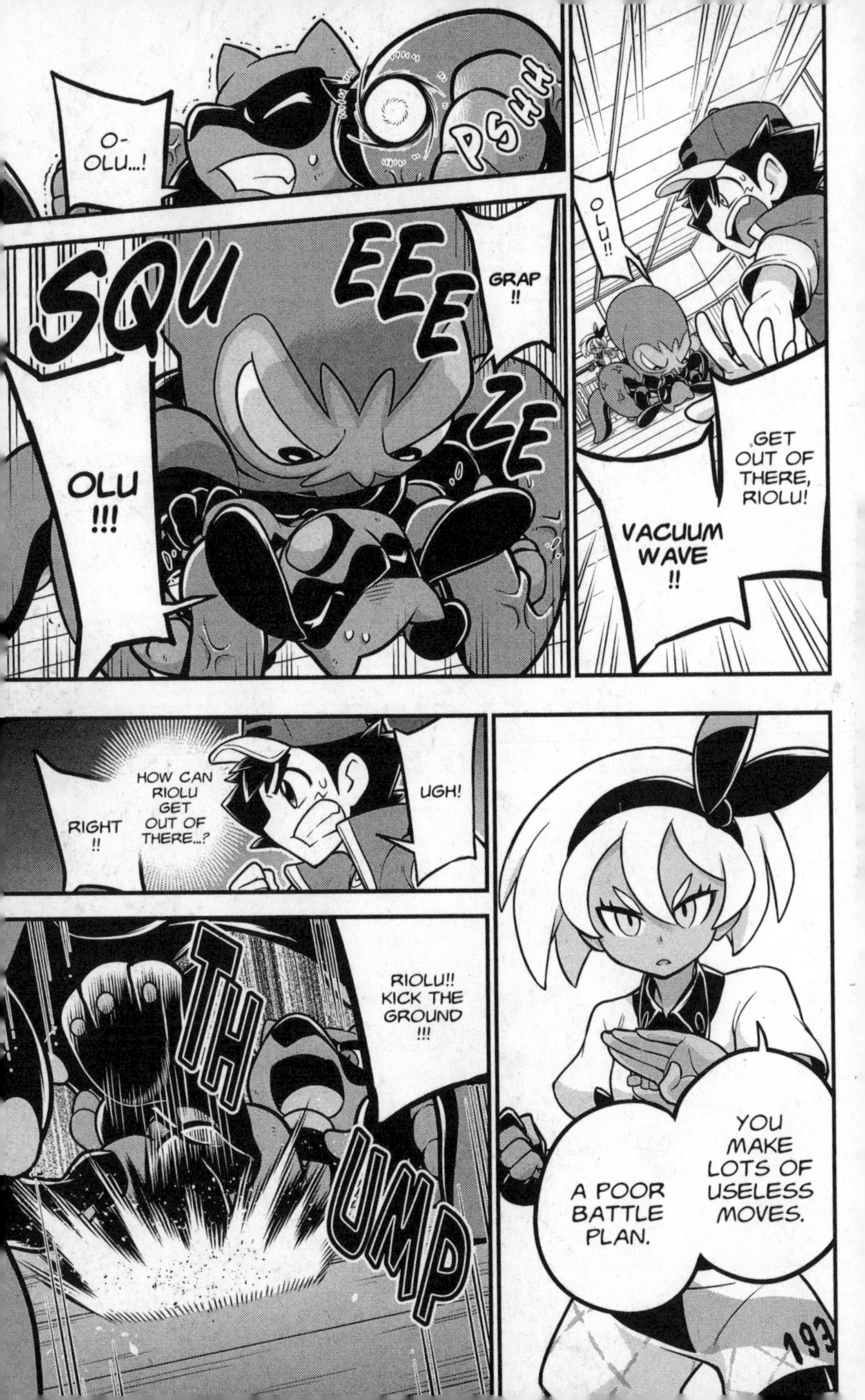
OLU!!
GET OUT OF THERE, RIOLU!
VACUUM WAVE!!
O-OLU...!
PSHH
SQUEEZE
GRAP!!
OLU!!!
YOU MAKE LOTS OF USELESS MOVES.
A POOR BATTLE PLAN.
UGH!
HOW CAN RIOLU GET OUT OF THERE...?
RIGHT!!
RIOLU!! KICK THE GROUND!!!
THUMP

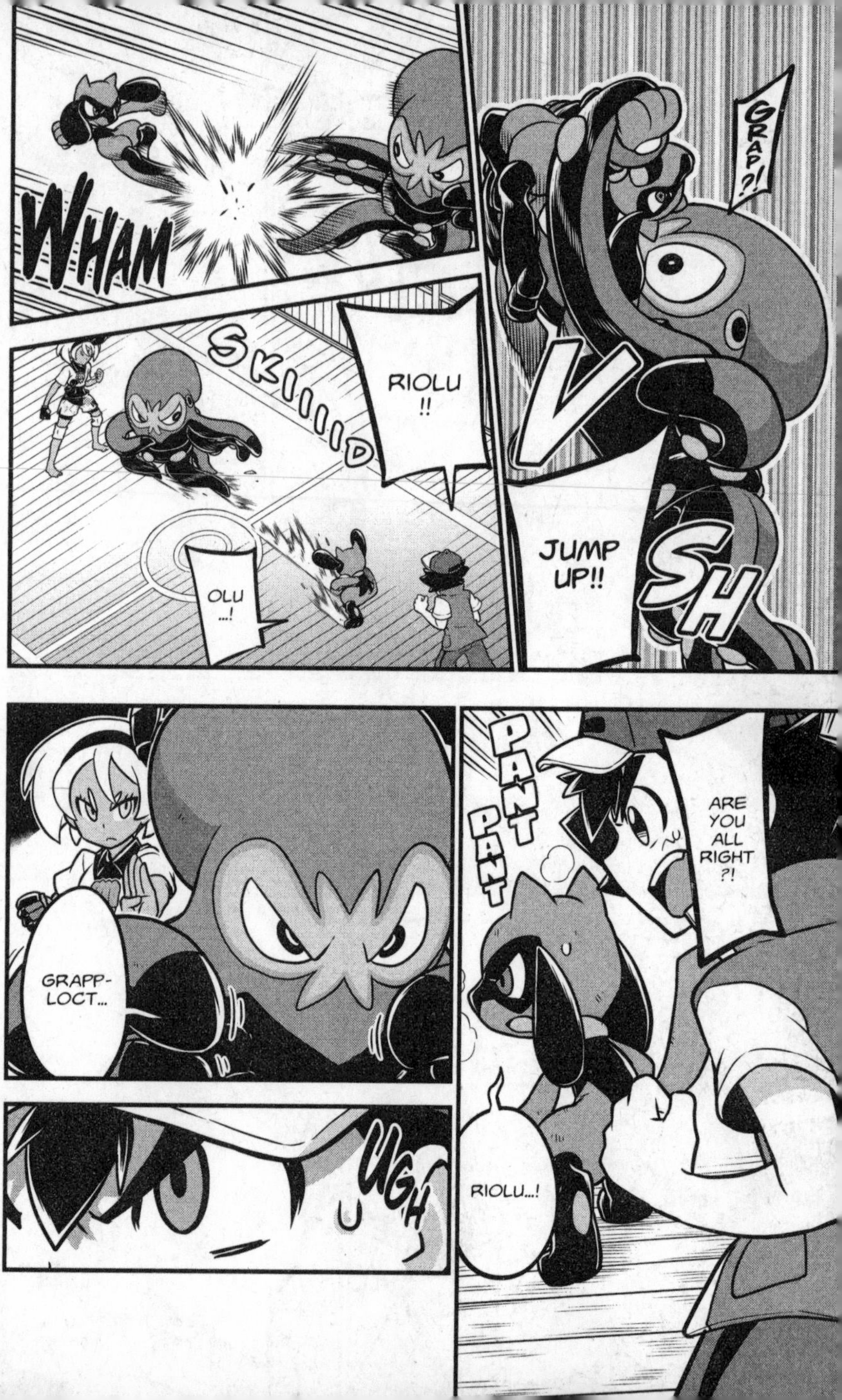
GRAP?!
V
JUMP UP!!
SH
WHAM
RIOLU !!
SKIIIIID
OLU ...!
PANT PANT PANT
ARE YOU ALL RIGHT ?!
RIOLU...!
GRAPP-LOCT...
UGH

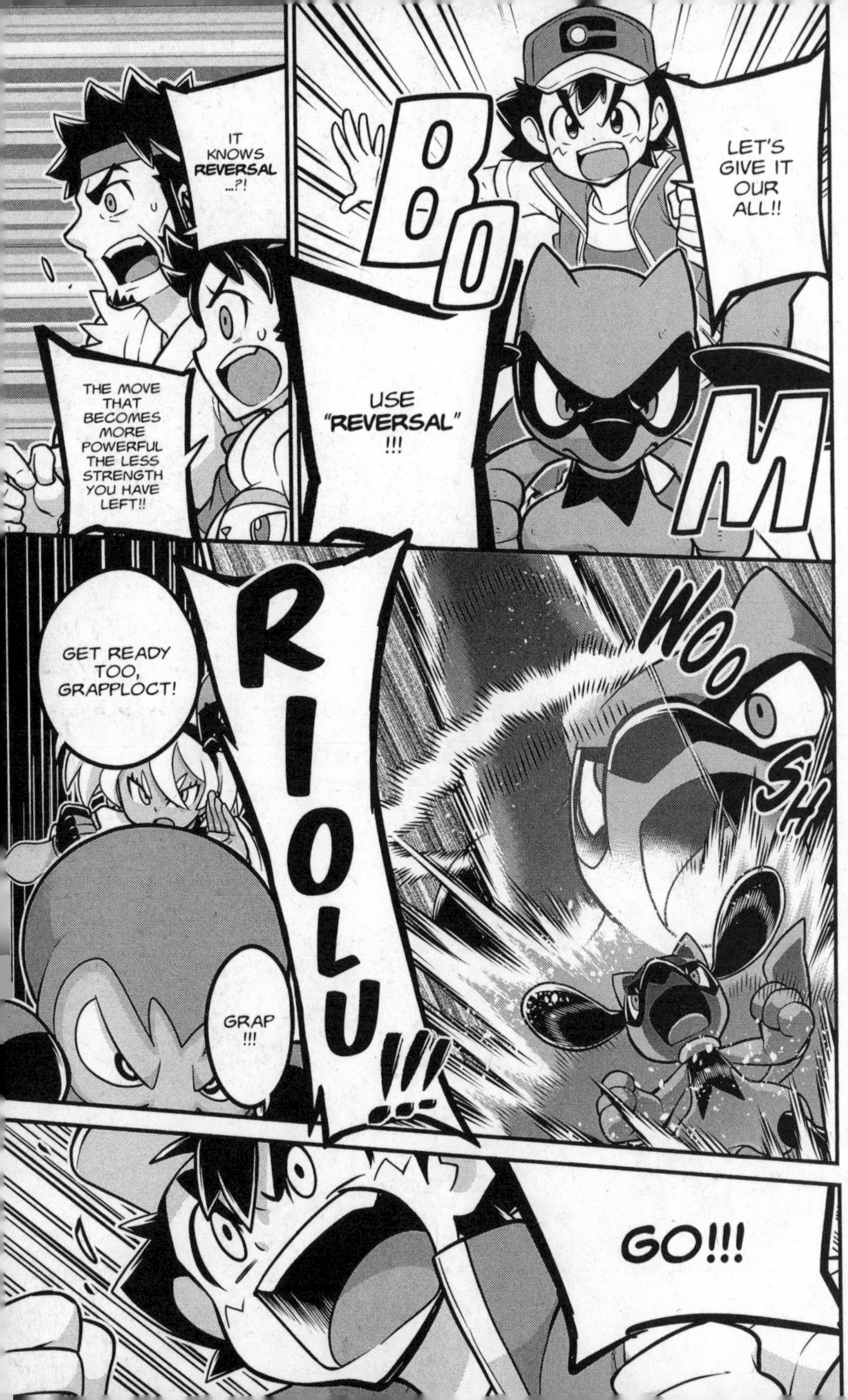
LET'S GIVE IT OUR ALL!!
BOOM
USE "REVERSAL"!!!
IT KNOWS REVERSAL ...?!
THE MOVE THAT BECOMES MORE POWERFUL THE LESS STRENGTH YOU HAVE LEFT!!
WOOSH
RIOLU!!!
GET READY TOO, GRAPPLOCT!
GRAP!!!
GO!!!

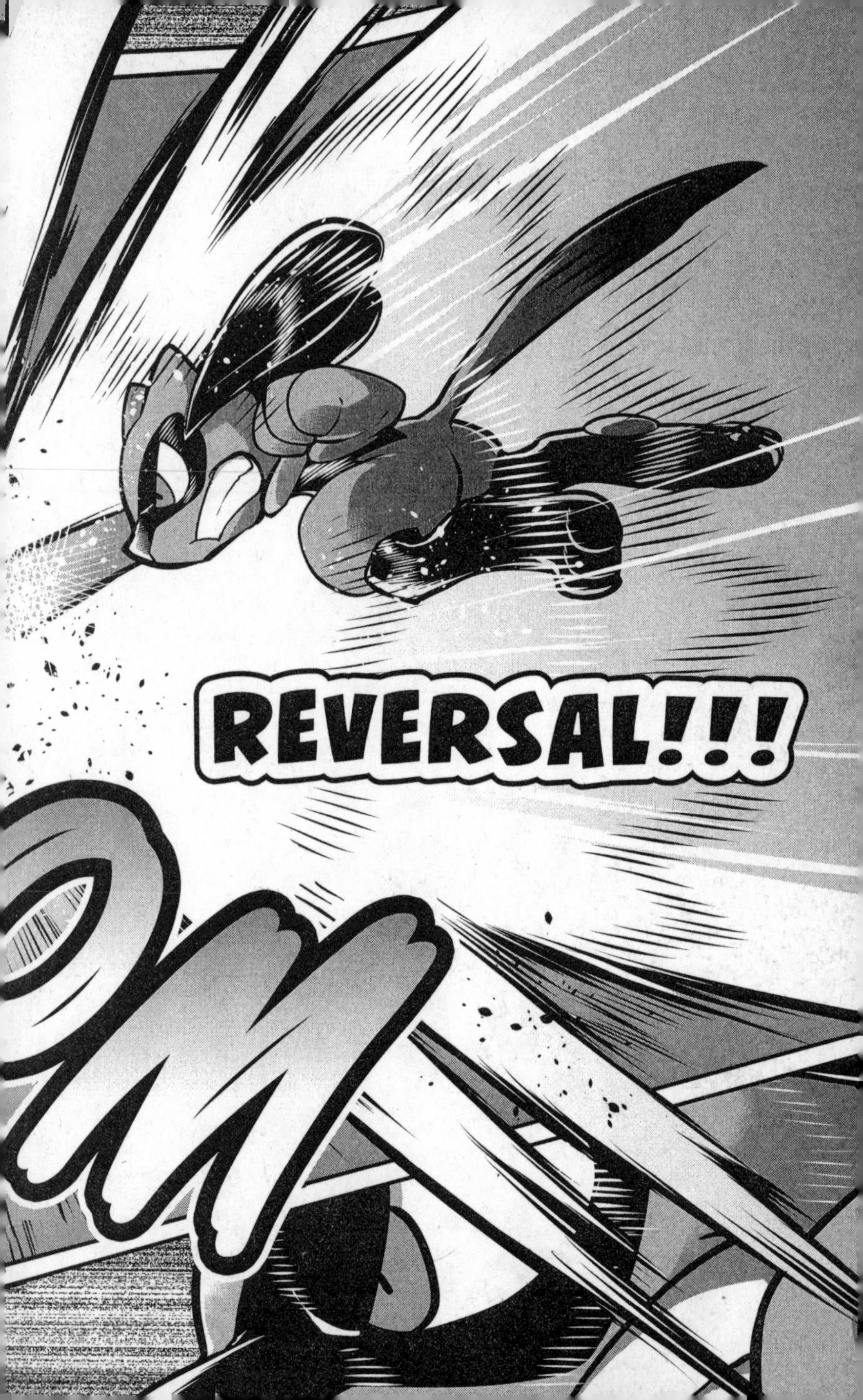
REVERSAL!!!

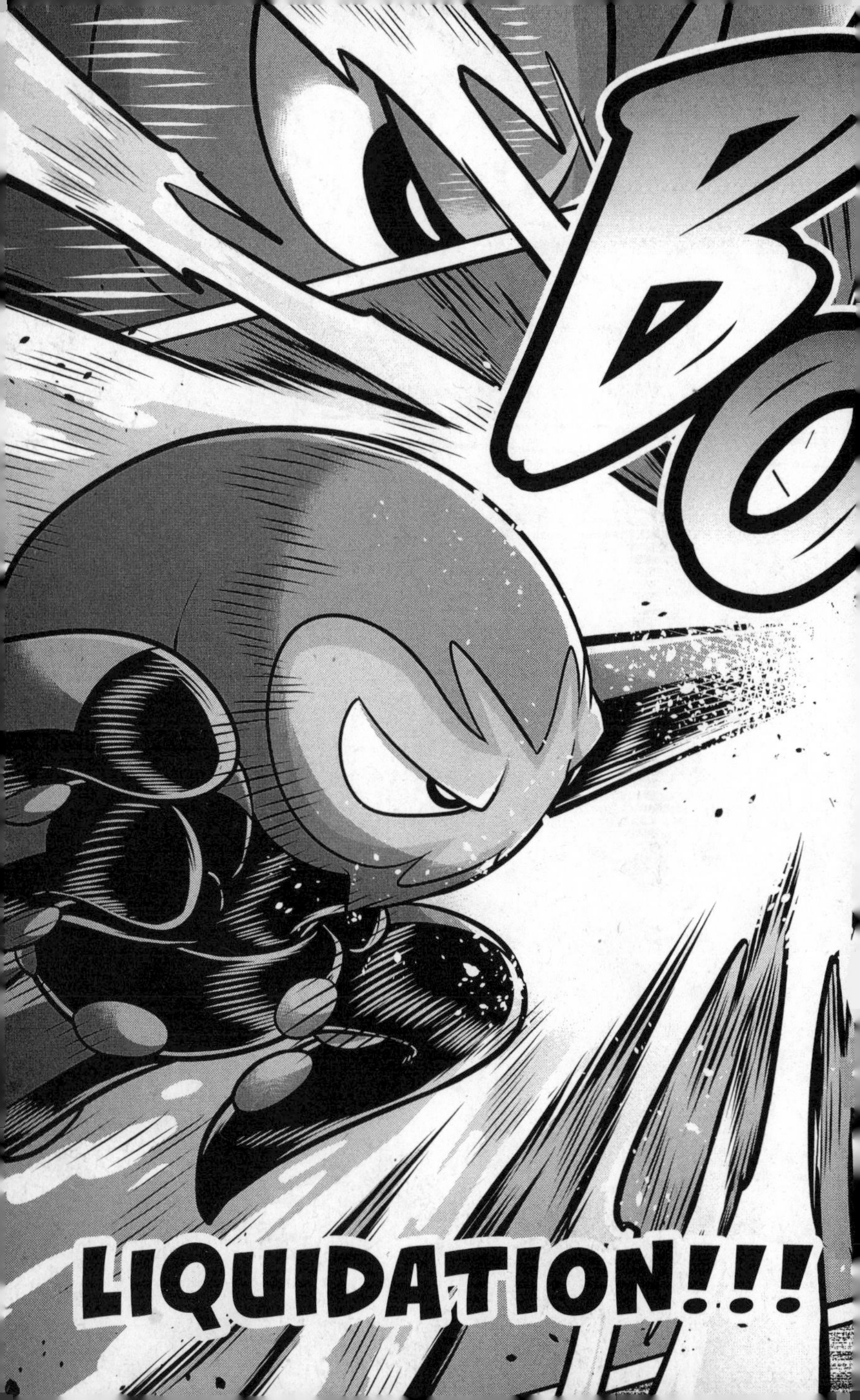
LIQUIDATION!!!

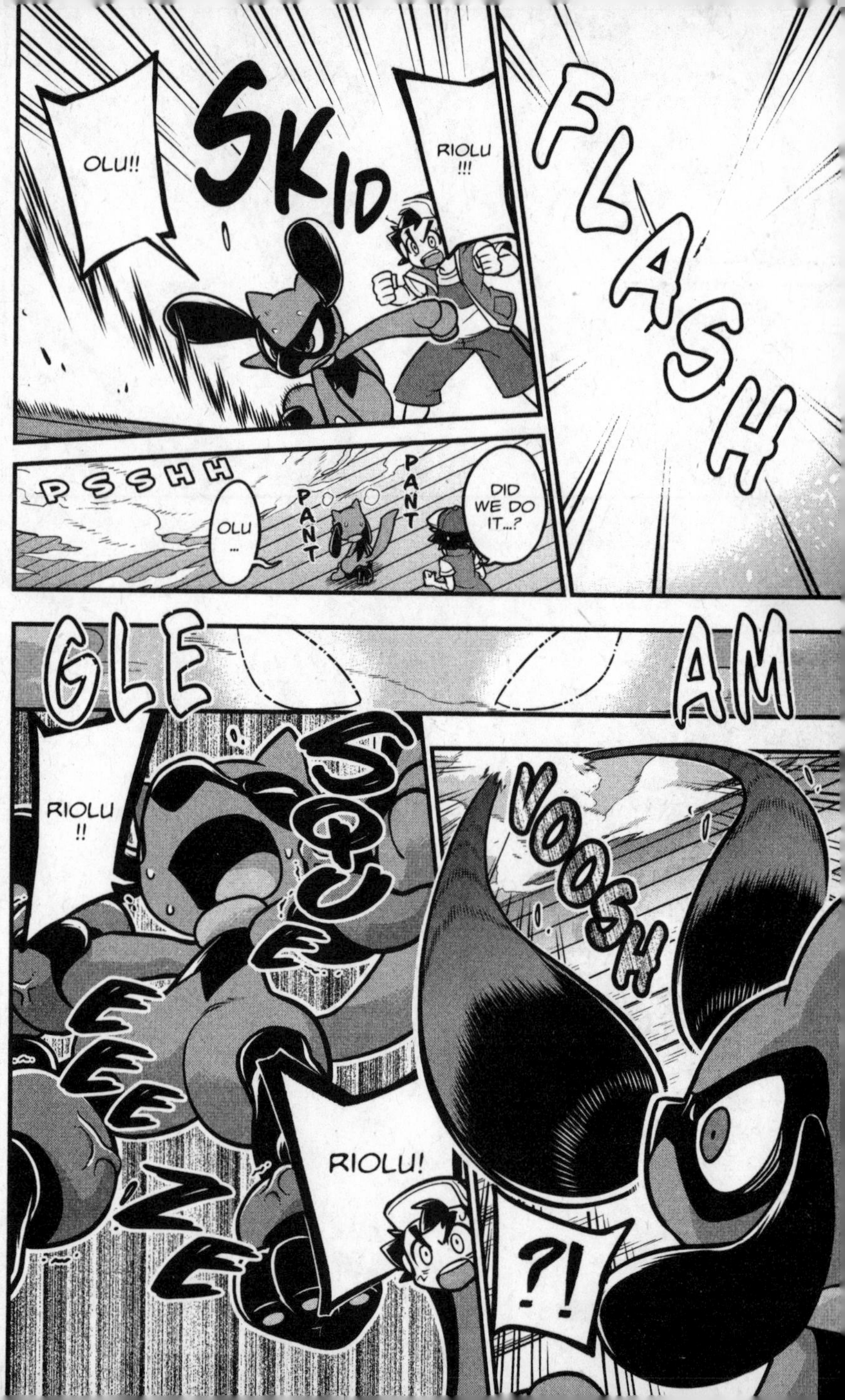
FLASH
RIOLU !!!
SKID
OLU!!
DID WE DO IT...?
PANT PANT
OLU ...
PSSHH
GLEAM
WOOSH
?!
RIOLU!
RIOLU !!
SQUEEEEZE

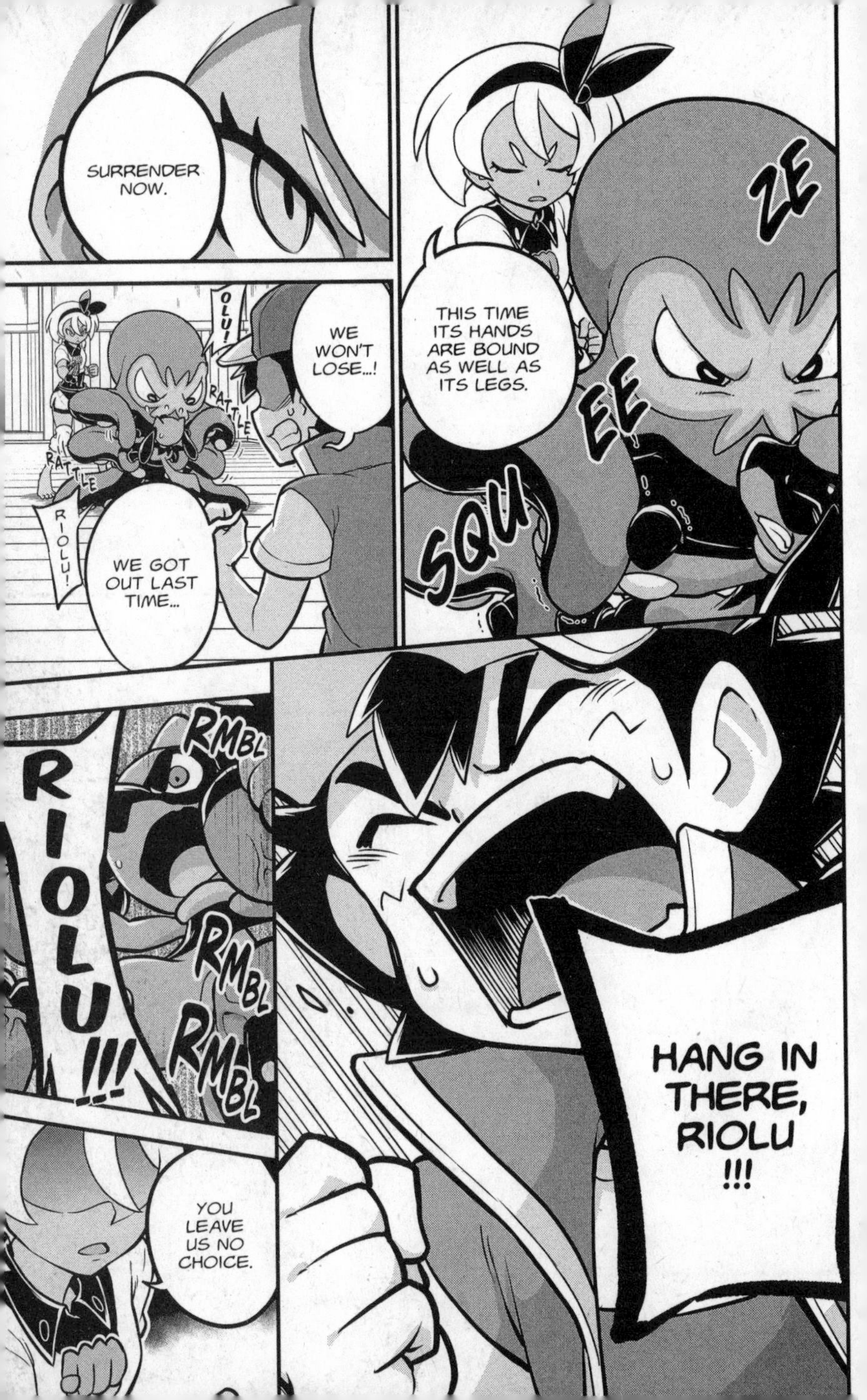
THIS TIME ITS HANDS ARE BOUND AS WELL AS ITS LEGS.
SQUEEZE
SURRENDER NOW.
WE WON'T LOSE...!
OLU!
RATTLE
RATTLE
RIOLU!
WE GOT OUT LAST TIME...
HANG IN THERE, RIOLU!!!
RMBL
RIOLU...!!!
RMBL
RMBL
YOU LEAVE US NO CHOICE.

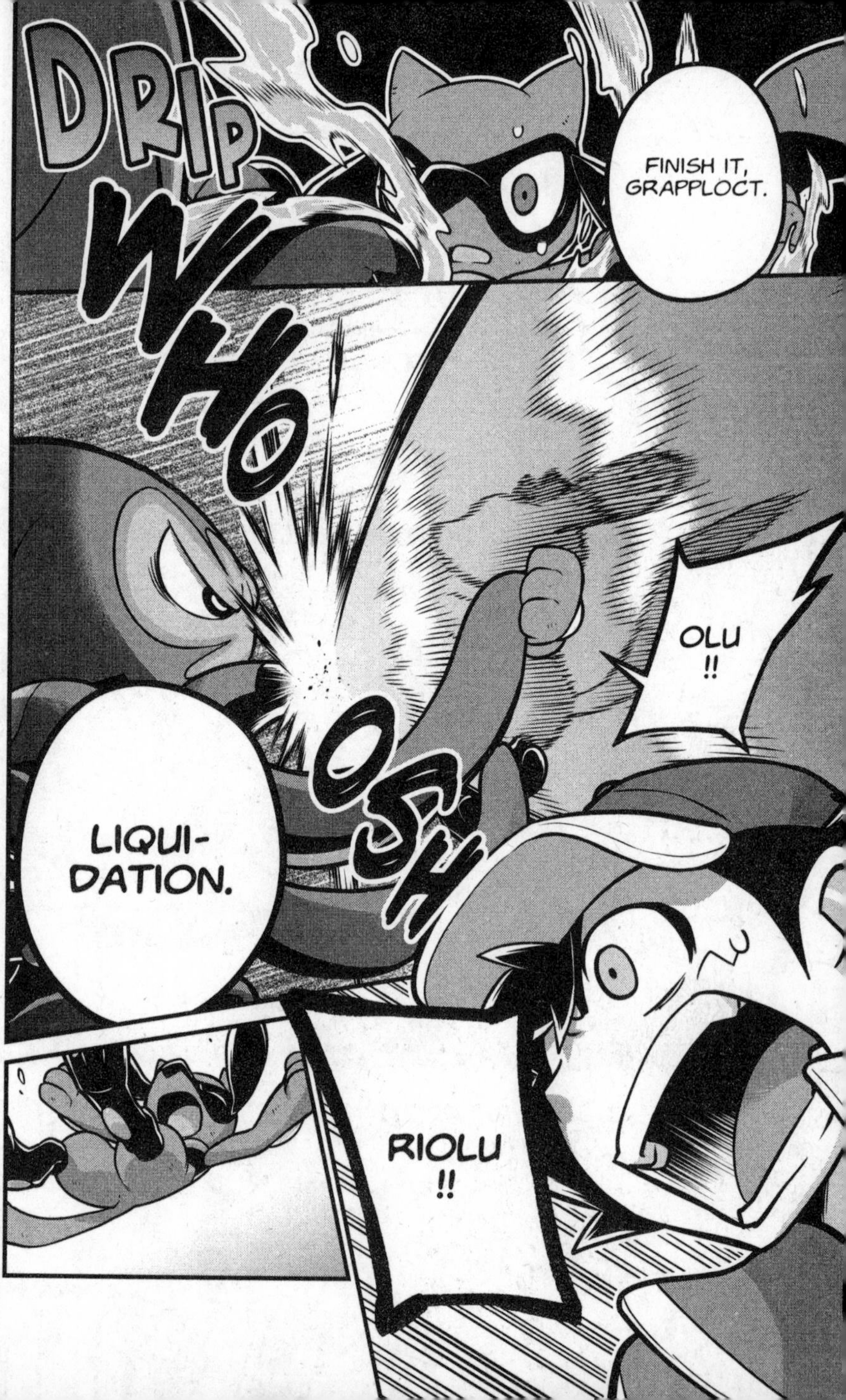
FINISH IT, GRAPPLOCT.
DRIP
OLU !!
WHOOSH
LIQUI-DATION.
RIOLU !!

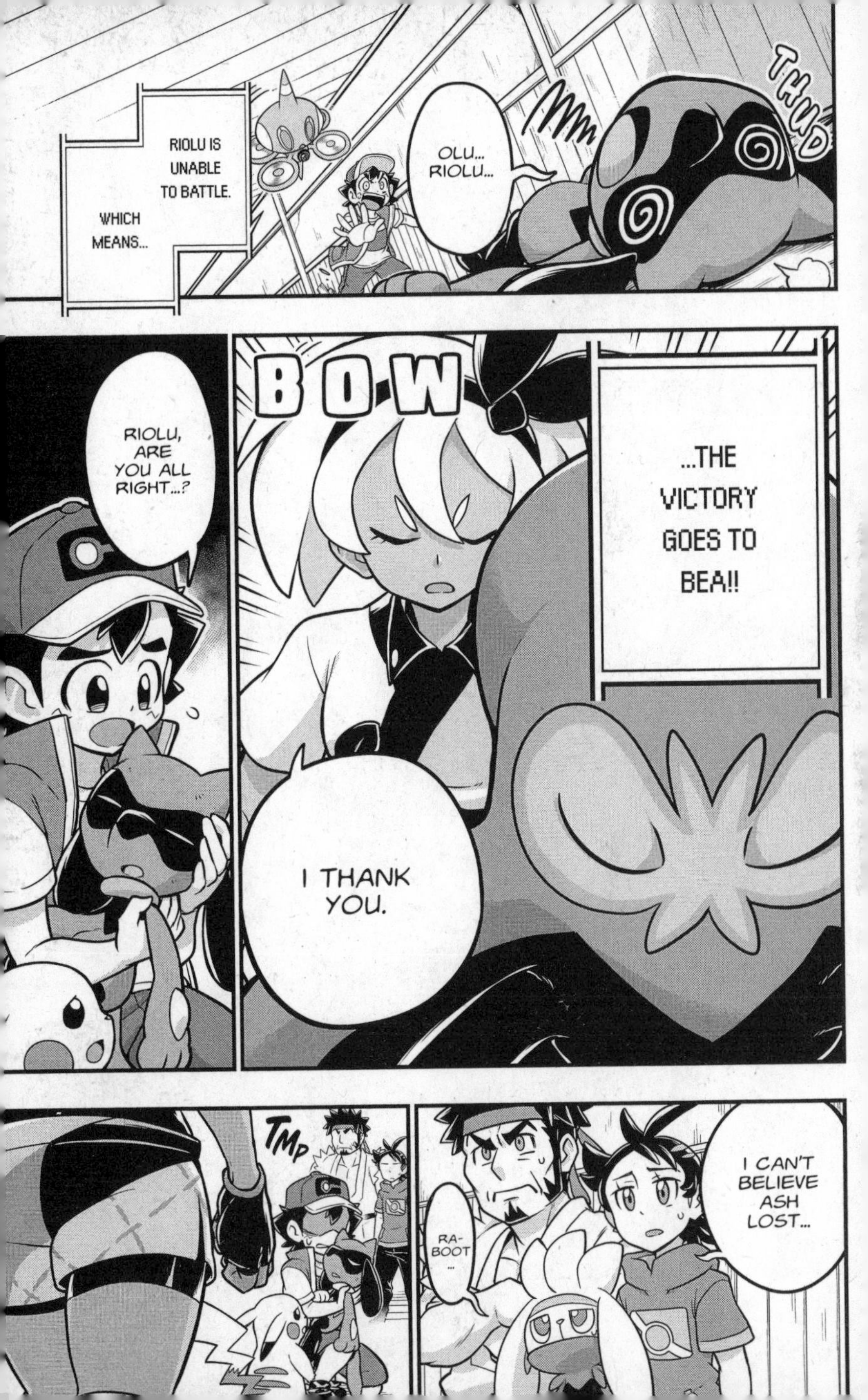
THUD
OLU... RIOLU...
RIOLU IS UNABLE TO BATTLE.
WHICH MEANS...
...THE VICTORY GOES TO BEA!!
BOW
I THANK YOU.
RIOLU, ARE YOU ALL RIGHT...?
I CAN'T BELIEVE ASH LOST...
RA-BOOT...
TMP

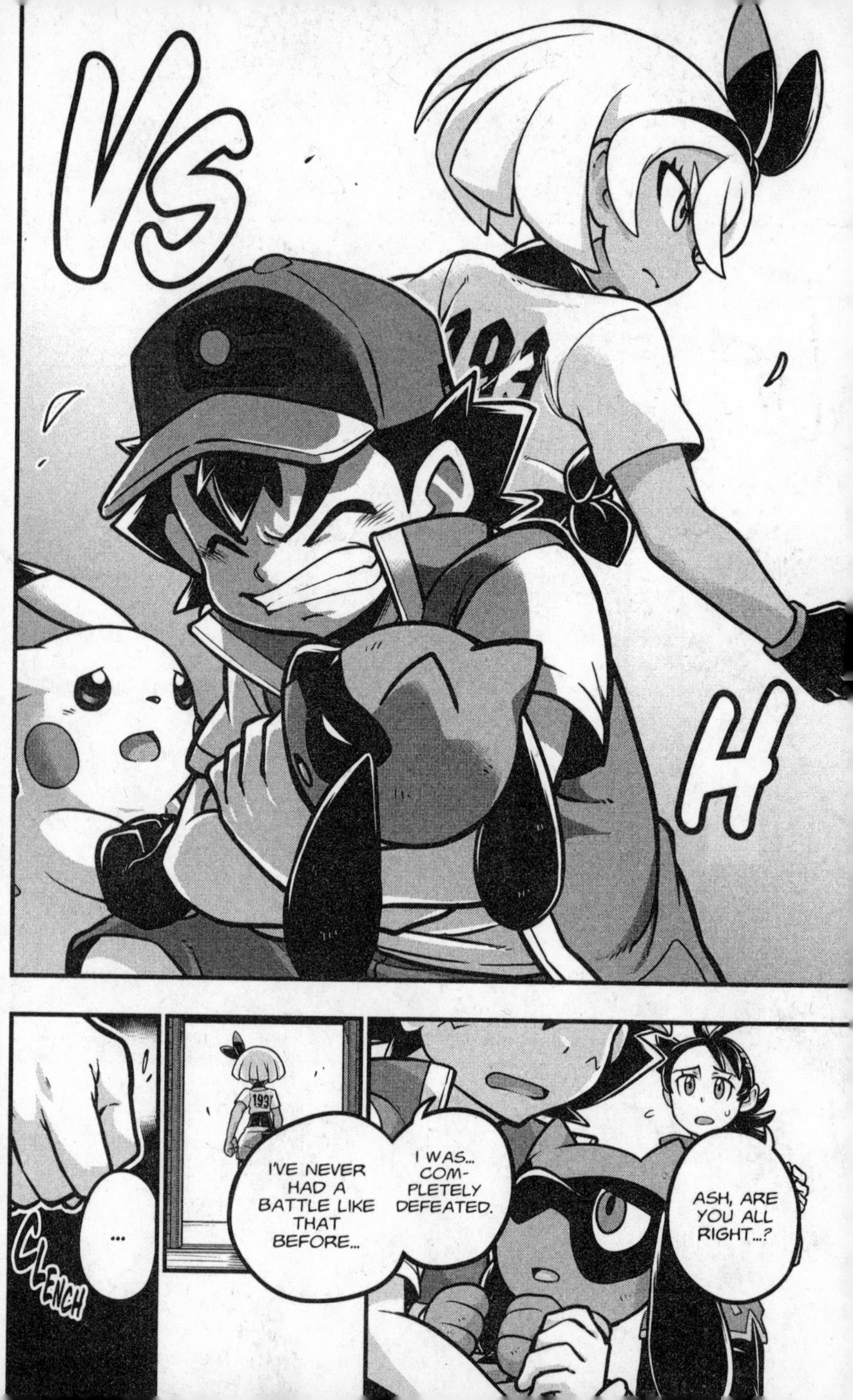
VS
H
ASH, ARE YOU ALL RIGHT...?
I WAS... COM-PLETELY DEFEATED.
I'VE NEVER HAD A BATTLE LIKE THAT BEFORE...
...
CLENCH

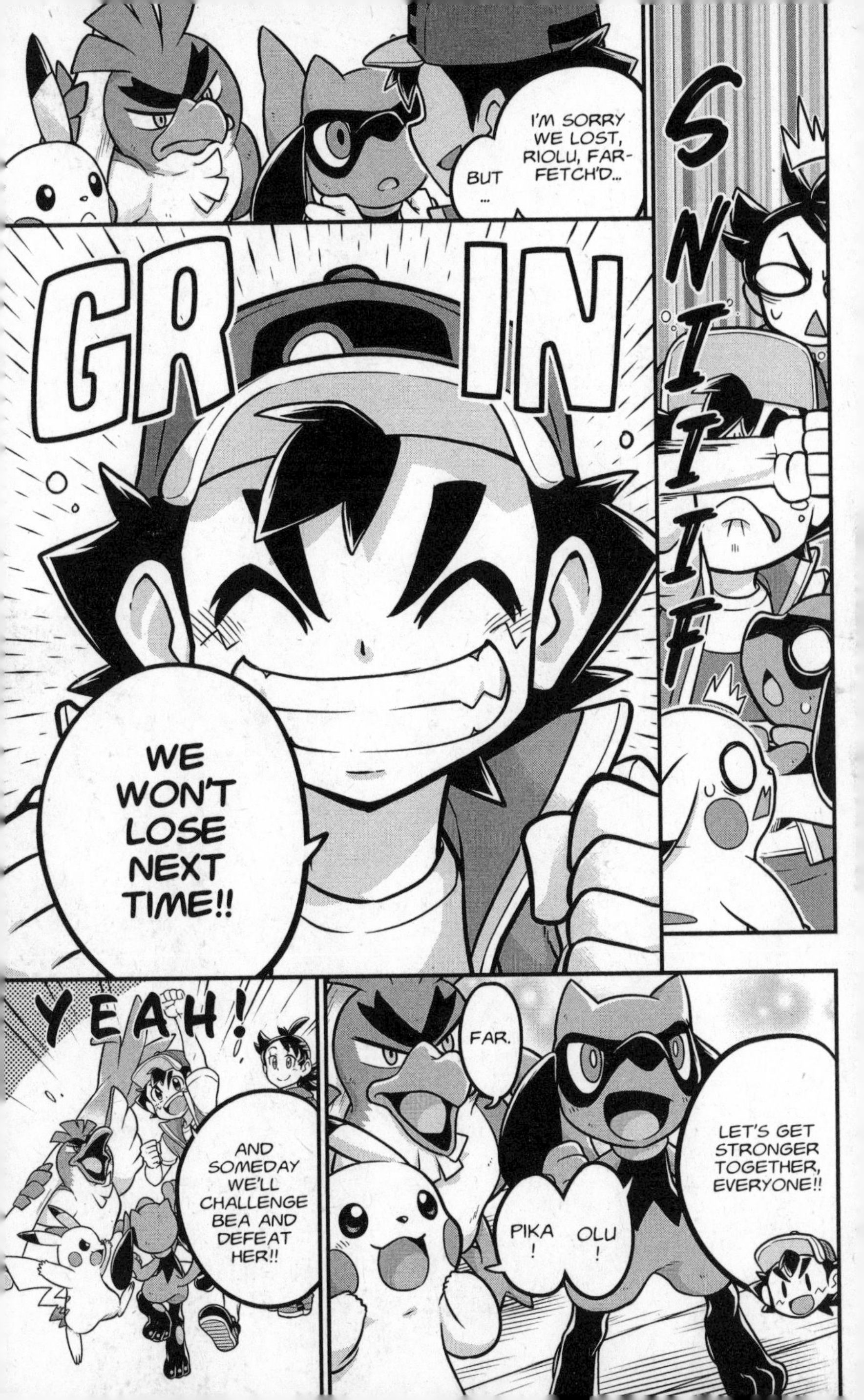
SNIIIFF
I'M SORRY WE LOST, RIOLU, FAR-FETCH'D...
BUT...
GRIN
WE WON'T LOSE NEXT TIME!!
LET'S GET STRONGER TOGETHER, EVERYONE!!
FAR.
OLU!
PIKA!
AND SOMEDAY WE'LL CHALLENGE BEA AND DEFEAT HER!!
YEAH!

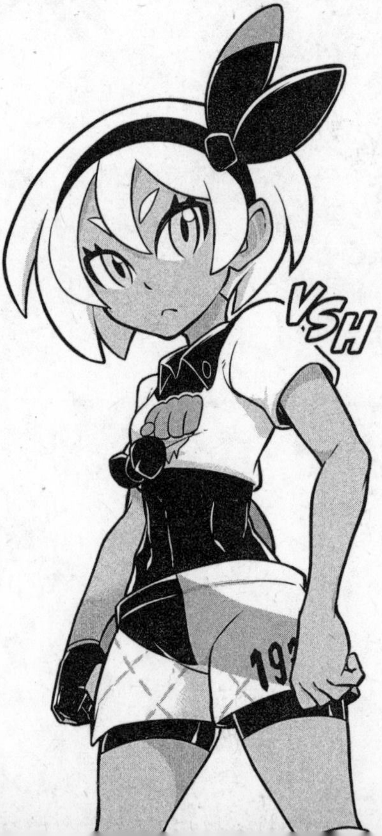
VSH

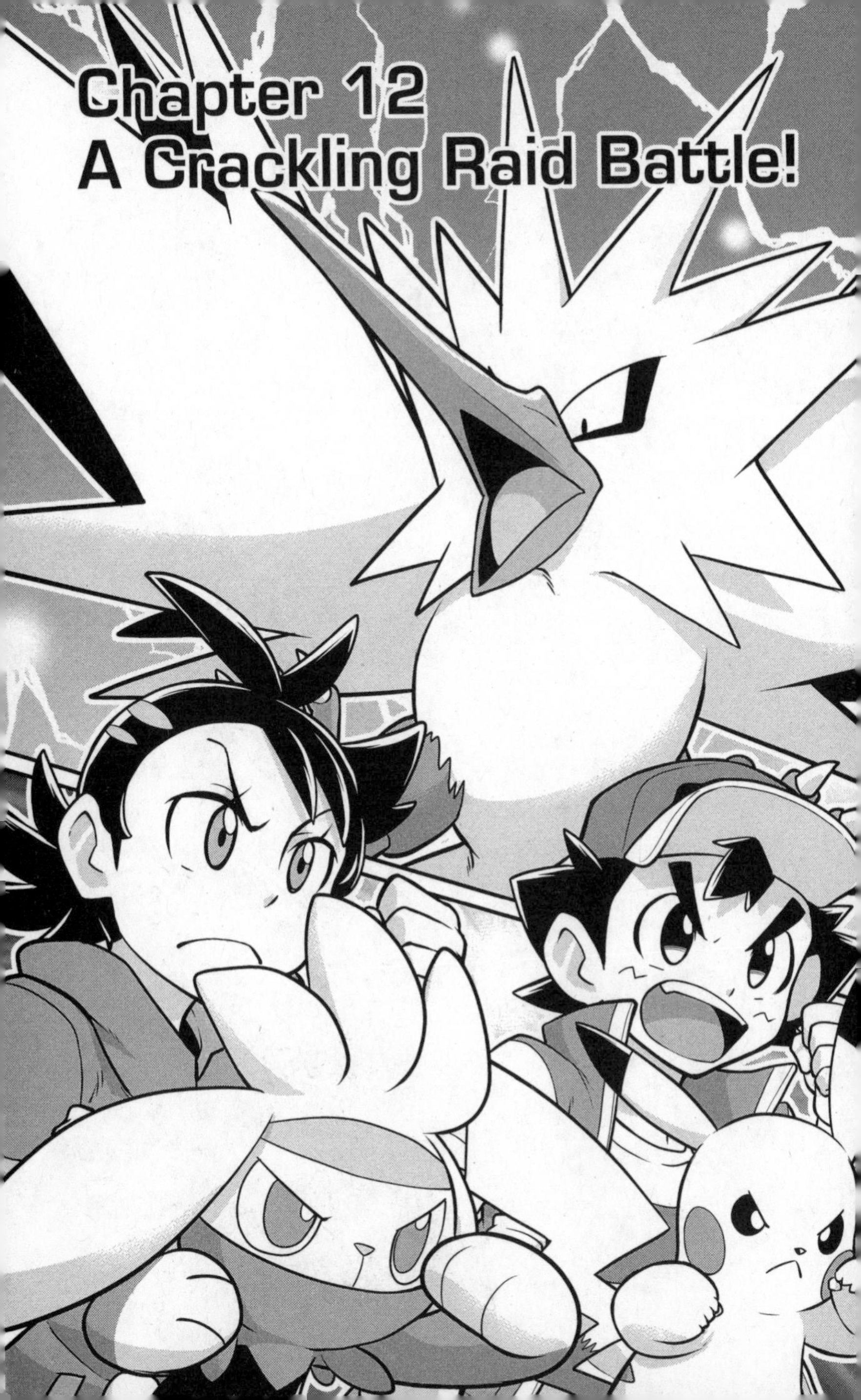
Chapter 12
A Crackling Raid Battle!

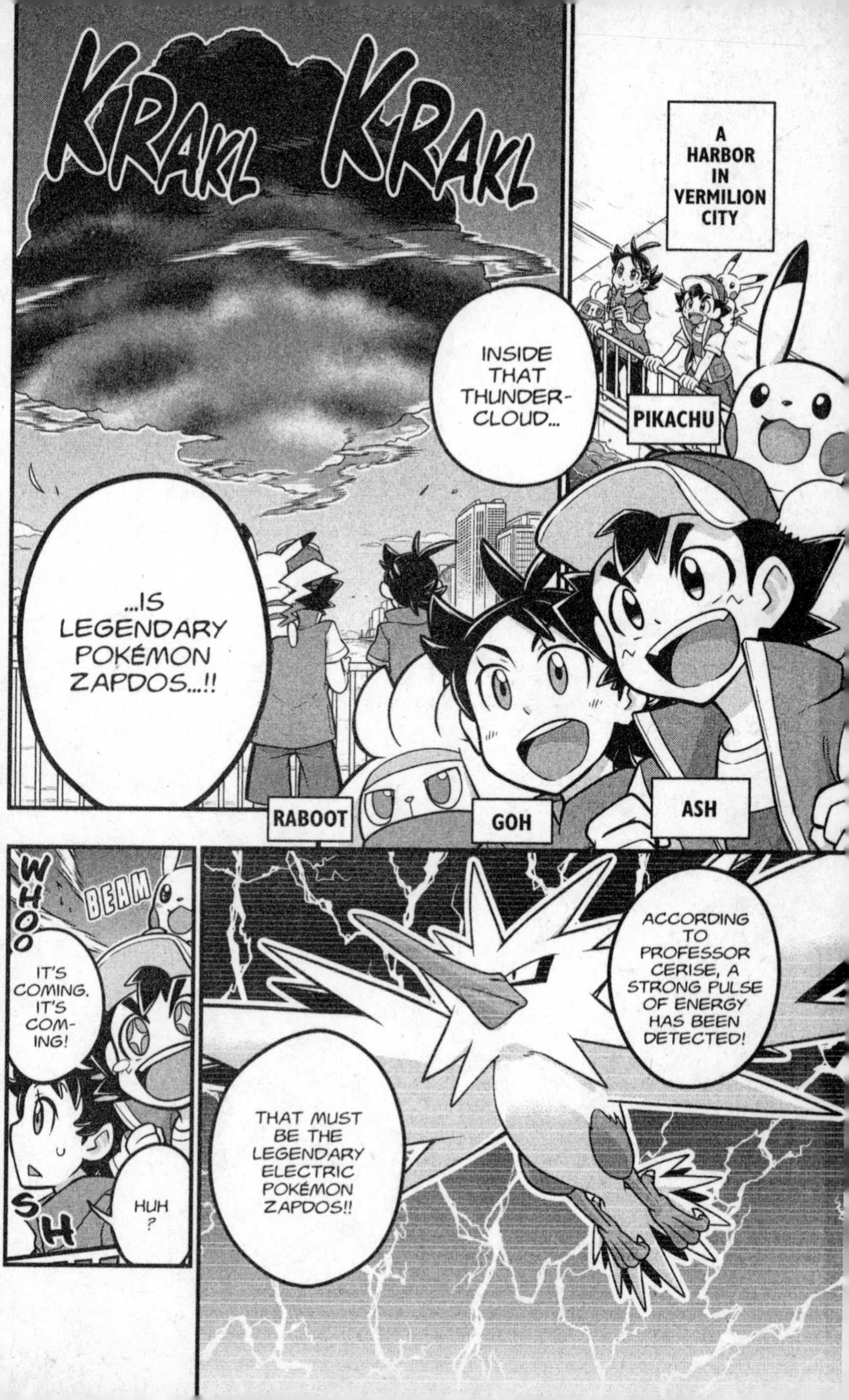
KRAKL KRAKL
A HARBOR IN VERMILION CITY
INSIDE THAT THUNDER-CLOUD...
PIKACHU
...IS LEGENDARY POKÉMON ZAPDOS...!!
ASH
GOH
RABOOT
ACCORDING TO PROFESSOR CERISE, A STRONG PULSE OF ENERGY HAS BEEN DETECTED!
THAT MUST BE THE LEGENDARY ELECTRIC POKÉMON ZAPDOS!!
WHOOO
BEAM
IT'S COMING. IT'S COM-ING!
SH
HUH?

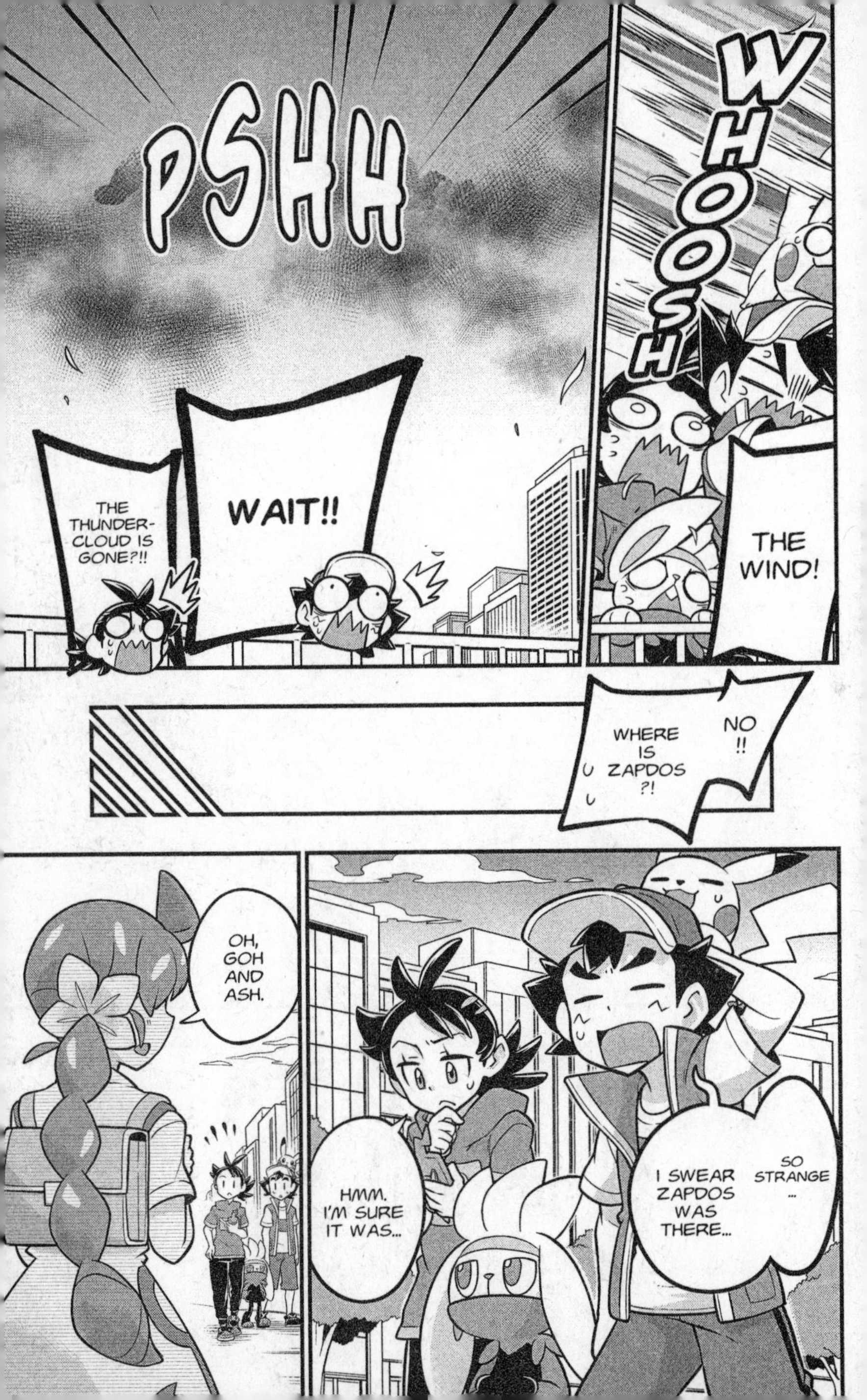
WHOOOSH
THE WIND!
PSHH
WAIT!!
THE THUNDER-CLOUD IS GONE?!!
NO!!
WHERE IS ZAPDOS?!
SO STRANGE...
I SWEAR ZAPDOS WAS THERE...
HMM. I'M SURE IT WAS...
OH, GOH AND ASH.

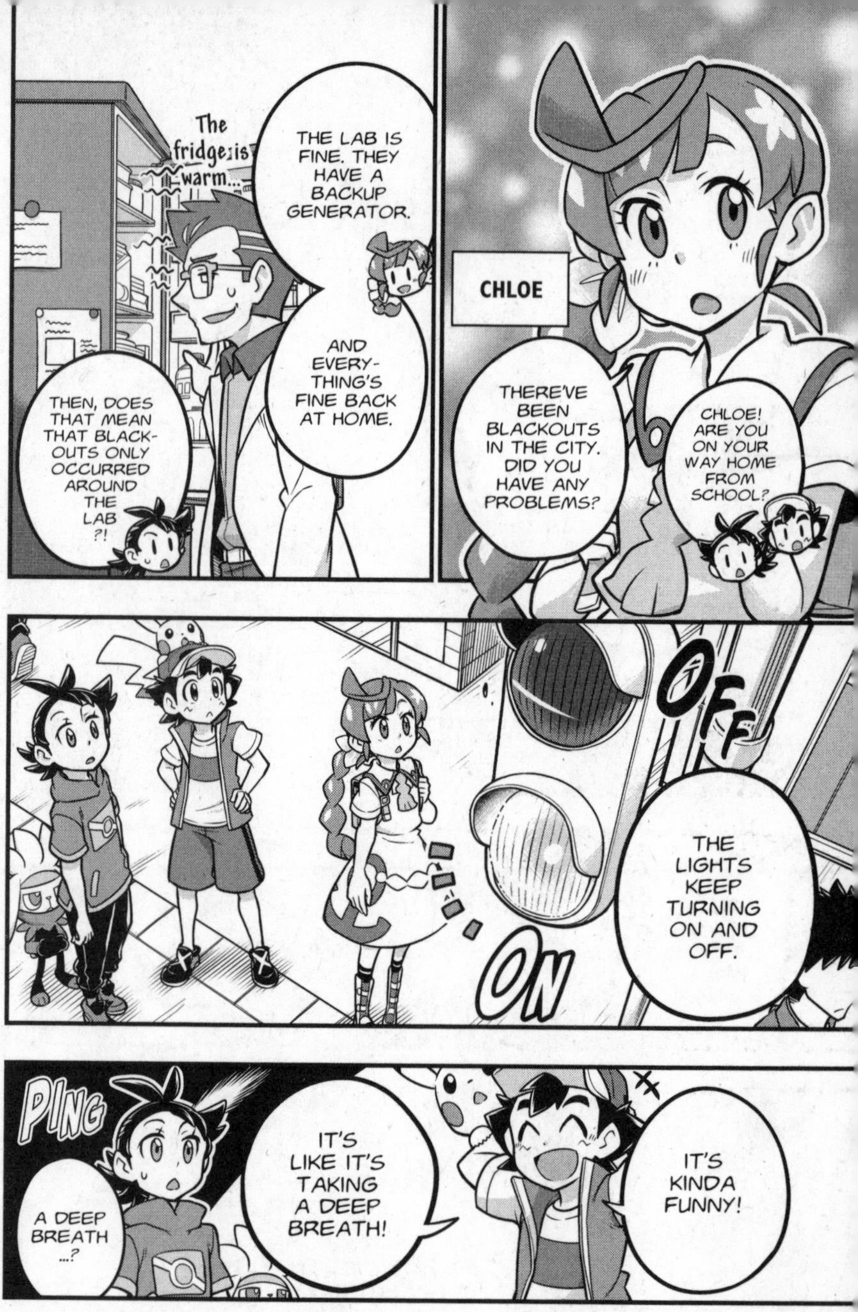
CHLOE
CHLOE! ARE YOU ON YOUR WAY HOME FROM SCHOOL?
THERE'VE BEEN BLACKOUTS IN THE CITY. DID YOU HAVE ANY PROBLEMS?
THE LAB IS FINE. THEY HAVE A BACKUP GENERATOR.
AND EVERYTHING'S FINE BACK AT HOME.
The fridge is warm...
THEN, DOES THAT MEAN THAT BLACKOUTS ONLY OCCURRED AROUND THE LAB ?!
OFF
THE LIGHTS KEEP TURNING ON AND OFF.
ON
IT'S KINDA FUNNY!
IT'S LIKE IT'S TAKING A DEEP BREATH!
PING
A DEEP BREATH ...?

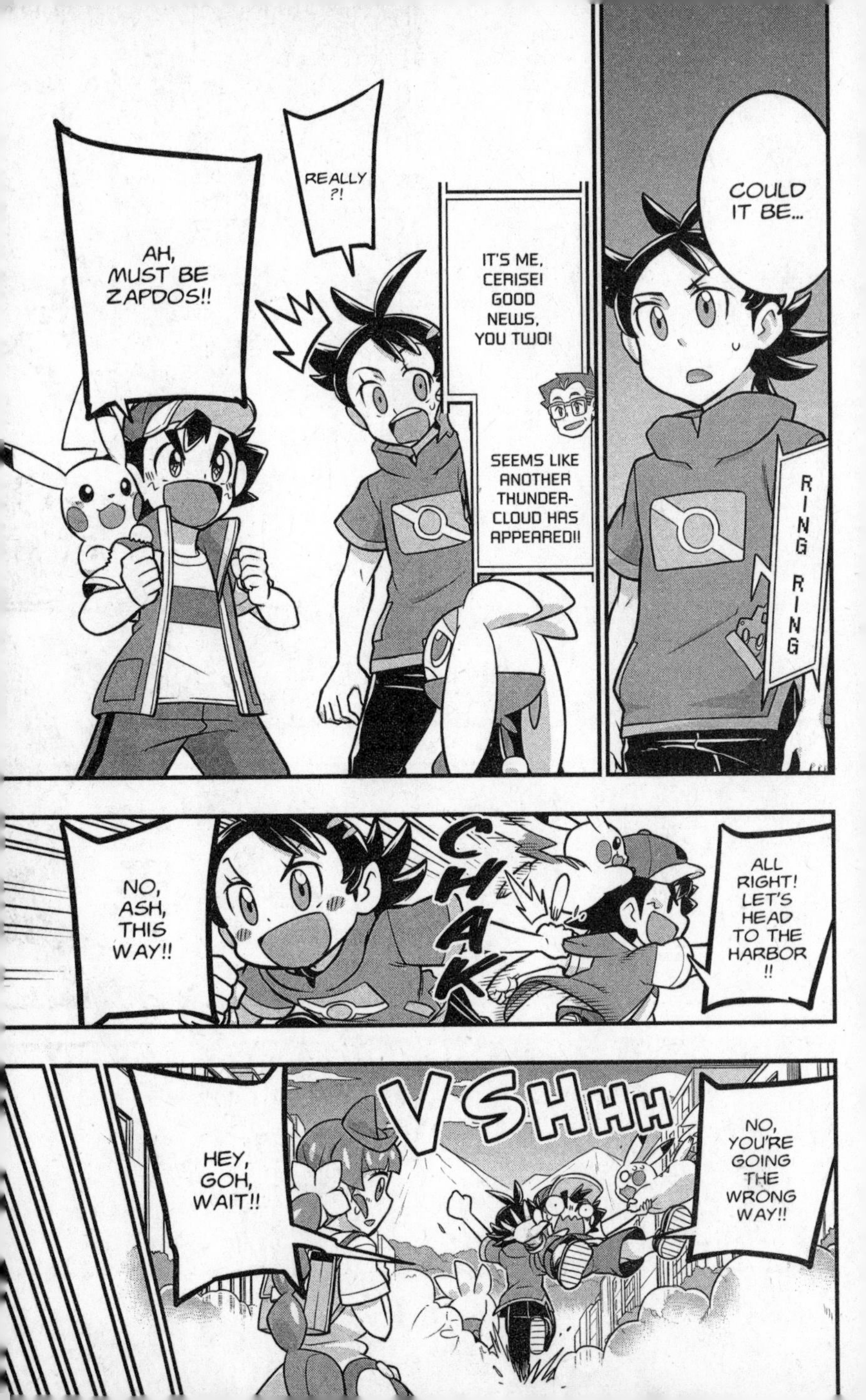
COULD IT BE...
RING RING
IT'S ME, CERISE! GOOD NEWS, YOU TWO!
SEEMS LIKE ANOTHER THUNDER-CLOUD HAS APPEARED!!
REALLY ?!
AH, MUST BE ZAPDOS!!
ALL RIGHT! LET'S HEAD TO THE HARBOR !!
CHAK
NO, ASH, THIS WAY!!
NO, YOU'RE GOING THE WRONG WAY!!
VSHHH
HEY, GOH, WAIT!!

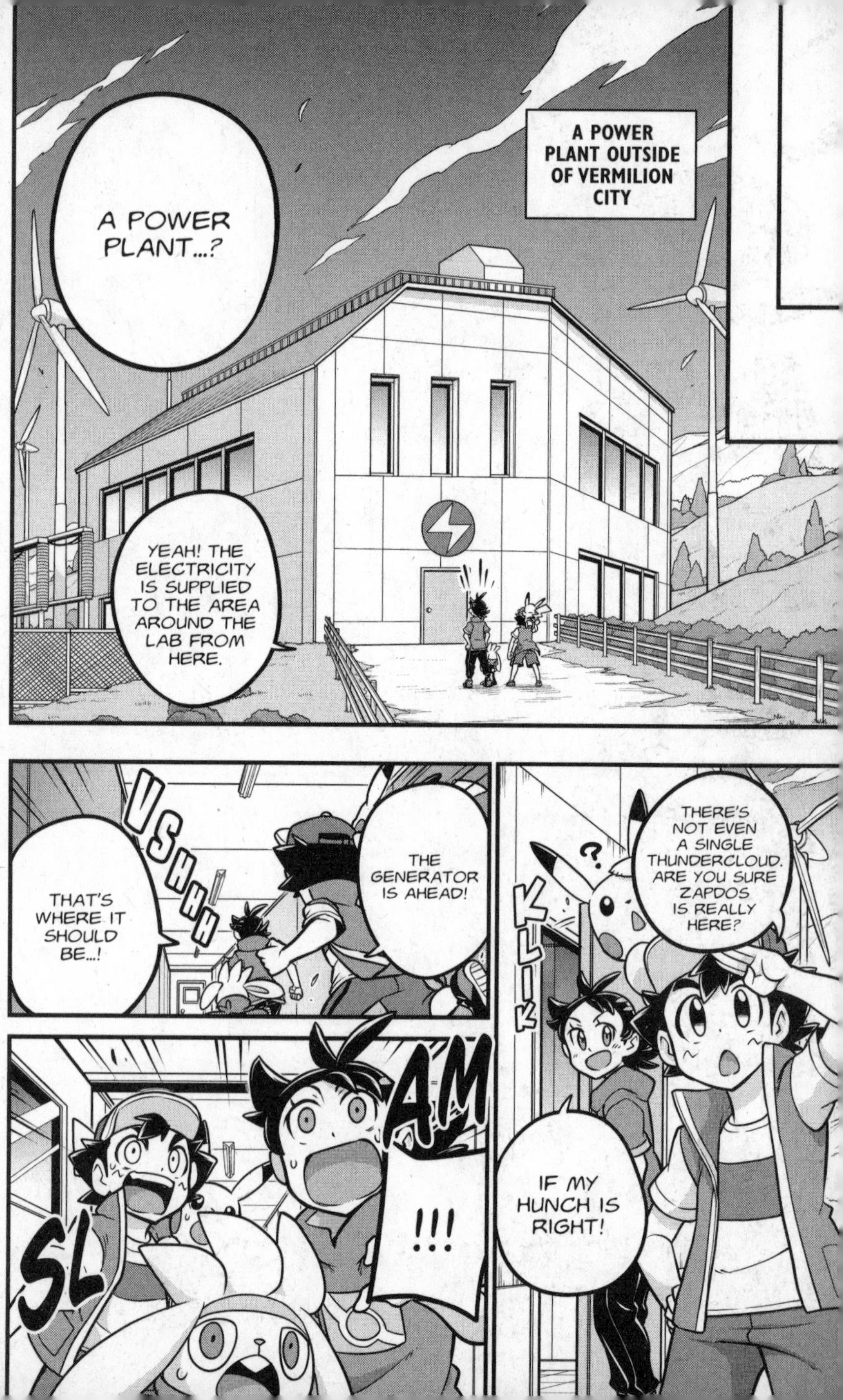
A POWER PLANT OUTSIDE OF VERMILION CITY
A POWER PLANT...?
YEAH! THE ELECTRICITY IS SUPPLIED TO THE AREA AROUND THE LAB FROM HERE.
THERE'S NOT EVEN A SINGLE THUNDERCLOUD. ARE YOU SURE ZAPDOS IS REALLY HERE?
?
KLIK
IF MY HUNCH IS RIGHT!
THE GENERATOR IS AHEAD!
VSHHH
THAT'S WHERE IT SHOULD BE...!
AM
!!!
SL

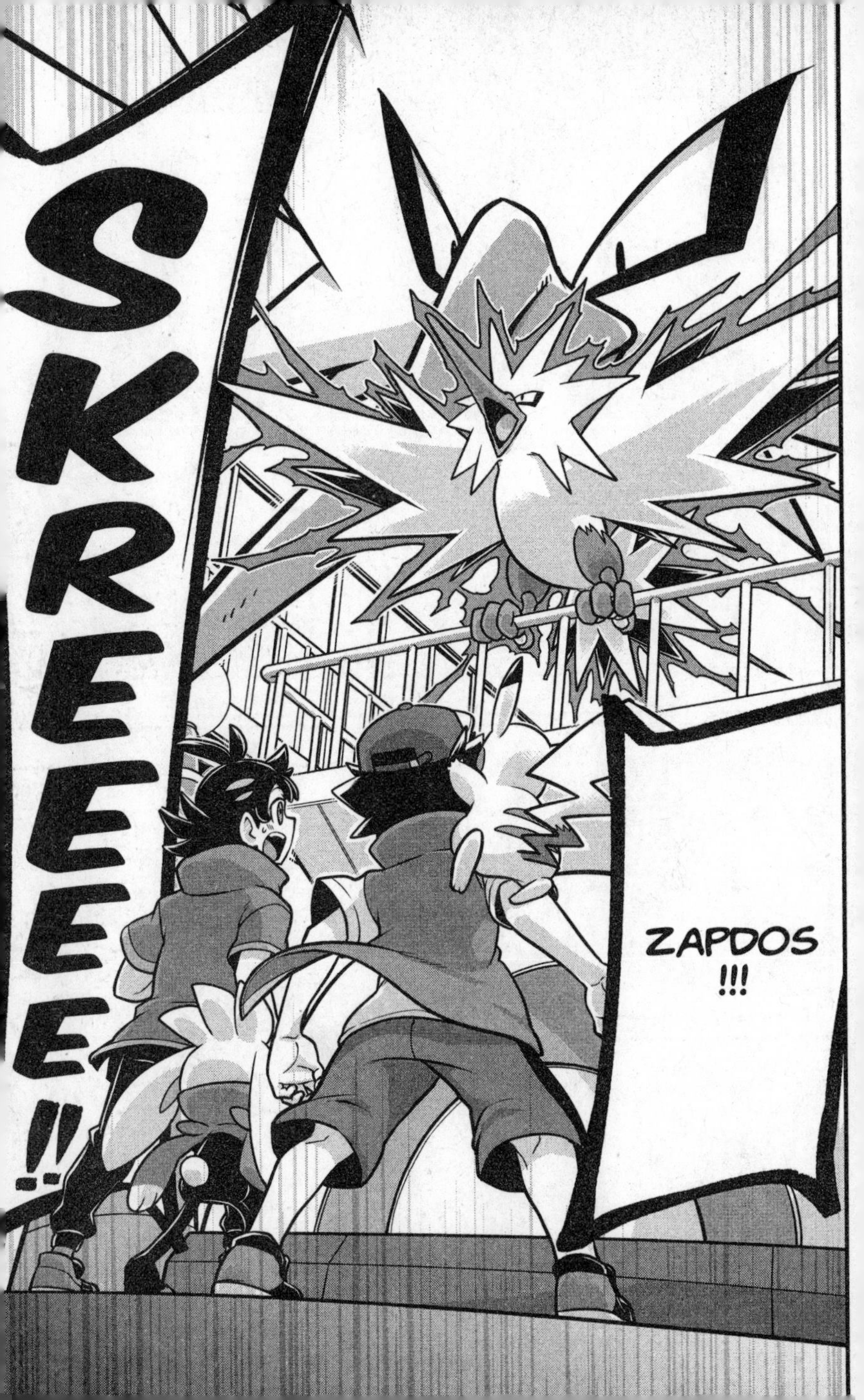
ZAPDOS
!!!
SKREEEEE!!

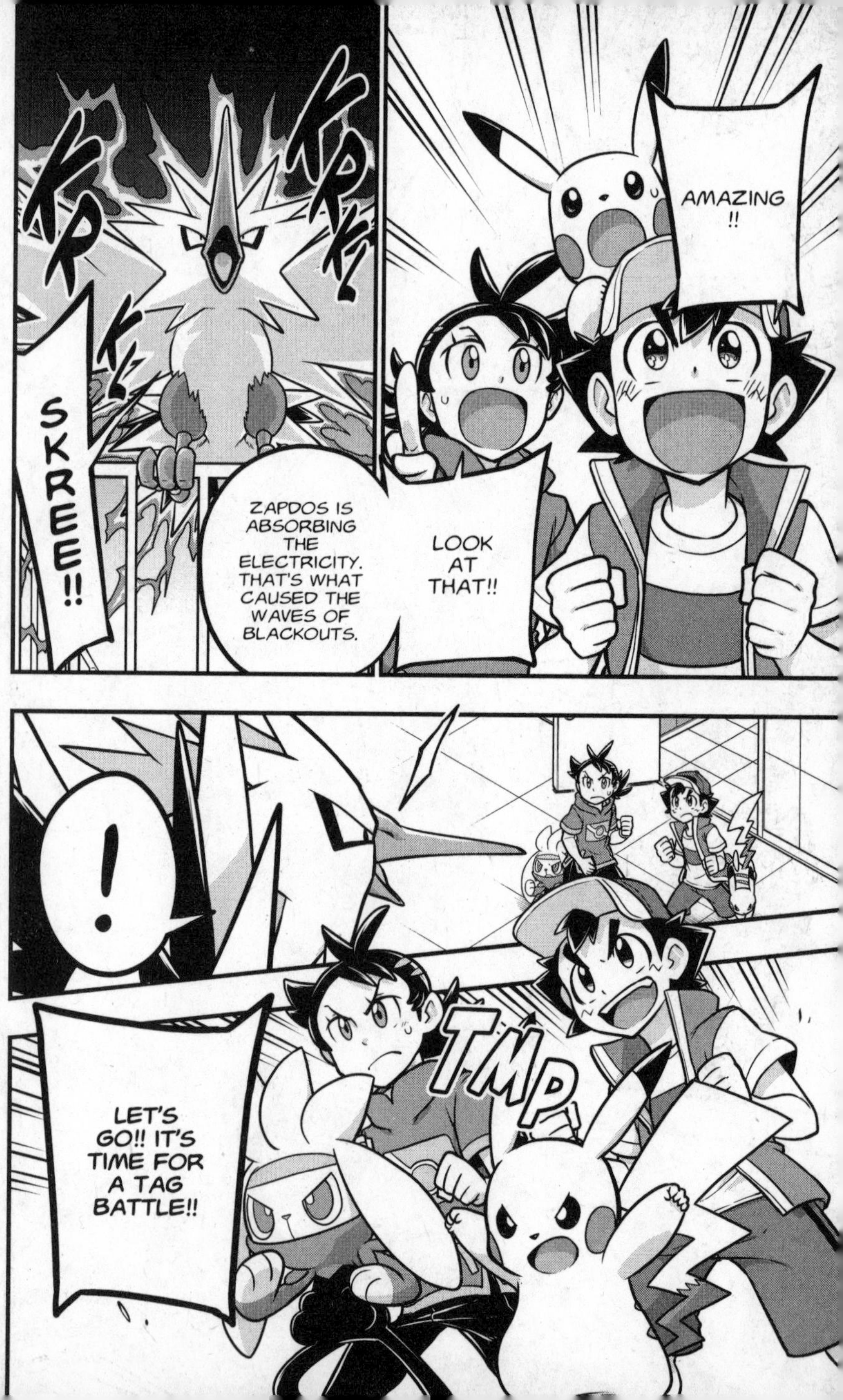
AMAZING!!
LOOK AT THAT!!
ZAPDOS IS ABSORBING THE ELECTRICITY. THAT'S WHAT CAUSED THE WAVES OF BLACKOUTS.
SKREE!!
!
TMP
LET'S GO!! IT'S TIME FOR A TAG BATTLE!!

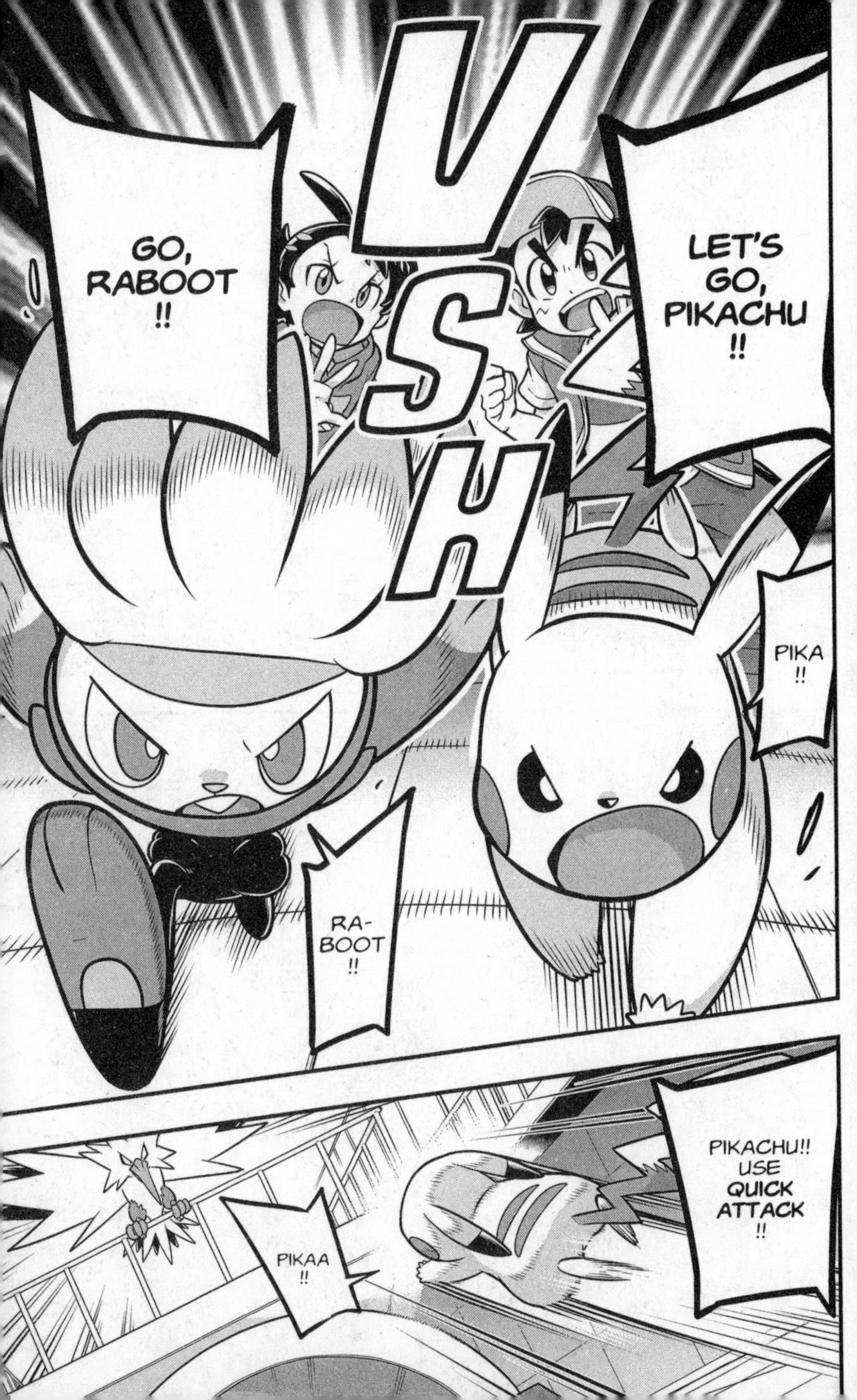
LET'S GO, PIKACHU !!
GO, RABOOT !!
VSH
PIKA !!
RA-BOOT !!
PIKACHU!! USE QUICK ATTACK !!
PIKAA !!

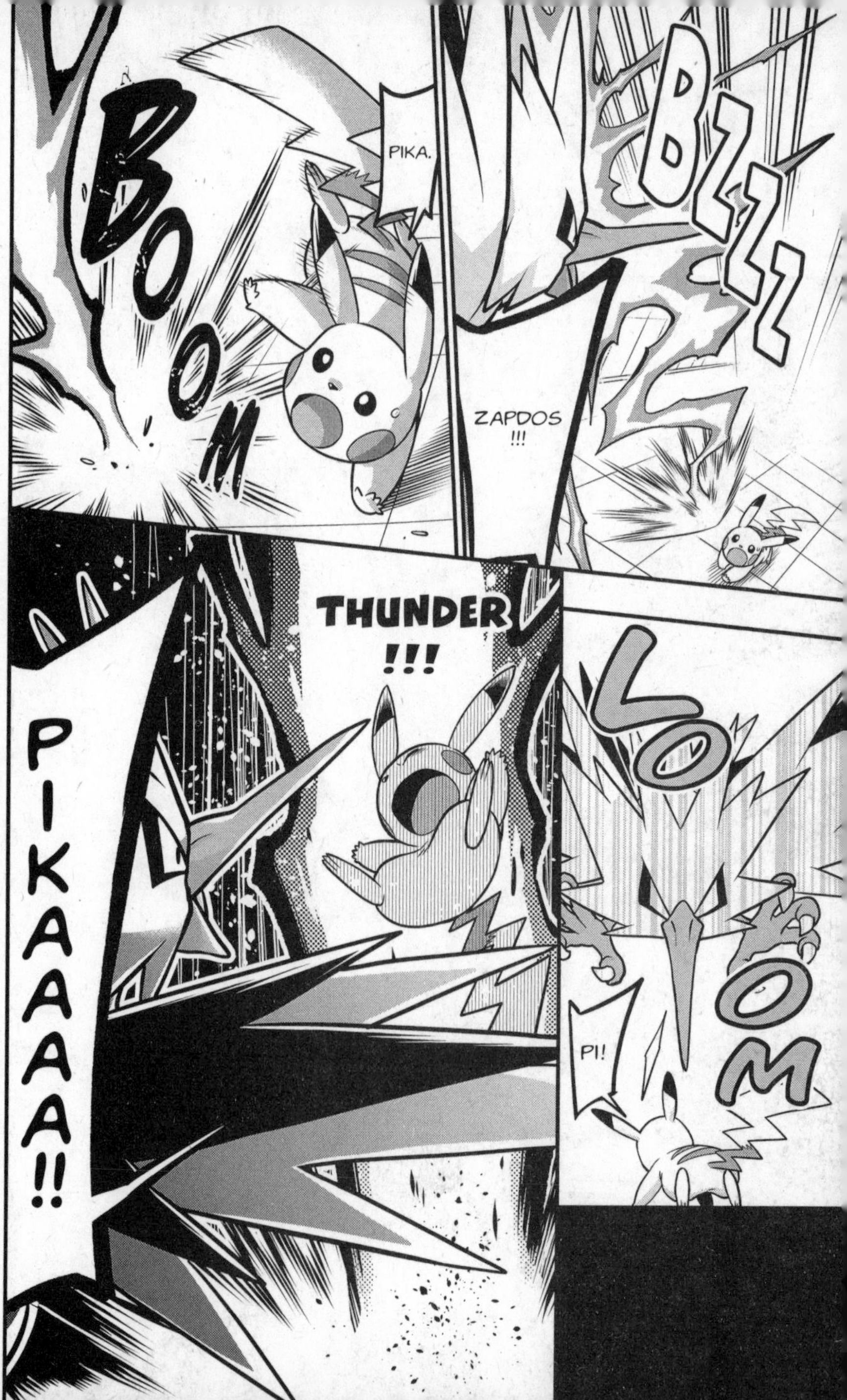
BZZZ
ZAPDOS!!!
PIKA.
BOOM
LOOM
PI!
THUNDER!!!
PIKAAAA!!

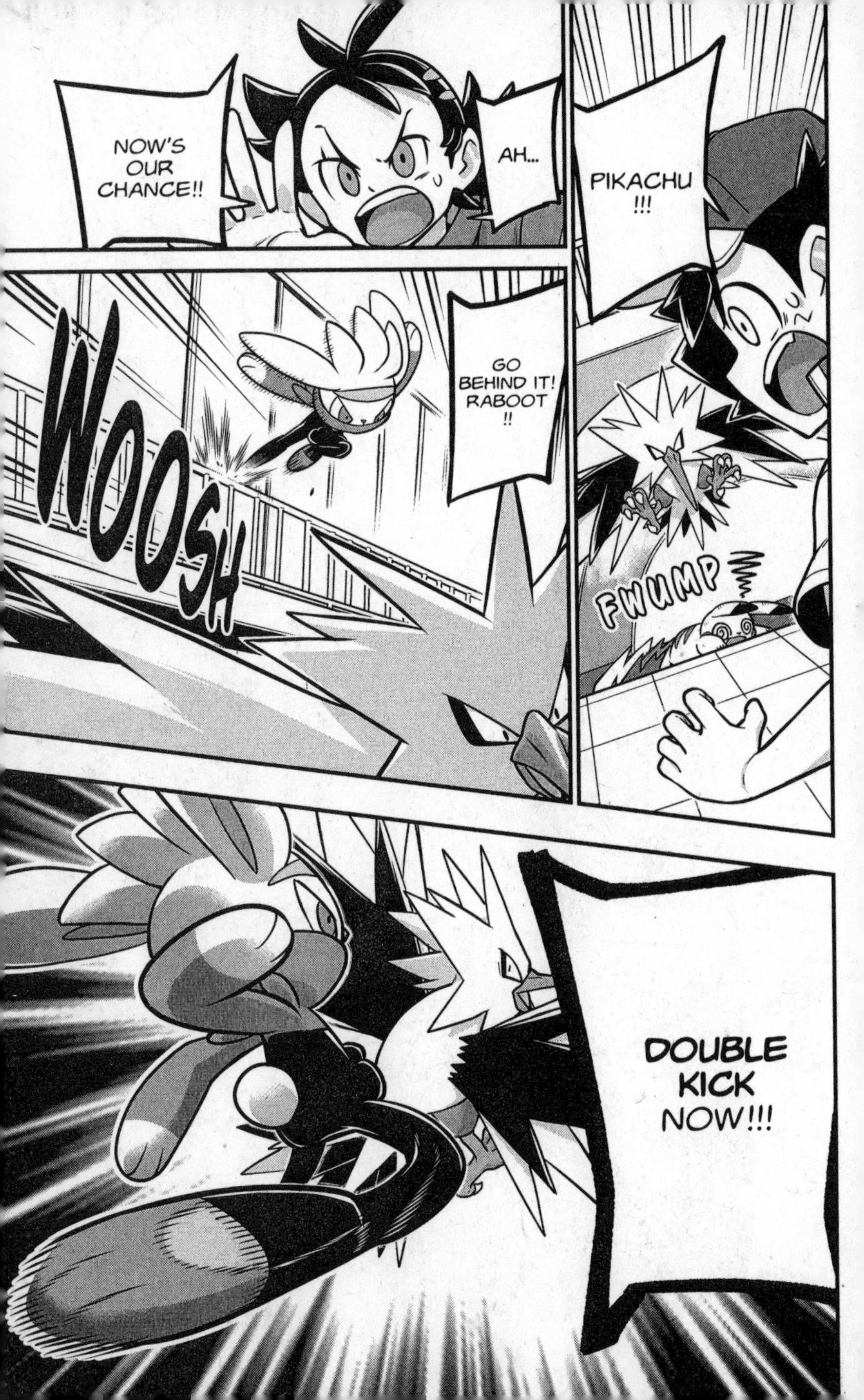
PIKACHU!!!
FWUMP
AH...
NOW'S OUR CHANCE!!
GO BEHIND IT! RABOOT!!
WOOSH
DOUBLE KICK NOW!!!

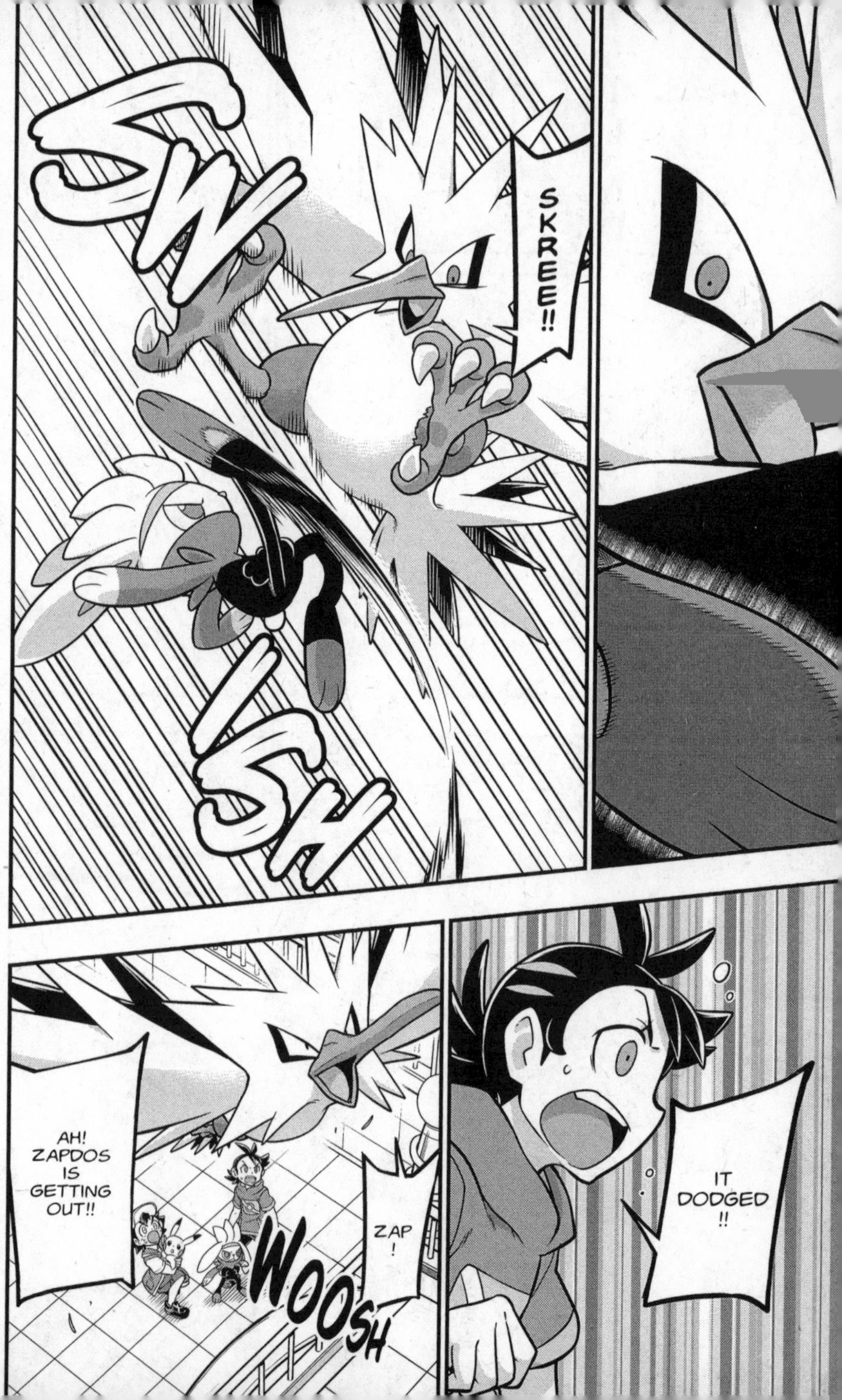
SKREE!!
SWISH
IT DODGED!!
AH! ZAPDOS IS GETTING OUT!!
ZAP!
WOOSH

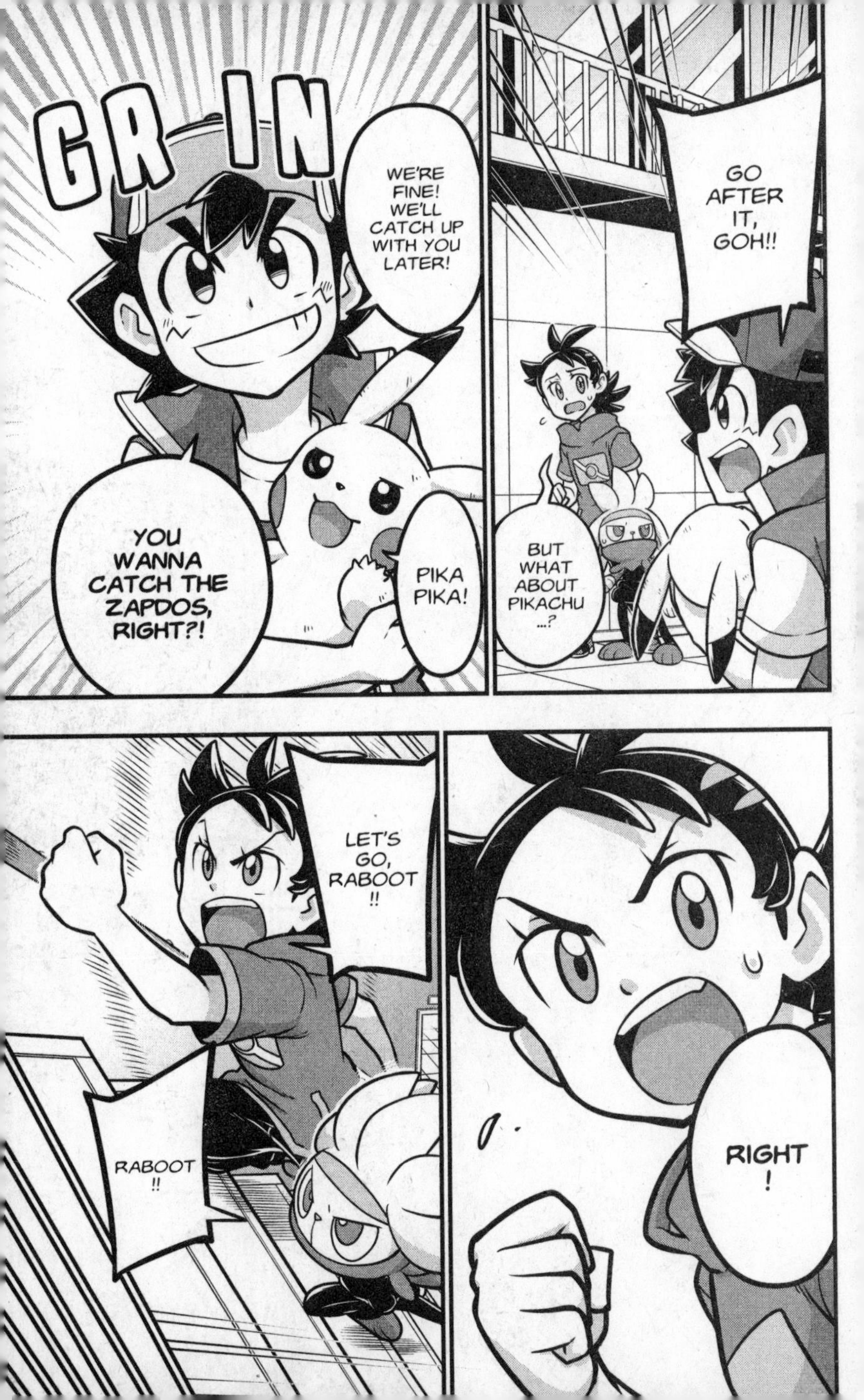
GO AFTER IT, GOH!!
BUT WHAT ABOUT PIKACHU ...?
GRIN
WE'RE FINE! WE'LL CATCH UP WITH YOU LATER!
PIKA PIKA!
YOU WANNA CATCH THE ZAPDOS, RIGHT?!
RIGHT!
LET'S GO, RABOOT!!
RABOOT!!

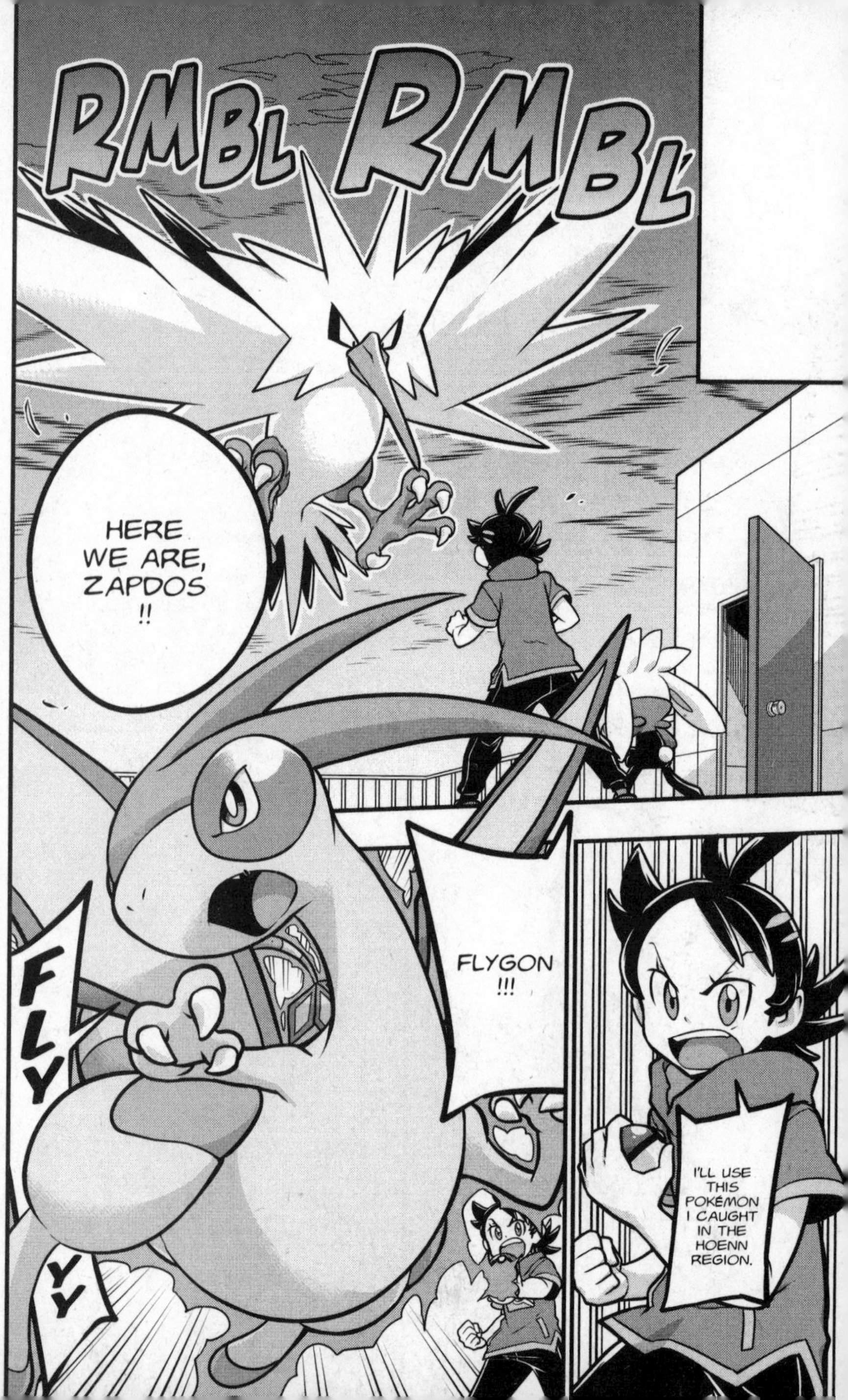
RMBL RMBL
!
HERE WE ARE, ZAPDOS !!
I'LL USE THIS POKÉMON I CAUGHT IN THE HOENN REGION.
FLYGON !!!
FLY
YY

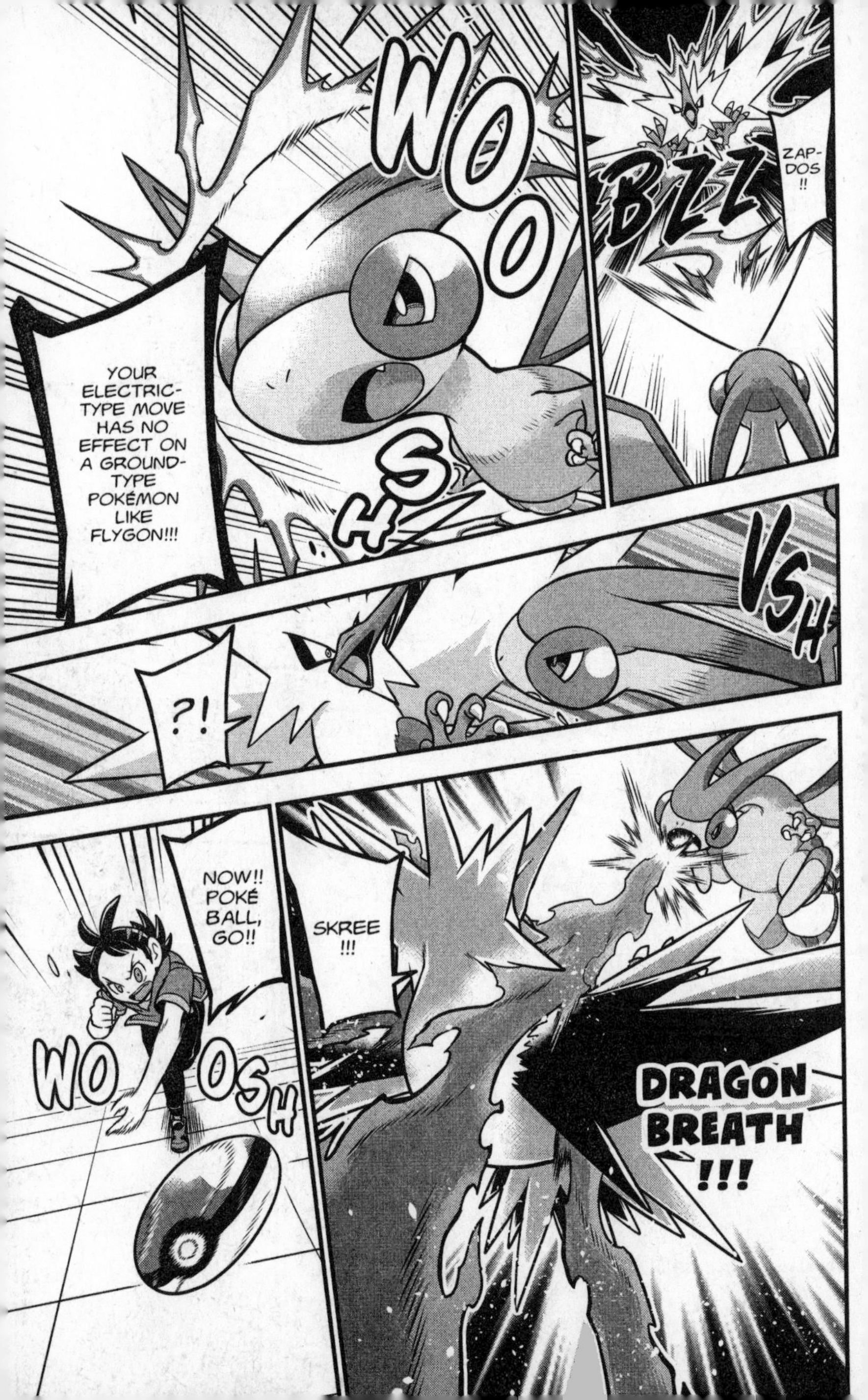

BZZ
ZAP-
DOS
!!
WOOO
YOUR ELECTRIC-TYPE MOVE HAS NO EFFECT ON A GROUND-TYPE POKÉMON LIKE FLYGON!!!
SH
VSH
?!
SKREE
!!!
DRAGON BREATH !!!
NOW!! POKÉ BALL, GO!!
WOOOSH

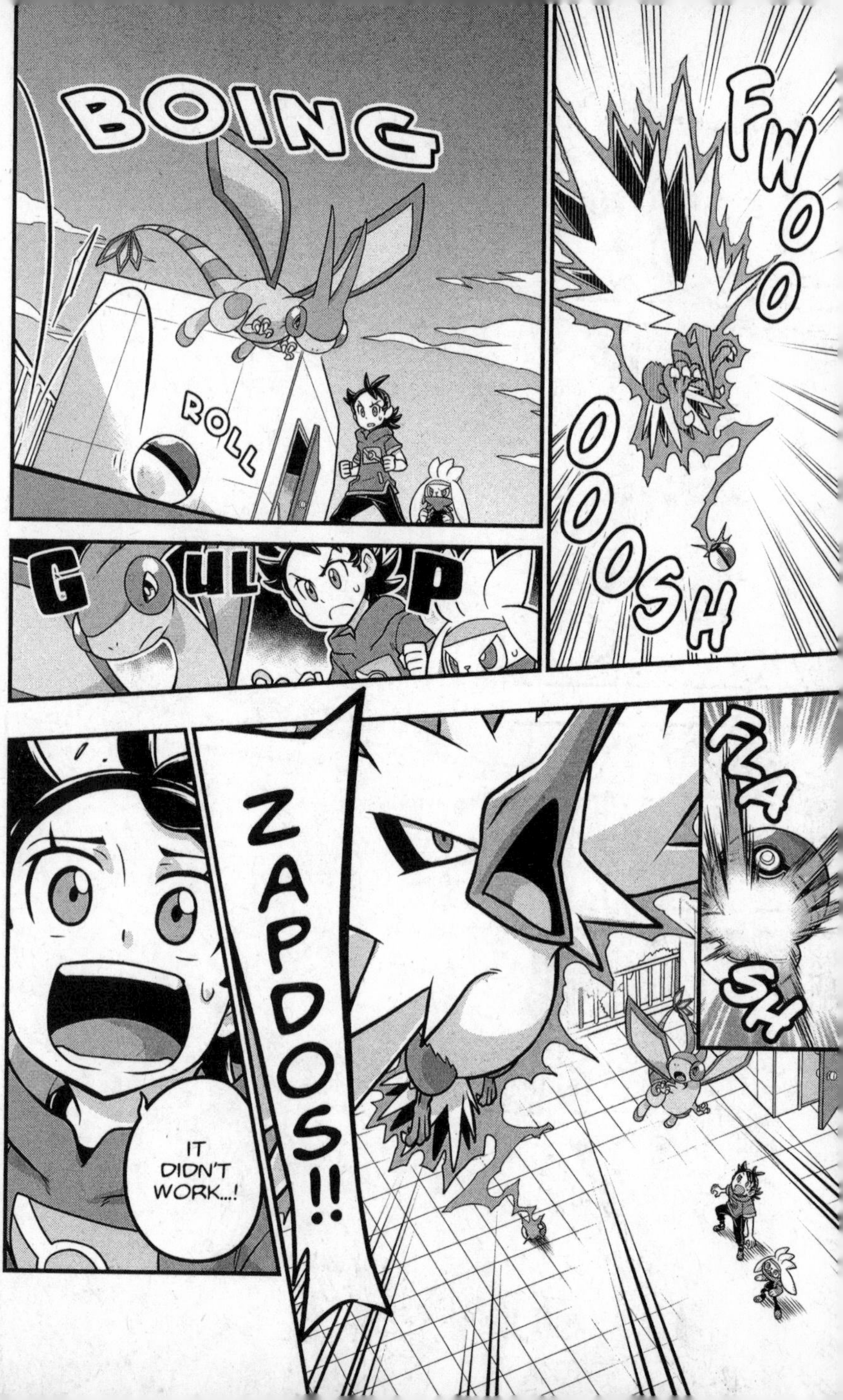

FWOOOOOOSH
BOING
ROLL
GULP
FLASH
ZAPDOS!!
IT DIDN'T WORK...!

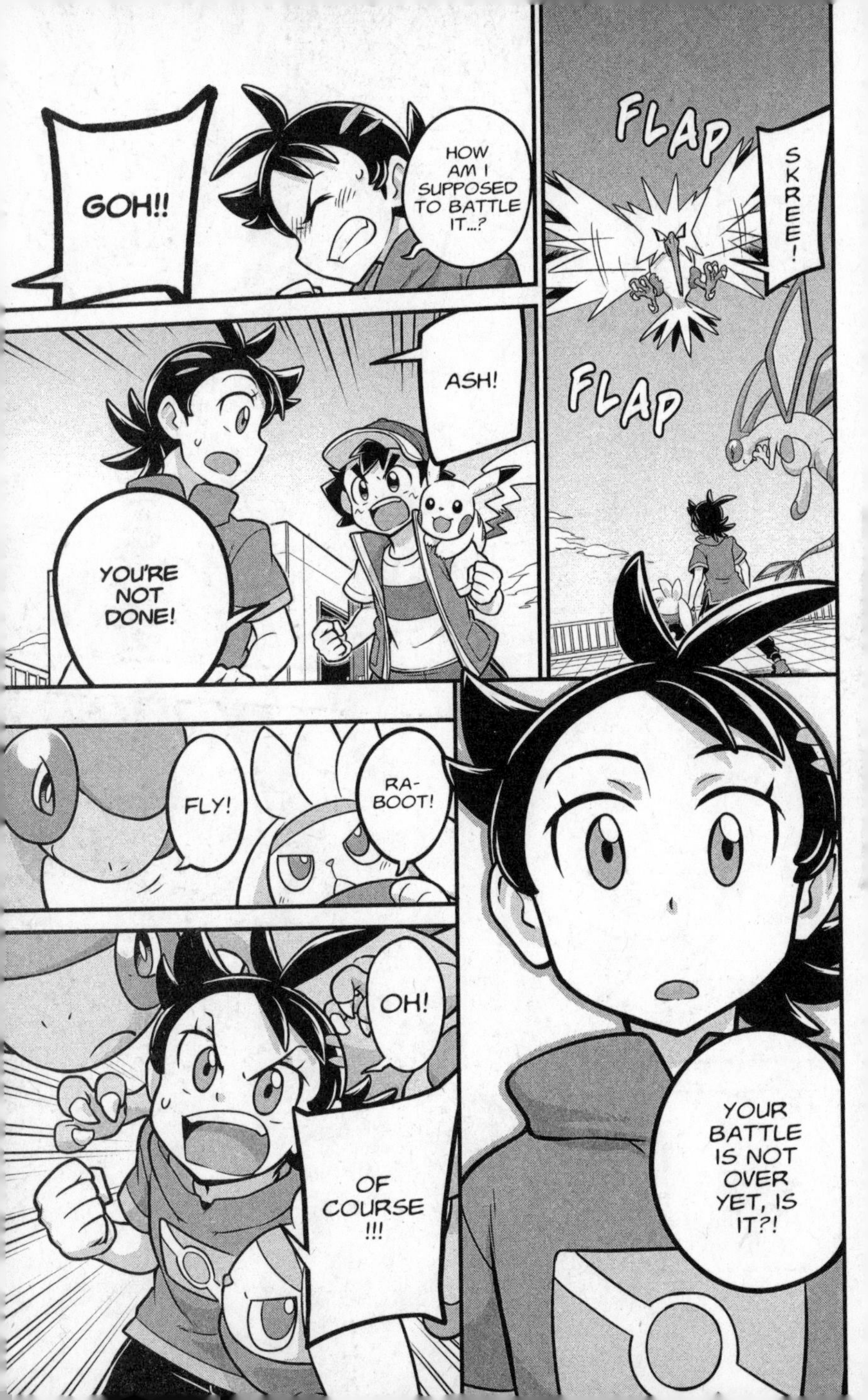
FLAP
SKREE!
FLAP
HOW AM I SUPPOSED TO BATTLE IT...?
GOH!!
ASH!
YOU'RE NOT DONE!
YOUR BATTLE IS NOT OVER YET, IS IT?!
RA-BOOT!
FLY!
OH!
OF COURSE!!!

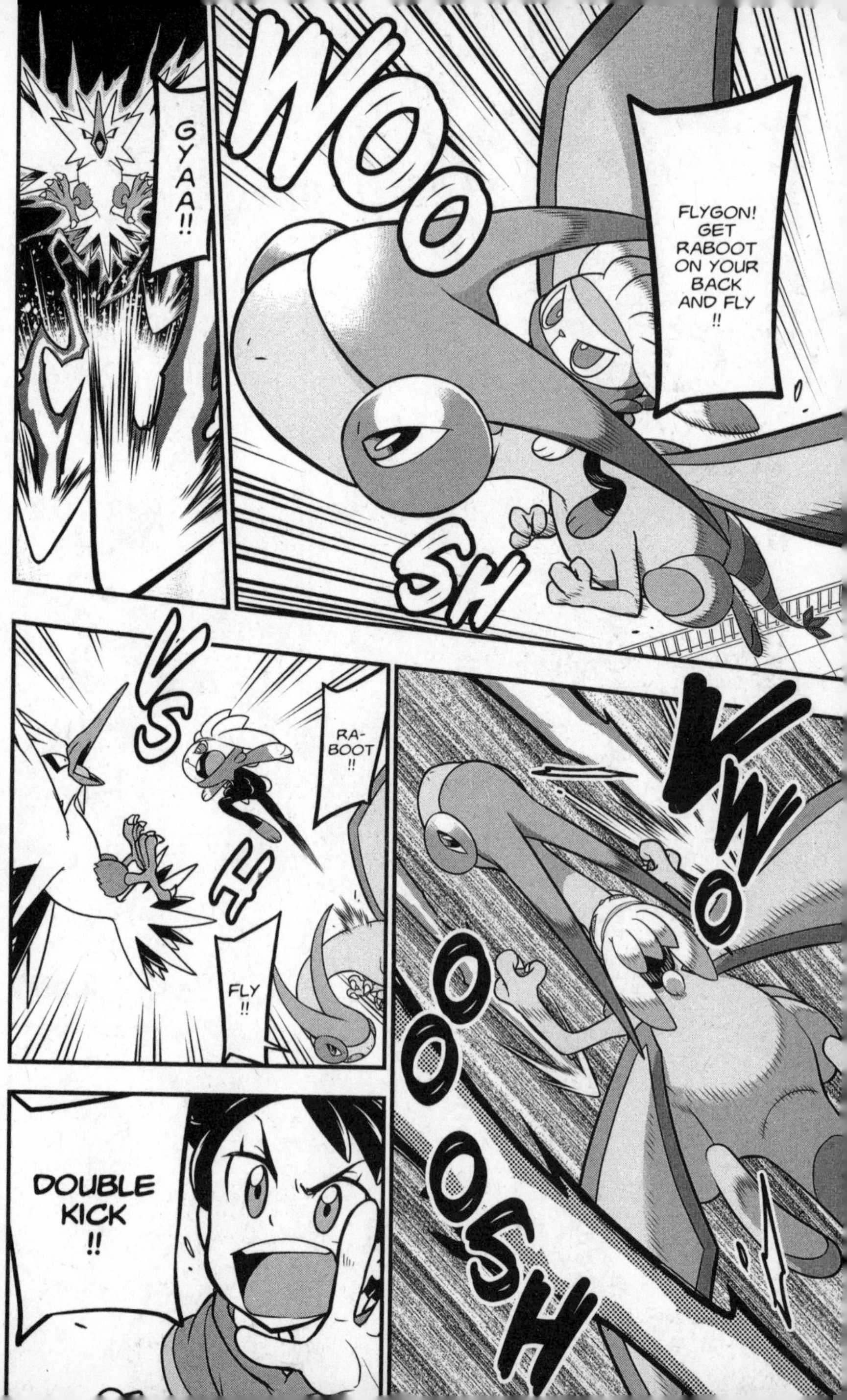
FLYGON! GET RABOOT ON YOUR BACK AND FLY!!
GYAAA!!
RA-BOOT!!
FLY!!
DOUBLE KICK!!

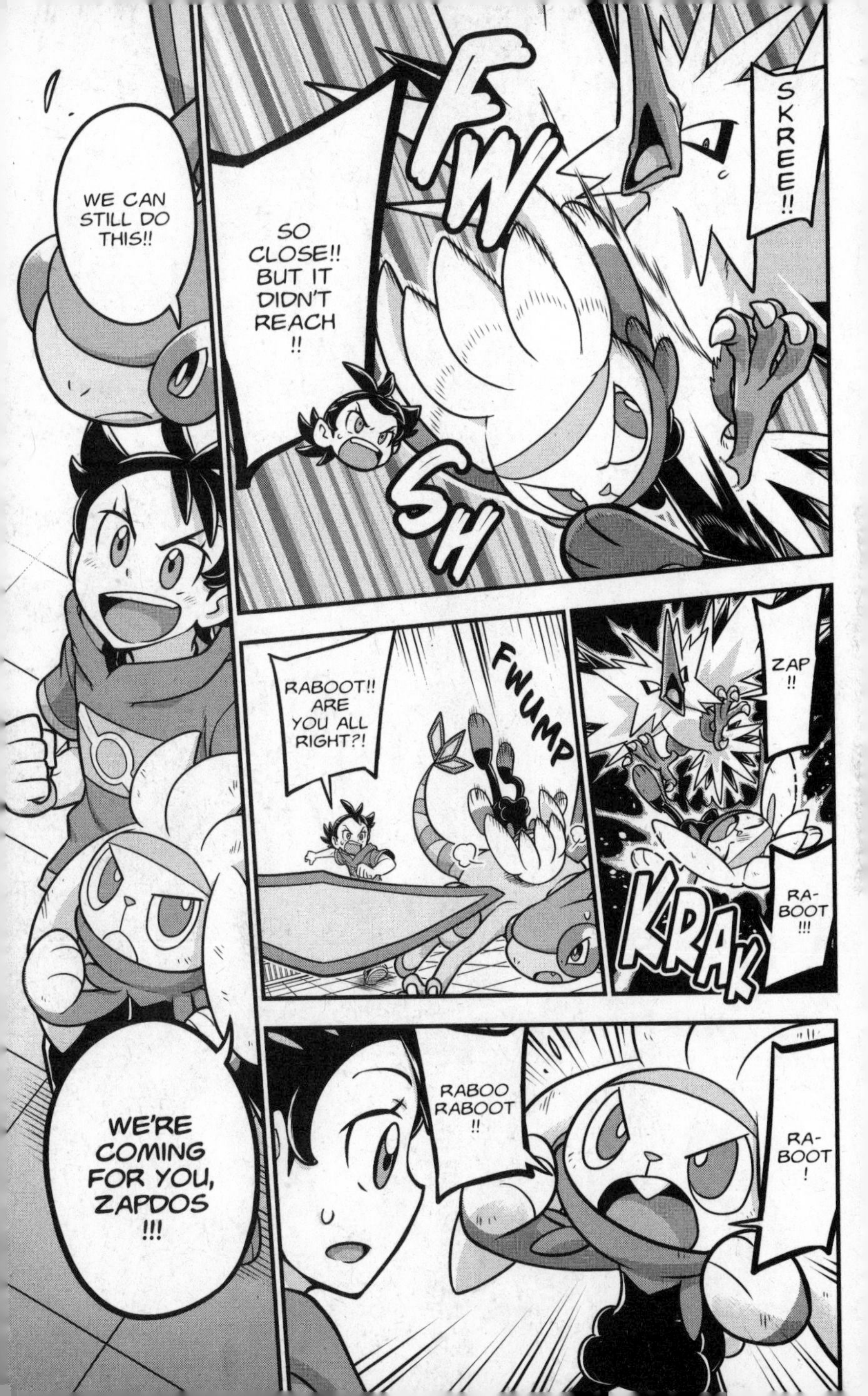
SKREE!!
FW
SO CLOSE!! BUT IT DIDN'T REACH!!
SH
ZAP!!
KRAK
RA-BOOT!!!
FWUMP
RABOOT!! ARE YOU ALL RIGHT?!
RA-BOOT!
RABOO RABOOT!!
WE CAN STILL DO THIS!!
WE'RE COMING FOR YOU, ZAPDOS!!!

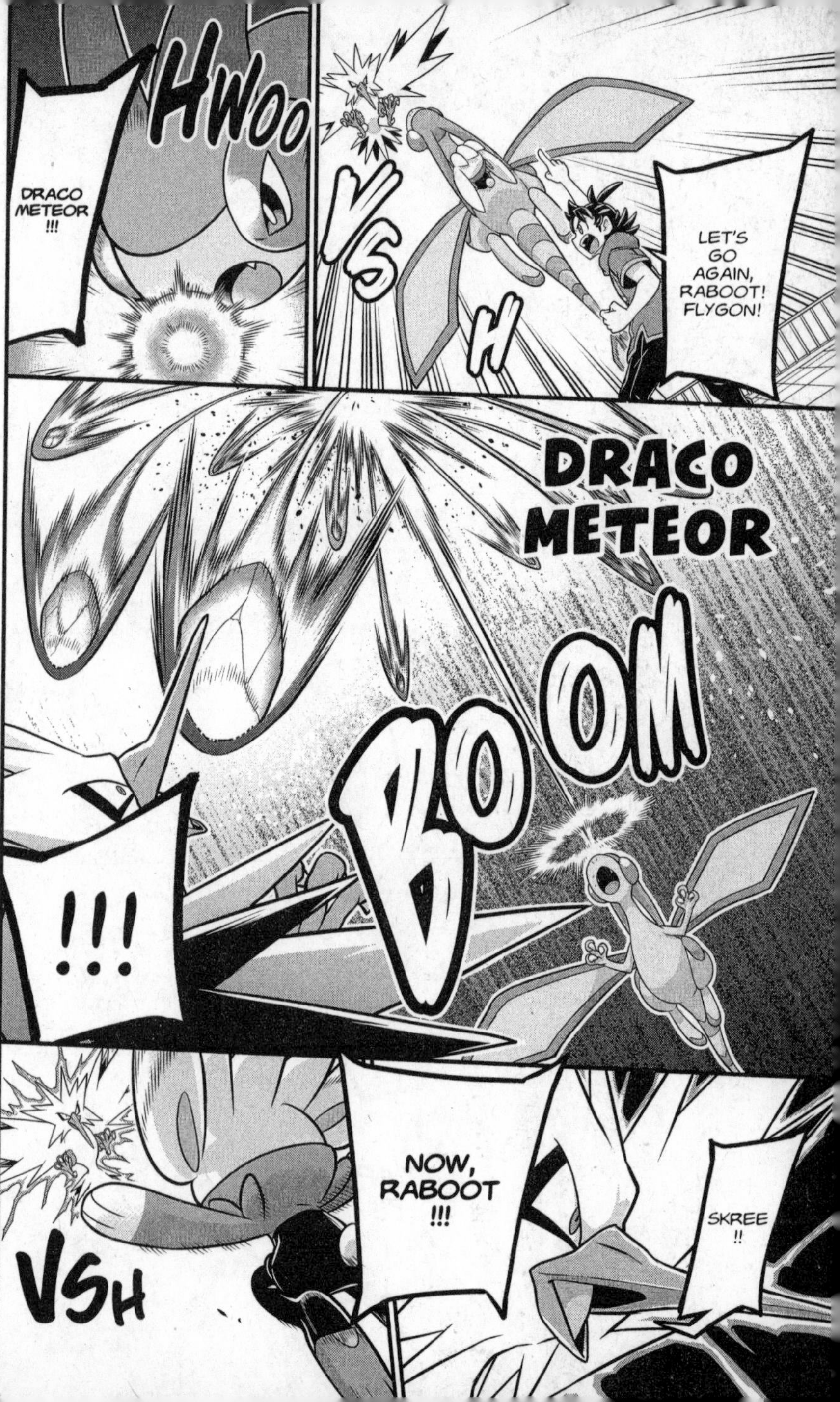
LET'S GO AGAIN, RABOOT! FLYGON!
VSH
HWOO
DRACO METEOR !!!
DRACO METEOR
BOOM
!!!
SKREE !!
NOW, RABOOT !!!
VSH

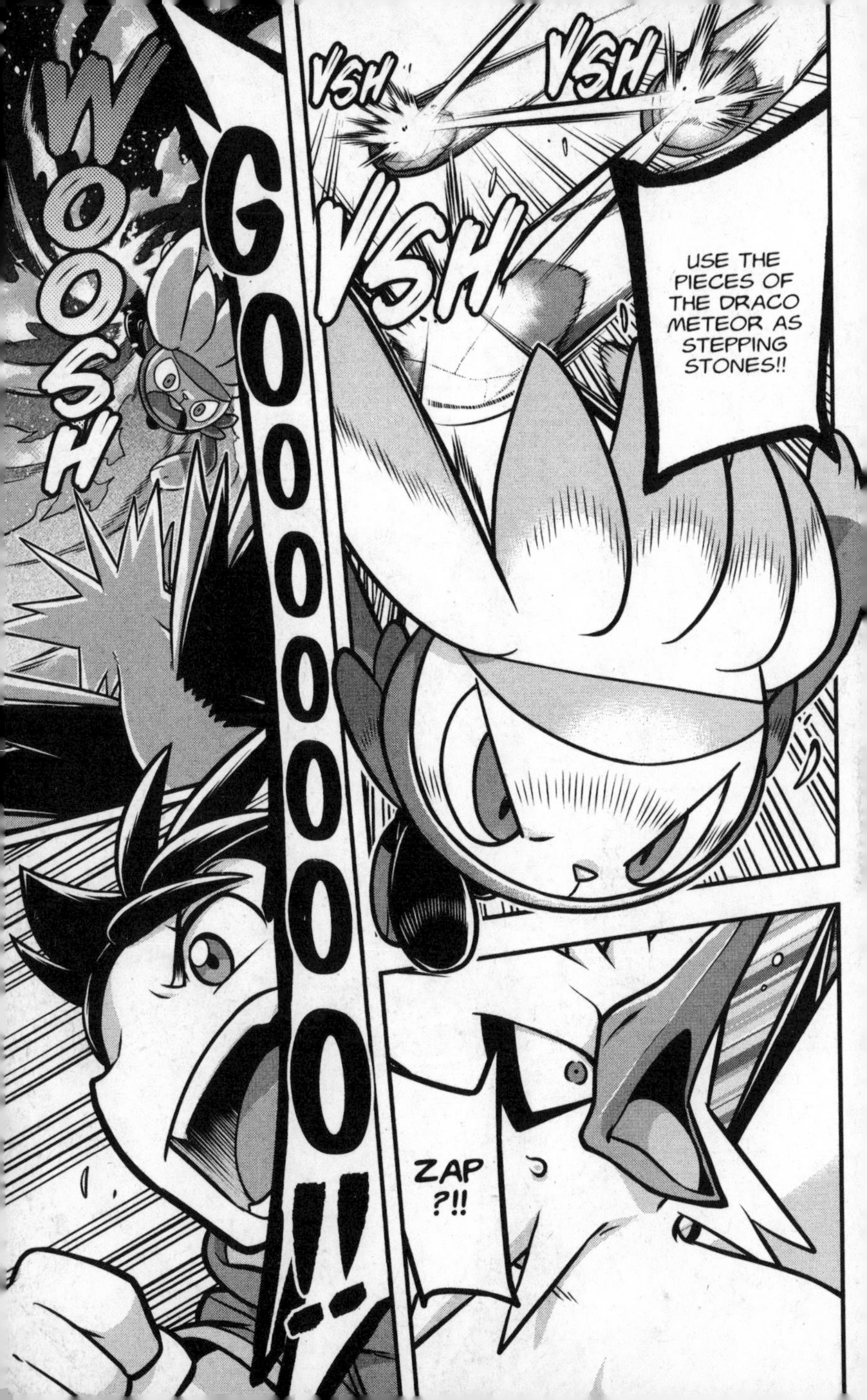
VSH
VSH
VSH
USE THE PIECES OF THE DRACO METEOR AS STEPPING STONES!!
ZAP
?!!
WOOOSH
GOOOOOOOOOO!!

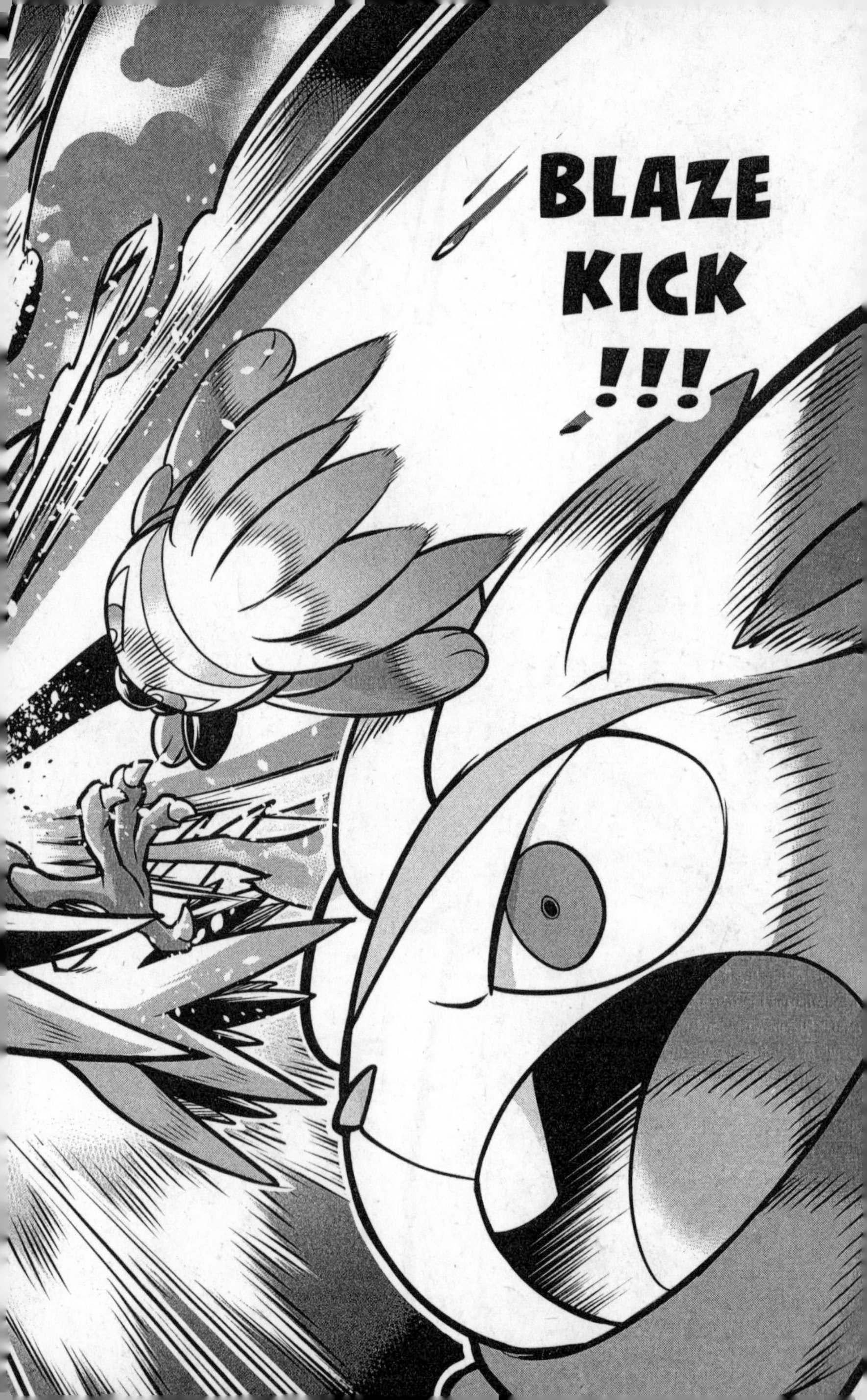
BLAZE KICK !!!

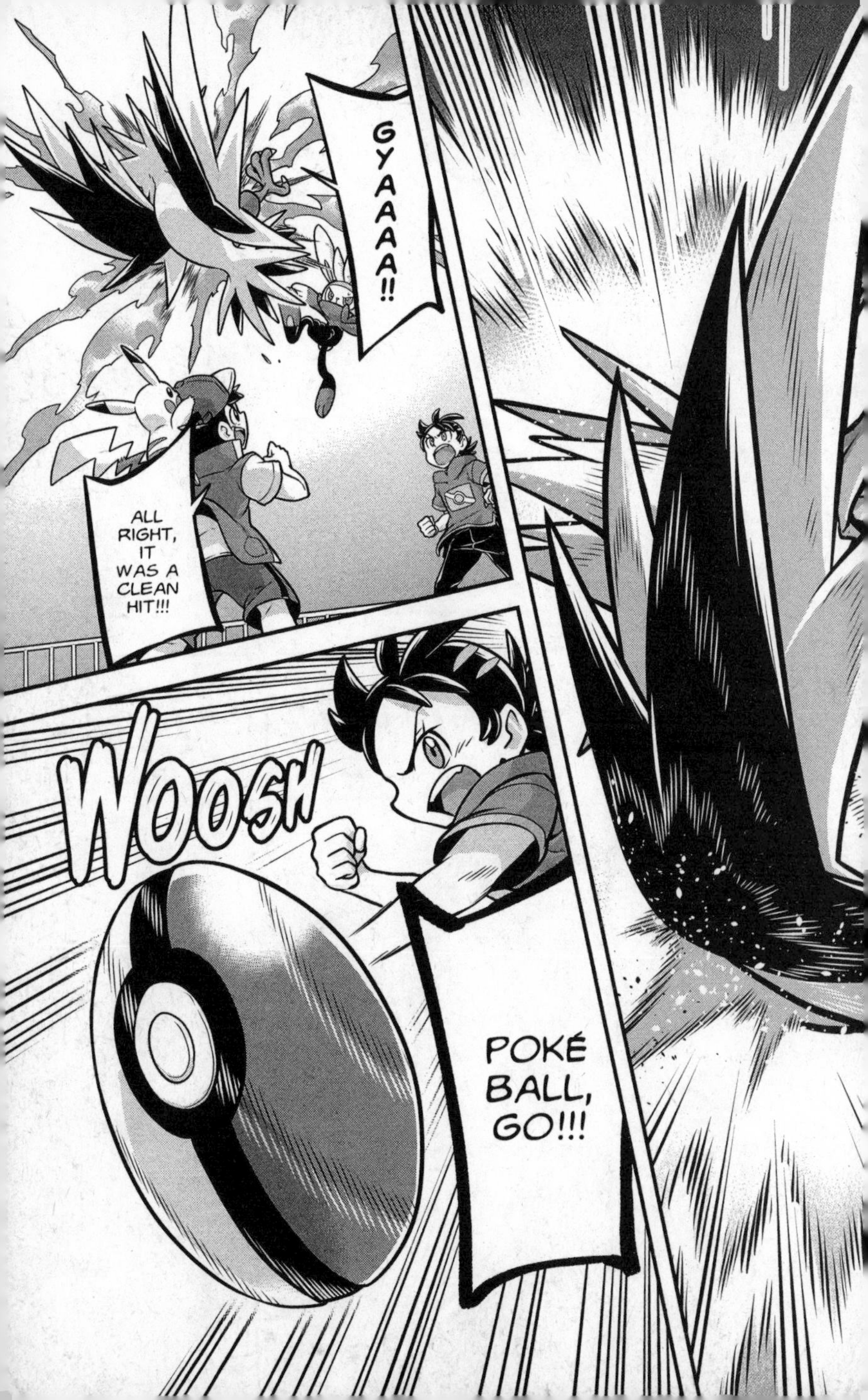
GYAAAAA!!
ALL RIGHT, IT WAS A CLEAN HIT!!!
WOOSH
POKÉ BALL, GO!!!

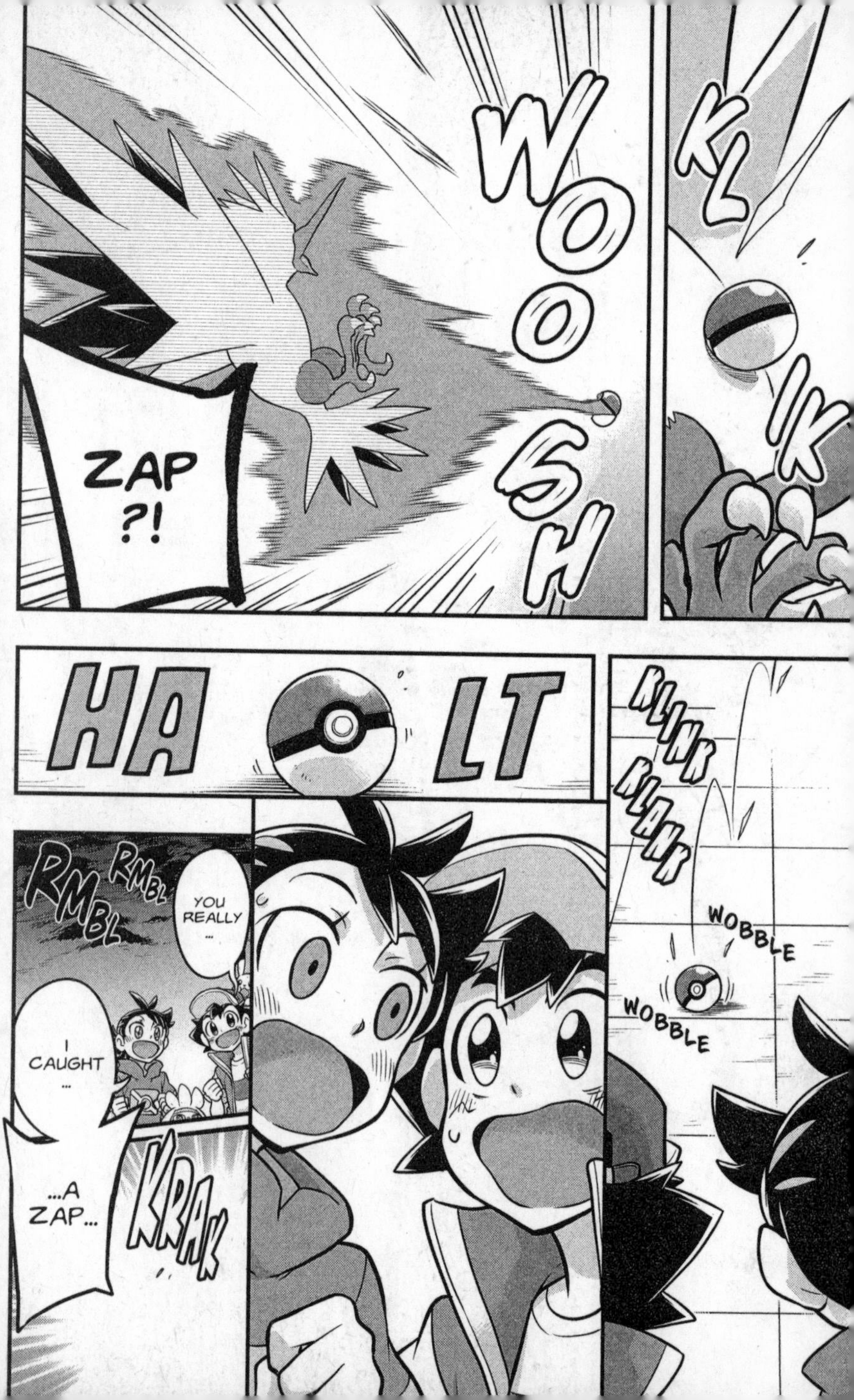
KLIK
WOOOSH
ZAP ?!
KLINK KLANK
WOBBLE
WOBBLE
HALT
RMBL
RMBL
YOU REALLY ...
I CAUGHT ...
...A ZAP...
KRAK

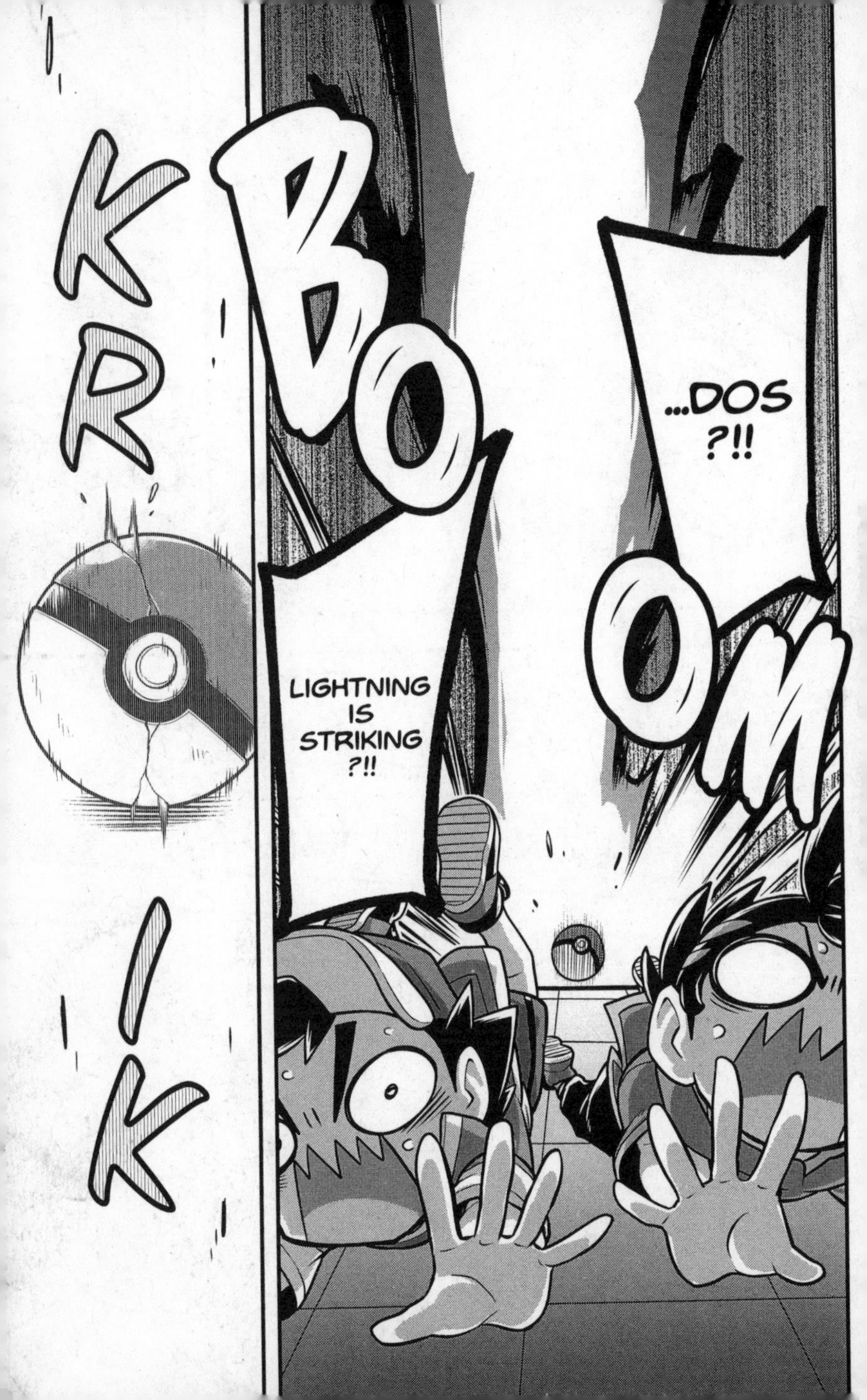
BOOM
...DOS ?!!
LIGHTNING IS STRIKING ?!!
KRIK

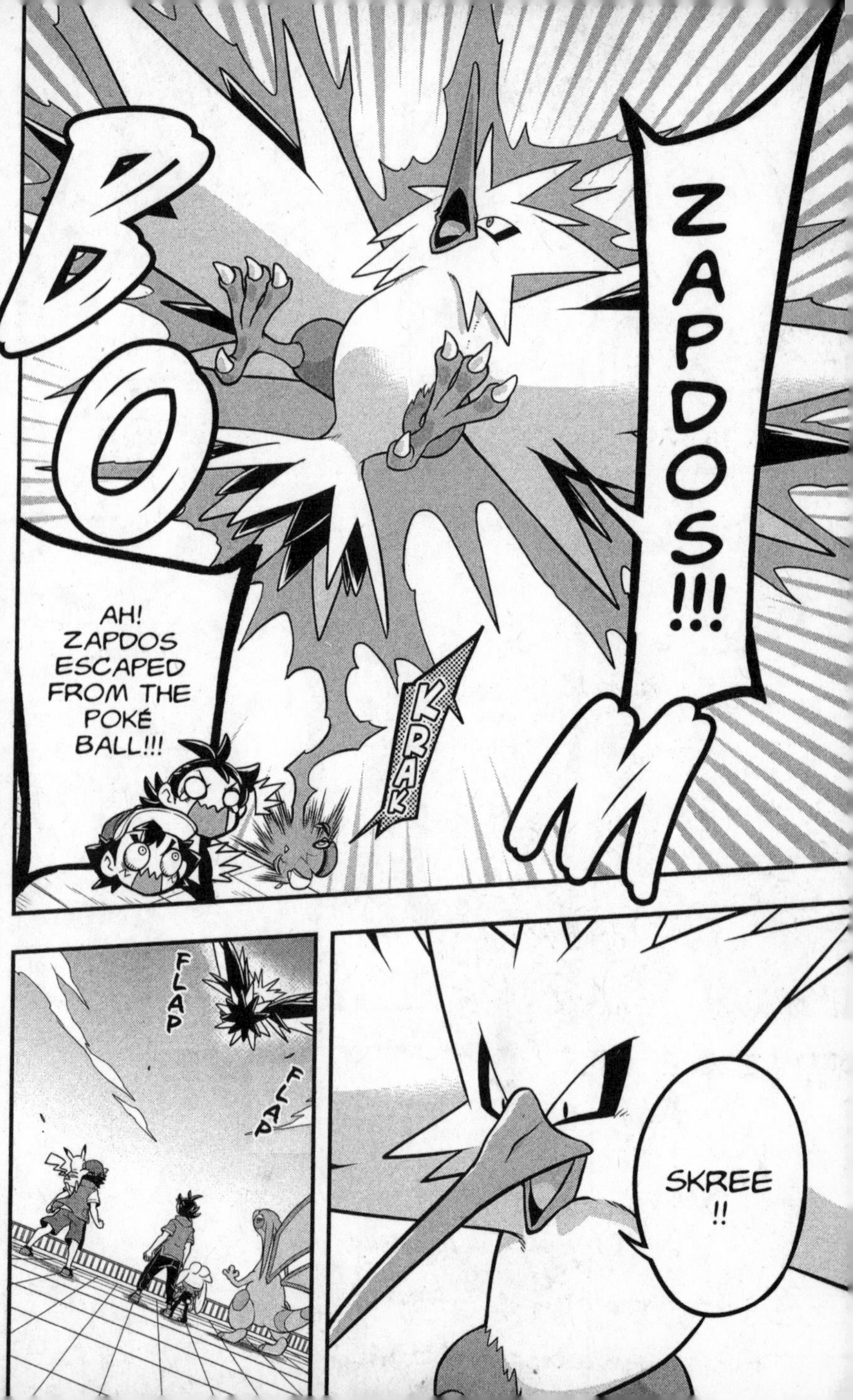
ZAPDOS!!!
BOOM
KRAK
AH! ZAPDOS ESCAPED FROM THE POKÉ BALL!!!
SKREE!!
FLAP
FLAP

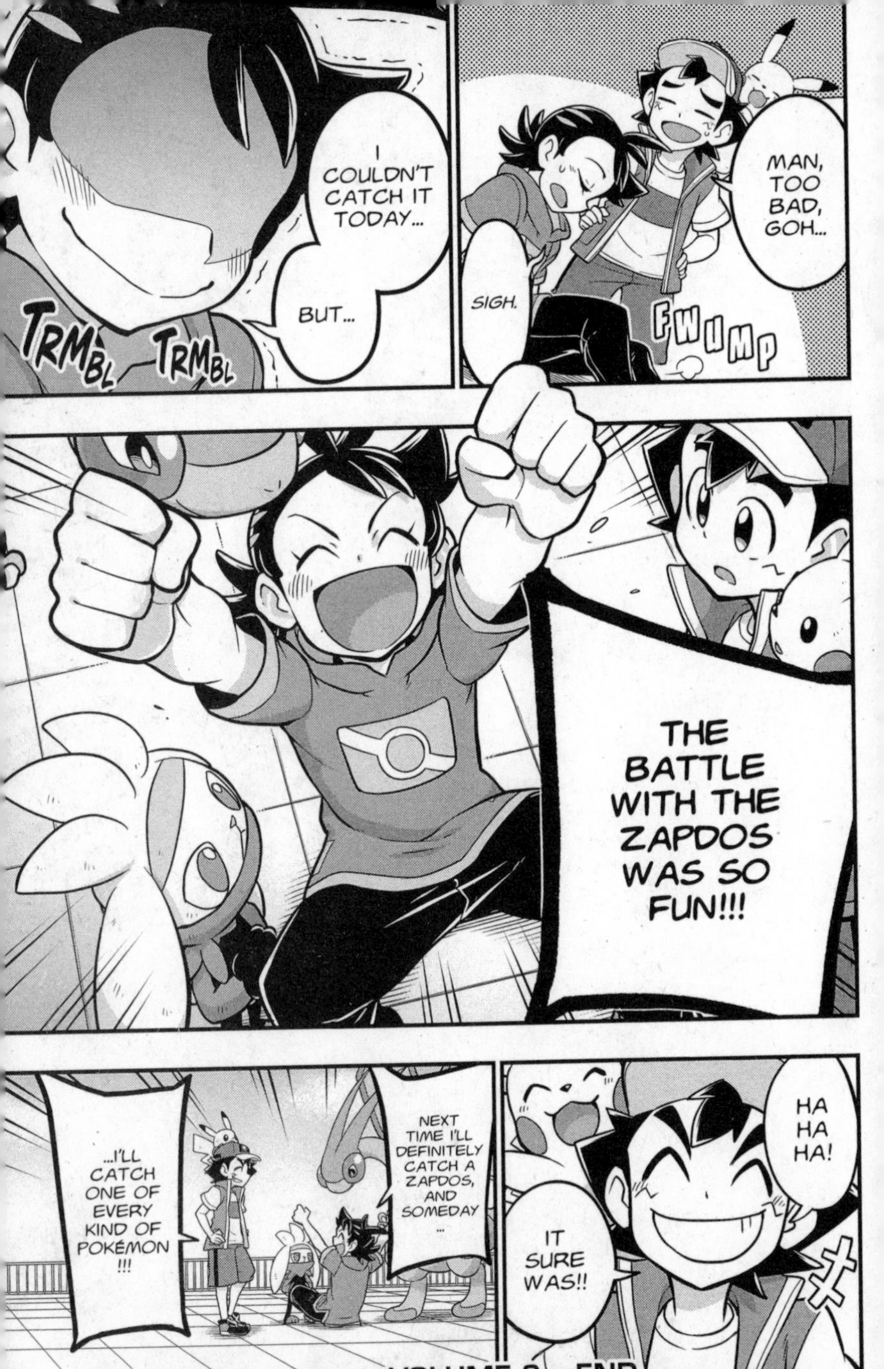
MAN, TOO BAD, GOH...
SIGH.
FWUMP
I COULDN'T CATCH IT TODAY...
BUT...
TRMBL
TRMBL
THE BATTLE WITH THE ZAPDOS WAS SO FUN!!!
HA HA HA!
IT SURE WAS!!
NEXT TIME I'LL DEFINITELY CATCH A ZAPDOS, AND SOMEDAY ...
...I'LL CATCH ONE OF EVERY KIND OF POKÉMON!!!

Pokémon Journeys – VOLUME 2 – END

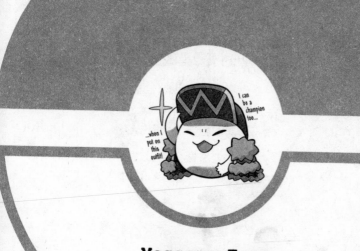

I can be a champion too...
...when I put on this outfit!

Message From
MACHITO GOMI

Ash and Goh are challenging themselves with things like catching Pokémon and battling! I would also like to challenge myself in lots of ways...despite being lazy!!

Machito Gomi was born in Tokyo on March 12, 1992. He won the Effort Award in the February 2013 Manga College competition. He is also the creator of *Bakejo! Youkai Jogakuen e Youkoso* (Bakejo! Welcome to Yokai Girls' School) and *Pokémon: Mewtwo Strikes Back—Evolution*.

Volume 2
VIZ Media Edition

STORY AND ART BY
MACHITO GOMI

SCRIPT BY
DEKO AKAO, AYA MATSUI, ATSUHIRO TOMIOKA & SHOJI YONEMURA

Translation **Misa 'Japanese Ammo'**
English Adaptation **Molly Tanzer**
Touch-Up & Lettering **Joanna Estep**
Design **Kam Li**
Editor **Joel Enos**

©2022 Pokémon.
©1995–2020 Nintendo / Creatures Inc. / GAME FREAK inc.
TM, ®, and character names are trademarks of Nintendo.
POCKET MONSTERS – SATOSHI TO GOH NO MONOGATARI! – Vol. 2
by Machito GOMI
Script by Deko AKAO, Aya MATSUI, Atsuhiro TOMIOKA & Shoji YONEMURA
© 2020 Machito GOMI
All rights reserved.
Original Japanese edition published by SHOGAKUKAN.
English translation rights in the United States of America, Canada, the United
Kingdom, Ireland, Australia and New Zealand arranged with SHOGAKUKAN.

Original Cover Design/Plus One

Printed in the U.S.A.

Published by VIZ Media, LLC
P.O. Box 77010
San Francisco, CA 94107

10 9 8 7 6 5 4 3 2 1
First printing, March 2022

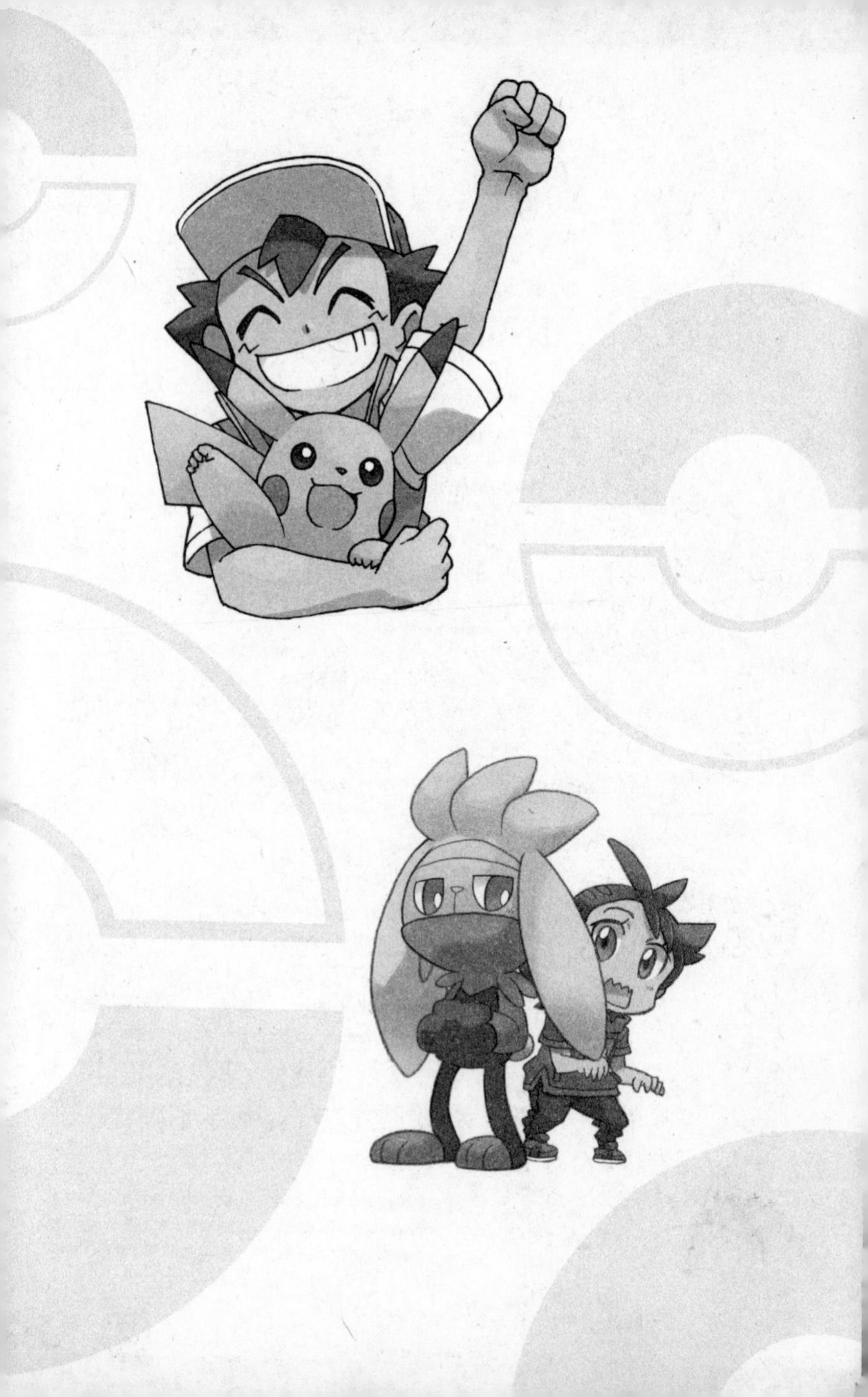

POKÉMON

SWORD & SHIELD

Story by
Hidenori Kusaka

Art by
Satoshi Yamamoto

*Awesome adventures inspired by the best-selling
Pokémon Sword & Shield video games
set in the Galar region!*

RATED A ALL AGES

 VIZ

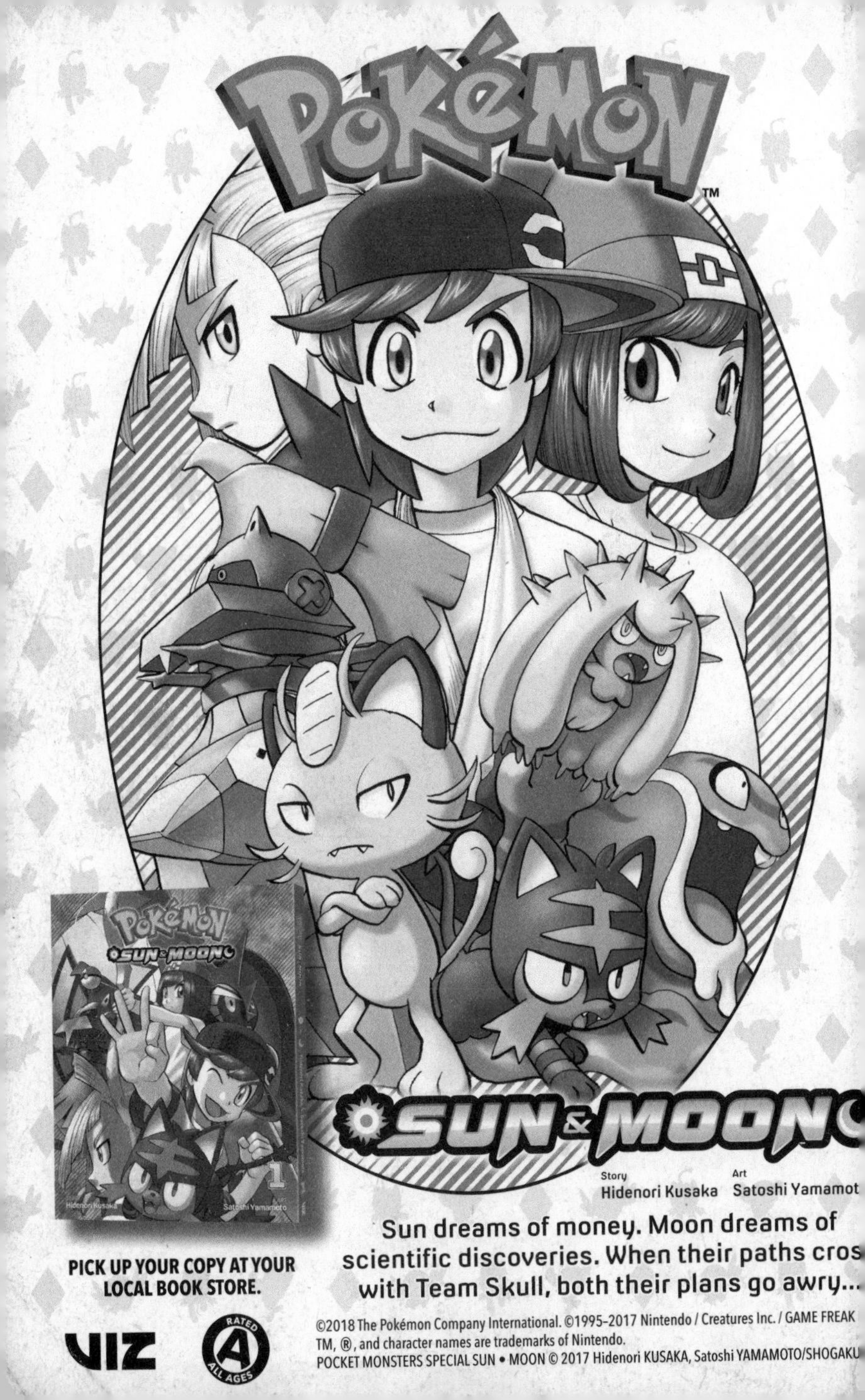
POKÉMON™
SUN & MOON
Story
Hidenori Kusaka
Art
Satoshi Yamamot
Sun dreams of money. Moon dreams of scientific discoveries. When their paths cros with Team Skull, both their plans go awry...
PICK UP YOUR COPY AT YOUR LOCAL BOOK STORE.
VIZ
RATED A ALL AGES
©2018 The Pokémon Company International. ©1995–2017 Nintendo / Creatures Inc. / GAME FREAK
TM, ®, and character names are trademarks of Nintendo.
POCKET MONSTERS SPECIAL SUN • MOON © 2017 Hidenori KUSAKA, Satoshi YAMAMOTO/SHOGAKU

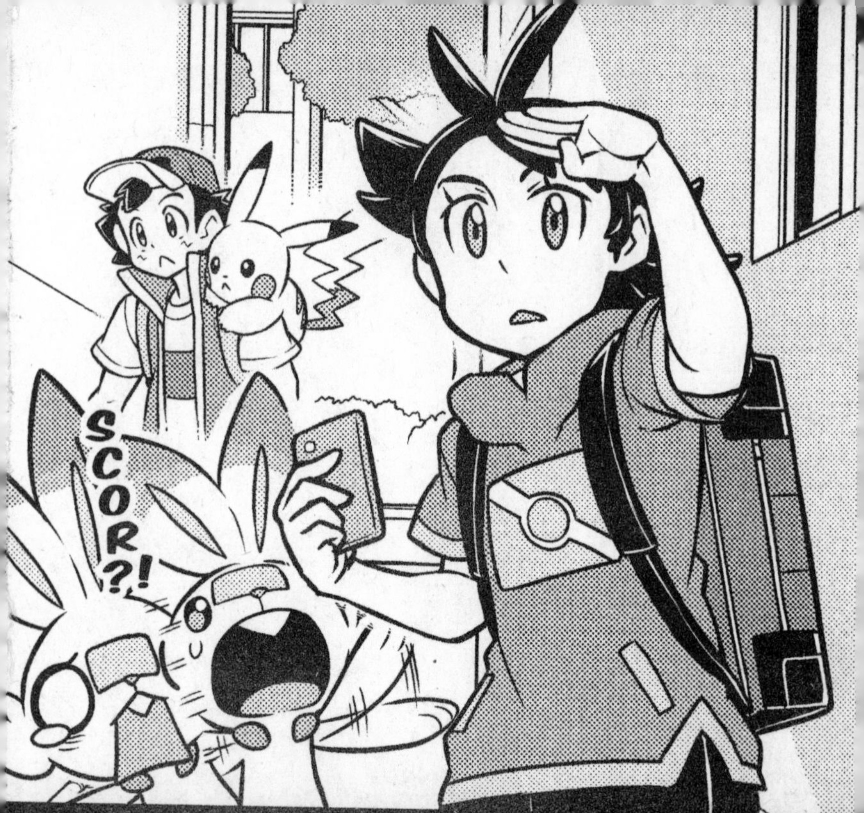
SCOR?!

THIS IS THE END OF THIS GRAPHIC NOVEL!

To properly enjoy this VIZ Media graphic novel, please turn it around and begin reading from right to left.

This book has been printed in the original Japanese format in order to preserve the orientation of the original artwork.

Have fun with it!

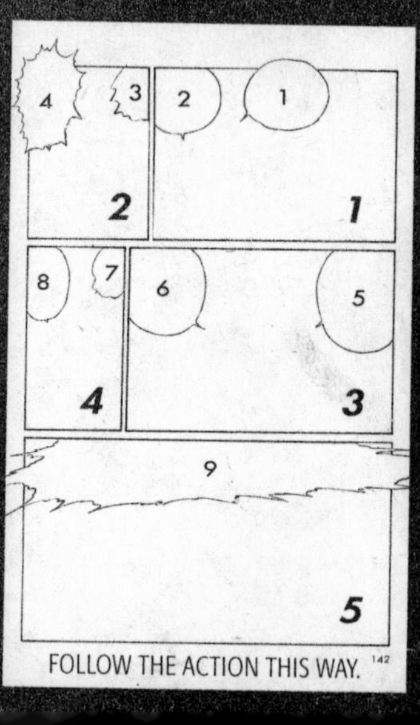
FOLLOW THE ACTION THIS WAY.